Hello, Heartbreak

Amy Huberman is from Dublin, where she still lives.
She is an actress, best known for her role as Daisy in the
popular RTÉ series *The Clinic*. *Hello, Heartbreak* is her
first novel.

D0513142

Hello, Heartbreak

AMY HUBERMAN

PENGUIN
IRELAND

PENGUIN IRELAND

Published by the Penguin Group
Penguin Ireland, 25 St Stephen's Green, Dublin 2, Ireland
(a division of Penguin Books Ltd)
Penguin Books Ltd, 80 Strand, London WC2R ORL, England
Penguin Group (USA) Inc., 375 Hudson Street, New York, New York 10014, USA
Penguin Group (Australia), 250 Camberwell Road,
Camberwell, Victoria 3124, Australia (a division of Pearson Australia Group Pty Ltd)
Penguin Group (Canada), 90 Eglinton Avenue East, Suite 700, Toronto, Ontario, Canada M4P 2Y3
(a division of Pearson Penguin Canada Inc.)
Penguin Books India Pvt Ltd, 11 Community Centre,
Panchsheel Park, New Delhi - 110 017, India
Penguin Group (NZ), 67 Apollo Drive, Rosedale, North Shore 0632, New Zealand
(a division of Pearson New Zealand Ltd)
Penguin Books (South Africa) (Pty) Ltd, 24 Sturdee Avenue,
Rosebank, Johannesburg 2196, South Africa

Penguin Books Ltd, Registered Offices: 80 Strand, London WC2R ORL, England

www.penguin.com

First published 2009

I

Set in Garamond 13.5/16pt
Typeset by Palimpsest Book Production Limited,
Grangemouth, Stirlingshire
Printed in Great Britain by Clays Ltd, St Ives plc

A CIP catalogue record for this book is available from the British Library

ISBN: 978–1–844–88214–4

www.greenpenguin.co.uk

Penguin Books is committed to a sustainable future
for our business, our readers and our planet.
The book in your hands is made from paper
certified by the Forest Stewardship Council.

For Mum and Dad

I

What in the name of sweet, gentle, divine and suffering Jesus did I look like?

A life-sized Zapf doll mixed with a half-melted Dolly Parton waxwork model.

'Keelin, you said these things were going to *boost* my confidence,' I whimpered, my bottom lip quivering again, 'so why do I feel like going outside, lying on the road and waiting for an articulated lorry to come and end this misery?'

'Izzy, for God's sake, you're such a drama queen. They're only a pair of Spanx,' she huffed, as she and Susie continued to hoist the horrific tube of flesh-coloured elastic up my body.

'But why would you do this to me?' I wailed. 'Have I not suffered *enough*?' I watched my reflection in the full-length mirror as the two traitors on either side of me continued to make me despise myself even more than I already did. Every upwards *whoosh* lifted my feet a few inches off the floor, and every time I thudded down my shoulders slumped even further.

'Izzy, you really aren't making this easy. Do you want us to put you in a back brace as well?'

'Oh, why not go right ahead, Susie? Then I'll be just about ready for the hair shirt and orthopaedic shoes you've lined up for me.'

'We're trying to *help* you here, Iz.'

'Then why exactly have you shoved me into a horrific, flesh-eating,' I twanged at the thick elastic digging into my thighs, 'tit-deforming, ass-annihilating *body condom*? Is this some sort of last humiliation I have to suffer before I become –'

'A martyr? Yes, that's right, Izzy. Now, arms up!'

'I hate you both.'

'*Up!*'

They slid something over my head, which I figured was most likely the hair shirt. But as I slowly prised open my eyes in terrified anticipation of the next bout of enforced dressing, I realized how badly I'd misjudged the situation.

'Oooh,' I cooed. I watched the silky material fall gracefully to my knees, and I knew that this was no hair shirt. Oh, no. This was my gorgeous new sparkly gold dress.

The dress.

As in, the one I'd bought especially for tonight.

The same one I'd thrown out of my bedroom window when I got home after trying it on in front of my full-length mirror. I seem to recall it had something to do with being a fat, violently unattractive pathetic lump, or something along those lines. Anyway, that didn't matter now. Not when it looked like *this*.

Not when *I* looked like this.

If I hadn't hated myself quite so much as I did at that moment, I might even have gone so far as to say I looked human. And not a fat-violently-unattractive-pathetic-lump human – oh, no. A passable human with a lovely cinched-in waist, pert boobs and tight arse.

My! My! My!

I flitted from left to right in front of the mirror, grinning inanely. 'Where would I be without you guys?'

'Lipstick?'

'Yep!'

'Perfume?'

I squirted some more on to my wrists. 'Check!'

Ow! That was stinging now. I must remember that I didn't have to spray myself with perfume or go again with the lipstick *every* time Keelin ran through the checklist.

'Don't forget your kohl eyeliner,' Susie warned, as she whizzed past me to get her coat.

Kohl eyeliner. Check. Eyeliner sharpener. Check. Bronzer. Rouge. Pen thingy to make under my eyes look less knackered. Check. Mascara: one lengthening, one thickening. Hairclips: one grippy, one knotty. Serum. Comb. Check. Check. Check.

Okay, one last quick look to make sure I hadn't slathered my fake tan on in cement-like mounds in the manner of an over-enthusiastic bricklayer. Damn, not so pretty workmanship around the ankles. Hmm. How long would it take to buff down about three layers of skin with an exfoliating loofah? Oh, bollocks to that! If men were looking at my ankles when I was wearing this dress, my troubles ran far deeper than I'd thought.

Front-door key.

Check.

Mobile phone.

Ciggies.

Charger in case phone dies.

Spare battery in case charger gets lost.

Spare sim card in case the spare battery freakishly turns out to be 'not charged'. Although charging it for around thirty-six hours ought to have done the trick.

I know this all sounded highly neurotic, but everything just *had* to go like clockwork. I'd been planning this for days, and far too much was at stake for anything to go wrong.

I wanted my life back.

I wanted it back!

Okay. Breathe.

Maybe, maybe, I was just about ready.

Shit. I couldn't close my bag.

Why the hell not? It wasn't like I'd thrown in any non-essentials, for crying out loud. Basics was all. *Basics!* For the love of God, could someone out there not design a bag to accommodate the measly *basics* of a woman's night out? *Please?* In the form of, say, an incredibly cute clutch? Was I really asking too much?

Fine. I suppose I could leave the curling iron and the hair straightener at home.

'Back in one, Izzy!'

'But – but it's in a pint glass.'

'*Back. In. One.*'

Christ, they were animals.

I necked it and grabbed my coat.

'Ready?'

'Ready,' I squeaked.

'I said, are you *ready*?' Keelin repeated, like a sergeant major on speed.

I gulped. The alcohol burnt the back of my throat.

'Ready!'

'Okay, let's do this!' Susie shouted, and bustled us out.

'Wait! Stop! For the love of God, stop!' I yelled, wedging my foot in the front door. 'I can't do this!'

'Izzy? *Whaaaaat?*'

'You don't understand –'

'Izzy, you have got to be kidding! I swear to God above . . .'

'Not like this!'

'Izzy, you're doing great. You're nearly there.'

'*I've forgotten my eyebrow brush!*' I half screamed, silencing them both. They blinked back at me.

I think they'd grasped the seriousness of the situation. I was one eyebrow brush away from complete and utter hysteria. This required sensitivity, the compassion of a loyal friend.

'Isobel Keegan, do you know that you're a fucking mentaller?'

I looked around the nightclub, searching.

Was he here?

He was here somewhere. He had to be.

I couldn't see him.

My stomach churned and my head spun with anticipation.

Of course, there was a fair chance the spinning was down to my having necked that pint of vodka and tonic. And now Susie was cranking open my jaw and pouring a baby Guinness down my throat. She pushed my chin up, allowing me to close my mouth.'Get that down you.'

'I think I may have had enough,' I slurred.

'Nonsense!' she said briskly, prising my lips open with two fingers. Even though my teeth were clenched, the Sambuca still managed to filter through and slide down my gullet.

'What if he doesn't come?' I felt like crying at the thought.

'Oh, he will,' Susie replied. 'He's a predictable wanker, I'll give him that.'

She was right. That was Cian. Predictable to the core. Predictable in all the *wrong* ways, unfortunately. Like being tactless. And stubborn and insensitive. Not to mention thoughtlessly cruel.

So why was I there? Same old, same old. For every reason I had to hate him, there seemed a million more why I couldn't shake loving him. For one, he'd been part of my life every day for the past three years. And he was Cian. My first and only love.

Had been. *Had* been a part of my life. It still didn't seem real. It felt like some awful half-dream that was slowly sucking the air out of my world. And I was stuck right in the middle of it, not knowing what to do, or where to go, or even how it had happened. And no matter how much it hurt or how much I cried, no one was coming to wake me up.

'Holy shit! He's just arrived!' hissed Keelin, as if she'd witnessed the second coming of Christ.

Uh-oh. *He was here!*

I wanted to puke. I wanted to cry. I wanted to run and hide behind the DJ box and curl up in the foetal position and call my mum.

But if I did that, then it would pretty much *definitely* be over between us. I'm not exactly sure how much more 'definite' I needed it to be, seeing as I'd found out he'd been having sex with another woman and all. But, you know, I still wasn't really getting it as such, so perhaps a little more clarity on that front might help to clear things up for me.

Anyway, I couldn't fail tonight's mission – not after all the work the girls had put into getting me here. The *mission* was for Cian to see me so that he could realize what an awful mistake he'd made. Then he'd drop to his knees and beg me to take him back. I would play hard to get for a suitable length of time, then jump his bones and straddle him for all I was worth. Simple.

After that, everything would be okay again. I'd be the old Izzy and life wouldn't seem like a steaming pile of shite. My heart was broken without him. After three years, he had to feel even a little heartbroken himself, right? He just needed to remember how great we'd been, and then he'd want us back.

'Izzy, what do you want to do?' Susie asked.

'Go over and say hi!' I shrugged.

'Are you sure?'

'Of course I'm sure. What else would I do? I'm cool, Susie, I'm breezy. I'm out with my friends, just casually getting on with my life, while coincidentally wearing a magnificent dress with my hair professionally blow-dried. It's going to be absolutely *fine*. You don't have to worry.' I went to rest my hand on her arm reassuringly, but I missed and ended up petting Keelin's boob. There were no two ways about it: I was trolleyed.

Keelin and Susie exchanged nervous looks as I made my way over to him. It felt like the longest walk in history. Like a pilgrimage to Knock from Dublin, trudging over broken glass, in bare feet, against 60 m.p.h. winds. I squinted, trying to pull his face into focus. He was standing with a group of his friends, his back to me. My stomach flipped at the familiarity of the back of his neck. Not far to go now, just across the dance-floor and over to the other bar . . .

'Iz, we're nearly there. What now?'

'You guys stand here and pretend you're just chatting and I'll come from over there to join you. It'll mean I'll have to pass him, and then he'll see me and I'll be a picture of nonchalance.'

'Okay, Angelina, go get your Oscar.'

After seven attempts at the same routine, the fish still hadn't bitten. God damn it! *Bite, fish, bite!* The girls even tried calling my name as I walked over, but the music was so loud he couldn't hear it. Then, on the eighth go, it happened. I was sashaying to perfection, like they do on *Britain's Next Top Model*, and my hair was falling perfectly around my shoulders and I'd just reapplied my lip gloss, when – good God – he saw me. Cue soaring music. Here we go. This was it. Finally, the Moment!

'Izzy?'

'Cian! My goodness! Hi, what are you doing here?' My heart was banging against my ribs and I had to steady myself against a bar stool so I didn't fall over. I could see Keelin and Susie in my peripheral vision, clinging to each other in suspense.

'Erm, well, it is Club Life, Iz. I mean, we always come here.'

That's exactly why I'd known he'd be here. *Here* was our social life. *Here* was where we ended up every Saturday night. It was where we all came to worship the gods of booze and cheesy music. Most of all, it was *our* spot, where we'd been known for three years as the couple who couldn't keep their hands off each other. Good Lord, how soon could we get the pleasantries out of the way and skip to that bit?

'I, eh, didn't expect to see you here,' he muttered.

Hang on a minute. He looked uncomfortable and his voice sounded cold. And he was staring at me like he'd just caught me out on something. I looked into his eyes and was suddenly overwhelmed by the feeling that coming here tonight had been a terrible mistake. 'Well, why wouldn't you expect to see me here?' I said, with a defiance I didn't feel.

I swiped a baby Guinness off a passing tray of drinks and slugged it back in one. 'I'll get you back,' I lied, replacing the empty glass on the tray and shooing the waiter with my hand.

'Maybe you should go home, Izzy,' Cian said.

I searched his face. Nothing. No emotion. Just . . . blank. If my heart was a shiny red helium balloon full of hope and love and expectation, he'd just popped it with a pin. And I hung there, withered and deflated, as the gas disappeared into the ether around me.

I had to look away. All of a sudden I felt so embarrassed.

8

So pathetic. He wasn't on his knees begging me to come back to him, proclaiming undying love. Far bloody from it. I was annoying him. He didn't want me here.

What had I been thinking? That I could come here tonight in a gold dress and some nice shoes and that would be enough to convince him to love me again?

Christ, how could I have been so stupid? I felt like my face was being slapped and each slap spelt out a different kind of hurt.

Rejection. Betrayal. Heartbreak. Slap. Slap. Slap.

Reality. Slap.

It was over.

He was gone.

My boyfriend, my lover, my confidant, my friend – all gone. Every little piece of our relationship had been pulled apart and discarded, as though they'd never fitted together in the first place. My heart ached for him, and before I knew it, trails of hot, salty tears were streaking my painstakingly made-up face. In that moment – the moment it dawned on me that it was over, that I'd lost him for ever – standing amid hundreds of people, I don't think I'd ever felt more lonely in my life.

Then something unexpected happened. It was as if someone had pressed 'play' on some 3D horror film in which I unwittingly had a starring role, but the sound was muted, so I couldn't quite figure out what was going on. A sequence of terrifying moving pictures started to unfold in front of me. *What* the hell? Why was an exotic beauty sidling up to Cian and draping her arm around him? Why was he looking at her like she was a Bond girl he wanted to have sex with? And why the bloody hell was she calling him '*baby*'?

Oh, fucking hell, it was *her*! The woman who'd been sleeping with Cian behind my back . . . my Cian. I felt unbearably hot, as if someone had buttoned me into an Aran sweater and locked me into a sauna. My head felt as if it was about to detach itself from the rest of my body and float away.

Jesus Christ, they were together. I'd thought, you know, it must have been a fling. A bit of excitement, maybe. A mistake, definitely. But here they were, standing in front of me, carrying on like a couple of lovesick teenagers.

I looked her up and down. So this was the owner of the voice at the other end of the phone. The shameless hussy who had called my mobile to leave a message with Cian's 'assistant'. At first I'd thought I was speaking to someone with crazily outdated views on gender roles and women's rights, but as she rattled on, I realized she thought I was his PA. Just as I was about to inform her otherwise, she told me to tell Cian thanks for the fantastic weekend away and that the little gift he'd sent fitted her perfectly, but he was so *naughty* to buy it for her. Then the phone went dead. Followed by my entire world. Shut-down.

And now here *she* was, with her long, elegant limbs and long, silky hair. This was the infamous Weekend-Away-With-the-Diamond-Thong Girl, as I had christened her in drunken rants to the girls. Of course, I didn't know what *little gift* had fitted her so goddamn perfectly, but I was pretty sure he hadn't bought her a pair of long-johns and some novelty socks. I'd convinced myself he'd imported diamonds from South Africa and hand-sewn them to an Indian silk pink thong.

Not that I'd thought about it much.

She opened her perfect mouth and crashed me back to the present. 'Who's this, baby?'

I swear to God, if she said 'baby' to him one more time, my ears were going to bleed.

Cian was swishing the end of his beer into a little vortex at the bottom of the glass. 'Erm, this is . . . eh, Izzy,' he muttered.

'I see,' she purred, scanning me up and down like a security camera. 'So *this* is Izzy!'

What the hell was I supposed to do? Wave? Shake her hand? Move in for the airkiss? All I wanted to do was punch her dainty little nose, but that might not sit too well with my 'nonchalant' thing.

'Ah, Cian,' she said, smiling at me like a reptile. 'She's so . . . cute.'

Excuse me? Was I wearing pigtails and dungarees? Did I look like a puppy?

I strove to cling to the last vestiges of dignity. 'Sorry, and you are?' Let's not be too hasty here, perhaps she was just some long-lost overly tactile cousin of Cian's whom I'd never met.

'I'm Cian's girlfriend. Saffron. But you can call me Saffy.'

I could, but I think I'll stick with *shameless hussy* if it's all the same to you.

'Izzy, I think you should head off,' Cian said quietly.

She snaked an arm through his. 'Yeah, maybe you should do that, Izzy. Things could get, you know, a tad *awkward* otherwise.'

I looked at Cian helplessly. Was he going to let her speak to me like that? As if I was someone insignificant, dismissible?

'All the best, Izzy,' he said, and turned away.

Yes, apparently he was.

The room started to spin in slow motion. She nestled into Cian like a cat, not taking her eyes off me for one second. I started to inch backwards, resisting the urge to get the hell out of there. I wanted to give them an I'm-so-over-it look of contempt, flick my hair and walk away, taking my incredible arse with me. But it was impossible – I couldn't stop staring at them. It was like watching a car crash, or an episode of *The Jeremy Kyle Show*. Even though it was making me nauseous, I couldn't look away.

The really painful thing was that she was a total ride. There were no other words for it. A ride. I had led myself to believe that the woman he'd chosen to run off and sleep with was a wiry-haired, overweight, overwrought minger, preferably with false teeth and a limp. That was how the story had gone in my head.

But, no, that wouldn't be how things worked out in the real world at all, now would it? No, here she was, with her sickeningly predictable long black silky hair and the longest legs I'd ever seen on anyone bar Naomi Campbell. (I saw her in Brown Thomas once when she pelted past me like an ostrich.)

And her dress. Oh, dear God, her *dress*! That was the final nail in the coffin. It was a backless gold number with long lace sleeves down to her wrists and an elegantly cut neckline. Stunning. Plus it was set off by the most amazing pair of Louboutin gold peep-toes, which looked like they'd cost about three pay cheques, where my crummy wages were concerned.

She was everything I wasn't. Tall and dark, with expensive clothes and killer accessories – she looked almost Asian. Her skin was flawless, clear and radiant. I felt like yelling, 'Good score!' and high-fiving Cian. 'Saffy' was an A1 boyfriend-stealer, I'd give her that.

She was eyeing me equally frankly, which made me feel unbearably vulnerable and exposed. I looked down at my gold dress, so tacky and cheap beside hers, like a sprig of lacklustre tinsel. There was no comparison, and it crippled me.

Had he always been too good for me? I'd never really

thought about it before, but he was gorgeous. Even now, when he was being so cold, I couldn't tear my eyes off him. He had an undefinable, inexplicable *something* that had me hooked. Some would call it sex appeal but it had always felt like so much more than that to me. His cropped sandy-blond hair, his big blue eyes, his tall lean frame and broad shoulders had become a blueprint for what I thought of as beautiful. Every other man on the planet paled beside him.

He turned back to me, catching me offguard. I half smiled at him, but he didn't smile back. 'It's time you made yourself scarce.'

'Yeah, Cian's right,' said Bitchface. 'It was lovely to meet you, but we really just want to enjoy our night together now.'

'Izzy, honestly, you should go before you make a fool of yourself,' Cian said, with an edge to his voice.

Well, all I can say in my defence is that he'd found the only button he hadn't already pushed and just pressed 'detonate'.

'I'm *sorry*? Before *I* make a *fool* of myself? *Fuck you, Cian Matthews!*' All the pain was suddenly replaced by an overwhelming fury. 'Fuck you, you self-righteous, self-satisfied, heartless, cocky *fuckhead!*'

'Okay, time to go,' Susie said, behind me.

I'd forgotten they were there. Anyway, where was I? Oh, yeah. '*You* are the one who made a fool of me in the first place by not having the *balls* or the decency to inform me you were shagging another woman behind my back!'

'Seriously, Izzy, abort!' Keelin pleaded, trying to pull me away. She would have had more luck trying to bridle a wild horse: this girl was not for turning.

By this stage a rather substantial group had formed around us, all wanting a slice of the action. 'What?' I shouted at the crowd. I think adrenalin had pumped the alcohol around my body because I was suddenly feeling out-of-my-mind blind drunk. Some of them looked away, others were cringing with embarrassment, while a good majority were shaking their heads as if I was the most pitiful sight they'd ever chanced upon.

'*Don't pity me!*' Was this really my voice? It didn't sound like it. 'Pity *them!*' I yelled, my arms flapping about wildly to illustrate my point. 'They are going to be miserable!' God, I sounded like Skeletor from *He-Man*. 'He is going to be *miserable* without *me*!' I roared, wrapping the entire argument up neatly for the crowd. 'Ha!'

I may have even bowed.

I didn't receive a round of applause or calls for an encore. Instead, the shocked, silent stares continued to burn through me until they'd melted all my resolve. I suddenly felt weak and pathetic, like some circus freak who'd stepped outside the tent. As quickly as it had arrived, the rage that had hijacked me departed, replaced by utter mortification.

I burst into tears. And, no, not the subtle tears I'd shed rather eloquently earlier on, but full on, snotty, wailing, heaving sobs. I stood there, swaying, with mascara staining my face, looking every inch the woman scorned. The last thing I remember is Cian, eyes wide, staring at me with horror. Then everything went blank.

2

One month p.m. (post-mortification)
iPod choice: 'I Will Survive'

I'd decided that flowing, silky hair and long, skinny limbs was just such a cliché. Far more intriguing and quirky to have to get every pair of jeans you buy turned up and to have hair that's slightly unruly, with a fringe that won't lie flat.

I'd also decided that Cian sleeping with the Cliché behind my back was possibly the best thing that could ever have happened to me: I'd dusted down *all* the shelves in my bedroom, something I always said I'd get around to but never found the time to do. Being single meant I had lots of time. And I'd put it to good use by vacuuming under my bed as well and pairing off all my socks. *And* sewing missing buttons back on to all of my blouses. I honestly couldn't believe I'd sacrificed all of this just so I could be with a boyfriend! I mean, was I mad?

I'd spent most of last week trying out different conditioners, which had been a right hoot. It wasn't an attempt to make my hair lovely and silky, no, just so I was up-to-date and well informed the next time I found myself in a discussion about haircare.

I honestly had to say I'd never felt happier in my life. People kept asking me was I 'okay'? Of course I was okay! What not-okay person goes and alphabetizes the food presses? Or sorts out all of the towels in the hotpress? Or scrubs the moss from the gutters? I was more than okay, was what I was! I had a new lease on life! I felt fresh and fantastic and wonderful, and all of my blouses had their buttons on them and the tins of beans were now so easy to find and my sock drawer looked so pretty and lovely.

I was just *so goddamn happy*!

Cian had been holding me back all this time!

3

Two months p.m.
iPod choice: 'Everybody Hurts'

I'd decided that Cian sleeping with the Cliché had ruined my life. For ever. I hadn't come out of my duvet cocoon in quite some time. It was really quite cosy and I'd made no plans to leave any time in the near future. Westlife and I had forged a new type of bond. I mean, I'd always been very fond of the lads, but now? We were *tight*.

I'd told my boss I had meningitis. (Must remember to look up symptoms before I go back to work so I can relay the horrors of what I went through.) People just didn't want to give you time off work if you told them you had brokenheartitis. Why not, for God's sake? This was far worse than anything else I'd ever had to suffer through before. Even worse than that full body rash I got when I was eleven and Mum had to slather me in anti-itch cream and wrap me in tinfoil for a week.

Keelin and Susie kept asking if I was okay and leaving sambos *with the crusts cut off* outside my door. Why couldn't they see that Blue Nun and Tayto were the only food groups I needed now that everything was ruined? Now that Cian had dumped me for the tall girl with the long, silky hair.

God. The *only* people who understood me now were Westlife.

If I propped all my pillows around me, I could sit up to drink my wine and *still* have the duvet over my head. What more could I want? A life? No, didn't have one of them any more. Not after the girls tried to make me go out last weekend. Not after I'd stepped into the pub and some drunk person shouted, 'Oh, my God! Look! It's that *psycho* from Facebook!'

That's right. My meltdown. Captured on camera phone. Uploaded on web. Posted on Facebook.

Hello, heartbreak. Hello, public humiliation. Goodbye, dignity. Goodbye, life.

It was official. Social reclusion was the new black.

4

Three months p.m.
iPod choice: 'Wind Beneath My Wings'

This was it for me. I was going to turn into that crazy lady who roamed the streets shouting at children, 'Enjoy your lives while you can, you little shits! One day someone will break your heart and then you'll be *miserable*! Just like *me*!' I'd be that bent-over old witch in the corner of the nursing home, rocking in my chair and stroking my beard, chanting, 'Cian Matthews broke my heart. Cian Matthews broke my heart,' while the staff had to restrain me to administer my sedatives.

Because he had. He had broken my heart.

And I felt hollow, bruised and raw.

This was how it would be for me from here on in. I'd never get over him. In fact, I'd make a stand against getting over it and win some award for being the Most Heartbroken Person Ever (also known as the Martyr Award) and then he'd finally know just how badly he'd hurt me.

Oh, he'd know all right.

They'd interview me under my duvet and say, 'So tell us, Isobel, where did it all begin?'

'Well, you see it was when Cian Matthews, my first love, shagged the tall lady with the long, silky hair behind my back. It nearly killed me because I thought we were going to be together for the rest of our lives. Because we just *knew*. We knew when we got together that it all fitted into place. Some said, "You're too young to know that," and we said, "No, we're not. People in the olden days got married at sixteen!" We didn't care what they thought because we *knew*. But then he went and spoilt it all and shattered my life. So, thank you for the award, but could you go away now, please? I'm not used to too much social interaction and it makes me nervous. Oh, but you couldn't just fill up my wine glass before you leave? And hit "play" on the Westlife CD on your way out?'

5

Still slightly traumatized over what had just happened, but Mum said sweet tea would help. She kept lifting the mug to my lips and making me drink. I didn't want sweet tea. What was the point if there was no alcohol in it? But I drank it anyway because if I didn't it'd spill down my front and scald my chin.

Mum, Emma, Keelin and Susie had staged an intervention. I kid you not. I hadn't seen it coming. I'd thought it was someone coming to drop off another crustless sandwich at the bedroom door, but all of a sudden I was picked up, duvet and all, wrestled down the stairs and into the back of Mum's car.

And now here I was. Back at home. Violated, defeated, held against my will.

'It's for your own good, love,' Mum said sternly. 'You cannot continue like this. Keelin and Susie are going out of their minds with worry, and so are we.'

'But I've been going to work!' I wailed dramatically.

'Yes, but you can't spend every other waking moment up in your room, under your duvet, drinking cheap wine.'

'Fine. I'll buy expensive wine. It's not like I've anything else to spend my wages on.'

'Izzy, it's *time*. Girls,' she called, waving her hand, 'be strong. I can't watch.'

Emma, Keelin and Susie took out huge scissors and started shredding my duvet.

'*No!*' I howled, as Mum held me pinned to the couch, her face turned to the wall.

An hour later, after I'd worn myself out crying, I was lying on the couch, curled up in a little coil of dejection. Keelin and Susie, two of the Scissor Sisters, had gone home. Dad came in to check on me every so often. I liked Dad. He wasn't as mean as the others.

Doris, our dog, was staring at me.

'Did Doris get a haircut?' I asked, looking at her. Why was she staring at me? Had she seen the clip on Facebook?

'Er, not exactly,' Emma – Scissors and real-life sister – muttered guiltily. 'I was sort of trying out these new curling tongs I'd got and they fried a huge chunk of her hair because I kept trying to make it go into ringlets. I ended up cutting the rest off.'

Oh, I see. Doris was actually pleading with me to take her to my home when I left.

'Izzy, you can't go on like this. I'm seriously worried about you!' Emma said gruffly. 'You have to get a grip now. You used to be such a cool big sister, but now you're –'

'I'm what?' My bottom lip began to quiver. 'I'm an embarrassment?'

'Exactly.'

'*Emma!*' Dad exclaimed.

'Sorry, Dad. Well, no . . .' she lowered her voice '. . . but you're not far off, Iz.'

'*Emma!*' Dad again.

Her big blue eyes went doe-like and cartoonish, as they always did when she was insulting me. She had this uncanny knack of verbally abusing people in such a cute way that it was virtually impossible to get mad at her. Like the time I got my hair cut into a bob and she told me I looked like a seven-year-old boy. She'd looked so sweet while she was saying it that I ended up apologizing and promising I'd grow it out.

'I'm sorry, Emma. I know you're disappointed, but I tried, okay? I really tried this time.'

'If you don't start going out and enjoying your life again soon, you'll go down in history as the Internet Bunny Boiler. *Not* that I'm saying people are calling you that – well, not *everyone* – but you have to come back fighting. Once you're out there, people will forget. But you have to face the music! There was a girl the year ahead of me who dressed up as a gimp for her boyfriend one Valentine's for a romantic surprise, but his flatmate caught her and took a photo of her on his phone and sent it to everyone in college. Okay, sure, she was humiliated and no one would sit beside her in tutorials and her boyfriend dumped her, but she got back out there! And now she only gets abused two or three times a week, tops. So, Izzy, please! You've got to get a grip before it's too late and you end up moving back home permanently, putting on fourteen stone and growing a *beard*!'

That didn't sound too bad to me. Apart from the beard. 'Why would I grow a beard?'

'Because, Izzy, when women lash on a speedy fourteen stone their hormones go haywire and they grow hair all over their face.'

'There you go, love,' said Mum, nestling in beside me on the couch. I took the mug from her and slurped the tea.

'Okay,' Emma said. 'I've gotta go now, Iz, but we'll talk more about your recovery plan tomorrow.'

'I'm not the economy, Emma.'

'Well, you kind of are. You're like one big nasty recession that we have to pump some resources into before you sink entirely.'

'Where are you going?' I asked limply. I was worn out with all this intervention and recovery talk.

'*Out*, Izzy. It's Friday night. It's what most people do, remember? And it's what you're going to start doing again. And, Dad, you're driving me over to Barbara's.'

'You could have asked,' he huffed.

'Oh, sorry. Dad, please will you drive me over to Barbara's?' she said, switching on the blinky cartoon eyes.

'On you come, you.'

Worked every time.

'You look great, Em. Have fun,' I said, eyeing her attire.

It was true, she did look great – but, my God, did she have crazy dress sense. She was like some superhero of bling. Bling Girl! Coming to save the universe from boring colours and lack of sparkle! I think she was wearing every shade of the spectrum in her outfit and the fifty bangles she had stacked up her left arm. It was a pity our tastes clashed so completely as we were more or less the same size. Ah, I remember my youth . . . going out clubbing, flirting, socializing. I was only five years older than my sister, but it all seemed so far away.

Psychodelic madness aside, Emma really was a stunner, no doubt about it. She looked more like Dad, while I was like Mum. We reckoned Stephen, our brother, looked a lot like Maurice Gibney from number thirty-eight, which we slagged him relentlessly about. Mum would just roll her eyes and tell him he was gorgeous and not to worry, that Maurice only moved onto the road in 1983 and Stephen was conceived in 1978.

'Thanks, Iz. Don't worry, we'll get you there,' Bling Girl piped, and trotted off, dragging Dad with her.

God, I was sad. Maybe it *was* time I got myself together. Here I was, wedged between Mum and half-shorn Doris on a Friday night, drinking a mug of tea.

Where had my life gone?

I sighed. Mum moved her hand to mine and stroked it gently. 'Emma has a point, sweetheart,' she said softly.

'I know,' I whispered. 'I'm fed up feeling disappointed and hurt, Mum. I want to move on so much, really I do, but it's like I'm stuck.'

'Well, some things do take time, love. But there also comes a point when we have to help ourselves.'

'But I just don't know how to do that. I've been trying to be more positive the last while, but it's like every time I move forward, I get stuck in all this hurt and shame and disbelief all over again.'

'Izzy, you've never been a quitter. And you know what? No one else is going to do the hard work for you.'

Jesus, she was right – Mum should get her own afternoon TV show. She could be an Irish Oprah. That'd be so cool. And we'd probably get loads of free stuff too. I'll run it past her once I get my life back on track.

Decision made. I was going to do it.

I was going to get back out there.

Goodbye, heartbreak! Hello, world (but hopefully not Hello, People With Access to Facebook).

It was official. Getting over it was the new black.

6

. . . Seven months p.m.
No iPod choice. No iPod. Fecked iPod against wall.
Blame Gloria Gaynor

I'll be honest, going to Odds and Sods always terrified me. Even after four years living on the same street, I didn't know anyone else who dreaded popping into the local newsagent's like I did. Okay, okay, I know it could have been worse. I could have been living in Beirut or Cardiff. But, then, Odds and Sods was definitely situated on *the* most frightening corner of Dublin City. Think screeching tyres and late-night police raids. Think shouting and screaming. Think twelve-year-olds in hoodies with fluffy moustaches – and that was just the girls. Honestly, it was a trip to the dark side.

There was nothing for it, though: Odds and Sods was the nearest local shop so we had to cross to the dark side fairly often. Whenever we discovered we'd run out of milk or ciggies or bread, Susie, Keelin and I would stare each other down, and the first to crack would be sent on a tour of duty.

'Izzy, you haven't gone in ages and it's serious this time – we're out of Skittles.'

'What? That's so untrue! I went last time.'

'Well, I went the last *two* times.'

'And I've developed some sort of wheat and lactose intolerance, so perhaps you guys should leave me out of the proceedings.'

'Well, if that's true, then what exactly are *these*?' Susie cried, pointing from the crusts of bread on a plate in the kitchen to the milk moustache on my top lip.

Jeez. Easy, Professor Plum. 'Fine, fine,' I said sulkily.

Some friends they were! How come they didn't hate going to Odds and Sods as much as I did? Maybe it was because Keelin had never been assaulted by a 'young hoodlum' with a Loop the Loop while she was innocently perusing the magazines. Hey, don't laugh, I know it doesn't sound very dangerous, but it sparked a lengthy hyperventilating and screaming fit in me. Or maybe it was because Susie had never suffered the misfortune of having a half-bald cat jump onto her head from above the shop door. (I can't elaborate on this because I'm still far too traumatized.)

As I scuttled towards Odds and Sods, I prepared for my 'safety measures', which involved a charming charade I liked to call Blending In With the Locals. In layman's terms, I adopt a tic and appear slightly pissed at all times. Take it from a woman who knows: the key to survival is attracting as little attention as possible. I know because – and call me a posh fuck – I once had a child lob a sliced loaf at my head because I'd had the temerity to inquire about semi-skimmed milk.

I pushed open the door, triggering the bell, which always made me think of a boxing ring. Okay, okay, concentrate, Izzy! Speed and precision! Quick and fast, like ripping off a plaster. We needed three things: bread, milk and Skittles. Go! Go! Go! Ooh, chocolate spread. Some bloke in a pinstripe suit jacket and swimming shorts was shouting obscenities at a jar of Hellmann's right beside the chocolate spread. I turned to him and said, 'Fucking mayonnaise,' so he'd think we had loads in common and therefore wouldn't mug and/or kill me.

'Tell me about it!' he answered, flashing me a smile. Sheer brilliance. My 'blending in' never failed. I plucked a jar of chocolate spread off the shelf and wished him luck.

Now that I was feeling a little braver, I decided I'd get some Cheerios and maybe a few eggs while I was at it. The girls would be *so* proud! It might even win me a bit of compassionate leave before I was forced to come back here again.

Hang on . . . was that . . . Jesus H. Christ . . . *No fucking way!*

I dropped the chocolate spread and pinned my back to the cereal shelf. I couldn't breathe! Christ, I was dying! Wait, no, I could breathe. I just had to . . . breathe. Like I'd always done. Same method I'd been using for the last twenty-seven years. In, out, in, out. But my hands were all tingly and my heart was doing a gymnastics routine in my chest.

I started to move, very slowly and very carefully, towards the voice I could hear. When I got as close as I could without being seen, I peered around the edge of the shelf.

Holy good Jesus! It *was* him. Cian.

I craned a bit further. He was talking to someone. A woman. *Oh, Christ, no, no, no!*

It was Edna McClodmutton, a.k.a. *Bitchface*, a.k.a. Saffron, *Saffy,* 'up-and-coming' actress-socialite and all-round robo ride who stole my man. I had renamed her Edna McClodmutton as 'Saffron' really was far too nauseatingly cool.

I closed my eyes and tried desperately to hear what they were saying. I willed my ears to translate their mumbles into recognizable words, but it was like doing an Irish-aural exam: I couldn't understand a bloody thing. They might have been discussing *Áine agus Ronan* going to *an phairc* to kick a *liathroid* for all I knew.

Now they were laughing, like love's young dream. It was enough to make me throw up right there in front of the All Bran.

I had to get out.

Now.

I couldn't see them. Meet them. *Face* them.

My God, I'd only managed to come out of hiding a few weeks ago. I'd only gone back into a nightclub for the first time last week. For the first time since . . . since Black Saturday. I went puce and light-headed whenever I thought about it or anyone mentioned it. Black Saturday, 10 November 2007, the day I did a Britney and lost my marbles. Not only that, but Black Saturday had become a hit on YouTube, thanks to whatever arsehole had recorded it on their mobile and put it on Facebook under the title 'Girl Has Shit Fit Over Ex-Boyfriend's New Girlfriend'. Thank you, arsehole, who-ever you are. I owe you one.

Anyway, there was absolutely no way I could face Cian and Edna McClodmutton now. It would set me back *months*. And what the hell was he doing in my local shop anyway? He lived nowhere near here.

Okay, okay, calm. Think. I needed a quick exit.

I peeped over the cans of beans to where the door was. Yes! It was still in the same place. God, you couldn't beat consistency in a world gone mad. Hang on, though. If I made a break for it, the heavily tattooed woman behind the counter might think I was shoplifting, impale me on a stick and parade me up and down the road. Hm, but that did sound far more appealing than meeting Cian and Miss Asia.

I checked the route again. A quick leapfrog over the stack of toilet tissue, past Mayo Man and out of the door, never to be seen again.

This was it. Now or never!

'Izzy?'

Bollocks!

'Izzy?'

Not knowing what to do, I panicked and began to swipe

random items off the shelves like some lunatic contestant on *Supermarket Sweep*. 'Izzy,' he repeated. What should I do? Keep ignoring him? His voice was closer now and my heart pounded violently as I turned to face him.

There he was, all six feet and two inches of him, as gorgeous as ever. Euch. He was still so bloody predictable.

Neither of us spoke. We just stood there in silence, gawping at each other for what seemed like an eternity. Like ten Palm Sunday Masses back-to-back. In Latin. He looked as if he'd seen a ghost, and I knew exactly how he felt. He struggled to say something, but failed. I allowed myself the opportunity to reacquaint myself with his face, his hair, his eyes, his mouth. Did I want to kiss or punch it? I wasn't sure.

The silence was broken by a high-pitched whine: 'Cian? Sweetheart? Will you ask if they have any sushi?'

Sushi? Was she having a laugh? We were in a shop where the mere mention of semi-skimmed milk could land you with GBH.

Cian turned to her, leaving me standing directly in her eye line. I felt like one of those timid gazelles you see on nature programmes, the ones the lions are going to be picking out of their teeth in about an hour's time.

'Oh. My. God,' she said.

'Hello,' I said, trying to sound dignified, confident and very much over it. Didn't work, of course. It came out as a pathetic squeak – the squeak of a scorned woman who was still alone and miserable and would be for ever more because she'd turned herself into a social recluse. Never knew one squeak could say so much about a person.

I wasn't at all happy with how this was panning out. I wanted to turn back the clock to this morning so I could get my hair blow-dried, my makeup applied professionally, a spray tan, choose a tailored skirt and sheer silk shirt from

Dita von Teese's wardrobe and buy a pair of skyscraper heels. In red. Not too much to ask, was it? After everything I'd been through?

This was not part of The Plan. You know how it goes: you bump into your ex a few months down the line and you're wearing Diane von Furstenburg? And there are people all around you in convulsions laughing at something hilarious you've just said? And then a man who is sex on legs walks up to you and asks for your hand in marriage, which prompts your ex to burst into tears and cry inconsolably? The Plan.

So how was the plan shaping up when I needed it most? Well, let's see. Smelly old trainers, bleach-stained raggy jeans, a dark green shapeless hoodie, greasy hair thrown together in a hideous scrunchie that had made its way straight from the 1980s into our bathroom, where I'd found it this morning. Yeah, not so much Dita von Teese as Rita von Shameful Sleaze.

Naturally, Edna McClodmutton looked amazing, which made everything even worse. (Murphy, if you're out there, I hate you and your bloody law.) Her shiny dark hair spilled over her shoulders, looking so soft and silky that in other circumstances I would have run my fingers through it and asked her what conditioner she used. Even without makeup her almond eyes were compelling: they were almost black against her honey complexion and her pouty bee-stung lips.

I shuffled uncomfortably from foot to foot as she strutted down the aisle towards us. Well, this was cosy, wasn't it? Group hug, anyone?

She smiled broadly, clearly savouring my discomfort. 'Izzy, darling, it's been a while.'

'Uh-huh,' I replied, trying to sound casual. As though I'd last seen her at the cinema or on the street.

'Em, Saff, could you just see if they have any . . . um, dish-washer tablets?' Cian muttered.

She looked from him to me and back again, let the perfect space of awkward silence choke the air around us, then sauntered up the aisle in her *gorgeous* lace-up ankle boots, her hair swishing like a sheet of black silk. Just as she was about to disappear around the corner, she turned and glared at me. Again, I had to restrain myself from congratulating Cian on what a ride she was.

'Listen, sorry – you know about what happened after . . .' he started.

'Please. Don't.' I had to look away. This was horrible. I moved away from him and went into the next aisle.

Her heels were clipping back already to where he was standing. This time I could hear *everything* they were saying. And it was awful.

'Is she going to have another public breakdown? Honestly, Cian, I'm not in the mood.'

'Sssh, for Christ's sake!'

'You said it yourself – she's probably still obsessed with you.'

Bastard!

'What? No I didn't, I said –'

'Seriously, Cian, she makes me really uncomfortable. My friends think she's clinically deranged. Remember last month when I went to that open audition for the part of a psycho lady in *Fair City*? Well, guess whose monologue I downloaded from YouTube and learnt for my audition? That's right, your crazy ex's. And, okay, I didn't get the part, but the director said my piece was very "real".'

Lord, take me now.

'Would you be quiet? She's still in the shop,' he barked.

'No! I will not pussyfoot around her just because she's mentally unstable. She lost. She needs to get over it.'

Bitch! I could not believe my ears. I *lost?* That was my *boyfriend*!

Not a bloody game of tennis! I sloped towards the counter, almost too numb to move.

'Izzy, wait.' I turned to see Cian whirring towards me like an annoying wasp. I wanted to splat him, the pretentious prick.

'Just leave it, Cian,' I said, plonking down the items I'd managed to gather during my fit of shopper's mania. There, laid out in front of me in all their embarrassing glory, were a packet of nappies, some nappy rash cream, an odd brand of toothpaste for 'problem bad breath', an aerosol can of Odour Destroyer and a jar of Bovril. Yep, any time now will do just fine, Lord!

'Izzy, I'm really sorry about that. God, this is awkward. Are you okay?'

'What are you doing here?' I asked.

'I dunno – we were just passing . . .'

'And you realized you'd run out of sushi and dishwasher tablets?' I fished around in my pockets for change as the incredibly-manly-once-you're-up-close lady totted up what I owed.

'There's no price sticker on this rash cream,' she roared. 'Go over and check the price on another.'

You. Have. To. Be. Kidding.

By this stage, Edna McClodmutton had snaked her way back into view and was surveying the scene. My cheeks flushed bright crimson. 'Em, yeah, just hang on.' I staggered back to the display and stood there muttering, 'Price stickers, price stickers,' like a mad woman. I could feel all their eyes on me. There wasn't a sticker on any of them. Someone, please, give me a break!

Just then, like a little ray from heaven, I spotted a bright orange glow shining out at me from the back of the shelf. Forgetting I wasn't an eight-year-old Cub Scout who had just stumbled on the final clue in an orienteering competition, I turned and spluttered, 'Three euro fifty,' waving a tube of the cream victoriously.

Edna raised an eyebrow and folded her arms.

I cleared my throat. 'It's, eh . . . three euro fifty, quite reasonable, really . . .'

Mute button, Izzy.

I kept my head down as I fished out a stash of chocolate at the counter and paid the cash-till beast. Then I walked straight out of the door. I didn't say goodbye. I didn't look back. And when I knew I'd walked far enough to be out of sight, I broke into a sprint.

One thing was for sure: chocolate alone was not going to cut it today. I needed something a lot stronger. I ran into my street, past my neighbour's front door, past my own front door and didn't stop until I reached the off-licence at the end of the road.

7

The next morning I woke up feeling like road-kill, the kind you can't believe is still alive, considering the state it's in. As I lay there, swaddled in self-pity, I had an overwhelming desire to be at home with Mum and Dad. Okay, I know I wasn't seven years old, but I wanted to be transported back to a time where my biggest problems were whether to watch *The Raccoons* or *The Snorks* or to make a den in my bedroom and dress the dog in my doll's clothes.

Maybe I'll call over to them, I thought, as I tried lifting my head. No luck there. It was as if someone had sewn my scalp to the pillow, which in turn had been sewn to the mattress. How much had I drunk last night?

I couldn't get up, so I switched my energy to attempting to bring different blurred objects into focus. It was a game I liked to play whenever I was lying in a hungover state of paralysis, killing time until feeling had returned to my body. The rules were simple: if I guessed correctly before managing to de-blur the object, I got five points. Points for what exactly, I wasn't sure. Although sometimes I'd award myself a cheeky McDonald's hangover treat if I did well.

My eyes rested on a small white bundle. What was it? A pile of unironed clothes? Probably. It started to move. 'Dermot!' I thought he was going to puke, as he normally did when he got a fright, but a moment later he was hopping towards my outstretched arms.

Dermot wasn't some weird one-legged guy with a weak constitution who lived on my bedroom floor. He was our pet rabbit.

We all adored him, even though Susie was seriously allergic to him. But what were a few hives and a couple of extra puffs on an asthma inhaler when you could have him in your life?

Keelin and I had rescued Dermot from an animal shelter about a year ago and since then he had become the centre of our little urban-family unit. We stumbled upon him one Saturday afternoon after we'd got lost trying to run an errand for Keelin's dad. Bored and frustrated driving around Rathfarnham looking for an address that clearly didn't exist (one of Keelin's dad's 'little quirks' was mixing up Rathfarnham and Raheny), we decided to follow the signs to an animal shelter 'just for a look'.

They say 'you just know' usually in reference to falling in love, but it's true of so many other things too, like the perfect pair of shoes, or knowing when it's time to eat some chocolate. Well, if any rabbit on this earth was for us, it was Dermot. As soon as we laid eyes on his little fluffy face, we just *knew*. He looked so lonely and miserable in his cramped little hutch that we couldn't possibly leave him to his animal-shelter fate. He looked as if he had been chewed, swallowed and regurgitated by an Alsatian, but it was nothing a warm bath, some volumizing shampoo and a dose of TLC couldn't cure.

Now I bent down to pick him up and nearly hurled over him. 'Sorry, Dermot, feeling a bit rough this morning,' I told him, as I placed him beside me on the bed. I hoped I wasn't going to knock him unconscious with my stale-gin breath. He nuzzled his little pink nose against my hand, looking to be petted.

'You've come a long way, Dermo,' I said, playing with his ears. 'I reckon we can stop backcombing your hair now that most of it's grown back . . . although it does give you a nice bit of volume on the crown.' He started to fall asleep as I teased his fringe with my fingers – he was a long-haired rabbit so we'd cut him a nifty side one. I felt so lucky to have him. My own little ball of love that was available for hugs round the clock. Better than a boyfriend. I sighed heavily.

'Did you know that bollocks didn't like you? Come to think of it, I don't think he liked me all that much either.'

I was so excited, phoning Cian to tell him of our animal-rescue operation. In hindsight, it probably wasn't the wisest way to tell him that the girls and I had adopted a rabbit.

'Cian,' I proclaimed giddily down the phone, 'we're going to be parents.'

I didn't know he was going to pass out and hit his head off a chair, did I? Anyway, after he'd come round and made himself a mug of sweet tea, he called me back. He wasn't too impressed.

'Who the hell keeps a rabbit in their house?'

'Lots of people, actually. You can litter train them and they don't need as much looking after as a dog. Cian, he's just so cute, you'll love him.'

'Izzy, it's a rabbit. Get a grip.'

'Yeah, but he's our little adopted rescue rabbit. Actually, he's far from little. He's humungous – we think he weighs about two stone. Anyway, Keelin reckons she can train him to collect the post from the doormat. You have to call around later and see him –'

'For God's sake, Iz, it's just *stupid*. Tenner says you'll have brought it back by the end of the week.'

Everything I did was 'stupid' in those last few months. Looking back now, I can't understand why I didn't see how impatient he was with me, how much I irritated him. Perhaps I hadn't wanted to see it. I remember thinking, Okay, he's a bit off-hand with me, but all couples go through phases like this, right? After all, it was me and Cian. We were in love, mad about each other, always had been. He said we belonged together, and I believed that one hundred per cent.

How. Bloody. Stupid.

Oh, God. Now I remembered why I'd drunk so much last night. After doing a three-minute-mile to the off-licence, I'd arrived home with a bottle of gin and informed Keelin and Susie that my aim for the day was to end up in A & E with alcohol poisoning, and would anyone care to join me?

Susie had still been greyish-green from the night before, but when she saw the state I was in she realized this wasn't something she could wimp out of. 'The hair of the dog that bit you!' she said cheerily, as she disappeared into the kitchen to get glasses and ice. I could have sworn I heard some stifled gagging but, fair play to her, she didn't complain and came back out a few minutes later with three tumblers in her left hand, a bag of ice in the right and a tortured smile plastered to her face.

We sat for hours, drinking and bitching about Cian and Edna McClodmutton, which made me feel *so* much better. Keelin told me all about the TV ad Edna had done after leaving drama school. I couldn't believe I'd never seen it.

'*No way!*' I screeched.

'Come on, Izzy, you remember the one with the girl on roller blades on Dun Laoghaire pier going on about how her new winged sanitary towels helped her period fly by? That's *her*!'

Talking about Cian was harder, but as the girls reeled off anecdotes about his less attractive moments, I started to laugh. Susie reminded me about the time he had handed everyone his 'new business card', saying he'd been promoted in work, only for us to discover later that he'd printed it himself in the local Spar.

'The stupid gobshite,' I snorted, through fits of laughter. 'What the hell did I ever see in him?'

An hour later I was crying so much Keelin thought I needed sedation.

'I want him back,' I wailed. 'I miss him *so much*.'

Susie sat there handing me tissue after tissue, while Keelin put the used ones into the bin. It was a perfect chain of command, which continued until my eyes stung and my chest heaved with long, worn-out, defeated sighs.

The rest of the night was a bit of a blur, but I think that after I'd cried myself to the point where I resembled a piece of dried fruit, I crawled up to bed and passed out. This morning, lying prone, I resembled one of those women you see on programmes with titles like *When Plastic Surgery Goes Horribly Wrong.*

'Oh, Dermot, I'm so fecking tired of feeling like this.'

I tried to look on the bright side. Maybe bumping into them yesterday was supposed to bring me closure. If closure meant ripping open the wound and hosing it with vinegar.

I wondered if he was in love with her, whether they had a lot of sex. And whether it was brilliant. Maybe she was into stuff like swinging upside-down in a gimp suit. Maybe he thought I was boring. Did they say, 'I love you,' to each other? Was 'Love you always, Edna McClodmutton' the new 'Love you always, Izzy'?

I rolled over and covered my head with the pillow, trying to block it all out. I'd have given anything not to be able to feel for one day. It was like that form of torture where someone has a drip of water landing on their head in the same spot over and over again. Drip, drip, drip, drip. Constant. Relentless. These miserable drips of thoughts would drive me mad soon.

I was so bloody fed up with it all – fed up with myself. It was *over.* They were together. That was how it was. I couldn't allow myself to go on wallowing. Getting nowhere. But how did I go about getting on with my life? Someone, anyone, just tell me what to do and I'll do it. I don't care what it takes. Give me a sign to show me the way out of the pit I'm in.

There was a knock on my door.

'Holy shit!' I shouted, bolting upright in the bed. 'Dermot? Did you hear that? Maybe it's an angel! Jesus, Dermot, what if I'm *blessed*?'

'What if you're what?' Keelin asked, opening the door and poking her head round it.

'Er, nothing,' I said breezily. I'd obviously been watching *way* too much *Highway to Heaven*.

Keelin bounded in and plonked herself on the end of the bed. Where the hell had she mustered the energy to pull off that little display? I thought I'd got her totally polluted last night, but now, even though her pyjamas were on inside-out and back-to-front and she had chunks of hair matted to her left cheek, she looked a lot less hung-over than I did. She couldn't look bad if she tried. She was the only chick I knew who could pull off a short black blunt-cut bob with a fringe, a nose-piercing, black nail polish, tank tops and jeans, and look absolutely *stunning*. Minus the PJs and with her hair brushed, she might have been on her way to a *Vogue* photo-shoot.

'How are you feeling?' she asked.

'Okay, I think. Although I'm not in a fit state for any public appearances today.'

'Oh, that's a pity. You haven't made any of the ribbon-cutting ceremonies you've been pencilled in for lately. Will I ring the mayor to cancel today's or do you want to call him yourself?'

'You ring him,' I said, lobbing a pillow at her head.

'Oh, Izzy! You look like one of those post-op plastic-surgery people on the telly.'

'Well, that's *exactly* how I feel.'

'You've been doing really well. Except for last night's mild to strong relapse, you've made serious progress, dipping your toe back into your social life after the recluse thing. Please don't let this little fall keep you down too long.'

'I won't,' I said, only half believing myself.

'Well, if you're not heading out to that ribbon-cutting, it's a darned good thing it's a rainy miserable Sunday. I reckon we sit ourselves down in front of the telly for the day and eat ourselves sick.'

'Sounds brilliant!'

And that was exactly what we did. Susie, Keelin, Dermot and I sat huddled under a duvet on the couch in our pyjamas – except Dermot, who doesn't wear them – and watched old movies all afternoon. And apart from the abject misery and feeling like a worthless unlovable cretin, I felt somewhat uplifted.

Until Aidan, Susie's idiot boyfriend, arrived. How I could love Susie so much and him so little remained a mystery to me. He let himself in (cheeky bollocks), came over and kissed Susie (euch), then flicked on the lights so he could read the sports pages in his tabloid. I did the squinting-and-shielding-my-face-with-my-hands thing in the hope that he'd get the hint, but he didn't.

'What's up with you?' he inquired. 'Don't tell me, you had another trial going-out night last night and someone abused you about Facebook again.' He laughed so hard he almost choked.

I wished he would.

'Aidan!' Susie snapped.

'Sorry, Izzy, sorry,' he said, still chuckling. 'You just look a bit mad is all, like you've been crying. And there you are under another duvet. I just reckoned you'd had another melt-down.'

I couldn't let this happen again. I couldn't go back there. I couldn't let *Aidan*, of all people, be right. I couldn't have someone like *him* laughing at me. A wannabe actor who pretended to come from the 'wrong side of the tracks', complete with hugely annoying inner-city accent when he actually hailed from Dalkey. What a plank! No, an idiot like Aidan laughing at me was too much to bear.

Mentally I gave myself two quick slaps across my face. I'll show him! I'll show *them all*!

8

I woke up on Monday morning convinced it was the first day of the rest of my life. A new beginning! I was going to transform myself into an updated, improved model of the old Isobel Keegan. I would be the 'Izzy Turbo 3000'. Okay, okay, so I might not be all that new and improved but, sure as hell, I was going to get back to normal at the very least. I was going to get back to *me*. Enough was enough.

First and foremost, I would make an effort to look like a member of the female species, starting with my legs even though there was no immediate prospect of any man seeing or touching them. I glanced down at them as I swung them over the side of the bed. Not a sight for the faint-hearted: they looked like two giant Velcro watchstraps.

A full-length mirror was propped against the wall opposite my bed. Through the ten inches of dust layered on its surface, I could just make out the reflection of someone who looked a lot like Wayne Rooney. That someone was me.

I shuffled over and wiped off the dust with a sock. Then I stood in front of it and forced myself to take a cold, hard look. Okay, not quite as bad as I'd thought, but still only some dim lighting and a Man U jersey away from you know who. So, what was needed? A haircut, pronto, and my highlights. Then I just had to pluck my eyebrows. Sorry, eyebrow.

What else? Well, I wasn't exactly fat, but I'd put on a few pounds over the last couple of months. What else was there to do at weekends? My initial intention had been to read the entire Jane Austen collection and learn a new language, but

43

I'd passed the time by eating non-stop and watching films about scorned women on the True Movies channel. I pulled up my pyjama top and prodded my pot belly. Yes, the time had come to wean myself off the mayonnaise drip I'd become addicted to. Food loves mayonnaise? Tell me about it. I can actually hear my sandwiches say, 'Go fuck yourself,' if I don't slap on lashings of it.

Every couple of weeks I'd tell myself that, starting on Monday – it won't work on any other day: it's a well-known fact that you're only allowed to wipe the slate clean on a Monday – I was going to look on life with a whole new attitude. It rarely lasted beyond Tuesday afternoon, but this time would be different because it had to be. I had two choices here: either I kept myself locked away and ate troughs of mayonnaise until I ended up with an arse I couldn't squeeze through the front door even if I wanted to, or I sorted myself out. Which meant no more pining for that bollocks, no more playing 'Spot the Difference' between me and Edna McClodmutton, and no more self-loathing. It was time to look forwards, onwards and upwards. Eat All Bran! Drink green tea! Wear mascara! I would say my affirmation in front of the mirror every morning: 'I will be a girl! I will be a girl! I will be a girl!'

I marched over to my wardrobe, flung open the doors and pulled out my old grey tracksuit bottoms – the ones that retained my body shape even when I wasn't wearing them – and threw them into the bin. They looked so abandoned. Would it be weird if I held on to them as a sort of comfort blanket? As a souvenir of what I'd been through? Okay, Izzy, they're just ugly, worn-out skank pants that will impede my new life as a hottie.

If I was going to look less like a native from the Land of the Dumped, I had to spruce up my work outfits too. Shiny black polyester trousers and a white shirt weren't going to get people wondering whether it was *Elle* or *Vogue* I subscribed to. On the mornings I didn't have time/couldn't be arsed to iron a shirt, I'd throw on one of my long-sleeve cotton T-shirts, which I had in brown, blue and black. They came in a handy multi-pack from M&S and I'd managed to get them for eight euro, reduced from fifteen . . .

Oh, sweet Jesus.

I just heard myself.

Hang on a second while I play that back in my head.

Yep. Just as I'd feared – shocking. Exactly *when* had I turned into a euro-saving, unfashionable, hairy *bloke* with bad clothes and one eyebrow?

A wave of nausea washed over me. Good God, if I hadn't rescued myself now, I might have been only days, hours, minutes away from heading to the shops in a pair of brushed cotton pyjamas and fake Uggs.

A hazy series of vague memories in which I was wearing nice clothes drifted from the back of my mind. I willed myself to bring them to the front. A sparkly pink hairclip . . . a gold handbag . . .

Concentrate!

. . . fitted jeans . . . a dusty pink wraparound dress . . .

All from my Before days. I'd kind of split my wardrobe into Before and After I was dumped. Pathetic, I know. Feminists would have set fire to my bra (while I was still wearing it) to teach me a lesson.

Back to those fitted jeans. I rummaged furiously through a mountain of threadbare hoodies and washed-out, oversized skater denims until I spotted a leg of my Citizens of Humanity jeans. I reefed the rest out and held them up triumphantly. I wanted to be a Citizen of Humanity again!

Well, I was going to have to remain at refugee status for

now because there was no way I'd fit into them any time soon. Not unless I lived off ice cubes for a month, got my stomach stapled and had a parasite implanted into my digestive system. Christ, I was a skinny bitch in my Before days.

I slipped the jeans on a hanger and balanced it on the wardrobe door. I scribbled 'Easy on the Miracle Whip, Izzy' on a Post-it and stuck it to one of the front pockets, as a reminder. 'Soon, my lovelies,' I reassured them. 'Soon we'll be back together. Walking down the streets together, sitting in fancy bars together. And if you're really good, I'll do my best to find you a nice manly pair of jeans to wrap yourself around now and again.'

Proactive and charged with enthusiasm, I rooted through my drawers for a photo of me in my pre-hermit days, so I could tape it to the mirror as a visual reference of my new goal. I stumbled on a photo of me, Keelin and Susie from a school trip in third year. We were no beauts – did we really think we looked good wearing our jeans up around our ribcages like that? With Paisley shirts tucked into them? I couldn't believe I'd let the head of the Paisley Cult – my mother – brainwash me like that. As for the blue mascara and the wild, unruly fuzz on our heads – well, it wasn't our fault the hair straightener had yet to be invented. No need to stick this one to the mirror.

Ah, here was a cute one of me, Emma and Stephen on the sofa at home as kids. Maybe 'cute' wasn't the right word. Emma and I looked traumatized, as if Stephen had just bashed us over the heads with the fire truck in his left hand. That stood to reason – he was always a grumpy little shit.

Shuffling around a bit more, I came across one of me and Cian – inevitable, really. I'd accumulated so many over the years, from different parties, family dinners, holidays. I'd taken this one when we were mucking about at his place.

We'd just watched *Notting Hill* and he told me he wanted photographic evidence to keep as proof the next time I gave out that he never watched chick flicks with me. He's holding up the DVD pointedly in one hand while taking the photo of the two of us, laughing, with the other.

God, it could have happened only yesterday. I could still smell him, hear his laughter, feel his cheek against mine. I wanted to climb back in and relive it. And, just like that, my resolve was melting like ice cream on a hot stove. I felt defeated and exhausted at the prospect of attempting anything other than schlepping about feeling sorry for myself.

But the longer I stared at the photo, the more I started to pull it apart. Had he met Edna McClodmutton at that stage? Had he cosied up on a couch with her? Watched a romantic movie with her? Had he already slept with her when it was taken? Bile rose into the back of my throat. I lunged for the scissors on my dresser and, with two swift strokes, hacked his face out of the photo. 'Well, you cut me right out of your life, so I'm gonna cut you out of my photo!' Hardly even stevens, but it was a milestone. Filled with a sense of purpose again, I taped the other half of the photo to the mirror.

I wanted that old Izzy back, even if Cian didn't.

I did.

I studied myself in the photo. Okay, so I didn't have long, silky black hair like Edna McClodmutton, or dark brown eyes and slightly Asian features, but I *did* have honey blonde hair that fell in nice waves. And Susie said my face had far more personality than hers and that my wide blue eyes had more sparkle than Edna could even dream of. Keelin had said she thought Edna was very striking – which made me cry: why did she have to rub my nose in it? Then she told me to shut up and let her finish her sentence. Edna was not

47

pretty, she said, but I was. And when I shook my head she furrowed her forehead and almost growled, '*Don't* give me that, Izzy. You *know* it. You've been told you're gorgeous your whole life.'

I'd never really considered myself 'pretty' but, then, I'd never considered myself 'not pretty' either. Perhaps it was my insecurities that stopped me thinking of myself as good-looking – and not in a fishing-for-compliments way. I swear if Giselle whinged to me that she was a fat minger I'd punch her – I *hated* when people did that. So, I never complained about my face or body, but I never celebrated them either. But, to call a spade a spade, I looked remarkably better in that photo than I did now. No two ways about it. I inhaled deeply. Well? What was I waiting for?

I fished out a pink linen ra-ra skirt from a back corner of my wardrobe, checked to see that there weren't any squatters in it of the moth/spider variety, and laid it out on my bed beside a plain white tank top and a silvery-grey button-down cardigan. I felt mildly overcome with nostalgia. I hadn't seen these little gems since the Before era. My choice was a little ambitious, perhaps, considering the weather of late, but it *was* summer. Apparently. Well, it was summer in Ireland, which meant it was really still winter but fewer people looked at you oddly if you went out in public wearing a T-shirt or flip-flops.

Half an hour later I'd made some fairly radical changes in the hair department. I had two eyebrows again, which felt good, and although I'd lacerated my legs with my deceptively innocent-looking pink razor, they were now silky smooth. I just had to remember to remove the plasters before I left the house – if those bratty kids who hung around Odds and Sods taunted me on my first day, it might sabotage the whole Fresh Start and have me running back to my tracksuit bottoms, begging for forgiveness.

I lashed on some mascara and counselled myself that, although it might appear otherwise, I did not look like a Goth. It was only one coat, and it probably looked strange to me because I hadn't worn eye makeup during the day for quite some time.

As I trotted down the stairs I admired my freshly painted pink toenails as they peeped out from a pair of silver wedges I'd forgotten I owned. I had also forgotten that exposing one's feet in different open-toed shoes and sandals wasn't a criminal offence, and that I didn't have to treat my feet as mere stumps at the end of my legs that had to be hidden in smelly runners or shoved into Irish-dancing brogue-type shoes. To top the whole thing off I'd gone wild and put on a pair of earrings, seeing as this was such a special occasion.

I went through stages of boycotting my jewellery, on the grounds that none of it was from Tiffany – which wasn't fair: it wasn't its fault. My last jewellery-spurning stint had lasted longer than usual, however. So much longer, in fact, that the issue of having to re-pierce my own ears came to light when I finally lifted the boycott this morning. It was worth it in the end when I finally pushed the chosen studs through, but it came with its fair share of pain. In fact, this looking-good lark had been a fairly painful process. Not only did my legs feel like I had been running through barbed-wire assault courses but I also felt as though I'd been shot on either side of my head with sparkly pink bullets.

'Jesus, Izzy? Who's the new bloke in work?' Susie exclaimed, dropping her spoon into her bowl of Coco Pops.

'Come off it, Susie – we can't fit fresh air into our office, let alone a whole new employee.'

'Fair point,' she said. 'I'm still convinced you're developing a hunch from having to squash yourself into your desk.'

49

'I don't have a choice. They needed all the wall space they could get for the shelving unit over my head.'

'Seriously, though, Izzy, you look great. What's going on?'

'I dunno,' I said, a bit self-conscious. 'I think it's time for a change. I just feel like I've had enough.' I sat beside her on the couch. 'I'm fed-up with feeling sad, and I'm the only one who can pull myself out of that.'

She nodded and I noticed the relief in her eyes. 'Was it seeing them the other day?' she asked.

'I guess.' I shrugged. 'Made it seem *real*. And made me feel stupid for giving up my social life over two people who don't give a shit about me. What have I been trying to prove?'

'You were hurt, Izzy.'

'Yeah. And *mortified*.'

'Well . . .' she tried to find the right word '. . . yes.' We both started laughing. 'That's the only way you can describe it, really.' She giggled. 'And, anyway, you've been seriously out-humiliated by that poor girl running down Grafton Street naked at two in the morning.' We burst out laughing again. 'You'll get there, Iz. I know you will.'

'Thanks, Suz.'

'And you look fab.'

'Thanks,' I said, as a lump formed in my throat. 'I'd love to return the compliment but, well, I just can't.'

'I completely understand,' she said solemnly. She was sitting on the couch in a Liverpool FC jersey, hospital-green pyjama bottoms and stripy bedsocks. I mean, I'm all for experimental fashion, don't get me wrong, but the jersey was Aidan's so, you know, enough said. If Armani was his favourite designer, I'd never wear it again. Although that wouldn't be too much of a chore, given that I couldn't afford it, other than the lipgloss. But it's the spirit of the thing that matters.

I left Susie on the couch and headed into the kitchen. I

simply had to have a healthy breakfast or my Fresh Start wouldn't have a snowball's chance in hell of lasting past lunchtime. All that seemed to be on offer, though, were two packets of cheese and onion crisps, some digestive biscuits, half a loaf of white bread (very bad, we all know about the evils of refined carbohydrates), an unopened jar of chocolate spread (cruel) and an empty Choco Flakes box. Any other morning that might have reduced me to tears, but not today, at the start of my new health buzz.

Jaysus, I'd love a bowl of Choco Flakes.

Was it more beneficial, psychologically, to *wean* yourself gently off the bad stuff? Hmm . . . I'd check it out later on that shrinks-on-line website. I was going to have to eat something, though. I didn't want to pass out on the way to work. I'd probably end up in some bus depot in the middle of the country, discovered by the cleaners on the back seat of the top deck, sprawled unconscious and fleeced of my money.

What were my options? A gnawed carrot, compliments of Dermot? No, that was just gross. I opted instead for the marginally less gross option of a liquorice allsort that had been sitting on the kitchen windowsill for about three weeks. Not a healthy option, I'll admit, but you know what they say about small portions. It was a nice compromise.

For some reason the weather was on my side and I wasn't greeted by the usual torrential rainstorm as I left the house. It actually felt quite warm and the sun was poking itself over the top of a tuft of candyfloss clouds. Bus, my arse! I was going to *walk* to work! It was only three stops anyway and, come to think of it, I was beginning to feel the strain of being called a 'lazy bitch' by my workmates. *Especially* Eve. She was a mid-thirties, anally retentive, low-fat, low-carb, one-hundred-per-cent-organic, caffeine-free, yoga-obsessed pain in the arse. And I had the untold misfortune of sharing a desk with her. Well, we had our own desks, really, but they were located within a hair's breadth of each other. At times I felt she could have been a parasite living on my body. A parasite that, over the past few months, had been sucking dry my will to live – and to come to work in the mornings.

Eve spoke to me and my colleagues as if we were brain-damaged. She bustled about like a schoolmistress, tutting and rolling her eyes at the stupid things that we, her remedial students, were saying and doing. Thank God I liked the rest of the bunch that worked at Lights! Camera! Action! The others made the office almost bearable.

Lights! Camera! Action! was a small film production company in the city centre. It didn't make blockbusters or fantastic art-house classics or even low-budget high-quality ones, but it had a steady stream of work on the go. They'd started out making TV commercials in the early noughties – mostly those crappy ones for furniture stores, with flashing photos of couches and voiceovers shouting that you were insane if you didn't buy your furniture from them. A few years ago they'd moved on to making low-budget movies in the West of Ireland, usually fairly appalling stuff, but the majority of their deals were pre-optioned DVD buyouts, so they always made their money back on top of a small profit.

I'd joined about a year ago on a work-experience placement after finishing a post-graduate degree in media studies. I'd done a bit of writing and producing and editing as electives during the course, but I hadn't really settled on which bit of the film industry appealed to me most, and I was hoping Lights! Camera! Action! would point me in the right direction. It hadn't, and I was still confused. The main thing I'd deduced was that I didn't want to make annoying furniture ads or dodgy vampire films set in Sligo, and that I did want to get into the creative side of things.

So, for now, I was still there, working as a general dogs-body, which everyone in the industry kept telling me was unbe*liev*ably fortunate when *soooo* many people were trying to get into the business. Hmm. Well, some days I didn't feel so lucky, let me tell you. Working long hours for not much money, spending weeks on end doing unfulfilling tasks, being shouted at regularly and rebuffing Eve's constant attempts to convince me that I had substantial learning difficulties did *not* make me feel like coming over all Kylie. At least it wasn't just me. The Lights! Camera! Action! office seemed to be a holding-pen for people who knew they wanted to be involved in film, just not in the way they were at the moment.

Laurence, the financial accountant, was an eccentric failed actor who, after years of brutal rejection by every casting director in the country, had decided he'd better resort to get-ting what he referred to as a 'real job'. He'd managed to amass a vicious loan over the twelve-year period he'd spent flirting with thespianism, so after securing only one single acting job in his career – an advert for a shoe polish that could also be used on door handles – he made an effort to appease his bank manager and went back to his roots: a BA in econom-ics. He also dropped his stage name, which, for the record, was Robert O'Niro.

The two other people who shared our rabbit hutch of an office were Geraldine and Gavin. Geraldine, the production assistant, was in her mid-fifties and more than a little hard to gauge at times. One minute she was as sweet as a missionary nun, the next she'd be thrashing around the place like some-thing out of your worst nightmares – the ones you get if you've watched *The Hostel* while eating cheese just before going to bed. She blamed her mood swings on the meno-pause and a lazy, inconsiderate husband called Ger. No joke, they were Ger and Geraldine FitzGerald. What are the chances? Quite high, I suppose, if you both grew up in a tiny village somewhere in County Roscommon with a total population of twenty-three, seven of whom, according to Geraldine, were already incarcerated in an old folks' home. You do the maths.

Geraldine had been involved in amateur dramatics at the Boyle Community Centre for a good few years before moving to Dublin and had a keen interest in the arts. But, as she said herself, her main reason for working in Lights! Camera! Action! was that she was 'officially in love' with George Clooney and he might end up in one of our films. There was more chance of me making Eve godmother to my first child, but everyone had to have a dream and who was I to crush Geraldine's?

Apart from being a part-time servant of Satan, Geraldine was pretty cool and I'd grown quite fond of her. She also despised Eve with a passion, so I felt we had a special bond. My way of honouring it was to open a window whenever she was having a hot flush. They say it's the little things that forge a friendship.

Gavin was my consistent saviour and companion in the office. In the time I'd been working there, he'd become one of my closest friends. The only disadvantage was that, as a freelance researcher, he was only there about two days a week. The rest of the time I had to fend for myself against the madness and try my best not to act out the fantasy I had of pinning Eve's head to the noticeboard with the fancy staple gun I'd won for being Employee of the Month back in March.

Gavin was more than a friend, though: he was my inspiration because he knew exactly what he wanted to do and why he was working there. He wanted to make documentaries. Pure and simple. It was the only thing he'd ever wanted to do. He'd made three before he even started his communications degree. He kept telling me they weren't documentaries as such, just a series of home videos he'd recorded as a child on the family camcorder. Well, he could say what he liked, but I certainly didn't know of any other child who had made a trilogy of short films about rounders, British bulldogs and Tip the Can by the age of eight.

He was also loved-up with a fantastic girl called Kate, and they were every inch the perfect couple. No tantrums, tears, mind games or shagging people behind each other's backs. If I could have bottled Gavin, I'd have happily injected him.

Now I prayed that Gavin would be in today. But I had vague recollections of him telling me he wouldn't be – something to do with Kate? Her graduation, maybe? That was it.

Shit one – not that Kate was graduating but that he wouldn't be in today. I wasn't sure I could handle a Gavinless day without an enormous amount of chocolate. It was great that Kate was graduating. She'd worked so hard, but it was still difficult to believe she was practically a fully qualified doctor. She was super-chilled and great *craic*, and I loved her almost as much as I loved Gavin. And, luckily for me, she didn't have any prejudices against Britney meltdown copycatters either. She'd even told me she would probably have done the same thing if she'd been in the same boat. Dr Kate was a liar, but a nice one.

Kate the doctor, Gavin the documentary-maker: don't you just hate sorted people who seem so grown-up? I envied everyone who found their 'thing' before they were thirty. I'd probably be some horrific age, like thirty-seven, when I finally had my lightbulb moment and figured out what I wanted to do. What if it was something weird, like farming guinea pigs? People wouldn't exactly pat me on the back for it. In fact, if I ever did decide to farm, it would be rabbits, not guinea pigs. And I didn't want to be an office lackey. So that was two things – guinea-pig farmer and office lackey – that I could scratch off my desired career hot list. It wasn't as if I was *completely* undecided about my future.

I hadn't much time to consider my options lately because Lights! Camera! Action! had been hectic because we were into the last few weeks of pre-production before filming was due to start on a new movie. That sounds exciting, doesn't it? It was anything but. Maybe it was me. Maybe I should have made more of an effort to be interested, but I really couldn't have given less of a shit about *Snog Me Now, You Dublin Whore*, which we were co-producing with a London company: 'An exciting adventure revolving around the lives of a misunderstood drug addict and his one-legged prostitute girlfriend.' The script was demented, as was the writer/director, who claimed he was 'going to create a modern-day Dublin-based cutting-edge and hard-hitting version of *Pretty Woman*'. Excuse me? Sacrilege.

So that was how my day was shaping up: no chocolate, no Gavin, a lot of Eve, mild starvation due to hopelessly inadequate breakfast, and a substantial amount of oohing and aahing about a film I hated. I might have to restrain myself from skipping the rest of the way to work.

9

By the time I arrived at the office I was sweating. I had lost track of time reading the magazine covers in the newsagent when I was supposed to be choosing a cereal bar and had had to run the rest of the way. Well, I kind of ran, but it was more of a maimed-animal scuttle because of the effect my Fresh Start silver wedges had on my capacity for forward motion.

As soon as I'd put my handbag on my desk I went to the window and leant out in an attempt to cool down, managing to burn my knees on the radiator. Aaargh! Why did they turn it on in June after leaving it off all winter?

Geraldine was sitting at her desk, nursing a cup of tea and nibbling a blueberry muffin. 'Hi, sweetheart, how are you today?' she asked. 'My, my, my! Don't you look like a little shiny button this morning!'

Was that good or bad? Had I gone totally OTT with my transformation? Damn, I *knew* I'd applied too much eye makeup . . .

'Izzy, you look fantastic!'

Yay! Being a shiny button was good.

'I love the outfit. God, I haven't seen you in colour since January. I thought you were going to start wearing a shroud to work. I know you were mourning your relationship with that gobshite Cian but, honestly, love, there were plenty of times I wanted to remind you he hadn't died. And, pet, I have to say I'm thrilled you finally plucked that slug over your eyes. I didn't want to say anything, but it was beginning to distract me from my work. Honestly, the phone would ring and then I'd look over at you and . . . well, anyway. What's with this super transformation anyway? Have we found ourselves a new man?'

'God, no. This is for me, Geraldine. I have to love myself before anyone else will love me.'

'Oprah?'

'The one where she gets all those whiny women into a circle and they group-hug and chant that affirmation over and over until they're crying?'

'Well, *no one* was going to love you with that hideous monobrow, love, but I'm glad you're coming out the other end of the Beauty Budget. Laurence named it that, not me, ever the accountant. I liked to call it the Dog Day Afternoons, Mornings and Nights.'

Way harsh.

'But you have to make an effort, love. Let me tell you, I don't enjoy wearing thongs, but I do it. The third Tuesday of every month I get out the thong. And I do it for Ger. Big thong man is Ger.'

The liquorice allsort was repeating on me. I needed to change the subject before I threw it up whole. 'It's roasting today, isn't it?' I tried.

'Nothing new to me, Izzy. I've been sweating non-stop for the past two and a half years now and counting. My doctor still won't give me HRT because I've high blood pressure, so I just have to put up with it. Feel like I'm being deep fried.'

'Where's Eve?' I asked, desperate now to move on. Once Geraldine got on to the subject of HRT, she was like a *Liveline* caller on crack cocaine.

'She's in talking to Fintan,' she replied, fanning under her arms with a copy of this week's *Now!*.

'Is she in trouble?' I asked hopefully.

'Ha! No such luck, love. She's after a raise again, so she's in there doing handstands with her skirt over her head, trying to convince him she's the most instrumental part of the film industry.'

Just then a fit of fake laughter erupted from Fintan's office. Seconds later Eve swung open his office door and trotted out of his room in her five-inch Louboutin heels. She was a knob *and* she had the most perfect pair of black patent Christian Louboutin court shoes – what's not to hate?

'You are too funny!' she squealed at him, wagging a forefinger, then made some bizarre clicking noise with her mouth.

Fintan Norris was our boss and the executive producer of Lights! Camera! Action!. He was quintessentially uncool, but somewhere along the way he had convinced himself he was a cross between Harvey Weinstein and Brad Pitt. He thought that an expensive suit, long glossy hair and a winking habit could make up for the fact that he wasn't funny, interesting or hugely intelligent. He was harmless enough, if a little cringy. He loved the way Eve flirted to get what she wanted. Luckily enough for Phyllis, his missus, Eve's interest in Fintan was only wallet-deep. He was too far beneath her for her to entertain any serious ideas about him. And thank God for that. He'd spent so much on the happy-family portraits on his office walls that it would have been a travesty if he'd had to take them all down. Every spare inch of hanging space was covered with black-and-white soft-focus photographs of Fintan, Phyllis and their three freckly, gap-toothed teenage daughters striking a thousand different poses. It was like Chevy Chase's *National Lampoon* meets *Miss Teen USA*.

'You are *so* the funniest person I know.' Eve gave him a sleazy wink and closed his door behind her.

'What did he say that was so funny, Eve?' said Geraldine. 'That the back of your skirt is bunched up into your knickers?'

'*What?*' Eve whipped around.

'Gotcha!'

'Shut up, you old wench, or I'll turn up the heat. You won't be so smart then, will you?' Eve plonked herself down at her perfectly dusted, polished and organized desk.

'Old wench?' Geraldine hissed back. 'Not exactly in the first flush of youth yourself, are you, pet? Ah, sure, you're not a hopeless case yet, I suppose. You've still got that blind boyfriend of yours. Maybe he'll agree to marry you one day.'

'Hilarious, Geraldine. Your jealousy is so transparent. If you did more exercise than simply trudging to the fridge for ice-cream refills, maybe you'd be able to keep that fat ugly husband of yours interested in you and that way you wouldn't need to pick on Philippe.'

Eve's boyfriend's name was plain old Philip, but he thought that too drab and uninteresting for someone of his social (climbing) status. He was the male version of Eve so they were a perfect match. Actually, it was probably Eve who had forced him to change his name, over a steamed-tofu stew, so she could refer to him as 'my Philippe' in a quasi-French accent.

'Now, if you'll all excuse me,' she continued, 'I just have to pop down to the boiler room to hike up the heating.' She marched out of the office.

'Izzy, pet, pass me over Eve's salad box there till I flush it down the loo.'

Brilliant!

I spent the rest of the morning trying to get Laurence to play 'Who Wore It Best?' by printing off pictures of two different celebrities wearing the same outfit. He refused to play after his third go, saying there was no way that Posh Spice wore the stripy pants better than J.Lo. It was after Geraldine started talking about smear tests that he got really pissed off and reached for his ear-mufflers. His cousin was a foreman on a building site and had given him a pair of industrial ones, which he wore whenever he'd had enough of us going on about 'girlie shite'.

Just before lunch he checked his emails and informed us that Gavin would be in that afternoon, thanks be to God – he'd feared he was going to grow a set of moobs, there was that much oestrogen in the room.

Yippee! Gavin was coming in! Today wasn't going to be so disastrous and mind-numbing after all. I was dying to see who he'd pick as the winner between Madonna and Rhianna in the pink jumpsuit.

Just before lunch, Eve put an end to my fun by making me fold 570 copies of the shooting schedule into halves and then quarters – for no other reason, I was convinced, than to bug the shit out of me. I tell you, the only shooting schedule I had in mind involved a revolver, a single bullet and her head.

I was applying a plaster to my *fourth* paper cut of the afternoon when I heard Gavin mutter, '*Snog Me Now, You Dublin Whore.*' He had walked into the room, talking into his mobile.

'Ah, Gavin, you come up with the cutest little nicknames for me. But I don't care how charming you are, I won't snog you. You have a girlfriend,' I carolled.

'Shut up, you!' He laughed, and sat down at Eve's desk. 'The financier keeps putting me on hold here.'

'I'm not surprised. Who the hell is going to want to give their money to fund this film? Gavin, you're not ringing senile old grannies again, are you? Promising you'll play bridge with them if they give you their life savings?'

'No, I'm offering them signed photos of Gerry Ryan.'

The door to Fintan's office opened and Eve sashayed out. When she saw Gavin, she almost purred. 'Gavin, *darling*! I'm delighted you're with us this afternoon. I need your help with something. Isobel was supposed to have sorted it for me, but I can't understand a word she says when she's confused, which, let's face it, is quite often!' She laughed, *haw, haw, haw*, and winked at me as if I knew what she was talking about. 'Let me just have a bite to eat and I'll be right with you!' she said, tapping his arm.

Round about the time I was praying that Eve wouldn't notice we'd stolen her lunch, she screamed, '*Who the fuck stole my lunch?*'

I could feel a sweat moustache on my top lip as I realized that my part in the great salad-flushing incident had not, perhaps, been such an award-winning idea. I gave Gavin a tell-my-parents-I-love-them-and-that-they-must-try-to-get-on-with-their-lives-when-I'm-gone look.

'*Well?*' she screeched, nostrils flaring.

Clearly sensing I might be bludgeoned to death with a five-inch Christian Louboutin heel (I could think of worse ways to die), Gavin took charge. 'Listen, Eve. I'm really sorry, I knocked against your desk and the lunchbox fell to the floor and popped open. I had to throw it in the bin. I'm really sorry. How about I run out and pick you up a sandwich?'

'Oh, don't worry about it, Gavin. I just thought those immature *children* had done something.' She glowered at us and I got back to my shooting schedule origami so I wouldn't have to look at her. 'But it's fine, Gavin, I'm on a diet anyway. Can't keep your buns this solid without a little sacrifice!' She chuckled, smoothing the back of her skirt.

Phew! God bless Eve's crush on Gavin. I'd live to be bludgeoned another day. Hoorah! Did he even realize how charming he could be? I don't think so. He was such a lovable rogue that he always got away with it. All people ever wanted to do was ruffle his scruffy black hair and pinch his dimpled cheeks. I mean, look at Eve. Us, she could happily eviscerate; him, she came over all coy and sweet, happy to do anything he wanted. He had never even so much as blinked in response to her come-ons, but he was the only one in the office who could coax her out of scratching someone's eyes out with her creepy, square-tipped gel nails whenever she was in a bad mood.

'Thank you!' I mouthed at him, and stuck on my fifth plaster of the afternoon. I was sorely tempted to ring that number from the have-you-had-an-accident-or-injury-at-work-that-wasn't-your-fault? ad and file a report about Eve. But I decided I'd cheated death once today and should quit while I was ahead. So I faffed around on the Internet instead. After half an hour of emailing friends, I perused the latest drool-inducing jewels on the Tiffany website, incandescent delights of silver, platinum and gold, diamonds, emeralds and sapphires. It was too cruel. The starkly contrasting reality of my multi-pack of sparkly bits from Accessorize taunted me. I could feel myself turning into Verucca Salt every time I looked at the website. But I resisted the urge to burst into song and decided to email Gavin instead.

Help me! Eve's evil stares are lasering into my brain. I'm getting a migraine here.

Serves you right. There's no rearing on you. Did your mother never teach you not to steal other people's things?

I didn't steal it! I flushed it down the loo!

Oh, well, then! I needn't have been so worried about your morals after all. I have to pop out on a few research-related bits in a while. If you promise to buy Eve some organic mung beans by way of an apology, I'll tell the boss I need to bring you with me to help me out.

Oh, my God, I love you! Yes! And I'll get her a kilo of the most expensive tofu in town! By the way, where are we going on our research mission? Perhaps we could do some research at the Brown Thomas summer sale while we're at it?

Em, not exactly outlined in the research guidelines of *Snog Me Now, You Dublin Whore*, but I'm sure we could manage it if we finish up early.

Thank you, thank you, thank you! Gosh, you are so important and authoritative! Thanks for agreeing to hang out with the lowly office muppet.

Any time, Miss Piggy.

This is Izzy, not Eve.

Now now, Ms Keegan! What did I tell you about being nasty? Nasty youngsters don't get to go on day trips out of the office.

Okay, okay. Eve is so beautiful and kind. One day, I hope to grow up to be just like her.

That's more like it. Get your bag, we're outta here!

After we had delivered a few files to an office at the quays, and after he'd spent a nerdy half-hour discussing boring business-related topics with one of the people who worked there, I was feeling rather scared about the prospect of having to get back on Gavin's scooter. He was a pretty safe driver so there was really no need for me to start screaming every time I climbed on to his Vespa but I always did, just as soon as I'd flung my leg over the seat. Maybe I wasn't such a scaredy-cat at all, really, maybe it was just the inner fashion victim in me freaking out because, as most women know, even those who don't read *Vogue* or shop on net-à-porter, a big black balloon helmet somewhat kills the ra-ra skirt and wedges look.

'Yes, Izzy, I promise not do wheelies at traffic-lights,' Gavin said patiently, as I sat behind him, flipping about like a fish with epilepsy. 'Just wrap your arms around my waist and hold on tight.' After ten minutes of Gavin zipping in and out past cars, trucks and articulated lorries, and me sitting behind him screaming like a chimpanzee in labour, we eventually pulled up in O'Connell Street beside a lamppost to which he could lock the bike.

'I think I'm deaf,' he said, tapping his left ear. 'You pierced the drum at a new octave today, Izzy. Well done.'

'Thanks,' I replied. 'I've been practising my technique to images of Eve telling me she's my long-lost sister.'

'What do you want to do now, so? Head to Brown Thomas? Though if you stand there and force me to decide which colour eyeshadow I prefer, when clearly they look exactly the same, I'll shoot you.'

'Hey, that was *one* time! And, I'm sorry, but the difference between fawn and soft beige is *huge*!'

'My ears are bleeding.'

'Oh! I think I should get a bike!' I shouted – anyone listening would have thought I'd just solved the last clue in a murder mystery. No one was listening, as it happened, except Gavin, who told me I couldn't wear a bike and would I not think of getting something a little more user-friendly, like a T-shirt or a pair of trousers?

'Hilarious. But how great would it be if I had a bike? I could cycle to work, or into town or to the shops. It could be my new exercise regime. And it's so friendly to the environment.'

'You're so ecotistical, Izzy.'

'Ha, ha.'

'You can't bear being on my bike, so how are you going to manage one of your own?'

'That's like comparing a racehorse with a one-legged Shetland pony. A one-legged Shetland pony I could handle.'

'Not sure they sell them in BT's. We may have to go to a rescue centre for one of those. Or Finglas.'

I folded my arms and frowned at him.

'Okay, okay.' He laughed. 'Let's go bike hunting.'

We strolled off in search of a bicycle shop and Gavin asked if I was going to start doing newspaper rounds on weekends. I told him I might, and that if he was really lucky, I'd nick some of the freebies from the Sundays and keep them for him. He said he was worried I had a problematic penchant for stealing things.

Finding a bicycle was more difficult than I'd anticipated. Usually I left it up to Santa to decide: I'd send a note to the North Pole saying something along the lines of 'Need new bike. Brother crashed and broke last year's one. Also need a Slime Ball to put in brother's bed when he's not looking. And I'm not saying you have to but my advice would be to ignore his request for a Scalextric and give him a lump of coal instead. Thanks and safe journey. PS Mince pies will be in the usual place. Help yourself.'

A bike was a bike, right? I knew there were different types, like apples, but you just choose one and get on with it. Let me tell you this: apples and bicycles are two totally different things.

The first one I climbed on to made me feel like a 1930s coal miner, with its enormous wheels and cast-iron black frame. The second made me look like a simpleton who hadn't accepted that the 1950s were over. It had a wicker basket strapped to the front and streamers dangling from the handlebars. Maybe it was the inner simpleton in me, but I kind of liked it. Vintage clothes were cool, as were vintage cars, so why not vintage bikes? Okay, so one of those crazy ones with the huge front wheel and the tiny back one would look a bit silly, but perhaps I could introduce Dermot to the sights of Dublin City on this little beauty. We could spend many a happy afternoon cycling around town, with his little head poking out of the top of the basket, his ears flapping in the wind with the multi-coloured streamers. We'd be like Elliot and E.T.! People would say, 'Ah, there's that lovely skinny girl and her gorgeous rabbit out for a cycle again . . .'

If I was going to stick to my aim of looking less like a boy, I suppose I shouldn't really have made inquiries about the blue BMX with the bright yellow wheels. But I had a pair of yellow wedges that would match it. OK?

No. It was still a boy's bike. Next.

Gavin had to talk me out of a cute little sparkly sky blue Raleigh bicycle on the grounds that it was for seven-to-ten-year-olds and had stabilizers.

I finally decided to take the wicker-basket number. I paid for it and the man took it off to pump up the tyres, but as I was pushing it out of the shop I noticed a beautiful shiny red and gold bell fastened to the handlebars that hadn't been there before.

'Gavin, that bell wasn't there earlier, was it?' I feared I was having one of my hunger-induced hallucinations. God, they could be troublesome. I was once convinced I'd seen Brian O'Driscoll walking down Grafton Street and decided to tell him what a disgrace that whole spear-tackle in New Zealand thing was. So I ran after him, asking how his shoulder was. Turns out it wasn't Brian O'Driscoll at all, just a guy wearing a number-13 jersey. Worst thing was, I knew him. He used to live on our road. *And* he was a complete ride. The stranger looked at me as if I was the most pathetic person alive in Ireland. 'Rugger-hugger,' he scoffed, and walked off. Which was so unfair because I wasn't *at all*. It's just I knew a girl who'd dislocated her shoulder and I wanted to tell Brian she'd made a full recovery. I went off and ate a sambo before I embarrassed myself again.

'No, it wasn't there earlier. I just got it for you as a little good-luck thing. Consider it a house-warming gift for a bicycle.'

'Ah, Gav, thanks a mill, I love it!'

I gave him a backer as we cycled around town, showing off my new set of wheels. Every now and again I'd get the opportunity to ring my lovely shiny bell at random death-wish pigeons who wanted to play dodge with my front wheel. Gavin suggested we pop in and say hi to Kate as we passed the Rotunda Hospital, where she worked. I swung a sharp left through the hospital gates, nearly throwing Gavin off the back and giving myself a wedgie in the process.

Kate was on a break when Gavin phoned her, so we waited in the car park for her to come out. She was working in obstetrics and had been overseeing a labour when the woman in question had suddenly decided she didn't want kids. Bit late, really, so one of the ward sisters was inside telling her to 'cop on' that she didn't have a choice at this stage. When Kate trotted down the front steps, Gavin scooped her up in a big hug. They were such a gorgeous couple. Kate was tall and willowy, with long brown hair and delicate features, while Gavin was taller again, with broad shoulders and a strong build. His dark messy hair was always unkempt in a non-contrived way and his green eyes had a glint of mischief. The Clothes Catalogue Couple. That's what I called them. But, thankfully, they didn't wear sweaters tied across their shoulders or point up at the sky, smiling at nothing.

'Hi, Izzy,' Kate called, and waved to me.

I wheeled my bike over to where they were standing. I always felt so small beside them. Like a little child. I could be a child in one of their catalogue shoots.

'Oh, cool! You got a bike!' Kate said.

I was feeling more like a child by the minute. 'Yeah just this afternoon. It was the basket and the streamers that really sold it to me!' I laughed. By. The. Minute. 'Listen, I'm going to leave you two lovebirds alone.'

'No, Izzy,' Kate said, 'you don't have to. Stay!'

'No, honestly, I need to go home and sort out my crayons.' (I didn't actually say this.) I told them I was going to have a look around the shops.

'See you soon, Iz,' they called, as I climbed back on board and headed out through the gates.

What a great day, I thought, as I cycled past the Gate The-atre and down past Clery's. Bunking off work with Gavin, check. Glorious sunshine, check. New bicycle *with* a basket on the front, check. So cycling in the city centre was pretty terrifying, but I'd get used to it soon enough and wouldn't scream *every* time a car zipped past me or feel the need to pull over and breathe into a brown-paper bag any time I spotted an oncoming bus. Cycling etiquette question: how bad is it if you knock someone's wing mirror in traffic and they shout after you but you don't stop?

Feeling all positive and invigorated about my Fresh Start, I decided I was going to head straight for Brown Thomas to buy the amazing dress I'd been perving over for the past six weeks. A shop assistant had asked me to leave the last time I was in (OK, so a little bit of drool fell on it – it was an accident). So, no more looking. I had to buy now. Hell, I deserved it! And purchasing it would help to mark the end of five long months of alienation and dressing like Misery Incarnate.

Yes, I was ready. I was going to break my self-imposed social-life ban. Facebook or no Facebook. Cian and Edna or no Cian and Edna. (It really would be preferable if there were no Cian and Edna, but I had to come to terms with the fact that there was.) It was time for Izzy Keegan to get back in the saddle, metaphorically speaking. This caterpillar was finally going to leave its fat furry existence and become a butterfly. But this little butterfly needed a fab set of wings if she was going to go out there and get flying, and that dress was perfect. It was seriously expensive and I hadn't a notion when I'd ever get a chance to wear it, given its incredible gorgeousness, but sometimes a woman had to act on the assumption that if she had the dress, the occasion would come and find her.

10

Its fri grls - I nd a drnk!!! Whos wit me?

Yippee! I cd murder a gin! Count me in!

Defo nd more than 1 - crap day at offce!

Ok amigos - where?

Smwhere we cn tlk. Ron blcks?

C u there!

There really was no gin like the Friday-night post-work gin. All day I had been staring at the clock, willing it to go faster. I had even thought about sneakily pushing the hands when no one was looking and bagging us all a half-day, but then I realized I'd need Susie, Keelin and the barman to back me up, and it wasn't fair to make them all lie on my behalf. Especially considering I didn't know the barman.

I was sitting there with my bag on my lap, coat on, and one foot off the ground ready to sprint when the minute hand clicked into place: gin o'clock! I'm outta here.

I was first to arrive at the pub, so I nabbed an empty couch down the back, away from all the loud, macho office types who thought that if you heard them say, 'A hundred and fifty K a year with a company car,' as you passed, you'd swoon and take off all your clothes before the evening was out. The trick was to get to your chosen seat without making eye contact. If you did catch someone's eye, you could bet your life he'd be making a mental note: later, when incoherent, I'll ask that up-for-it little minx to have a kebab and sex with me. She's sure to want both because she made eye contact. Oh, yes, I'm getting lucky tonight.

I made it through without anyone noticing me, then felt miffed that I could be so invisible to the opposite sex. I got a drink. Ah, Gordon was always there for me, no matter what. Isn't that right, Gordon? Hmm, perhaps that was where I was going wrong – forging strong attachments with my drinks instead of connecting with the real-live menfolk. I scanned them again. Did I really *have* to? Was this what 'moving on' was all about? Maybe if I zoned out and replayed *Love Actually* in my head while they talked at me, I could just nod and smile every now and then, and when the girls saw me 'flirting', they'd think I was coming on in leaps and bounds.

I settled down on a couch to watch how Keelin and Susie fared in the eye-contact-avoidance game. First up was Susie, who came barrelling through the door, talking nineteen to the dozen into her mobile. She didn't even register the ranks of drinkers, just strode past, oblivious. I smiled to myself – you can always spot a woman in a long-term relationship: she's the one who's forgotten what 'flirt' means and has no idea of the effect she can have on men. Susie used to be brilliant at getting us free drinks from amorous lechers, but those days seemed to have gone, thanks to Aidan. I missed that Susie.

'Sorry, Your Honour, I really have to go now. I have a five thirty with the Lynch crowd. They're still pleading innocent. 'Bye.'

'I'm the Lynch crowd? What did we do?' I was hoping for a juicy one, like maybe I'd run over my ex's new girlfr– Wow. I should probably stop watching so much True Movies. Tempting Fate. Besides, Susie dealt with leasings and conveyancing, so a good old-fashioned murder wasn't in the offing.

'Sorry, Iz, couldn't get him off the phone otherwise. And sorry, I can't say, you know how it works.'

'I'm so glad I'm not the only one who works with a megalomaniac. I mean, Eve hasn't exactly told me to call her "Your Honour" but close enough. . .'

'Izzy, that was my supervisor on this story. He's a judge.'

'Absolutely. I knew that. Hey, I got you a vodka. Get it down you.'

'Oh, God bless you. My brain's crying out for a decent dollop of alcohol. Why did I sign up for this again? And how the hell did I end up writing for a legal journal?'

'Because you're a fantastic writer and you have to start somewhere. So you're a journalist for now. And you're brilliant at it.'

'Iz, I write about banks repossessing people's homes and inheritance tax. Not exactly the stuff of top crime novels, is it?' She drained her drink in one. 'Where's Keelin?'

I pointed at the door, through which Keelin had just appeared. Now there was a woman who knew what flirting was all about. Keelin looked sexy no matter what she was doing. She could have moonwalked in wearing a full-body Lycra leotard and still looked cool. I watched her walk slowly past the tables, letting all the stripy-shirt men get a good look at what they'd never get their hands on. It was a masterclass. If I tried to do that, I'd probably trip over a stool and send them all flying, like a set of dominoes. But nothing fazed Keelin.

'Hello, ladies. You started without me, you sluts.'

'Here, I got us all one to start. We're only one ahead of you, so lash into that and it's even stevens.'

'Great. Okay, guess what?' she said, skulling it back and slamming the empty glass on the table.

'Em, you bought a pair of shoes?'

'No. Guess!'

'You passed your driving test?'

'God, no. Guess!'

'You found the back of the remote control?'

'Come on, girls, you can do better than that! *Concentrate!*' Good God, it was relentless. Keelin should give up her job and become a host on one of those crazy Japanese game-shows.

'Keelin, I'm going to torture you slowly and painfully if you make us guess any more,' Susie said calmly.

'Okay.' Keelin took a deep breath. '*Simon winked at me this morning!*' she screeched – at such a high pitch that I could have sworn I heard a dog somewhere in the distance bark in pain

'Wowser!' I said. 'That sure is . . . woweeee . . .' I could give up my job and become an American game-show host.

'I know. I was over at the photocopier, just casually doing a bit of photocopying while butt-cheek flirting with him at the same time –'

'Sorry, Keelin, have to stop you there,' I interrupted. 'Decode.'

'Izzy, have I taught you nothing?'

'Keelin, I've no idea what you're on about either.'

'Listen and learn, Susie. Okay, basically Simon is standing behind me, waiting for me to finish so he can use the photo-copier.'

'Right,' we say in unison, taking our lesson seriously.

'So I tense up my butt cheeks, then relax them, then tense them again so that when he looks at my arse, he sees that, you know, I'm flirting with him.'

Susie and I collapsed into laughter.

'Keelin, you're a mentallist,' Susie gasped.

'Why don't you just laugh inanely whenever he opens his

mouth? Or bat your eyelashes at Olympic speed or –'

'Izzy, I've tried all that stuff. And there was that time I laughed hysterically when he told me his granny was in the final stages of bowel cancer because I hadn't bothered to listen to what he said. It was time for a different technique because *nothing* had been happening.'

'He's probably just not that into you,' hovered on my lips, but I couldn't say it. It sounded way too harsh. Anyway, I didn't quite believe it.

I think what was killing her was that she rarely, if *ever*, got rejected. Keelin had always been the wild, sexy, crazy girl that guys couldn't get enough of. And, on top of that, she was *always* the one in control. A true heartbreaker. When she got bored, she'd just flit right on to the next, leaving misery in her wake. But she was never cruel about it – that wasn't in her nature. Keelin would never *intentionally* hurt someone. She was always upfront and honest with these guys, telling them from the start that she wasn't looking to settle down and play 'boyfriend and girlfriend', but inevitably they fell head over heels and wanted nothing more than to play 'boyfriend and girlfriend' with her. And by then their fate was sealed.

But this time, I think for the first time *ever*, it hadn't worked. The guy hadn't responded. Until that morning. Apparently.

'Normally when I butt-cheek flirt, I get results. You two can laugh all you want, but it's *never* failed. Well, not until Simon.'

'So what happened next, then?'

'Well, as luck would have it, Fate handed me a perfectly timed damsel-in-distress moment and the photocopier jammed, so Simon had to come to my rescue.'

'Did you jam it on purpose?'

'Obviously.'

'Good work. Continue.'

'Thanks. He opened the paper drawer to remove the jammed sheets, and because the machine is so old and crap, a load of dust blew into his face and – oh, my God, it was such a Clark Kent moment. I bent down and removed his glasses for him so he could wipe the dust off his face and we sort of just knelt there for a moment or two. Then, out of nowhere, he winked at me. Like he couldn't say, "Thank you," so he said it without words. It was so endearing and cute – I wish you'd been there.'

Too right we should have been there – to divert a potential sexual harassment case! Or, at the very least, to suggest that maybe he was trying to blink the dust out of his eyes.

I couldn't blame her for being so excited, though. 'The Wink', regardless of the motive, was a milestone. She'd been chasing this guy for the past eight weeks, ever since she'd got the job. She'd only answered the ad to appease her parents. She'd told them she'd accepted a voluntary redundancy package from her old firm to save any of the single mothers losing their jobs, when really she'd been fired for stealing éclairs from the vending machine. She was afraid her parents would start to suspect something if she didn't act soon so she decided to look for another job quick smart. While she was waiting to be interviewed, Simon walked by and that was that. She gave the interview of her life, claiming she'd saved a puppy from drowning in a neighbour's pond and that she'd once made a splint out of lollipop sticks for a blackbird that had broken its wing flying into her kitchen window. As a result, she was now the receptionist at a dogfood company called Ruff Justice. I know – painful. Her boss believed he could win over the public and part them from their money if he made them laugh. So now Keelin spent the day answering the phone, 'Ruff Justice,' only to be met by unamused silence. It was all a far cry from her commerce degree, but for some reason she seemed to think Simon was worth it. And, besides, she did have a soft spot for dogs, so organizing nice food for them wasn't the worst.

Once we'd all agreed that this morning's wink might quite possibly lead to a candle-lit dinner in Paris next weekend, Keelin said she had a proposition for me.

'No,' I begged. 'Please don't make me ring Simon to ask him if he fancies you.'

'Izzy, if you did that, I would legally divorce you as my friend. When have I ever made you do that since 1997?'

I racked my brains. She was right. June 1997: she'd made me ring Cormac Doherty. And, yes, he did fancy her.

'What I was actually going to say was that Caroline has decided to have a dinner party at her house tomorrow night for her birthday. And you're coming. For the *whole* night. Look at you here, out in a pub on a Friday night and doing great!'

I didn't want to tell them I had a beanie hat in my bag to pull over my face in case any randomers started shouting, 'Facebook freak,' at me.

'So, are you up for it?'

Hell, yeah! This was my no-nonsense Fresh Start after all, wasn't it? 'Bring it on!'

'Great,' she said, getting ready to go to the bar. 'Okay, gin, red wine and vodka it is. Now, when I come back, I want a considered opinion from each of you on whether or not you think there's any truth in the story that George Bush is actually related to an orang-utan in a Californian zoo.'

11

'Izzy, you *stink* of curry, do you know that?' Greg demanded, and covered his mouth as if he was about to puke on the table.

'Em, really, Greg? Well, I think everyone must stink of curry considering Caroline made us a curry and we're all eating it.' I hadn't blinked in quite a while and my eyes were starting to stream. My manic save-me stare at Keelin wasn't having the desired effect, and I felt like lobbing a bread roll at her head to get her attention. Why did she have such crap peripheral vision? And what on earth could Marcus be saying to her that was *that* interesting?

I smiled pathetically at Greg, hoping he would read the pain in my face and leave me alone.

No such luck.

'Actually, I think you'll find I don't stink of curry,' he droned. 'It's because after every few mouthfuls I pop one of these handy little breath fresheners into my mouth. See?'

As he exhaled a waft of minty curry breath into my face, I wondered how I'd managed to forget just how annoying he was. I did my best wow-that's-amazing-I'm-so-happy-for-you look as I shovelled another forkful of chicken into my mouth. If nights like this one had been all I'd missed out on, I'd gladly have chosen a bar of Galaxy, the couch and *The Woman Who Never Got Over Him* on True Movies, thanks very much.

No, Izzy, focus. This was my first committed, no-bullshit attempt at staying out past nine thirty on a weekend night. And if that meant sitting beside a Ginger Pain in the Arse to make a start, then so be it. Just for the record, I was *not* happy with

Caroline and her seating arrangements or the fact that she had a brother like Greg. But that wasn't her fault, I suppose. If this ever happened again, I'd have to re-evaluate my friendship with her. Susie was convinced she was trying to set me up with Greg. Horrific.

Apart from wanting to leave, I was doing quite well. This was the first time since Cian had dumped me that I was going to stay out *all* night, no matter what. Keelin and Susie had my key, and Mum and Dad had told me they'd Chubb-locked the front door, drawn all the curtains and disconnected the door-bell so I couldn't escape home. They were being so supportive. It wasn't a particularly challenging night – I was at a dinner party at a close friend's house – but I had to take things slowly. I was relatively safe here, just a casual evening in the company of friends, with zero chance of bumping into Cian and Edna. I sipped my wine and started to relax a little, zoning out Greg's droning.

'Do you want a mint, Isobel? I have loads – well, not loads, but I do have . . . let me see . . . seven! I could definitely spare one. I think you should take it, see how you get on. You don't have to go out and buy a whole packet or anything, so it's not much of a commitment . . . you might as well . . .'

People often joke about being bored to death. Well, it's no joking matter. If I listened to Greg any longer, I would be the first case of death by boredom in Ireland and there would be a slot on *Nationwide* about me. Oh, God – they'd re-enact the bit when they'd had to lift my face out of the plate of curry to check my pulse. And they'd probably get Edna McClodmutton to play me! My stomach dived. They wouldn't get Edna to play me because her hair was long and silky and she was far too tall and skinny to be me.

I decided to entertain myself with a daydream in which I was going for a long, romantic walk with Josh Hartnett along the Amalfi coast. Josh and I loved the seaside and we could spend hours sipping ice-cold cocktails and watching the sun dip slowly behind the twinkly ocean . . . 'No, Josh, I think it's too soon for marriage, let's just enjoy our time together now. I know you're obsessed with me, but we've only known each other for three days . . .'

'You're right, darling Izzy. It's just that I don't want you to run off with Brad Pitt. I know he's been hounding you again. Did I mention that you're so lovely and your hair really suits you up like that and that I don't think I've ever felt this way in my entire life?'

'Only a *million* times, Josh! Now don't be worrying about Brad, you silly big ride, and take off your clothes. Ooh, are you going to finish your strawberry daiquiri or can I have it?'

I was jolted back to reality when I missed my mouth with my wine glass and drowned my chin and my top in a huge splash of sauvignon blanc. I grabbed a napkin and tried to dab it away.

'. . . spearmint or peppermint, but the Ice Cool is definitely up there as my favourite flavour. You can't beat it. It's so refreshing and I find it really clears your nostrils so all you want to do is take really deep breaths, but then sometimes you feel light-headed, so you have to be careful . . .'

Dear Lord, if you could just send Josh Hartnett to save me right now, that would be greatly appreciated.

'Izzy, did you know that if you ring a certain number, I can't remember what it is now, I think it could be . . . No, it's gone – God, I just hate when that happens, don't you? I know all the numbers there are, you know, ones like six, three, seven, nine, five, for example, it's just I don't know necessarily what order they go in for certain phone numbers. Because there are so many. Like what's yours?'

'Our house phone got cut off because Susie spent all our

money for the bills on . . . tomato ketchup [*What?*] . . . she just loves the stuff. And my mobile phone fell down the loo the other day so I don't have any phone numbers at all! Pity, isn't it?'

'You're right, Isobel, it is, because I could have phoned you to give you this number I was talking about. When you call it you can choose from loads of different songs to have as your very own ringtone on your mobile phone!'

Although I wanted to very badly, I didn't shout, '*I don't care! I want to go and talk to someone else. I don't care!*' in his face. Instead I said, 'That's incredible.' I wondered if my face would ever go back to normal after holding a rictus grin for so long.

'Right? Well, I chose from a list of Eurovision winners so anytime anyone rings my mobile, Johnny Logan's "Hold Me Now" starts to play and I can sing along to it. Classic hit. Except I've learnt the hard way not to sing along when I'm on the bus. One time I was on the number eleven going home and just as I was singing the really emotional bit about tears having no place in her heart – you know that bit? – well, some – sorry to use the word – skanger who was sitting at the back of the bus threw a can of cider at the back of my head. See that scar there? The hair on that patch doesn't grow any more. Bald.' He started to fondle a tiny bit of his scalp. 'You can still see the scar, even though I put Bio Oil on it every night before I go to bed. Give me your finger there so you can have a feel . . .'

Just as he was reaching for my hand, I jumped up and blurted, 'My phone is buzzing in my pocket! What if it's an emergency and someone's in trouble? I must leave the table and check it *immediately*!'

Had I not just told him my mobile was broken? Had I been watching too much *Inspector Linley*? Not to worry, I was up now and nearly out of the room. I legged it past everyone and up the stairs to the toilet just as Greg was shouting across the table to Susie that if she wanted any tomato ketchup there was some on a saucer in the fridge.

'*Freedom!*'

Wow, *Braveheart* had inspired me more than I'd thought. Not that getting away from Greg was in the same league as Scotland being liberated from centuries of English oppression, but it was enough to make me want to jump on the back of a horse and, with blue warpaint slapped on my face and a sword raised over my head, ride up to him and roar, in a Scottish accent, for heightened effect, 'You can try to take my sanity, but you can never take my *freeeeeeedom*!'

I ran into the bathroom and banged the door shut behind me. Silence – at last! I took a few deep breaths, and refreshed my makeup. Keelin had told me that a few more of Caroline's school friends were arriving after dinner, so perhaps there'd be some potential flirtees. It had been a while, but I reckoned there had to be a pulse beating somewhere in my charm department.

I practised fluttering my lashes in the mirror and doing a little coy, pouty sort of a thing. Hmm, looked more like Bell's palsy than 'come hither' – but nothing a few more glasses of *vino* couldn't fix.

As I applied more lipgloss, someone knocked on the door. 'Isobel, are you in there? Hello? Isobel, are you in there?'

'Yes, Greg. I am. I'll see you downstairs in a while, okay?'

'How long will you be? It's just that I found that number for the ringtones and I've written it on a napkin. Do you want me to give it in to you?'

'Oh, thanks – don't come in, though! Em, you can just pass it under the door.' Will, Caroline's flatmate, had been meaning to install a lock on the bathroom door for the past year and a half. He was still 'getting around to it'. Apparently the choice at Homebase was 'mind-boggling'.

'Okay, and I think you should get the Johnny Logan song too because then we could get people to phone us at exactly the same time and do a duet together when our phones ring!'

'How lovely. 'Bye!'

Thank God he didn't walk in. I didn't know how Greg would have reacted to seeing me sitting on the loo peeing. He probably would have roared laughing and traipsed everyone up the stairs to have a look. But then, just as I was pulling up my jeans, the door swung open.

'Greg, for God's sake, I'll ring the number later on,' I muttered.

'Oh, I'm so sorry – em, it's not Greg. I'm Jonathan.'

I looked up and froze. Oh, holy divine God!

Incredibly good-looking random stranger standing in the bathroom. Jeans half-way up my thighs, hideous ratty old pair of knickers on full display. Were there any strays poking out? I'd say most definitely. Hermits who have only recently come out of hiding are not, as a general rule, well groomed. All of a sudden, the heady mixture of panic and alcohol became too much and I tripped over my foot and stumbled awkwardly towards the bath, arms flapping madly, desperately searching for something to grab on to. Missing the sink, I lunged at the shower curtain, pulling the whole thing down on top of me as I landed arse first in the bath.

'Shit! Are you okay? I'm so sorry. That was completely my fault. Did you hurt yourself?'

I opened my eyes to see the incredibly good-looking random stranger leaning over me as I sat wedged in the bath with my legs dangling over the side. I turned bright red, muttered, 'Em, I think so,' then tried to hoist myself out. All I managed to do in the process was knock a bottle of Head and Shoulders off the shower rack and on to the floor, where I watched it ooze out over his shoes. How had this little mini-disaster crept up out of nowhere? I'd been doing so *well*.

'Here, grab my hand and I'll pull you out,' the getting-better-looking-by-the-minute guy said, and pulled me to my feet. Had he said his name was Jonathan? I couldn't remember. I could barely remember my own name, such was my shock and embarrassment.

Eureka! I'd tell him my name was . . . Lorna! Lorna Quigly! Then I'd leg it out of the bathroom and into Caroline's bed-room, where I would rummage through her wardrobe and change into a different outfit. After that, I would come back downstairs as Isobel Keegan and tell Jonathan that Lorna had had to go home early, which was a pity because although she was very clumsy she was also a genuinely lovely girl. It was the perfect plan, and I could totally get away with it as my face was currently disguised by a bright red glow. He'd never know.

'You're Izzy, aren't you?'

Shit. Shit. Shit.

Gutted that my plan had been foiled, I didn't even lift my head to look at him.

'Lorna Quigly,' I whispered, a little sorrowfully and in such a hushed tone I barely heard it myself.

'Hey, you banged your head when you fell – you have a bit of a bruise coming up on your forehead.' He swept my hair back from my face. 'Do you feel okay?'

'I think so.'

I tried to button up my jeans on the sly without him notic-ing. Thinking I'd got away with it, I looked up to see that he was doing a fairly convincing impression of someone who was fascinated by bathroom tiles.

'Listen, I'm so sorry about that,' he blurted, when he thought a sufficient amount of jeans-buttoning time had elapsed.

'Don't be silly – it wasn't your fault,' I replied. 'I'm Izzy, but you already knew that, and now you know the colour of my knickers.'

'I could show you my boxer shorts if it'd make you feel any better.' He laughed.

Ding-dong! Yes, please!

After a moment or two of silence, and Jonathan looking increasingly uncomfortable as I stared expectantly at his crotch, I realized that he had been joking.

'Okay!' I clapped my hands together. 'I'm going to head back to the party.' Before he had time to respond, I was out of the door and down the stairs. 'Who the hell was he?' I asked the contents of Caroline's fridge as I grabbed more wine from the shelf and refilled my glass. He was so bloody gorgeous. I shut the door and leant against it. Was he a friend of Caroline's? Who else did he know here? When had he arrived?

Stop the press.

What if it turned out he'd only been some kind of vision that had appeared before me in the bathroom and no one else believed me when I told them I'd seen him? Had it been so long since I'd been with a guy that I was imagining chance meetings with good-looking strangers? Now that I thought about it, Jonathan had reminded me a bit of Josh Hartnett. And I'd definitely made up chance meetings with him.

So, getting back to Jonathan. Perhaps it had been just another Josh fantasy, but as I was now mildly pissed, I'd only come up with a second-rate Josh. Alcohol can easily cause things to get muddled in your head.

I wasn't buying this. My fear was that an incredibly hot man had in fact seen (a) me fall backwards into a bath with my jeans half-way down my thighs, ripping a shower curtain in the process, and (b) that I hadn't had a bikini wax since the

Before era. Oh, and (c) me mildly sexually harassing him by staring at his crotch for an uncomfortable length of time.

An hour and a half and five more glasses of wine later, I had completely recovered from the trauma caused by points (a), (b) and (c) and was rechoreographing a Beyoncé song on top of the dinner table with Keelin. 'Look at me, Keelin! I'm out past nine thirty on a Saturday night!' I beamed proudly, waggling my arse at her like a feather duster.

'I'm so proud of you, Iz,' she slurred back, 'but what happened to you? You look like you've a boob growing out of your forehead.'

'You know on *Dr Phil* when someone's repressed something so horrific from the past that when they finally tell someone they have an emotional breakdown?'

'Yeah.'

'Well, the same thing might happen to me if I drag up what happened, so I'm not going to tell you.'

'Fair enough.'

Shit. I was kind of hoping she'd ask me if it'd involved a complete random stranger called Jonathan. When she didn't, I asked, 'Who's Jonathan?'

'He's Will's cousin, from London. He works in film too, so Will said. He's quite hot, isn't he? Not Simon hot, but definitely hot.'

Was he *what*? Why had Will never told me he had a cousin? I was so hurt – although I didn't think Will knew much about my extended family either so I'd leave him off.

So it appeared I hadn't been plagued by the Single and Desperate Virus and that Jonathan was indeed a real live person and not a fevered hallucination. Good to know, too, that my desire to sleep with Josh Hartnett wasn't morphing into a morbid obsession that I'd need to speak to a professional about.

'I'm gonna go find him,' I said to Keelin, who'd now started break-dancing.

'Do! Go find him!' she encouraged me, spinning around on her elbow. She was going to be one sore little madam in the morning. I hadn't seen her bend like that since Sister Eileen's gym class in the early 1990s.

Time to go and find Jonathan and try out my Bell's palsy face on him. If I was really lucky, he had a bad memory and/or wasn't the sharpest tool in the box so had already forgotten what had happened in the bathroom. It might also help to distract me from the few Cian thoughts that were creeping into the back of my mind.

Go away, Cian Thoughts! *Please!*

But I couldn't help wondering where they were tonight, Cian and Edna McClodmutton. Were they out at Club Life? Were they having a shagfest lockdown weekend? Was she participating in some beauty pageant while he sat in the front row clapping? When was I going to stop missing him, thinking about him? When would the day come that I didn't crave seeing him, talking to him or just hearing him laugh? When was it going to stop kicking me in the gut every time I thought about it?

When?

Wheeeeeeeeen?

No.

No, Izzy! Stop this!

I slapped myself across the face. Snap out of it. I wasn't going to let this happen. Not tonight. Not when I was dolled up and out for the night, bravely being a butterfly after months of living like a caterpillar. I was out past nine thirty, having fun with my friends. This was progress. Of course there were times when I allowed myself to indulge in daydreams – little fantasies of being back with him, watching a movie together, going for a drink, sitting on his knee, him twirling his fingers around loose strands of my hair. Well, bollocks to that! Now wasn't going to be one of those times. Especially not when I'd been drinking buckets of cheap wine. Good God, I'd have to move back home altogether if I got upset now, rang Cian and left a ten-minute '*WWWWWHH-HHHYYYYY?*' on his voicemail.

No, this was the time to brush off the cobwebs, to tell myself that Cian was a prick of the highest order and that I was better off without him. Onwards and upwards!

I wished Gavin were here. He'd slap some sense into me quick smart. I'd only have to mention Cian's name and he'd roll his eyes and mumble, 'Prick,' under his breath.

'Izzy, I just saw you slap yourself across the face. What's wrong? Tell me. Do you wanna take your mind off it by teaching me some of your Buoyancy dance moves?' Greg whined, as I trotted past him.

'My *what* moves?'

'Hello? Your Buoyancy moves! Lead singer of Density Child! Although maybe you shouldn't, now I think about it. I have a corn on my little toe and my chiropodist has warned me that excessive –' That was all I heard before I disappeared out on to the balcony to see what the others were up to.

A drinking game, as it happened.

At five thirty, when everyone else was long gone, Will had to carry Keelin, Susie and me in from the balcony and out of the front door to where a taxi was waiting impatiently for us.

'My shoes. Susie threw them over the balcony.'

'Why?'

'She wasn't impressed when I told her there were no size fives left in the shoe sale. Like it was my fault! She's had *way* too much to drink,' I scoffed. 'Excuse me,' I protested, as

Will shoved my head through the door of the taxi. 'I need to get my shoes!'

'I'll drop them round to you tomorrow.'

'What if one of your neighbours nicks them? Will? *Will, my shoes!*' I croaked into the night sky as the taxi drove off. *'My lovely new peep-toes from the Brown Thomas summer sale!'*

I sat back into the taxi seat and wondered if Will's old pensioner neighbour Mrs Boyle would be spotted clopping along in my new peep-toes on her way to Mass in the morning. Then I started to think about Will's gorgeous cousin, Jonathan, whom I hadn't seen at all after the bathroom incident. Where had he been for the rest of the evening?

'Jonathan!' I shouted.

The taxi driver rolled his eyes and asked me if I'd forgotten my boyfriend and did we have to turn back.

'Not my boyfriend, Mr Taxi Man,' I slurred, 'but your positivity is touching. Thank you.'

'Come here to me,' Keelin mumbled, grabbing my face awkwardly in her hands and leaning in to me as if she was about to enlighten me with the most amazing piece of information. 'You gotta shag him.'

'I do, don't I?' I accepted bravely.

'You must!' Susie piped from the front seat, then slid across her seat and rested her head on our driver's shoulder.

'I must,' I repeated to myself.

'He's the perfect get-over-Cian guy. You must sleep with him!'

'You must! You must! You must!' Keelin, Susie and Mr Taxi Man chanted.

'I must! I must! I must!' I murmured, then slumped onto Keelin's shoulder and fell asleep.

12

'*Excuuuse me!* Get your rotten grubby notes off my desk. Yes, *my* desk – you have your own, you know. Just because you have issues with slovenliness does *not* mean you burden me with them.' She patted her scraped-back bun without even looking at me, but I could see that her nose was flared in disgust. She had quite a hooked one already, but when she was cross the tip of it curled down so that it almost touched her top lip. The orange lipstick she'd just reapplied was painful on the eye and I had to look away.

'Eve, for God's sake, they're not even *on* your desk,' I said.

'Isobel, I think you'll find that they are, in fact, on my desk. Did we or did we not discuss that my desk also includes the space around my desk, which, if I remember correctly and I always do, is exactly another two and a half inches from where the edge of my desk ends? Now, you may be going blind but I most certainly am not. I take two antioxidant tablets every day, as well as a vitamin A supplement, both of which have proven effects for one's eyesight. By my judgement your notes are invading the extra two-and-a-half-inch periphery of my desk. What's more, you haven't stopped sneezing all morning, so those notes are going to be covered with your filthy germs. Well, get snappy. *Move them! Off, off, off!*'

'Eve, relax, I don't have SARS,' I grumbled, as I gathered my splayed papers together and attempted to arrange them in neat bundles.

'Well, I wouldn't be surprised if you did. I know how fond you are of Chinese takeaways.'

Chinese takeaways? How ignorant was this woman? I resisted the urge to slap her. 'Eve, the only reason I'm sneezing is because you insist on burning incense at your desk. It smells vile, like a mixture of fish slop and toilet freshener.'

'Well, that would be the new cinnamon and orange ones. They're very good at relieving stress. You see, I work the hardest in here, Isobel, so anything that soothes my mind helps me to perform more efficiently. Who knows? They might do you some good too! Although, I don't think they're miracle-workers – *haw, haw haw*!' She was snorting wildly, like a donkey choking on a bread roll.

'I'd get that cough to the doctor, if I were you, Eve, sounds nasty.'

'What cough? I don't have a cough!'

'Oh, sorry, were you *laughing*?'

'Shut up.'

I looked back at my computer screen to see that I had spent the last five minutes typing 'jfdiauijfdnife djifoaius fdkj hguyrb hi hiyeyhl uihb jdiryttjhdjjhfuid jfkdfiafguighje htbbwpojan HUHAUEHH oiroejkmkppwo23jji***&&%$ ieooiej'.

'By the way,' Eve sneered, 'you spelt committee wrong in your notes. It has two *m*s, two *t*s and two *e*s.'

'Tell me, Eve,' I asked her sweetly, 'how many *m*s, *t*s and *e*s are there in Complete and Utter Pain in the Hole?'

Torture.

I think I'd rather spend five years in the Bangkok Hilton listening to Abba remixes than have to sit here day in, day out beside Eve, listening to her whine on *ad nauseam* about nothing. My nose tingled again. Another sneeze coming on.

Fantastic! I'd sneeze right at her, not covering my mouth or nose. Brilliant! Quite gross, but brilliant. I poured every bit of energy I could muster into making it the biggest sneeze

I had ever sneezed in my entire life. I inhaled a steady stream of air until my chest had expanded to its full capacity and waited. Ready for action, my eyes scrunched tightly shut – '*AaaaaCHOOOOOOO!*'

'*You filthy mutant!*' Eve shrieked, as I shrugged my shoulders helplessly, pointing towards the incense sticks that stood on her desk releasing plumes of smoke. 'No, sorry, not you, Mr Breen – hello? Are you still there? You think I may have deafened your right ear? Hello, can you hear me now? Hello? If you can hear me, I'm so sorry . . . Give me a sign that you can hear me. Press three if you're not deaf,' she pleaded down the phone to whoever she'd been speaking to. I think Mr Breen was one of the head honchos at BCM Films. Ha, ha!

I got back to the task in hand and deleted the garbage I'd spewed onto my screen during my heated exchange with Eve. What time was it? Nearly eleven thirty! For the first time in my life I wanted it to be nine o'clock again. Lovely, clean, fresh, unpanicky nine o'clock. Not shit-yourself-only-an-hour-and-half-left-until-lunch eleven thirty.

Lunchtime meant briefing my boss about practically everything to do with *Snog Me Now, You Dublin Whore* – shoot dates, castings, location managers, costume departments, catering, wage deals. Lunchtime also meant no lunchtime. No nice deli-made sandwiches with melted cheese, sundried tomatoes and red onion. Just my own handmade ones, which were always gross, limp, squished and over-buttered. I'd known when I was getting ready for work this morning that I wouldn't have time to leave the office for lunch so I'd come prepared with a sandwich and a soft, wrinkled apple for one of my five-a-day. Somehow I can convince myself it counts even if I don't eat it.

I stole a quick glance at the office clock. Were the ticks getting louder? Eleven forty! This was awful. It was like a real-life version of one of those horrible Leaving Cert dreams I get when I'm stressed. You know the ones I mean: you're there with only seven minutes left to finish five questions, all the instructions seem to be written in Greek, the ink in your pen has just run out and your claw-like writing hand has knotted itself into a spasmodic cramp. I was in exam hell. Only worse. I had approximately three months' work to do in one hour and twenty minutes.

'Isobel?'

'Yes, what — what, yes?' I looked up from the computer to see Fintan's expectant face glaring at me.

'How's the brief coming along?'

'Well,' I joked, 'it's brief.'

Nothing. Not even a charity chuckle.

'Right, Mr Cunningham from BCM will be coming in at lunchtime to go through all the facts and figures with us, so just make sure the presentation is up to scratch. We know how important BCM Films are to us, don't we? Yes, we do.' He winked, did some crazy hand charade and was gone.

If it hadn't been highly inappropriate, not to mention absolutely disgusting, I might have pissed myself there and then. Someone from BCM was coming in? *Here?* To go through the presentation? *Presentation?*

Looking down at my desk, I wanted to cry. Grubby little yellow Post-its littered every square inch of the surface. Underneath them bulged mountains of random A4 pages. I looked at the computer screen — blank, apart from the little cursor at the top left-hand corner that blinked incessantly at me. Someone from BCM was coming in? Leaving Cert double hell. Like the minister for education reading out your exam answers on national television.

BCM was basically the patron saint of Lights! Camera! Action!. If anyone should so much as mention its name in our office, a chorus of angels could be heard singing an accompanying '*Aaaaaaah*'. The day Fintan found out that BCM had accepted a deal to co-produce *Snog Me Now, You Dublin Whore*, he brought us all out to dinner and even ordered champagne. (Well, it was only *cava*, but I like to pretend sometimes that I'm living the dream.) The kitchen was also stocked with Kimberley biscuits for an entire week, courtesy of himself. *That's* how important it was.

Eleven fifty-five! How in God's name had that happened? The computer cursor continued to blink expectantly at me.

The next time I raised my head it was exactly seventeen minutes past one. I had somehow managed to arrange random names, dates, figures and estimates into what just might pass as a 'presentation'. I even had a cute smiley face with its lips pursed printed next to the *Snog Me Now, You Dublin Whore* title. I stood over the printer and watched with blurred vision as my efforts were spat out in efficient-seeming blurbs.

'Isobel? Could you let Mr Cunningham in? He's down at the front door,' Fintan called from his office. I longed for the cool authority of buzzing someone in but, no, we had to leg it down the narrow, winding staircase past the cluttered filing cabinets. It was like an office-furniture assault course.

The rug was wedged under the front door and for the life of me I couldn't shift it to let Mr Cunningham in.

'Hang on, I'll just give it another tug,' I called, through the letterbox.

'Do you want me to push the door from out here?' he answered.

The hallway was as narrow as Victoria Beckham's waist, so I was afraid he might kill me if he pushed too hard.

'Here, I'll try and squeeze round it,' he offered, and a leg appeared through the gap between the door and its frame.

The poor man. I winced as I watched him try to wedge himself through.

Nice shoes, I thought. Well, shoe. I assumed he was wearing a matching pair and that the other one was equally nice. Hmm, impressive expensive trouser leg and, hang on, a lovely muscly thigh to fill it! Was this Mr Cunningham going to be young and handsome? No way! Never! I'd pictured him as a clone of my dad's friend Ned Hogan, just a regular middle-aged balding man with a sleazy moustache.

Another excruciating shove and in came his torso, lovely and toned through his white shirt. This was like unwrapping the best Christmas present ever! The sleeves of his shirt were rolled up to reveal tanned forearms and strong, manly hands.

'Nearly there!' he called, as I stayed motionless on my hunkers, clutching the rug with bated breath. Please, please, please let him be good-looking . . .

With one last heave he was through the door.

I froze. Then I dropped the rug, let out an embarrassingly audible yelp and stared up at him in a complete, shock-induced stupor.

'Hi, Isobel,' he purred.

'Hi . . . Jonathan,' I squeaked.

Holy shit!

'How have you been?'

'Stupendous!'

Did I just use the word 'stupendous'? Yes, I believe I did.

His brown eyes hovered over me as he smiled and offered his hand. As he pulled me to my feet, he whispered teasingly, in my right ear, 'I think I've done this for you before.'

My cheeks were burning. To disguise the emissions of radioactive waves from my face, I headed for the stairs. 'We'd better go up or he'll think we've got ourselves into some kind of trouble.'

'Oh, what kind of trouble?'

'No. I think – we – seriously, I think we should just be serious,' I replied completely deadpan, like the talking clock. What was I doing? Here was my chance to be smart, witty and outrageously flirty, but all I could muster was the voice of an automated answering service. I tried to redeem myself. 'It's jusht that we're to be very busy with the whore from Dublin. Ha ha. Ha.' I sounded pissed.

As we walked up the stairs in an awkward silence, I tried to figure out how Mr Cunningham from BCM was that absolute ride from the dinner party. Images of myself hovering over the toilet with my jeans around my ankles, horrific grey knickers on show, then falling drunkenly into the bath mushroomed in my mind. I felt like Lois when she discovered Clark Kent and Superman were one and the same person.

All of a sudden I became acutely aware that my arse was directly in front of his face as we trudged up the narrowest staircase ever fashioned by the hand of man. He was looking at it – he had to be! It was right in front of him! It suddenly felt huge – no, gigantic, so horrifically enormous I was afraid it was about to get stuck between the wall and the handrail.

After what felt like a month of Arse Watch, we reached the top of the stairs. I held open the office door for him without facing him; I couldn't bear to.

'Thanks,' he murmured. As soon as he'd disappeared into Fintan's office, I twisted my head over my shoulder to see if my arse had indeed mutated into the size of a small country in the time it had taken me to get up from my desk and answer the front door. Thank God, it appeared to have stayed the usual size.

'I wasn't going to say it, but you've obviously noticed it now yourself. You have serious VPL in those trousers,' Eve said, as she blew on her steaming mug of green tea.

That was the least of my worries. To hell with VPL: I was more concerned with the acute FES I was suffering from — Feckin' Eejit Syndrome. The man must think I'm mentally impaired, not to mention socially inept, I mused. I bet he thinks I'm here doing work experience on a community outreach programme designed by the Department of Social Services to help integrate mentally impaired and socially inept individuals into society. How could I convince him I was reasonably sane? The thought of what lay ahead of me for the next hour was enough to make me and my oversized backside want to turn and run all the way to Dun Laoghaire, jump on a ferry, sail to Wales and hide there for the rest of my life under the assumed name of Gladys Cllewenyllwyn.

That would be a rash and foolish decision. I had nothing packed or organized for emigration. I was stuck here, whether I liked it or not. And now I had to go and sit in a confined space in front of the incredibly good-looking random stranger and try to convince him of the advantages of Section 481 of the government tax incentives with regard to indigenous film-making. And not to have me fired when he discovered my presentation looked like an eight-year-old's homework. Oh, and to fancy me.

Leaving Cert triple hell! Like going in to do your Irish oral only to discover that the examiner is the guy you have secretly been in love with for the last three years. And it turns out that it's not a secret at all. In fact, it's on the syllabus. And you have to discuss your love of him with him for an entire hour in Irish.

'Isobel?' Fintan called. 'Can you come in so we can get started?'

13

What was that smell? Oh, yeah. Tuesday Night Smell. Keelin's experimental cuisine night. I dumped my keys on the
hall table and rifled through the mail. As usual, there was
nothing of interest. Still I always held on to the tiniest glim-
mer of hope that I'd find a handwritten letter hidden in the
bundle. From whom, I wasn't sure. My Finnish pen-pal still
hadn't replied to my last letter. And, okay, I'd sent it in March
1994, but I hadn't entirely given up hope.

At least my credit-card bill hadn't surfaced. My stomach
lurched at the thought of what I might owe this month – on
second thoughts maybe I felt a bit off because of the pun-
gent fumes of fried penguin or roasted walrus wafting to me
from the kitchen. I glanced down at my pink sparkly wedges
and cut-off white jeans. Were they worth such abject guilt?
Yes, actually, they were. And they were kind of free because
I hadn't gone out at weekends for so long that the money I
would have spent had been clawed back into my wardrobe.
To think that one of my tutors at college had had the cheek
to fail me in my financial management assignment!

I'll admit that the bag had, perhaps, been slightly excessive,
but it had really cute dancing elephants on it. And the only
reason I hadn't brought back the seriously overpriced giant
pink glitterball was because that cute little boutique in Sandy-
mount only offered store credit on returns. And then I'd only
buy something silly instead. Once more, practical financial
management.

Penguin or no penguin, I was starving. A mixture of a two-hour-long presentation meeting plus the shock I'd suffered at discovering Mr Cunningham from BCM was in fact Jonathan Ride Cunningham from the party meant that I'd dumped my sandwich in the bin. Forget dieting! Excessive stress was where it was at.

'Izzy? Come and check this out. Someone's about to wake up,' Susie called from the sitting room.

'On my way,' I replied. I had no interest in *Big Brother*.

'Oh, no . . . Wait . . . he was just turning over. Yep, he's still asleep. False alarm!'

I was afraid of what might happen if Susie started watching regular TV again. The excitement could kill her.

'What's Keelin cooking?'

'Rainbow trout stuffed with peanuts, coriander and pineapple. It's Malaysian, I think.'

No mention of chocolate. Disappointing. I really felt like chocolate this evening. It sounds vile, but Keelin had once made chocolate soup and it was *amazing*.

I pushed open the sitting-room door and was even more disappointed: Aidan.

'All right?' he said, without having the grace to look up from the television.

'Hi, Aidan. You staying for dinner?'

'Smells fuckin' shit. I got stuff from the chipper.'

'Fair enough. What's going on in *Big Brother*?'

'Dunno. It's fuckin shit.' At least we had that in common.

'Izzy, come and sit down,' said Susie.

'Have yiz got ketchup?' he asked, in his put-on northside accent. I wondered how Mr and Mrs Costello, Aidan's golf-playing, Spanish-villa-owning, Lexus-jeep-driving, Dalkey-residing parents felt about his preferred choice of Dublin accent. Probably none too chuffed I'd say after his three-thousand-euro-a-term private education.

99

'I'll get some for you now,' Susie said obediently, and got up to go to the kitchen. *Lazy* bollocks.

We passed a few moments watching a *Big Brother* contestant yawning and scratching his private parts.

'So, you ridin' anyone at the moment?' Aidan asked, as he shoved a fistful of greasy chips into his mouth.

'Em, no,' I responded, slightly mortified. I felt as if I was back in junior school and someone had just said 'willy'.

'Why? You still obsessed with that Cian bloke or something?'

'What? No! I . . . I'm just happy to be single at the moment.' *Rude* bollocks.

'You not dyin' for a ride?'

'No!'

'Why? You got a shit sex drive?'

'No!'

'So you've got a high sex drive, do ya, ya dirty bitch? Love to be lashin' the fellas out of it, do ya?'

'Here we go. Ketchup,' Susie chirped, as she came back in and plonked herself down beside him.

I was so stunned by what Aidan had said that I couldn't even tell her that that particular bottle of ketchup had been sitting around since I'd last heard from my pen-pal.

'This ketchup's a load of shite.'

'Oh, sorry, I'll open a new bottle.' She raced back into the kitchen. Lazy *prick*.

'So you and that Cian fella? Ridin' every fuckin' hour, were yiz?'

Should I say yes or no? Which answer was worse?

'No? No fuckin' surprise the poor fucker dumped ya so!'

'Any auditions coming up for you, Aidan?' I asked, cutting across him.

'No. Me agent isn't gettin' me any at the moment. Is there

anything in the film you're workin' on for me?'

'No, unfortunately. Our film is about people who've lived very hard-knock lives and come from a very raw underbelly of society.'

'Eh? Are you jokin'? *Hello?*' he says, pointing at himself.

'Oh, sorry, Aidan, I'm confused ... are you not from Dalkey? Your folks have a place in Soto Grande right?'

'Brand new bottle of ketchup – there you go.'

'Nice one. You're a fuckin' legend.' He pulled her down to him and kissed her, his greasy hands all over her. Images of Susie's mum rocking back and forth in a strait-jacket, whimpering, 'Aidan. His name is Aidan,' flooded my mind, as they always did when he was around. He let her go and she giggled as she sat down beside him again. He turned to me and winked without her noticing. 'Fuckin' love a bit of that, wouldn' ya?' He grinned.

'Huh?' Susie asked.

'I'm talking 'bout me chips, babe, you'd love some, wouldn' ya?'

Lying bollocks.

'No, thanks, I'm grand. I'll wait for the trout.'

'Here, Suz, whaddya reckon we try and set Izzy up with Redzer or Buzzer or one of the lads? I reckon she's dyin' for it.'

More images of mothers poured through my mind, this time Redzer and Buzzer's. 'Three thousand euro a term!' I heard them wail. '*A term!*' I could never remember whether Aidan's crew were actual scumbags or just pretend ones, like Guy Ritchie. Either way, I'd rather have had to live with Greg, have little ginger children and exist on a diet of mints for the rest of my life than hook up with any of Aidan's skanger mates. The one thing Aidan had going for him was good looks – the others looked like a pack of anaemic ferrets.

'Em, I don't know. Eh ... what do you reckon, Izzy? They're really sound – they're coming over in a while to watch the match so you can have a look for yourself.'

I'd rather have chewed dried shite off a donkey's arse. What was it with my friends wanting to set me up with people who repulsed me? First Greg, and now I'd have my pick of the anaemic ferrets. Had any of them actually got to know me over the years at all? Or had they been zoning out all along, just pretending to listen to me anytime I'd opened my mouth?

And what match?

'What match?' I asked.

'Liverpool versus Bolton. It should be a terrific game,' said Susie, smiling broadly. Definitely feigned interest.

'Oh. What time does it start? *Sleepless in Seattle* is on later.'

'No fuckin' chance, man, we're not watchin' that fuckin' poncy shit about girls wantin' a ride and cryin' and shit. The fuckin' match is on!' He closed the discussion by shovelling another fistful of greasy chips into his mouth.

Should I remind him that I lived here and he didn't?

Better not. I had a lot of work to do tomorrow and I wouldn't get much done in a neckbrace and an arm sling. I decided to hunt Keelin down for some post-Jonathan re-encounter discussions instead. Hopefully she'd tell me I hadn't made too much of an arse of myself.

'And then you did *what?*' Keelin shrieked, as she whipped her head out of her wardrobe. She was taking off her work gear. 'You must have looked like a beast – you haven't waxed in months!'

Obviously this was not going to be one of those compassionate-lying moments. I'd been kind of hoping to hear something along the lines of 'No, listen, I'd say he's actually fallen in love with you. Honestly, guys love it when you do quirky, stupid stuff, they find it *endearing*. And perhaps he's spent a lot of time on the Continent and is used to hairy women.'

I stared at her pleadingly. Lie, woman, lie! I'd started from the beginning and told her about my slight indiscretion in the bathroom at Caroline's party. And now I wished I hadn't.

I also wished I was dead.

I watched her as she rooted through her wardrobe for something to wear. Silence, as she crawled even further into it. What was she doing? Looking for the door to Narnia?

'Here they are, my new jeans – had to hide them from Susie. She's such a thief.' She reefed the tag off and poured herself into them. Wow, they were gorgeous. I might have to steal them some time. I'd just blame Susie. She's such a thief.

'Listen,' Keelin said, as she surveyed her arse in the mirror, 'I bet he didn't even notice the grey knickers . . .'

'Do you think? So maybe it wasn't *that* bad, then?'

'No, not at all . . . *snughf, snughf.*' Was she sneezing? Was Keelin allergic to Dermot now, too? Ah, poor Dermot . . .

She wasn't sneezing.

She was *laughing*!

'. . . I'd say he didn't notice the knickers because he was too distracted by your thigh brows,' she shrieked, as she collapsed into a heap at the end of her bed. 'Izzy, I'm sorry for laughing, but it's just so . . . funny!' she wheezed.

'Keelin, shut up! I already feel like such a twat. It's not funny.'

'It *is* funny.'

'It isn't.'

'It is.'

'I know.'

After Keelin had got over the hysteria of my flashing

episode, we spent the next hour chewing over the details of that afternoon: the encounter at the front door, my flame-red cheeks, the awkward walk up the stairs with my bum in his face. She even offered the well overdue 'No, seriously, it's *graaaaaaand*!' lie once or twice when I told her about my severe sense-of-humour malfunction.

'But I couldn't think of anything funny to say – he probably thinks I'm a boring shite.'

'Well, it was better than coming over all girlie and pathetic and laughing insanely at every little thing he said.'

'But –'

'Seriously, it's *graaaaaaand*!'

'No, but I eventually *did* come over all girlie and pathetic. And I'd say the laughing was more manic than insane.'

'Oh.'

'I'd even go so far as to say my laughter was disturbing. Think the Joker in *Batman*. My makeup probably wasn't too far off his either, with the amount of sweating I'd done.'

'Makeup meltdown.'

'Literally. So after we went into my boss's office to discuss the presentation, I knew I shouldn't be doing it, but I couldn't help it! I must have been trying to compensate for all the damage I'd already done, but I just couldn't stop. I was like an eight-year-old at a McFly concert. I'm telling you, all he'd have to say was "profit shares" or "Revenue rebates" and I'd literally collapse into a fit of laughter, stamping my foot and slapping the desk. It was horrific. And, of course, I couldn't spell or write or add . . . and when he did try to help me sub-tract four hundred euro from nine hundred and fifty, all I could do, after an agonizing three-minute pause, was snort-giggles!'

'Oh, Izzy . . .'

'And to make matters worse, all my boss could do was

make awkward, apologetic tut-tuts and say, "I don't know what her problem is, she's usually quite articulate," over and over again. I'd say he'll send me for a drugs test tomorrow.'

'I wouldn't blame him if he did.'

'Neither would I.'

'Well, either he'll send you for a drugs test or he'll set up a crèche in the office for you so you'll have somewhere to play with your bricks and do your colouring-in assignments.'

'Ha-bloody-ha.'

Keelin had just launched into her latest update on getting Simon to fall in love with her when the doorbell rang. All I managed to piece together before we both moved off was that his stapler had broken so he'd asked for the lend of hers, which on Keelin's terms was pretty much him saying he wanted to sleep with her. I really was incredibly out of touch. I didn't understand the intricacies of flirting at all. Laurence had asked if he could borrow my yellow highlighter today, but I'm fairly sure it wasn't a ploy to have sex with me. Anyway, I was glad that at least one of us had had a successful day at the office.

As we made our way down the stairs, no one could have blamed us for thinking we'd been teleported to Ballymun *circa* 1988. Keelin inhaled sharply as she executed a Chinese burn on my right arm.

'Keelin! Ow! For the love of God, woman! Are you trying to break me? You know the kind of day I've had.'

'Looks like it's about to get a whole lot worse.'

'Sweet Jesus,' I whispered, as Redzer or Buzzer or Scuzzer, or whoever the hell he was, launched into a bargaining war with either Anto or Shanno or Deco or whoever the hell he was. The anaemic ferrets had arrived.

'No, man, fuckin' six cans of Dutch for five yo-yos [euros?].'

'Bleedin' robbed, man. Me oul one got seven Dutchies for four snots [again, euros?]. If not, that guy definitely got a raw deal there, especially when there were yo-yos on offer too with the fuckin' club points in Crazy Prices.'

'Crazy Prices, me hole! They do be robbin' all the cents off ya!'

'Wha'? How the fuck do dey rob the sense off ya? Dey're a supermarket! You've got your bird to be doin' tha', robbin' the sense off ya.'

They all high-fived each other. I clung to Keelin, who was hunched beside me, her hands hanging limply under her chin. I wanted to tell her she looked like a little squirrel. Maybe later.

'No, cents.'

'Yeah, I know, sense!'

'No, *cents*!'

'No sense? Wha'? Are you callin' me fuckin' thick, are ya?'

'Bleedin' robbed me so, the oul baldy prick in the offy.'

'Well, fuck it, at least you got your wacky half price cos you were ridin' yer man's sister.'

'True, man. Did ya get the bumper box of skins and the free lighter off your man for the two jips?' (Euro. I think. I hope! Either these guys had little pet names for our national currency or they were involved in all sorts of sexual favours.)

'No, the pigs came along an' fuckin' hauled his arse away before I got the skins, but I did manage to swipe four pairs of Adidas socks off him before they dragged him away. They're only fuckin' gorgeous, man.'

At this rate if someone had thrown in seven rolls of wrapping paper and a free singing Santa we'd be set for Christmas.

Keelin and I eased our way down the stairs, hoping we

wouldn't be spotted. Then we could leg it into the kitchen and hide there for the rest of the night. I had never had the pleasure of being introduced to Aidan's friends, and if birds of a feather do flock together, it was a pleasure I think I could just about manage to live without, thank you very much.

'Aido, man, you were right! Your bird's mates are fuckin' rides!'

Too late.

Three heads turned to face us: two shaved and one with spiky hair and a badly peroxided fringe. (I was fast becoming obsessed with silky hair and I wanted to run over and put leave-in conditioner in his damaged tresses.) We stood at the bottom step, grinning back at them as if we were tickled pink that Aidan's friends had finally come to visit us and show us what the world was really all about. It was probably nerves. And who could blame us?

'I could get you some if you liked,' said the scariest-looking one in the green tracksuit.

'Sorry, pardon?' I asked, still grinning like a little girl on her First Communion day.

'Some Adidas socks, man, they're dead handy.'

'Socks tend to be a bit that way, I suppose,' I replied. It was like being back in Odds and Sods, where I'd felt like I'd just come off the set of *Sense and Sensibility*, as if no one would understand me without subtitles.

Eventually Keelin broke the silence: 'Anyone for trout?'

Keelin, Dermot, a bottle of wine and I spent the rest of the evening in the back garden to keep out of the way of the football hooligans. How did Susie survive the night? She was so slight and delicate. Anytime a Liverpool player scored a goal, was fouled or sent off, I could imagine her caught helplessly in a cyclone of kicking and punching tracksuits, gold chains, hair gel, sovereigns and Adidas socks. Maybe she'd got into an anti-thug protective outfit after we'd gone outside. You can find just about anything on the Internet, these days.

About halfway through the match, our next-door neighbours phoned to see if we were okay. 'We're fine honestly,' Keelin assured them.

'Are you sure? It's just that we can hear people screaming, "Come on, move it, yous lazy fucks! Faster, faster or we'll kick the fuckin heads off ya!" We were worried you were all being kidnapped by a drugs cartel or something.'

'Just some extremely excitable Liverpool fans over to watch the match. Sorry, we'll try to keep it down.'

After ninety minutes of gangland warfare in the sitting room, Aidan and his friends flooded the kitchen to roll more joints and get more cans from the fridge.

'Bleeding robbed we were, man,' Green Tracksuit moaned, as he plonked a gigantic chocolate fudge brownie in the microwave. 'Three fuckin' two to those Bolton bastards!' The microwave beeped and he took out the brownie. I would have had him earmarked as more of a raw-pig's-flesh type. It was only when a distinctively sweet smell clawed its way through the air that it dawned on me that the giant chocolate fudge brownie was not actually a chocolate fudge brownie but was, in fact, the largest slab of hash I'd seen in my whole life.

I watched as Green Tracksuit diced it into twenty smaller portions with our kitchen knife. Hey! That was the knife my gran had bought me as a moving-in present: the handle was shaped like a cute little housewife wearing an apron and slippers and holding a steaming apple pie. I felt sorry for her as I watched her hack away at the dark brown slab. If Gran had been here to witness it, we'd be calling for a priest. Poor Gran. She'd thought the knife would unearth a repressed desire in me to make my own apple pies. It hadn't.

'Sorry, I can't sort ye out with some wacky. It's just that it's already been bought, ye know, and they're comin' around now to collect it off us.'

I couldn't find my voice to answer Green Tracksuit and tell him I was already sorted, that I had my own enormous block of hash upstairs on my dressing-table beside the picture of my gran and my powder puffs. It was only then that I noticed the large bag of white pills perched on the counter. And just as the fudge brownie had turned out not to be a fudge brownie, I doubted that the little white pills were actually an industrial quantity of Tic Tacs.

They were using our house to sell drugs. To God knew who! Probably some tattoo brigade out on parole for murdering their own families! Coming to *our* cute little house with the pink walls and the fairy-lights!

I looked at Keelin. She was staring wide-eyed at the pills. I could see beads of perspiration on her forehead. I figured she'd just ruled out the Tic Tac possibility, too.

I stormed out of the kitchen to find Susie. This was *not* going to happen here.

I found her in the sitting room having a blazing row with Aidan, surprise, surprise.

'Izzy, hi,' she said nervously, as I pushed open the door.

'What the hell's going on?' I knew she was already upset, but I just couldn't help it. I was shaking with anger. Aidan shrugged his shoulders. How on earth had she got herself involved in all of this?

'It's nothing. We're just having a bit of an argument.'

'Does it have anything to do with the drugs operation about to take place in our kitchen?'

'I'm so sorry, Izzy, I didn't know they were going to do it here,' she mumbled, unable to look at me.

'Aidan, get them out of here *now*!' I heard Keelin screech

from the top of the stairs. I turned to see the Adidas-sock lover with the badly peroxided fringe strutting down the stairs, shaking his head.

'He was in my bedroom! Poking through my *underwear drawer*!' she yelled, her cheeks purple with rage.

'Would ya fuckin' relax? I was just lookin' for a lighter or a box of matches,' he replied, calm as ever.

'In my *underwear* drawer?' Keelin's eyes were bulging so much I was sure they were about to pop out of their sockets and plop down the stairs. Suddenly, she ran down after him and grabbed the black silky thong that was sticking out of his back pocket. '*Pervert!*' she roared, while he just looked at Aidan with a nice-one grin and a nod. I could see Susie was mortified.

This was a nightmare. I'd rather have pitched a tent in aisle three of Odds and Sods for two weeks solid than be with this mob. I wanted them out so I could disinfect the whole house.

Just as Green Tracksuit poked his head out of the kitchen to ask me if I had any freezer bags to separate the pills into, the doorbell rang.

The family slayers!

Everyone stood eyeballing each other. Nobody spoke.

'Well, it's your fuckin' gaff . . .' Thong Thief said to me, as he jerked a thumb towards the door.

Where were my manners? How inhospitable of me.

Well, I was going to sort this situation. I didn't care who they were, or how many of their family members they'd killed. I was going to tell them that they had the wrong house and that the only drugs we had here were Nurofen Extra and the contraceptive pill. And they were welcome to them if they left us alone.

I grabbed Keelin, then picked up Dermot and tucked him under my arm. I didn't want to run the risk of one of the knackers eating him while my back was turned. We scuttled towards the front door, propelled by pure adrenalin. The blood was pulsing through my head so fast I thought I was about to have a brain haemorrhage.

'Open it!' Keelin ordered, under her breath.

'No, you!'

'You do it – just tell them to piss off. Tell them they have the wrong address.'

My heart beat in sync with the thudding on the front door. 'Okay, okay!'

I leant forward slowly and opened it.

'Hello. Is everything okay, ma'am?'

'Sorry, what? Yes! No! What?'

I didn't know whether to laugh or cry as I blinked at the two uniformed policemen standing at our front door.

'One of your neighbours reported a few disturbances coming from your house,' one of the guards explained. 'Ye're looking a bit shook up, girls. Is everything okay with ye?'

I struggled to bring the two blurred navy blobs standing in front of me into focus. 'It was the football!' I answered, a little too enthusiastically 'Bolton won three–two! Can you believe it?'

'Football?' the navy blob on the left asked.

'Yes,' said Keelin. 'We were watching the match and we all got a bit excited and were making lots of noise so our neighbours probably thought there was something dodgy going on, like a robbery or something, but we told them we were fine because they asked us were we being kidnapped by a drugs cartel or something – can you believe it? So we said no, we were grand, that there were no drugs here at all. Because there are no drugs here *at all*. There's an ashtray on our coffee-table that I stole from the pub around the corner, but I'll put it back if you want me to . . .'

Keelin had gone mad. I could actually see steam rising from the top of her head.

'Em, okay. Well, it's standard procedure for us to have a quick look around to make sure everything's in order,' the navy blob on the right affirmed. I still couldn't focus properly and I was beginning to sweat profusely.

'Very kind, but no need. Thank you and goodbye.' Keelin tried to close the door, but one of the navy blobs wedged his foot in it.

'Excuse me, girls, step away from the door, please,' they chorused sternly.

There was nothing we could do. We pinned our backs against the wall as we watched them head into our house.

'Come on in, yiz shower of fucks!' Green Tracksuit called from the kitchen. 'We have all the stuff sorted out for yiz!'

'Is that right, lads?' one of the policemen asked sarcastically, as he strolled into the kitchen. 'Well, well, well, what do we have here, then, hah?'

After a two-minute silence, Thong Thief and Aidan simultaneously burst into tears. I might have roared laughing at them if I wasn't already preoccupied with the thought of rotting in jail for the next forty years.

The policemen insisted we go down to the station, too, despite all our protests about being innocent bystanders. Keelin, Susie and I climbed into the back seat of the 've-hickle' – could they not just say 'squad car' like they do in the movies? By this stage, most of our neighbours were on their porches or peering out of their windows to have a good nosy at all the commotion. And if the entire neighbourhood's attention hadn't already been sufficiently procured, that was promptly taken care of when one of the officers flicked on the siren. Keelin and Susie were white with fear. They kept their heads down as we drove off, the sound of short, sharp bips bouncing off the houses as the bright blue light threw itself around in speedy circles. Well, at least I'd have great street cred the next time I needed to pop in for groceries, I thought, as we raced past Odds and Sods.

What a day! I glanced out of the car window to check that Jonathan wasn't in sight. As this day was turning out, I wouldn't have been at all surprised to spot him driving along in the lane beside us witnessing this whole sorry mess. Or perhaps Edna McClodmutton and Cian having a good gawk as they whizzed past on a tandem while out for a romantic evening cycle.

I closed my eyes and imagined myself curled up on the couch with Dermot and a trough of junk food watching *Sleepless in Seattle*. It seemed a million miles away as the car jerked to a halt outside Pearse Street Garda Station.

14

Keelin, Susie and I sat slumped on cold metal chairs in a poky little room off the reception area. We'd been there for hours, with no one bothering to tell us what was going on. None of us said a word. Susie kept her head low, unable to look at us. The bearded man with the bald head and the beer belly who'd put us here hadn't been back since. The floodlit room had a grey concrete floor and walls. I'd never been a fan of grey, had always been more of a pink person. I supposed I was just going to have to get used to it. But I'd never get used to porridge, overalls and woodwork classes. And never mind what they said about Stockholm syndrome, there was no way I could grow to fancy the man with the beard, bald head and beer belly – although we hadn't been kidnapped, just arrested, so that probably wasn't an issue.

I hadn't noticed I'd nodded off until I heard a heavy door slam in the distance. How long had I been asleep? The horrific details of the nightmare I'd just had came back to me. I'd dreamt I was in my jail cell five years from now, sitting on the chair I'd personally hand-crafted (turns out I'd excelled in woodwork), when a smug-looking security officer handed a newspaper in to me with a photo of Cian and Edna at their wedding reception. She was wearing a beautiful lace dress, her silky hair tumbling in loose curls around her face and a stunning pair of drop pearl-and-diamond earrings. The caption read: 'Groom claims he has never been happier as gorgeous couple seal their love with wedding vows.'

I have no idea why on earth it made front-page news but it

was *horrific*. Perhaps it was a punishment method carried out by the prison system: find your weak points and flaunt them as pretend newspaper articles to chastise you.

Well, it had worked.

I wanted to tell Keelin and Susie about my dream, but they were caught up in their own thoughts of porridge and over-alls and woodwork classes, and I didn't want to make it all about me. I wasn't really talking to Susie anyway.

I slumped in my seat, resisting the urge to cry. If Cian hadn't gone and fallen in love with Edna, he'd be on his way over here to get me. He'd look after me, mind me, sort it all out like he'd always done. But he was off minding someone else. Making someone else feel better. The tall, skinny Edna with the long, dark, silky hair. I was on my own.

Before the lump in my throat could take hold, the large steel door creaked open.

It was our captor.

'One of the young men has confessed to the charges and has informed us that ye girls had no knowledge of the crimes that were taking place, so you are free to go.'

I wanted to scream, 'I told you so, you fat, bald, bearded man whom I could never love!' but I thought it wiser to opt for a simple 'Thank you.'

We walked out of the station and stood breathing the fresh air for a minute, then grabbed each other in a fierce embrace. Even though I was still pissed off with Susie, I was so relieved to be going home I couldn't find it in me to be cross with her.

'I'm sorry,' she sobbed. 'I'm so, so sorry.'

A police car pulled up and two officers struggled to get a very drunk woman out of the back seat. She was shouting abuse at her partner, a diminutive, skinny man with a black eye. I wanted to hug him and tell him he could leave now and choose a different life. But then I remembered I wasn't Jeremy Kyle, so I refrained. The three of us looked at each other and started to run. We didn't stop until we reached the bottom of Grand Canal Street.

'Wait! Stop! I have to sit down for a minute,' I pleaded, wrapping myself around a lamppost, sliding down it and landing with a plop on the pavement.

'I haven't run that fast since Karen Millen announced they were having a one-off mark-down on stock due to water damage,' Keelin gasped.

'Guys, I'm so sorry about tonight, I really had no idea they were planning to do that,' Susie blurted, and started to cry.

'We know you didn't.' Keelin and I went to her side.

'What are you going to do?' I asked her, reminding myself that this whole mess was so much worse for her than it was for either of us. She had to end it with Aidan now once and for all, and it would break her heart. Even though he was the world's biggest twat.

She looked up at me with confused eyes. 'What do you mean what am I going to do?'

'About Aidan.'

'What about Aidan, Izzy? It wasn't his fault! He wasn't selling the drugs, his friends were.'

I stared at her in disbelief. Frustration sparked inside me. 'Susie, are you that *stupid*? What the hell is happening to you?'

Keelin backed me up. 'Susie, listen,' she counselled, 'I know you're upset at the moment, but you can't let Aidan away with this, you just can't. Even if he wasn't personally going to sell the drugs on, he still knew that his friends were and he shouldn't have put you in that position.'

'But he never said anything . . .'

'Obviously he never said anything!' I erupted. 'Until they were all there and there was nothing we could do about it!'

'He was the one who got us out of there. He told the police we had nothing to do with it.'

'Jesus, Susie, *after how long*? We've been in there for hours! It's now five thirty in the morning! Yes, you're right. I'm sorry. He's so goddamn noble!'

'Stop being such a bitch, Izzy,' Susie wailed.

'Do *not* blame me for this! If you want to be a complete doormat for that arsehole that's up to you, but you've made it our problem this time, Susie. And, like always, you're going to sweep whatever Aidan's done under the carpet and pretend it hasn't happened. You'll be the first one he'll come to looking for sympathy and you'll give it to him. But he's gone too far this time. Susie, please wake up and smell the coffee. You've had your fun, now just walk away.' I gazed at her imploringly, hoping I'd got through to her. 'This isn't you.'

'Well, I'm sorry, Izzy, but this *is* me, like it or lump it. *I've had my fun?* This isn't some sort of *game*. I happen to be in love with Aidan. And you may think he makes me miserable, but you don't see what we have together. He makes me feel I'm more than just some boring, predictable, sensible girl who always settles for "good enough". It's the first time I've ever taken a risk on something in my entire life – and you know what? *That feels good!*'

'Susie, you've never been boring or predictable or sensible. Ever. What's made you think that?' Keelin asked sadly.

'Keelin, please. You've always been the alternative, kooky one that people want to be around, and, Izzy, you're the funny, crazy girl everyone adores. So what makes me stand out?'

'Your wit and your intelligence and your amazing heart. My God, you don't have to be loud like me and Izzy to get attention. *Or* be with some guy who's wrong for you just because he makes you feel different.'

'Well, does being in love not count for anything?'

'It does, of course it does. But it can't count for *everything*. Especially when he's let you down this badly.'

'Oh, and you've stuck by that philosophy, have you, Izzy?' Suddenly she was fuming. 'You let Cian walk all over you. He was off sleeping with somebody else and then running back to you, for Christ's sake! And, deep down, you probably knew. What's more, six months on you're *still* pining for him. It's insane!'

I felt as if I'd been slapped across the face. I stood there, frozen with shock. How could she say that to me? She knew that Cian had been the love of my life. That he'd left me devastated. I hadn't been *pining* for him. I was utterly heartbroken. We stared at each other as the words hung in the air around us. Just at that moment a woman in one of the houses near us opened her window and screamed at us to shut up or she'd pour boiling water over us. I hadn't realized we'd been talking so loudly. She slammed the window shut and the only thing I could hear then was the sound of my breathing.

'I'm so sorry, Izzy, I didn't mean that,' Susie whispered.

I turned away from her and started to walk back down the road, my pace quickening with every step.

'Please, Izzy, wait! I shouldn't have said that – I'm just upset about everything. Please – just wait. Where are you going?'

I couldn't answer her. I had a lump in my throat that felt like a ball of soggy dough. If I tried to speak, I'd really start crying this time, and if I did that, I was afraid I'd sit down on the kerb and sob until it was time to go to work. And then Window Woman would pour boiling water over my head.

I could hear Keelin and Susie trotting up behind me. 'Izzy,

wait,' Keelin begged. 'Look, we're all upset and tired. How about we go home, put on the kettle and make some French toast?'

That sounded so heavenly I nearly got lost in it. But there was no way I was going back to the house tonight. 'Keelin, I'm not setting foot back there. What if the guys who were meant to pick up the drugs come for them? And what if they think we tipped off the police?'

'Holy shit, you're right! What will we do?'

'Izzy, are you okay?' Susie said quietly. She looked so worried I couldn't help feeling a pang of guilt.

'Let's not talk about it now, okay? We should figure out what to do next.' She gave me a defeated nod.

Susie decided to hail a taxi and head for her parents' house. I couldn't face going home and getting another seven-hour grilling. I was so tired I'd probably end up blurting everything to my mother, who would be so shocked and horrified I'd be sent off to boarding school down the country. Even though I was too old for boarding school.

Keelin couldn't go home either because her parents had a houseful of guests. She decided to call over to Caroline and Orla's and crash on their couch. Their apartment was far too small for us both to stay there. Keelin had already bagsed the couch, so I'd be left with one of the wooden chairs in the kitchen. Now, call me fussy but that really wouldn't do it for me tonight. I persuaded Susie and Keelin to go, telling them I'd sort something out. We hailed a passing taxi.

'Let us know you're okay – text me, all right?' Keelin demanded, before the taxi pulled away.

It was already starting to get bright and a little choir of birds were practising their morning songs. A cold breeze whipped around me and I blew into my hands to warm them.

I took out my mobile and phoned Gavin.

He was there exactly eight minutes and twenty-seven seconds later. Believe me, I know, because I counted every single second out loud to keep my mind off the cold. And everything else.

'Izzy,' he called, climbing off his Vespa. 'Izzy, are you okay?'

I stood up as he wrapped his arms around me and pulled me close to him. His fleece smelt of cinnamon, Bounce and toast and I inhaled it deeply into my lungs as I buried my head in his chest. He was so warm I could have fallen asleep standing there.

'You okay?' he asked again, in a whisper, as he stroked my hair. It was the nicest anyone had been to me all day, and I burst into tears of relief and exhaustion.

15

I'd been staying at Gavin's for a few days now. Susie was still at her parents' house and Keelin was still squatting on Caroline, Marcus and Will's couch. She told me that, apart from the few soggy Pringles and the empty condom wrapper she'd found squished between the cushions, she was very comfortable. She had gone back to our place the next day, Marcus and Will flanking her, to rescue Dermot from the crime scene. Will said she'd looked ridiculous, creeping through the house on her hunkers looking for him, a can-opener poised in her right hand, ready to decapitate any lurking drug-dealers who might have it in their heads to use Dermot as a mule. Now she assured me that our rabbit was fine and that he was delighted with all the attention he was getting at his new abode. Caroline had given him a bath, blow-dried his fluff and straightened his fringe.

I hadn't spoken to Susie. We'd missed each other's calls a few times. Maybe it was as well, until things settled down a bit more.

I felt like a complete burden to Gavin, but he kept insisting I stay at his place. He seemed genuinely concerned about the danger of going back to the house and I was happy enough to agree with him. The idea of being there frightened me, especially since we'd found out that one of the family-killing tattoo brigade was some notorious drug gangster called the Terminator or something. I laughed when I heard his name and said I was going to start calling myself the T-Rex so they'd know not to mess with me. But Gavin said it really wasn't a joking matter. The Terminator was a well-known gangster with a pretty nasty reputation. I still thought I could get through to him if only I could sit down with him and explain that the whole mix-up hadn't had anything to do with us. But then Gavin told me that this guy had allegedly kneecapped some bloke for skipping ahead of him in a queue in Tesco, so I decided against it. (Although, I hate queue-skipping *so* much that I could empathize slightly there.)

I hadn't been back to the house at all since the night in question so I'd bought a few bits of underwear from Dunnes and some cheap makeup and shower gel from a bargain bin in the local chemist. Unfortunately, the foundation was about five times too dark for my skin, the shower gel smelt like pigeons and the work trousers I had bought in Penny's for €7.50 looked like 1930s men's breeches. I'd definitely looked better. Maybe it was time I went back to the house and collected some of my stuff.

'I've decided, Gav. I'm going to head over to the house after dinner to pick up some things, including some pyjamas so you can have your Velvet Revolver T-shirt back. And I want to let you in on a little something. People who wear concert T-shirts while not at a concert always look like loner oddballs who still live at home with their mums. They send out all the wrong signals. I had to tell my dad to stop wearing his Céline Dion Live at the RDS jumper after I'd heard rumours that some of our neighbours thought he was gay and I felt sorry for Mum.'

'How can you say that, Izzy?' Gavin said, with a straight face 'Slash is my life. I spend all of my spare time up in my room, with my hair dragged down over my face, in a big black baggy jumper and dirty jeans, smoking a cigarette, listening to Slash and writing poetry about how no one understands me and how shit my life is.'

'I thought all you weirdo music heads were well over that stage by the time you hit sixteen. I mean, don't get me wrong, I was into that for a while, except my depression was offset by Boyz II Men. But that phase pretty much passed with adolescence, when it finally dawned on me that the chance of my marrying Edward Furlong was slim.'

'I'm coming with you,' he said, smiling through a mouthful of spaghetti Bolognese.

'To Boyz II Men at the Olympia?'

'Eh, no. To your house.'

'Oh, Gav, honestly, you don't have to, it's fine. I'll be in and out in no time . . .'

'Forget it, I'm coming with you.'

'Okay. Sure. That would be great. Thank you.'

After we'd finished dinner and washed up, we decided to walk over to the house, seeing as it was a beautiful summer's evening. Which was a good thing, really, as the Vespa and I still weren't seeing eye to eye. I doubted we ever would, to be honest. I really missed my little E.T. adventure bike, but Gavin had said there was no problem leaving it on his balcony. Which was also a good thing because the plastic flip-flops that had come free with the magazine I'd bought earlier had already left a rather unsightly collage of red blisters across my feet.

As we walked along, chatting about this and that, I couldn't help wishing that every day could be filled with this easy summer feeling. The past week had been so great – except for intermittent thoughts of being gunned down by balaclava-wearing criminals in a Hiace van – and there were a lot of positives to focus on, like not being sent to jail for a crime I hadn't committed. Which meant that my chances of seeing Jonathan again were quite high. Which was good.

Or was it?

God knew what might happen if I bumped into him. Given my track record, I'd probably fall and break my legs, burst into song, or start dancing around like a five-year-old with my skirt over my head, saying, 'Look! No hands!'

Hmm. It was probably best that I *never* saw him again. But I had made a solemn promise to Keelin, Susie and the taxi driver that I'd sleep with him.

More positives? Well, staying at Gavin's had helped take my mind off a certain person. Perhaps it was the change of scenery or that I was a guest in someone else's home and had to make more of an effort not to walk around in a T-shirt and underwear, crying. More than anything, though, I'd been so busy that I hadn't really had time to indulge in any self-pity parties. Work was more like a sweat factory by the day. Not only were we working insane hours with no breaks, but the thermostat was jammed at 30 degrees centigrade, so we were slaving away in conditions similar to a Turkish bath. In the evenings, Gavin and I usually ended up going for a drink or popping along to an event or a show.

I'd never realized there was so much to do right on our doorstep – I'd always thought the only options were the cinema, the pub or bowling. But Dublin was alive with stuff to do in the summer evenings. And Gavin seemed to have antennae that picked up on all the cool things to go to. One night, he, Keelin, Kate and I went to see a movie outdoors in Meeting House Square in Temple Bar – although we were asked to leave before the film started, after buying cider from a sixteen-year-old (in our defence, he did look eighteen). Another night Gavin, Kate and I headed to a Lebanese food festival over in Merrion Square. Although I sort of stopped eating after Kate told us about the woman in her ward who'd needed twenty-five stitches after giving birth to a fourteen-pound baby. I didn't want to be rude and tell her to keep her vagina-stitching stories to herself while I was eating, so I just told them instead that I'd found the lentil parcels very filling.

Most nights I was so wrecked by the time I got to bed, I didn't even have the energy to think about Edna McClod-mutton and Cian. Or the awful rumour Emma had heard about them moving in together, which caused me to run to the bathroom and throw up when she'd phoned to tell me. But I'd been so busy that I hadn't had much time to obsess about where they'd buy their bedlinen and if they'd get his and hers dressing-gowns.

'Are you ready?' Gavin asked, as we reached my house. We stood on the opposite side of the road, looking at number five, our cute little two-up, two-down townhouse with the red door. I shuffled from foot to foot to ease the pain. My feet were throbbing so much, I thought my toenails were about to shatter. Gavin asked if I usually walked like a half-eaten gazelle when I was scared or was it just the flip-flops? I told him it was just the flip-flops and that I wasn't scared at all.

I was shitting myself.

Gavin turned the key in the lock and pushed open the door as I hovered behind him, having entertaining conversations with our landlord in my head.

'Well, Mr Kavanagh, it's as much a surprise to me as it is to you to see every wall from floor to ceiling graffitied with "Die, bitches, die". No, none of us saw a thing, the girls were working late and sure I was out getting milk . . . but, em, I'd say with a bit of Jif and a bucket of hot water we'll have the place back to normal in no time. Sorry? . . . Oh, it's called Cif now, ha ha, sure that's lovely altogether, rolls off the tongue.'

'Izzy, do you want to wait here or come in with me?'

'Em, what do you think?'

'The Terminator could drive by and shoot you if you wait out here by yourself.'

I went white.

'Iz, I'm kidding, but maybe you should come in with me. What would I tell your mother if I allowed you to get shot?'

'Gavin, look! At the window! Someone has used one of those glass-cutter yokes and cut a circle out of it! The Terminator got in! *Phone the police!*'

Gavin went over to it. Why were men always so calm and collected in times of drama, break-ins, drug-lord avengers avenging and other such crises?

'Well?' I squeaked, in an octave even Mariah Carey couldn't have aspired to.

'Izzy, the glass hasn't been cut. It's just a mark left by that "Honk If You Like Fibre" car sticker you got free with your cereal. Glad to see you've taken it off, actually.'

'Oh, yeah, Susie used it last week to wrap her mum's birthday present. We couldn't find the Sellotape anywhere.'

Satisfied there were no visible signs of any *Mission Impossible*-type break-ins, we went inside and closed the door behind us. To my surprise, everything was just as we'd left it. There were no death threats spray-painted across the walls. Or horses' heads lying on the couch. Or pictures of Keelin, Susie and me pinned to a dartboard with darts through our heads. Everything seemed normal.

Somewhere along the way, without me even noticing, Gavin had taken my hand.

'You all right?' he asked, the dimple in his cheek appearing as he smiled reassuringly, giving my hand a squeeze.

'Uh-huh,' I answered.

Despite the circumstances, as well as my bouts of hysteria whenever I stepped on a creaky floorboard, it felt sort of odd. I looked down at our hands, entwined in a firm grip as I trailed behind him. Had we ever held hands before? I racked my brains. I was pretty sure we hadn't.

Neither of us said anything. And, not knowing what else to do, I left my hand in his as we climbed the stairs on our continued search for desecrated walls and voodoo dolls.

This definitely felt weird. Being led up the stairs? By *Gavin*? Holding my hand? It didn't mean anything – *obviously* – but it was just sort of . . . *odd*. I wasn't sure whether it was the feeling of impending doom at what we might find, or that it just felt strange to be there with him, holding hands, walking up to my room. Either way, my heart was pounding wildly in my chest.

Why should this feel weird? It's probably just fear! Right? Maybe the drug lords had ransacked my room looking for the pills and had burnt my clothes and broken my hair-dryer. Maybe this was how a girl felt when faced with the possibility of having no clothes, makeup or nice sparkly jewellery. Right?

I looked up at Gavin as he turned to smile at me. 'You okay?' he asked.

'Yeah – I may need trauma counselling, though, if all my stuff has been burnt to ashes and I have to live out my days in these polyshitamene men's breeches,' I muttered, giggling awkwardly.

Maybe Aidan had been right. Maybe I was dying for a ride. Maybe if I was being led up the stairs by Mick Hucknall I'd be feeling weird with my heart pounding. I mean, loneliness can do some pretty strange things to you.

A long silence swelled in the air around us and I wanted to say something to break it. But I couldn't think of anything. I couldn't even remember the last thing either of us had said. How long had it been since one of us had spoken? I racked my brain. I just wanted things to get back to normal. Get back to how they were just *five minutes ago*! Back to not caring what I said. Not feeling awkward. Being able to break into a random song or say something completely pointless or silly and not feel shy.

That was it. I suddenly felt cripplingly shy. What the hell was going on?

Gavin turned the handle of my bedroom door and creaked it open. He tightened his grip on my hand. My stomach danced and I swallowed hard to quell it.

'I think the coast's clear, Izzy. That is, unless they've left masses of unironed clothes around your room as a means of terrorizing you.'

Finally! One of us had spoken!

Now it was like I'd just dropped out of a daydream and landed with a thud back on earth.

'Do you want to get some of your things together?'

'No!' I felt like saying. 'Stop talking! Just stay here and don't speak. Let's go back to that weird trippy moment we just had.'

He walked into my room and took a bag down from the top of my wardrobe. 'Just throw your stuff in there – it's big enough, isn't it?'

I don't care about the case. Please come back and hold my hand again, I said. To myself.

Not out loud. Of course not out loud.

I still couldn't speak.

And, anyway, I couldn't say that to Gavin! It was *Gavin*!

None of this made any sense whatsoever.

I was rooted to the floor, my knees pressing against the edge of the bed. He stood at the opposite side, unzipped the case and laid it in front of him. The lid made a *pouf* sound as it hit the duvet.

Then there was silence again.

He looked at me. This time he didn't say anything, just stood looking at me with an expression I couldn't read.

A mobile phone trilled and we both looked away. Awkward. It seemed to ring for ever before Gavin reached into his back pocket. He studied the caller ID, diverted the call and the ringing stopped. I fumbled with the zip on the suitcase. I still couldn't find anything to say. I could feel him looking at me. The resonance of the ringtone continued to dance in my ears.

His phone rang again. This time it sounded louder and more intense, as if the caller was saying, 'Answer my bloody call!'

It rang and rang.

And rang.

'Kate . . . hi,' I heard him say.

Kate!

Oh, God!

I was such a *bitch*! I'd just been fantasizing about kissing her boyfriend. I hated girls like me! But it was Gavin!

What?

Even as I said it to myself it seemed ludicrous. I mean, it wasn't like I'd ever fancied him before. This had come out of nowhere – a moment of insanity! It's *Gavin*, for God's sake!

Gavin, who probably thinks I'm touched. Or that I melt into a mute mess when I'm scared shitless and fall into a trance, and should he call my next of kin for advice?

'Sorry, I'm just going to take this,' he said, covering the mouthpiece.

'Cool,' I said, shrugging my shoulders with forced apathy.

He brushed past me as he left the room. I listened to him chat to Kate as he loped down the stairs. I felt sick.

What a stupid moment of craziness. Gavin was so happy

with Kate. He was my friend. And so was she. Gavin and I had a totally platonic relationship, one hundred per cent. People always say that platonic friendships can't exist between a guy and a girl, but we had one. Ha! Freud, you may not rest in peace!

I do not fancy Gavin! Even if he does have those dreamy green eyes.

'Hey.'

I jumped and screamed. 'What the hell are you doing here with green eyes?' I blurted, overcome with surprise at my own thoughts. Gavin leant his shoulder into the doorframe and folded his arms. His eyes were dancing. 'What?' he asked.

'Oh, nothing. Sorry. Here – I'm just going to lash a few things into my case and I'll be right.'

'Cool.'

'How's Kate?' I asked, not knowing why.

'She's fine. She has a work thing on tonight so they're all in the pub.'

'Is she happy there, do you think?'

'In the pub?'

'At the hospital.'

'She seems to be. It's tough, though, she works hard.'

'How long did it take her to qualify?' Why was I suddenly so interested in Kate's life? Guilt?

'Four years, then an extra year as a junior on a ward.'

'How many babies is she going to welcome into the world?' I gushed. I sounded like one of those children with the plaited hair from *Little House on the Prairie*.

'Ah, Izzy, you big softie.'

'It is amazing, though, isn't it? She's going to be the first person in the whole world that all those babies meet.'

'Yeah.'

Kate was so lovely. She deserved to be with Gavin, and him with her.

I looked up at him. 'She's lovely.'

'I know,' he agreed, as he raked his fingers through his hair. His T-shirt lifted slightly as he rested the back of his head in his locked hands, showing his tanned, toned stomach. He shifted his gaze away from me and fixed it on something out of the window, possibly because I was holding an assortment of bras and thongs. I shoved them into the case so fast that I broke two nails.

I rifled through my drawers while Gavin perused my CDs. 'Michael Bolton?' he asked sarcastically.

'Don't slag. Those were hard times. I was fourteen and chubby with spots and greasy hair. No one fancied me and I felt that Michael was the only one in the whole world who really understood how much of a tortured soul I was. I moved on to him after I'd graduated from my Boyz II Men phase.'

Gavin laughed and put the CD back into the holder. 'What are these, Iz?' he asked, looking at a few sketches I'd propped against the back of my dresser.

'Oh, just some old stuff.'

'You drew them?'

'Yeah.'

'They're fantastic. I never knew you could draw.'

'They're okay. It's been a while since I've done anything, though.'

'Why?'

'I . . . dunno.'

'Well, you should do more,' he said, turning back to them and bending down to study them closely.

Most of them were of faces – people smiling, frowning, laughing, crying. I was going to start drawing again, and painting. I really was. I'd already decided that. But right now we just had to get out of here and shake this unbelievably weird atmosphere. I zipped up my case and swiped it off the bed. 'Right!'

'Right,' he echoed. He took the suitcase from my hand and I felt the warmth of his skin against mine. I told myself that once I left this room it would all be forgotten. My moment of madness. Back to normal again.

He didn't move, so I stepped forward to indicate that we should leave. I just wanted to get beyond that door. It was so close, right in front of me. Beyond it things would go back to normal. If Gavin would just move to the side and let me out . . .

He cupped his hand around my arm. 'Izzy . . .'

I held my breath.

'Are you okay?' he whispered, too close to justify speaking any louder.

His eyes looked sad. I was afraid mine did, too. But I wasn't sad. I was fine. 'Yeah,' I whispered. 'I'm fine.'

And with that I edged past him and out of the door.

16

I was already starting to regret my over-enthusiastic gymnastic display to get Fintan to pick me as the Lights! Camera! Action! on-set representative. It was probably a learnt response I was still carrying from my junior-school days that I jumped up, waving my arms wildly in the air, and shouted, 'Pick me! Pick me! Pick me!' when he asked for a volunteer. No one else moved a muscle. They were certainly not looking to be selected to go down to the set. That should have silenced me, but no, I still reacted like they were choosing teams for Red Rover.

Today was the first day of shooting on *Snog Me Now, You Dublin Whore* and, from what I could deduce, it was chaos. My guide – and saviour – amid the madness was Margaret, a straight-talking, practical woman whom you could trust to *get things done*. The only problem was, she was so efficient that she talked a mile a minute and her sentences were peppered with strange acronyms and film-English terms. I was a bit rusty in film-English – we'd talked nonchalantly about best boys and grips in college, but I was struggling to remember exactly what everyone did. Every time Margaret spoke to me, I watched her mouth move, trying to catch all the words as they spilled out. There was a good chance that this would make her think I was a lesbian trying to seduce her, but it was my best chance of not misinterpreting her.

Anyway, it might be chaos, but a day out of the office was *always* exciting. (Like school trips, right? Honestly, was there ever anything more exciting? I remember a trip to Government Buildings where I bought a postcard of the minister for trade and commerce as a souvenir. Don't laugh – at eight years old nobody is cool.) Another reason I'd begged to come today was because I was secretly dying to meet Tina Barrett, the lead actress. I'd read an article about her over the weekend, her starring role in a soap, her stint on *Celebrity Crusade*, her charity work for homeless Egyptian camels, the usual celeb stuff, and, of course, about her starting *our* movie. I couldn't wait to see her in the flesh. Keelin had instructed me to brush against one of her boobs to find out if they were fake or not.

Margaret was speaking in bullets again. *Ping, ping.* Tina Barrett. *Ping, ping.* Not coming . . .

What? Hang on.

'Did you just say Tina's not coming, Margaret?'

'Yes! Haven't you been listening to me hyperventilating for the last five minutes, Izzy?'

'But why not?' I asked, trying to hide my abject disappointment.

'She tripped coming out of Chinawhite in London over the weekend, and pretty much broke her face,' Margaret growled, clearly unimpressed. 'Highly disfigured at the moment apparently, with huge dental restructuring to be done, so that's that, unfortunately. We had to do a crisis recasting late yesterday and, at such short notice, it proved quite difficult, but I think we're sorted with a replacement. Not much experience but she looks good. Beggars can't be choosers and all that.'

Oooh! Maybe her replacement would be Reese Witherspoon . . . or Keira Knightley! Unlikely. They both had a considerable amount of experience under their belts. And the film was shit so there was no way on this earth they'd agree to be in it.

'What I need you to do, Isobel, is call down to the actors,

get them to sign their contracts and bring them back to me.' She handed me a stack of paperwork and a pen. 'Most of them will be down there in their little cabins.'

I looked to where she was pointing and saw a cluster of caravan-type yokes jumbled together like a halting site. I headed off, but just as I was approaching it, something caught my eye and instinctively made me hide behind one of the Portakabins.

'Isobel? Izzy, is that you?'

Holy shit! It *was* him! Jonathan Ride Cunningham!

'Er, yes, it's me!' Why was I still hiding? 'Em, how are you?' I called. In the grand scheme of things, I knew Jonathan didn't have any responsibility to contact me whenever he was coming over, but I would have liked a bit of forewarning. And thereby know not to wear grey T-shirts when really it was far too warm (sweat marks), or do experimental trails with crazy purple eye shadow. Did I have any chance whatso-ever of rubbing all of it off before he –

'Hell-o!' I sang merrily, spotting his head craning around the side of the Portakabin.

'Izzy.' He smiled. 'I thought it was you. What are you doing back here?'

'Who – me?' Was this going to be another choice display of mental ineptitude? 'I, em, well, I forgot my sunglasses so I, eh, just popped into the shade for a few moments so I could check I have all the contracts before handing them out. It's just, you know, my eyes are very . . . photosensitive.' I squinted to highlight my point.

'So, first day filming?' he said, in his smooth London accent. *Oo-er, Mr Darcy!*

'Yes it is,' I replied. 'Yes. It. Is.' *And* . . . nothing. I smiled awkwardly at him. Wow. I was now utterly convinced my sense of humour had a personal grudge against this guy. It always disappeared when I met him, so it was the only reasonable explanation. All I could think of was Susie, Keelin and the taxi driver chanting that I should sleep with him, but there was no way I was sharing that with him. I didn't care how short on conversation I was.

'So . . .'

'So!' I chimed in enthusiastically, wishing I hadn't when I realized how stupid it had sounded. He really was quite yummy, wasn't he?

'You've heard we've lost our lead actress?'

'Yeah, mangled face and all that.'

'Pretty much.' He laughed. 'Fingers crossed the replacement will work out. I mean, she hasn't much screen experience, but she does have a profile as an up-and-coming actress here, so that may help things slightly on a publicity front.'

'Oh, I agree,' I said, trying to sound knowledgeable, but the logistics of how these things worked didn't interest me hugely.

'You've heard of her?'

'Who?'

'Saffron Spencer.'

'Oh, yes!' I lied. 'Sure, who hasn't?'

Wait a second? Saffron Spencer . . . Saffron Spencer . . . Why was that ringing a . . .

Oh, Jesus . . .

Christ . . .

Saffron . . . Spencer . . . *Edna McClodmutton*!

When I came round, Jonathan was fanning my face with the contracts. 'Are you okay?' he asked, seeming incredibly concerned.

Was I dreaming? Nice dream. Nice Jonathan Ride Cunningham was looking at me as if he cared and loved me . . . 'I must sleep with him! I must!' I mumbled groggily.

'Sorry, Izzy, did you say something?' he asked, leaning in closer.

And with that I came round properly and jolted upright.

'You really are photosensitive, aren't you?' he observed. 'You gave me a right fright there, Izzy. We'll have to get you a decent pair of sunglasses.' He smiled at me warmly.

'Saffron Spencer?' I asked, in a daze.

'Yeah! Listen, if you're up to it I can introduce her to you now. That way you can get her contract signed too.'

How could I tell this man that even with twenty-eight pairs of industrial light-diffusing goggles I would never, *ever* be ready for that?

It all sort of unfolded in front of me like a dream. Sorry, a *nightmare*. I watched, in slow motion, Jonathan's hand knocking on the Portakabin door. We waited. Then the door slid open and there she was. Standing right in front of me. Edna McClodmutton of the long limbs and the silky hair.

'Come in! Come in!' she said grandly, patting the couch for us to join her. 'Isobel, how lovely to see you again.'

'You two know each other?' Jonathan asked.

'No! Yes!' we said at the same time.

I stared at her, resisting the urge to cry. She looked fantastic, as always, in a pair of skinny jeans, a plain white tank top and cute little sparkly flip-flops.

'So, isn't this great?' She stared straight at me. 'I'm just so *thrilled*. My big break. Over the last few months everything has really fallen into place for me.' She twirled a strand of her luxuriant hair around her finger. 'I just seem to have been so lucky and got *everything* I've gone after.'

'Well, we were delighted you were able to join the team, Saffron.' Jonathan nodded.

'I just hope you know how much I appreciate it, Jonathan,' she said coyly, gazing up at him like one of those women in the Magnum ads.

He smiled and she giggled shamelessly.

'So, Isobel,' she said, in a loaded tone, training her eyes on me again. 'What have you been up to? Still haven't been going out much, have you?' She turned to Jonathan. '*Poor* Isobel has been forced to hide away for the last few months due to a certain *incident* that appeared on the web. *Awfully* embarrassing.'

That sounded dodgy. 'It wasn't a sex tape!' I blurted. Bollocks, why had I said that? And why was I playing her sick little game? I couldn't believe this was happening. Edna was here. At *my* work. Fucking hell. Was she going to start taking over my entire life? Would I go home to find out that Keelin and Susie had kicked me out and rented the room to her? Oh, no, sorry, she was now living with the man she'd stolen from me so I was safe enough there.

She smiled sweetly at me, relishing my embarrassment. I needed to get out of there or I'd faint again. The Portakabin suddenly felt claustrophobic and airless. Prince Jonathan of Ridesville came to my rescue again and suggested we leave Saffron alone to learn her lines.

Outside, he asked if I was okay, and I nodded. 'I wasn't in a sex tape,' I repeated, wondering if he was thinking of firing me for being a slag. Now, on top of thinking I was a simpleton, he probably thought I had loose morals. And that was how he would see me for ever more – a thick slut with photosensitive eyes. And what man wants to sleep with one of those? Well, lots, I suppose, but not the nice ones.

'It was, just, this thing when I was drunk and, God, it was so embarrassing . . .' I stumbled, trying for damage control.

'Hey, hey.' He stopped me. 'It's okay, you don't have to explain. Now, are you sure you'll be okay if I leave you on your own?'

As soon as Jonathan had gone about his business, I called

Keelin and told her she had to meet me in Whelan's at five thirty on the button or else she risked losing my friendship for life.

Bless her, she tried desperately to cheer me up, but her attempts were futile. Did God hate me because I'd stopped going to Mass and lighting candles for the missionary nuns? Or because the change we'd collected in the poor box at home over Easter had ended up paying the gas bill? (We'd promised to pay the poor back, of course, which we were definitely going to do.) Was that why I was being punished? My life had become some cruel, evil joke. And the only person laughing was Edna McClodmutton. After all the progress I'd made, too – the socializing, the attempted flirting, the wearing of nice clothes, the All Bran . . .

So, Edna was the new lead actress in *Snog Me Now, You Dublin Whore*. Quite fitting, when you thought about it. I could see Cian saying that to her before he ravished her during one of their secret, sordid rendezvous. Saffron Spencer, 'up-and-coming actress and all round social butterfly', the press release read. I know because *I* was the one who'd had to send it out. Oh, but of course. She'd be in all the papers in the morning. Saffron Spencer. The up-and-coming actress and all round Diamond Thong Girl who'd stolen my guy.

And the final straw? At the end of the day Margaret happily informed me that I'd be joining their production team on-set to help out, and that I wasn't to worry one bit because she'd sorted it all out with Fintan.

Like I said, she was a woman who got things done.

Keelin and I had a few consoling drinks, and afterwards we went our separate ways – her to Caroline's and me to Gavin's. I teetered towards his place, lightheaded with alcohol and exhaustion. I was really hoping he'd be at home and still up so I could tell him about my day. Keelin understood the heart bit, but I knew Gavin would help me with the head part. He'd have me laughing at myself in no time, making me see what an idiot Saffron Spencer was. He'd make it seem not as bad.

I turned the key in the front door and pushed my way into the hall. The TV was on. Yippee, Gavin was home! Just as I was about to swing open the sitting-room door I heard the hum of two voices.

Oh.

Kate was with him. She'd been there nearly every night this week. I paused at the door and watched as my hand hovered over the handle. No, that was cool, I didn't mind. Sure I'd talk to him tomorrow. Or maybe I'd just say a quick hello and go to bed.

'Yo!' I said, heading into the living room and slumping on to the other couch.

'Hey, Iz.' Gavin smiled. 'How you been, little lady?'

'All good. Was on-set today, which was a bit mad.' Mad wasn't the half of it, but I didn't want to go into it now. Not with Kate there. I didn't want to barge in on their evening together and whine about how God was playing a cruel joke on me because we'd paid our gas bill with the money for poor people in Africa.

I looked at the TV. 'Hey, I didn't have you two pegged as the *Footballers' Wives* types.'

'Have you had a few?' Kate asked, laughing.

'Just a few. Was really just coming in to say hi and 'bye. Need sleep in a big way.'

'Any updates on your house?' Kate asked, as I turned to leave.

'How do you mean?'

'When can you move back home?'

Was it just me and my exhausted brain or was there a chill in her tone? I looked at Gavin, then back to her. 'Well, we haven't really heard too many updates. Aidan's been let off the hook because they didn't have enough evidence to charge him, but this Terminator guy is still at large . . .'

'But he could be for months,' she said. 'You'll have to go back some time.'

Kate didn't want me here. I'd never even stopped to think that it might be a problem. She knew Gavin and I were just friends, right? That he was helping out a mate? Gavin didn't think that too, did he? Had I outstayed my welcome?

Maybe she was one of those mind-reading, sixth-sense people who burn incense. And maybe she'd looked into my brain and seen that I'd sort of, for a split second, wanted to kiss Gavin last week. Oh, shite! *But I didn't fancy him!* I really didn't! Should I tell her so?

Gavin gave her a steely glare, obviously warning her to be a bit more tactful.

No. I hadn't done anything wrong, and if I told her here and now that I didn't fancy him, it might create a problem out of nowhere. 'Yeah,' I said, not sure whether I should feel hurt or apologetic. 'Hopefully we'll make a decision on that soon.' Kate had never been like this towards me before. We'd always got on so well. I suddenly felt quite isolated.

'Izzy,' Gavin interrupted, 'you're more than welcome to stay here for as long as you need to.'

Kate stared at the television.

'Em, okay,' I replied awkwardly. 'Well, I'd better head to bed. Night.'

'Night,' they both said.

I shut the door and climbed up the stairs. Had I done something wrong? I wouldn't have stayed with Gavin if I'd thought it would cause problems. Maybe I should move back to Mum and Dad's for a bit. But then I'd have to share a room with Emma and all my evenings would consist of watching her doing fashion shows of her entire wardrobe and listen to her pressing me on my progress in becoming less of a social embarrassment to her.

I heard them talking to one another in the living room. My tummy took a dive and I couldn't shake a feeling of disappointment. It was probably just tiredness. And gin. *And* I hadn't seen *Footballers' Wives* in ages. *And* Edna McClodmutton was now going to be an everyday feature in my life for the foreseeable future. Things like that couldn't help but make you feel disappointed.

What a day.

Still fully dressed, I lay on my bed in the spare room and stared at the ceiling until my eyes felt blurry and I drifted into sleep.

I was woken by my mobile beeping. The cruelty. I couldn't believe it was morning already – I felt like I'd only just nodded off. Plus I hadn't even managed to change into my pyjamas. Not to mention that it was still pitch dark. It couldn't be time to get up yet, could it? What time was it? I reached for my phone and squinted at the screen: two thirty-three a.m. It hadn't been my alarm. The screen showed one missed call. Keelin ringing with drunken updates on Simon? She'd been heading on to a work thing after we'd left Whelan's. Or perhaps she was phoning me to tell me that she was over Simon and had fallen in love with a different bloke, some guy she'd spotted at a bus stop.

I yawned and felt under my pillow for my pyjamas. Then my phone beeped again. This time it was a message. I opened my inbox and saw that it was a voice message. Here we go – a slurred communication from Keelin about Bob who takes the number ten. I listened as the familiar voice of the messaging service informed me that I had one new message.

'Izzy. Hi. Izzy, it's Cian . . .'

Sweet fuck.

'. . . I'm sorry for ringing you so late, but I really just . . . well, I just wanted to talk to you. If you're around over the next couple of days, I'd love to see you . . . if that's okay. Anyway, I hope you're well and I'll talk to you soon. 'Bye.'

I dropped the phone, then watched it slide off the side of the bed and thud onto the carpet.

17

When the sun finally rose at five thirty-two a.m., a wave of relief washed over me. I sat at my bedroom window and greeted the morning's swell of sunlight, comforted that the rest of Dublin would soon be waking up, taking their showers, having their breakfast, scrambling off to work. Maybe now I wouldn't feel so alone.

The last few hours had dragged by painfully slowly. It had seemed like one eternal witching hour. No sound. No movement. No nothing. I felt as if I was the only person in the world who was awake, watching the rest as it slept peacefully.

Since I'd listened to Cian's message I hadn't slept. I hadn't dared to. Falling asleep would have meant having to remember again in the morning. Those first few cruel moments when you wake before it all comes back to you. And you don't see it coming.

I slipped out of bed and shuffled down to the bathroom. Standing under the hot shower, I began to feel partially human again.

It had been nearly three months since I'd seen Cian on that fateful day in Odds and Sods. Nearly three months since I'd come face to face with him and Edna McClodmutton. Nearly three months since I'd heard that husky, gravelly voice. Nearly three months since I'd cried myself inside out and told myself, 'Enough, Izzy, time to get over him.'

Now she was working on the film and he was making late-night calls to my mobile phone.

Unable to stomach any food, I left the house and made my way to the set production office. Work was a welcome distraction. It was insanely busy again and I enjoyed the simple tasks of photocopying and stapling as there was a mechanical routine to it that numbed my brain. I spotted Jonathan at one point, chatting to the director down at the halting site, but I scooted back to the production base so he wouldn't see me. I couldn't face him today. I was too wrecked and distracted to try to make him want to have sex with me.

On my lunch hour, I flitted in and out of the shops, looking at clothes I couldn't afford, vacantly trying on crazy costume jewellery. I nearly walked out of one shop with a pink feather boa around my neck – I glimpsed myself in a mirror before I was on the street and ran back. I really didn't want to get arrested again. Shoplifting wasn't as bad as drug-trafficking, but I wasn't up for another go of the squad car and holding cell. Once was definitely enough. A bit like going to Holyhead.

I thought my usual happy pill – trying on Terry de Havilland shoes – would make me smile but it made me feel worse. What was the point? I was never going to be able to buy a pair.

The last straw was finding myself in Hickeys, comparing curtain fabrics. My mother would have exploded with joy if she'd witnessed it. It didn't matter where I was so long as I had something to occupy my mind. The day hadn't gone too badly, considering I felt like I was on another planet.

My phone beeped – a message from Keelin: **Wot u doin after wrk? Me and Susie wnt to c u. R u free?**

I sighed. I'd been putting that one off, but it was high time I saw the girls and straightened things out. Anyway, with Kate and Gavin clearly needing their space, I couldn't stay in any longer.

i'm free. Where u want to meet?

*   *   *

I pushed open the door of the Metro Café on South William Street and searched along the tables. When I saw Susie, I instantly wanted to hug her. She looked so lovely in her flower-print tea-dress, her long, ashy brown hair tumbling past her shoulders and her makeup fresh and pretty, with just a hint of blusher, mascara and lipgloss. She was on her own with an untouched mug of coffee in front of her. I could tell that she was nervous because she was sitting on her hands, which always gave the game away. I hadn't seen her since the drugs episode. I'd spoken to her on the phone a couple of times but that was all. We were on speaking terms, but there was still an awkwardness between us. I had been so judge-mental about her relationship and had said some pretty awful things to her. But she had said some nasty things to me too – maybe they had hurt because they were true.

I shuffled anxiously into my seat.

'How are you?' Susie asked.

'Fine, yeah. You?'

'Yeah, fine.'

She took a sip of coffee, then put the cup back on the saucer. 'Oh, God, Izzy, I hate this, I'm so sorry,' she said.

'Suz, me too! I've felt so rotten. Can we just forget the whole thing? I know it wasn't your fault and I'm so sorry for what I said to you.'

'Same here. And I want to forget it all too. But I just want to say . . .'

What? That she'd been wrong about Aidan? That she'd dumped him? That she'd finally seen the light? 'What?' I asked gently, encouraging her.

'I just want to say that I know you hate Aidan. But we're trying to work things out.'

Oh, no.

'I think it's going to be okay,' she went on. 'As you know,

he didn't get charged for the drugs thing but his friends did, and he says he's not going to have anything more to do with them.'

'But, Susie . . .'

'No, Izzy. I'm not going to apologize to you for wanting to be with him. And I'm not going to ask for your permission either.'

She was right. Of course she was. I couldn't tell her not to be with him, not to love him. 'Of course not. I'm sorry. It's your business.' I was so frustrated that I couldn't help her. Not yet, anyway. And when she needed me, I'd be there for her just as she had always been there for me. For now, all she wanted was my acceptance.

'Thank you,' she said, with a smile of relief, as if I'd just thrown her a lifeline.

A few minutes later Keelin joined us, smiling broadly. 'Shall we order?'

I was looking through the menu when I spotted Keelin doing something weird. Had she just winked at someone? I looked around and saw this very cute guy wink back at her.

'Keelin, what are you doing? You look like some sleazy old man at a strip club.'

'Seen many of them, have you, Izzy?'

'Jesus, I wish.'

'I'm just checking to see that I've still got it.'

'Got what?' Susie asked. 'A sleazy streak?'

'God, no, Suz, I *know* I still have that. I want to know that I've still got *it*. My sex appeal. That guys still find me attractive.'

'Oh, please!' We rolled our eyes.

'I'm serious!' she protested. 'Honestly, guys, this Simon thing's driving me crazy. He literally pretends not to notice me. I fell off my chair at a board meeting last week in an attempt to catch his eye with my cleavage. But he refuses to acknowledge me when he isn't forced to. He only ever nods at me when he's dropping faxes over to my desk or something. I sent him an email last week, saying, "Hey, Sexy! Do you fancy grabbing a coffee downstairs?" I got *nothing* back! And I'm afraid I'll get fired if I go ahead and just jump on him.'

'Yeah, I wouldn't recommend that.' I was cringing for her a little bit. She really wasn't great at taking hints, was she? Maybe she just wasn't used to rejection.

'Maybe he has a girlfriend,' Susie offered.

'Nope, he doesn't. I checked with Katie in Marketing – she knows him quite well.'

'Maybe he's gay,' I threw in.

'Please! I have the most in-tune gaydar out of anyone on the planet. I can *smell* gayness. Anyway, it was our work night out on Tuesday. Remember we'd sold a record number of rabbit-flavoured doggy snacks in June, so our managing director was taking us out for dinner and drinks to celebrate?'

We nodded, although I'm pretty sure neither of us knew what she was talking about.

'Well, we'd outsold our rival dogfood company by an unprecedented twenty-three per cent – their duck and orange treats haven't been doing too well lately, or their pork and bacon bits biscuits. Sad for them, really, but – where was I? So, yeah, for the first time in ages, I didn't chase Simon around. [Had he issued her with a restraining order? Hired bodyguards?] I know you'll find that really hard to believe, but I didn't go near him. [Definitely a restraining-order cover-up.] And I saw him chatting up some girl at the bar. Anyway, Katie from Marketing started snogging Ed from Accounts. I decided to leave after I saw Dave from Research attempting to dance to the Pussycat Dolls. On my way out

I bumped into Simon leaving with some girl! So he is definitely *not* gay!'

Susie and I eyeballed each other. I couldn't believe Keelin had got to the ripe old age of twenty-seven without ever having come face to face with the harsh realities of unrequited love.

We paid for our coffee and sandwiches and let someone else have the table, but decided we weren't finished chatting so headed into the nearest pub and settled into a corner booth. I told Susie all about Edna McClodmutton, and she thought I was taking the piss. 'Could you imagine?' she shrieked.

'No need,' I replied.

Her eyes darted from me to Keelin like one of those Action Man dolls, scouring our faces for hints of sarcasm. When there was none to be found she screamed, and I nodded bravely. I toyed with telling them about Cian's phone call too, but decided against it. I didn't want to over-analyse it until I'd convinced myself to call him back. Naturally the temptation was to pull at the little thread he'd offered, but the danger was that I'd just keep on pulling and pulling and pulling until everything had come undone again. I didn't trust myself not to do that, and I didn't have the energy to stitch it all back together again when I was left with another mess. I was going to ignore that little thread. Anyway, he was probably only ringing out of obligation. A little twinge of guilt had probably nestled into his head after Edna had mentioned she'd bumped into me on-set. Probably jogged his memory that he still hadn't got round to that apology he'd been meaning to issue more than eight months ago. Now he could tick it off his to-do list.

Either that or he was calling me to get Edna's and my work address so he could send a big bunch of roses with a note that said, 'Dearest most beautifullest Edna McClodmutton, I am so proud of you getting this wonderful part. I love you so much – more, in fact, than I have ever loved anyone in my entire life. And I just know that you're going to make it big in Hollywood and that everyone will see you *every day* on the television, in magazines and in newspapers, everywhere. And possibly even on huge billboards where my ex lives too. All my love, now and for ever, Cian.'

The barman came over and asked us to leave because we were getting too 'rowdy'. Susie apologized and said she'd only screamed because she'd seen a spider, which wasn't true but he'd hardly understand about Edna and my heartache. He said he didn't care if she'd seen a rhinoceros, took away our drinks (oi!) and kicked us out.

We trundled back onto the streets, wondering where we could go to next. We were a little tipsy after an afternoon of boozy chats, and the most popular option seemed to be to eat again. I told them not to judge me but I'd been secretly obsessing about chipper chips all through Keelin telling us about the incessant flirting she'd witnessed Caroline and Marcus doing with each other while she'd been staying with them. Keelin had told us they were still acting as if nothing was going on between them and kept insisting they were just friends. Then she shot me a look.

'What?' I asked her. 'What did I do?'

'Nothing.' She smiled. 'Let's get chipper chips.'

We went to the nearest chipper and ordered a bag each. I told the lady behind the counter that I had bought a lip exfoliator in town earlier on, but she didn't seem to care. It had seemed perfectly normal to share this little nugget with her, but it had probably been the gin and tonic talking. I stayed silent for the remainder of the wait and only spoke again to tell her I didn't want vinegar on my chips, but she lashed some on anyway. Don't they always?

Outside the chipper we got giddy about the prospect of returning to our house. Aidan's jailbird mates were safely locked away, we were pissed enough to take the edge off our fear, we hadn't hung out together in ages and there was a bottle of vodka in one of the kitchen cupboards. I asked if anyone thought the family-killing tattoo brigade might be waiting there for us. They insisted we'd be fine, that the drug lords would have got bored by now and that I'd have to give up watching so many crap detective shows. Susie looked a bit sheepish and I didn't want to start another row, so I just nodded even though I never watched crap detective shows. Only *Murder She Wrote* and the odd *Columbo*. And maybe one or two *Midsomer Murders*.

Keelin said she was dying to get back into her own bed again as she was convinced she'd developed spina bifida from sleeping on Caroline's couch. Susie said you couldn't get spina bifida from sleeping on a couch, but Keelin didn't seem convinced.

My phone rang as we headed for home. I fished it out of my bag and saw a number I didn't recognize on my screen. It couldn't be Cian again, could it? I answered, trying to steady my voice.

'Hello, love.' It was Mum.

'Hi, Mum.'

'Listen, just phoning to remind you about this weekend, Dad's birthday? We're having a Sunday roast at four.'

'I remembered!' I lied. Phew, thank God for mothers who knew you inside-out.

'I knew you would,' she lied in turn.

'Where are you calling from? Have you and Dad moved house and forgotten to tell me?'

'No, I'm over at Charlotte Noonan's — thought I'd give you a buzz now in case you were heading out later and I didn't get a chance to speak to you.'

'Thanks, Mum, see you Sunday.'

So it hadn't been Cian. Good. If it had been important, he would have called again. Just as I'd guessed, he had put in a courtesy call to check what stage I was at along the Heartbreak Scale, and exactly how horrific it had been coping without him.

I thought about his friends, his apartment, his mother, and his cosy family house that always smelt of home cooking, about his dad who always cracked inappropriate jokes, and his smelly brother. It was like a different world, a world I'd left one day and was never allowed back to. I couldn't imagine ever not missing it, even just a little bit.

I caught up with the girls and we continued on our way to our own little world. Criminals and silly tiffs aside – not to mention the boiler that needed a good kick now and then – it was one I'd always feel at home in.

18

Thank God it was finally Saturday. I'd thought it would never come. I knew it had to, as it has every week with the same regularity since I was born, but sometimes on a Tuesday afternoon, Saturday just seemed so distant.

I had been drifting in and out of sleep ever since the sun's first rays had crept between the curtains. Telling myself it was my duty to stay in bed past ten o'clock simply because I could, I forced myself to engage in semi-conscious dream-like images of myself dressed in Oscar de la Renta ball-gowns, driving champagne-coloured convertibles, doing photo shoots for my campaign as the new face of Tiffany's, all the while screening calls from Madonna, who was hounding me relentlessly to come to *another* of her parties. And, of course, being bombarded with requests for dates from an endless line of gorgeous men. I think I remember Jonathan Ride Cunningham floating among my bunch of delicious stalkers. That's right: he had been the one who'd arrived at my villa with the truckload of Christian Louboutins, begging me to sleep with him. Then Josh Hartnett had called around to say he'd organized an anything-you-see-you-can-have day at Brown Thomas for me and was going to take me for steak and chips in Shanahan's afterwards.

The bliss of enforced Saturday morning semi-controlled dreaming.

I wondered when I'd see him again. Jonathan Ride Cunningham, that was. I didn't know how long he was going to be hanging around Dublin and I needed due warning before

I ran into him. Time to practise standing up without falling over, speaking without going red in the face, talking about work-related topics without sounding like a brain-damaged chimpanzee, not fainting when the sun came out. I'd set aside ten minutes every day to rehearse in front of the mirror.

Oh, what was the point? He already thought I was a social leper. I should probably admit defeat and bring a bell to work to signal when I was coming. Give him a chance to scarper.

Speaking of bells, one was ringing downstairs. Huh?

'Everyone downstairs, please! Tea is being served in the kitchen!' Keelin called. Susie and I shuffled out of our bedrooms, groggy and confused.

'Great. Everyone's still alive.' Keelin smiled as we plodded into the kitchen.

'Did Will, Caroline and Marcus brainwash you? Are they all in some weird army cult?'

'No, I just wanted to make sure everyone survived the first night back. And that no one was murdered in their sleep by the Terminator, like I was in my nightmares.'

'Oh, me too!'

'And me!'

'How did he kill you?' Susie asked me.

'Axe. You?'

'Chainsaw.'

Keelin stared at us earnestly. 'I just want you to know that it's normal to feel what you're feeling. A lot of people experience trauma as a result of being victims of crime, and go through what you are now.'

Wow. And they thought *I* watched too much *Murder She Wrote*.

I decided to call Gavin and see if he was about so I could tell him about our move back to the house. I could collect some of my stuff from him too.

Much later, when I got there, he had a full spread of lunch on the go, which was great as I was starving. I told him about sitting down to eat a scone on that new river boardwalk near O'Connell Bridge on my way over to his place, but before I'd managed to take a bite I was attacked by a seagull. I ended up throwing the scone at it and running the rest of the way.

'What?' He laughed.

'I know! Feckin' scared the hell out of me!'

'You sure you didn't imagine it? Maybe you've been watching a certain Hitchcock film recently. Remember that time you thought Chucky was chasing you?'

He *was*! Well, near enough. How was I to know a little red-haired kid with ADHD had just moved in down the road? I did feel bad in the end, though. I'd legged it so many times when he was just trying to say hello to me that he ended up bawling one day and his mum told me off for screaming every time her five-year-old son came near me.

We sat on the two wooden chairs on the balcony with our plates on our laps and basked in the warm afternoon sunshine. Our glasses of cool white wine glistened in the sunlight as a myriad noises sputtered out of the radio in the kitchen.

I filled him in on my eventful few days on-set and told him exactly who Tina Barrett's replacement was.

'You're joking me?' he asked, his voice full of disbelief. 'Saffron Spencer is Cian's new girlfriend?'

'Yes!'

'Well, who on earth is Edna McClodmutton, then?'

'Gav! You didn't think there was actually someone in this world called Edna McClodmutton, did you?'

'Well, there was a Nuala Norrisflap in my class in college, so I guess you never know.'

I snorted wine up my nose in an attempt not to spray it all over myself. Ouch. 'Nuala Norrisflap?' I laughed.

'She was a lovely girl, I'll have you know, and if you continue to laugh at her unfortunate name, I'll feed the rest of your lunch to the seagulls.'

'I christened her Edna McClodmutton to substantially lessen her hotness.'

'Izzy, she is not hot.'

Wow. That sounded almost as nice as 'two-for-one' in Topshop. Music to the ears. But I didn't believe him so I couldn't quite enjoy it. 'Gavin, please, she's a ride.'

'Not my cup of tea at all. She's fake and tacky and . . . well, not to mention the fact that she's an out-and-out annoying muppet.'

'Really?'

'Really! Izzy, nobody respects that girl. She's made an awful name for herself around town over the years, schmoozing and back-stabbing wherever she goes.'

'Yeah, but now she's got the lead in this movie and she's gonna be a huge star and I'm going to have to see shots of her and Cian on holiday in Barbados in *OK!* magazine.'

'Sorry, are we talking about the same movie here? Iz, I honestly don't think *Snog Me Now, You Dublin Whore* is going to propel the girl to stardom.' He took a slug of his wine. 'Can't believe Saffron Spencer's Cian's new girlfriend. Well, no, I *can* believe it. Given that he's also a total and utter twat.'

'Really?'

'Really.'

Yay for Gavin!

We talked some more about how awful we thought *Snog Me Now, You Dublin Whore* was going to turn out. And then we chatted about the next project he was working on for Lights! Camera! Action!.

'It's *marginally* better,' he told me.

'As in you'd only be *marginally* embarrassed to put your name to it?'

'Exactly. Jesus, Iz, I wouldn't say this was hugely rewarding, would you?'

I shrugged. 'Well, at least you have a plan. I just have some blurry picture in my head with no clear direction. How's your own stuff coming along?'

'Good, yeah. Slow, which is frustrating, but I think I have a new idea for a project.'

'A documentary?'

'Yeah, maybe. Hopefully.'

'It's so fantastic, it really is, that you have this goal and work so hard to fulfil it. Oh, Gav, please don't tell me I'm going to end up a dogsbody for the Edna McClodmuttons of the world. I couldn't bear it.'

'Why don't you try de-blurring the picture a bit?'

'Ha! Easier said than done.'

'You can at least try.'

'I'm already doing bits of everything for the production company I'm in now.'

'Start drawing and painting again.'

'Huh?'

'Izzy, you've always said you wanted to get more involved in the creative side of film-making, but I never even knew you were artistic because you don't use your gift. *That's* what you should be concentrating on.'

'I'm not that good.'

'You are incredibly talented,' he said, getting all serious. 'Your stuff is amazing.'

'They were only a few old sketches.'

'Well, if that's all they were, imagine what you could do if you really put your mind to it.'

I looked out at the trees in the distance, letting it mull over in my head for a while. 'But what can I do? Unless I get into animation, and that's not really my thing.'

'I don't know – just paint, draw, whatever. You'll figure it out eventually. But you're not going to get anywhere just talking about it.'

He was right. What was I afraid of? I didn't have Cian in my life any more, looking down his nose at me whenever I expressed any interest in art.

'Draw me,' Gavin said suddenly.

'Have you gone mad?'

'Honestly. Draw me.'

'Not a chance.'

'Don't be such a wuss, Izzy. Come on. Now or never. Draw me.' I looked at him. He looked back at me, tapping the side of his glass casually and raising an eyebrow at me expectantly. 'Well?'

I bit my lip. It had been so long – I hadn't drawn a thing since *that* portrait. The one I'd given Cian for Valentine's Day. The one I'd been bursting to show him because I'd worked so hard on it and was convinced it was the best I'd ever done. And what had he said when he saw it? 'Aw, that's lovely, Izzy. It's great. And fair play to you, you didn't have to spend a penny either. Jaysus, I wouldn't have booked such a posh restaurant if I'd known you were doing my present on the cheap!' He laughed, and I forced a smile. I will never, ever forget that disappointment.

I jumped up. 'Fine! Stay where you are. Don't move.'

'Yee-ha!' Gavin whooped, rubbing his hands. 'That's my girl!'

I was back two minutes later with a biro and the inside cut out of a cereal box. It was all I could find. I got to work, scribbling away furiously. 'Stop moving!'

'Sorry,' he said, smiling. 'This is kind of unnerving.'

'Tough shit, you asked for it. Now shut up.'

I held the cardboard away from me and studied what I'd done so far. Was it okay? I looked back to Gavin's face. 'You should be a model,' I told him.

'Shut up and get on with it.'

But I was serious. As I drew the details of his face, I saw how technically perfect it was: strong cheekbones, a defined jaw, the slightly large nose that I'd always thought very attractive on a man. And he had the longest, darkest eyelashes I'd ever seen on a bloke. I shaded in his stubble. That was so Gavin. He was always a bit unkempt. And his long, dark shaggy hair was raked back and tucked behind his ears. He had a good neck. Great shoulders, too. He was strong without working too hard at it.

'I need to sneeze,' he said.

'Permission granted.' His dimple appeared and I drew it in quickly. That was my favourite feature.

'Nearly there?' he asked, sneaking a glance.

'You're so impatient!'

'Just give me a little peek.'

'No, it's not ready.'

'Just a tiny one and then you can take it back.'

'No.'

He suddenly reached over and whipped it out of my hands.

'Oi!'

He studied it intently. And kept studying it. For *ages*! He wasn't saying anything. Uh-oh, he thought it was shit and now we'd have to sit here and figure out another career path for me. Or maybe he was insulted because I'd drawn his nose a bit too big.

'Izzy . . .' He looked up.

'You have a lovely nose,' I said quickly.

He laughed softly. 'Thank you. I grew it myself. Izzy, this is amazing.'

'*Really?*' I asked, squirming a little.

'Really. And, as I said before, you're extremely talented.'

Wow! Gavin had a way of taking you by surprise when he was serious. Usually he was messing or joking or so laidback that when he spoke to you seriously, it was as if he was directly connected to you.

'Give it back,' I said, getting to my feet to take it from him. He held it out of my reach. I swooped for it and he trapped my hands with one speedy manoeuvre and held them pinned. How the hell did guys do that with absolutely no effort? I had to twist and contort every muscle in my body to open a pot of jam.

I moved my foot to dig him in the shin, but he shuffled his legs quicker than I could blink so that mine were locked tightly between his. I wriggled to get loose. Although I guess you couldn't call it wriggling, really, because I didn't budge an inch. It was more like I'd just twitched. Like when I get trapped in a size-six dress after I've tried to convince myself that I might get away with it – I always end up having to call an assistant to help me out.

I suppressed a grin as I stared down at him.

'Lovely weather we're having, isn't it?' he asked, tapping his fingers on the arm of the chair.

'I could spit on you,' I threatened, my face hovering above his. Even for a girl, I think I could probably have aimed it okay. Gravity was on my side. If I missed, I really would have to rethink taking up darts.

'I've hung people over the balcony by their ankles for less. And I must warn you that I have a zero-tolerance policy for spitters.'

'You wouldn't have the nerve.'

'Well, actually, your mum called over last week with a fresh baked apple and raspberry crumble. I dumped it straight into the bin, grabbed her by the ankles, swung her over the balcony and told her I only ate chocolate fudge cake, and if she *ever* called over with a fruit crumble in future, I wouldn't be quite so lenient.'

'Is that why she hasn't been in contact with me?' I asked.

'Probably.'

'Fine, you win this time, Balcony Bully.'

'Good. I'm keeping this,' he said, holding the picture defiantly in his other hand.

'Fine. I'm going to get more wine. Release me, you brute.'

I plodded into the kitchen to open another bottle of wine. My eyes were dazzled by a collage of shifting white speckles from being out in the sunshine. I blinked, and headed to the fridge. Which turned out to be the oven. Definitely no wine in there. My next guess was right and I plucked a cool bottle from inside the door.

Wasn't this lovely? Sitting in the sunshine, chatting, drinking . . . *drawing* again. It'd been far too long. And I'd forgotten how much I enjoyed doing it. I was kind of disgusted with myself that I'd more or less given up on account of Cian. I was so used to hearing him say that art should be a hobby that I'd allowed it to sink in. 'Enjoy it in your own time, Izzy,' he'd say, 'but it's the tangible things like law, business, accountancy that'll impress people. They're the stepping-stones to success.'

Puke. What an arrogant, self-righteous prick. Gavin was right: he was a twat. A twat who thought phoning his ex-girlfriend in the middle of the night eight months after he'd broken her heart was acceptable behaviour. Euch. I was angry, though, that it still bothered me. It had been so easy for him to call me out of curiosity or some other selfish impulse and I hated him for making me think about him. It was too cruel.

I went back outside and Gavin and I chatted for a while longer, laughing about Laurence's love of primary colours. He said it was his only outlet of creativity these days – his little colour-appropriate rhymes. Gavin let me in on this week's display of ingenuity: 'If it's debit loans you said, simply file it with the red!'

Then he told me about Geraldine setting Eve up on 98FM's morning crew, getting them to phone her and tell her that she'd won the Most Fantastic Employee Award in Ireland. And she'd totally believed it! She'd told them live on air how she was at her desk before anyone else in the office and it wasn't unusual for her to work straight through her lunch hour.

Priceless.

Before I had any more wine, I headed upstairs to pack some of my stuff before I got too pissed to care. I threw a few things into a holdall and bundled some other bits and bobs into a pile to collect in a few days' time. Just as I was about to head back downstairs my phone beeped.

Did u get my msg? Call me when u get a chance. Cian X

What the fuck? X as in a kiss? Well, kiss my arse, you pretentious anti-art capitalist Philistine! Little shit couldn't bear to be ignored. Could he not see that I didn't *want* to speak to him? I shoved the phone back into my pocket before I got so angry that I flushed it down the loo.

I headed downstairs in the hope that Gavin would distract me. When I walked out to the balcony, he was engrossed in some article in *Hot Press*.

'I'm going to miss it here,' I said, and suddenly realized how much I meant it.

'I'll miss having you here,' he said softly. 'You know, for a girl, you weren't too bad a flatmate. Except for all the crying and screaming and leaving boxes of tampons around the place.'

'And I got used to your empty beer cans thrown in the bath too.'

'Yeah, baths are no fun without a six-pack of Bud.'

I sighed. 'Right, I'd better head,' I said. 'And, Gav, thanks so much for everything.'

'Izzy, before you go . . .' He paused. 'There's something I need to ask you.'

Sounded serious. What did he want to say? That Kate officially hated me for being a squatter? That I hadn't removed all the hair from the bathplug?

'Sit down,' he said, indicating the empty chair on the balcony. I inched towards it, my heart racing.

'Listen.' He stalled. Listen, *what*? 'Remember I was telling you about the documentary thing I had in mind?'

I nodded.

'Well, it's a pretty big deal, really. It's a competition and only ten get in out of a possible five hundred entries. The winner gets a contract with *the* best documentary production company in Ireland and the UK.'

'Wow.' I was seriously impressed.

'As you can imagine, the selection process is pretty hard and other entrants will have way more experience than I do –'

'You're gonna get in!' I yelped, jumping to my feet.

'Not so fast, Ms Positive. Here's where you come in . . . hopefully.'

Oh, shit! Gavin wanted to make a documentary about me! Uh-oh. What would it be about? My shit taste in men? My hermit era? The length I'd allowed the hairs on my legs grow to? Hmm. Would I be able to say no, considering he'd been good enough to let me stay in his apartment?

'To be accepted as an entrant, you have to get chosen on the merits of your proposal.'

Here we go – proposal as follows: My Friend the Hairy Desperado.

'Izzy, I'd be honoured if you'd draw the storyboards for me.'

'Sorry?'

'It's okay if you don't want to. I wouldn't be able to pay you what you should be paid –'

'Gavin, are you mad? If you think I'm good enough, I'd be happy to do them for free.'

'Really?'

'Of course.'

'Izzy, thank you so much. Really.'

'Done.'

'Brilliant. I'll get some of my plans down on paper and then maybe we could get together to have a meeting about it over the next few days.'

A *meeting* no less. Someone thought my drawing was good enough to entail a *meeting*!

I skipped off into town to get some art supplies so I'd be fully equipped with nice cartridge paper, graphite blocks, charcoal, ink, pencils, and markers for whenever Gavin wanted to get together for our *meeting*. I didn't actually need markers, but it was always nice to buy some. Who doesn't love a brand new set of every-colour-under-the-sun markers?

What a day!

19

On my way over to Mum and Dad's on Sunday, I darted into town to buy Dad a birthday present. Question: why is it virtually *impossible* to buy presents for men? It's not like they're a minority group or anything. They account for fifty per cent of the world's population. Why hasn't someone come up with a few viable options other than socks and golf balls?

Guys reckon *we*'re high maintenance, but we're so easily pleased in comparison. If it sparkles, smells nice or comes in a Brown Thomas bag, we're sorted. But what do you buy for a man in his fifties? One who doesn't play golf, only wears the aftershave his wife buys him, owns every book that exists in the world and has so many socks that if he were to tie them all together they'd stretch from here to St Petersburg (rough estimate).

I resisted the urge to leg it into Sock Shop and splurge on a three-pack of knee-highs. Instead I wandered aimlessly from shop to shop, looking at the assistants, hoping they would instinctively know by my pained expression that I faced the near-impossible task of Buying a Present for a Man. Maybe then they'd rush over and cradle me and tell me not to worry, that together we'd work it out.

I ended up buying Dad a karaoke machine and some posh hair gel. I knew Mum would shoot me, seeing as Dad only liked to sing Céline Dion songs. And he was completely tone deaf. But at least he'd look good while he was at it.

After the mandatory half-hour wait for a Sunday bus, I was on my merry way out to the leafy suburbs of Blackrock.

There, I walked up our driveway and before I'd even taken my keys out, Emma swung open the door, leapt forward and hugged me.

'Thank God you're here! Mum's freaking out because the parsley's not organic and she's making me scrub the potatoes! Izzy, look at my hands! They're *raw* red!'

My sister, the drama queen.

'Will you peel the carrots? I don't think I can cope with them too,' she pleaded, on the verge of tears.

'Yes, Emma, I'll peel the carrots.'

'Thank you.' She did some tortured-smile thing I'd only ever seen in Danielle Steel movies.

Far from freaking out, Mum was in the kitchen whistling along to some Joe Dolan song on the radio. Knowing my health-food-junkie mother, she probably had let out a whimpery squeak when she'd discovered the parsley wasn't organic, but not to the extent Emma had made out. Dad was perched in front of the TV, watching a programme about owls – he'd been excused any chores because it was his birthday. I gave him a big hug and made him open his birthday present. At first he thought the karaoke machine was a microwave, and seemed delighted to discover that it wasn't. Then he headed off to the bathroom to 'style his hair' for lunch while I went into the kitchen to deal with Carrotgate.

I peeled while Emma sat on the counter with her hands slathered in eight-hour cream, 'recovering'. She pawed through the fashion supplement of the *Sunday Times* and complained about not having any Roberto Cavalli clothes. I told her not many people did, let alone third-year arts students. She sighed and nodded nobly like the trooper she was. Mum finished making the stuffing and we bunged the whole lot in the oven and set the table.

'Where's Stephen?' I asked, wondering why he wasn't

already there, tucking into a beer and complaining about football. My brother supported the worst team in the world – some club in the third division that wore a dodgy pink-and-yellow strip. He'd met one of their players when we were on holiday in Wales years ago and followed them ever since. The only other famous people he'd met were Stephen Roche and a retired RTÉ weather presenter.

'He'll be over soon,' Mum said. 'He has to pick his girl-friend up on the way.'

'He has a *girlfriend*?' I screeched. 'But he's a sl—'

Good God! I'd nearly told my mother that her son was a slut. Which he was, but I shouldn't tell her that. 'But he's usu-ally . . . always single,' I told her instead. No, it didn't make grammatical sense, but I'd saved her from the truth.

'I know he's usually single. Your speech is slurring, love, are you hungry? Your blood sugar's probably low. Have a barley sugar,' she said, unwrapping it and forcing it into my mouth.

'Thanks,' I replied. I wondered if anyone under the age of fifty ever bought barley sugar.

'Can't wait to meet her. She probably looks like Jodie Marsh,' Emma joked.

'Who's Jodie Marsh?' Mum asked. 'Someone in college with you?'

'Eh, not exactly.'

'Oh, right, probably someone off the telly, some stunner. Your brother is a handsome boy so I'm sure she's gorgeous.' And with that she scooted out of the kitchen 'to put on a bit of lipstick'.

'Can't believe Stephen has a girlfriend!' I said to Emma.

'It's mad, isn't it? He's so gross.'

'He's not gross, Emma, but he's such a slut. I never thought he'd be able for a relationship. Being in one generally means you can't shag loads of other people.'

'She's probably a porn star.'

'He's not *that* bad. Actually, he is. You're right, she's probably a porn star. Or maybe he's changed. Maybe he's in love!'

'Don't be ridiculous. Gross people don't fall in love.'

'And how about you? Still hankering after that guy in Commerce?'

'Richie? God, *no*! Found out he was as tight as a cat's arse.'

'Wouldn't buy you an Aston Martin Vanquish, then?'

'Never heard of them! Are they the new Louboutin? Can you get them in Harvey Nicks?'

Stephen arrived a short while later and, embarrassingly enough, we all barged off to answer the door. Stephen looked horrified to see his entire family wedged between the walls of our narrow hallway. His girlfriend went red and I liked her instantly.

'Hi. Eh, this is Deirdre.'

'Hi, Deirdre,' we chorused.

'Hi,' she said, her cheeks turning purple.

'Come on in, Deirdre,' we chanted in unison.

'Thanks.'

We spilt into the sitting room and sat down. Deirdre was pretty and understated and shy. We were so engrossed in scanning her for evidence of being involved in the sex industry that we forgot to speak. She shifted nervously in her chair and Stephen shot me an evil look. I jumped up and introduced the whole family. Mum started chatting about the weather, and Dad informed her that owls' life spans ranged from five to twenty-seven years. That was 'normal' conversation for him. Emma told her she liked her shoes and I said that Deirdre was a lovely name. I fixed them both a drink, which seemed to help them recover: Stephen sighed with relief and Deirdre's face returned to a more normal colour. Then we all sat down to eat.

I stayed at Mum and Dad's that night – Emma had pestered me non-stop for about half an hour.

'Please.'

'No.'

'Please.'

'No.'

'Please.'

'No.'

I won't keep going or you may get bored so I'll skip to the bit where I gave in.

'Please.'

'Okay.'

She said she really wanted the company and that it was no fun talking about boys with Mum as Mum would usually interrupt and ask why she wasn't going out with Colin Farrell. We slept in our old bedroom, which Emma now had to herself but my bed was still there. Somewhere. It took me a decent ten minutes to locate it under the gargantuan mountain of my sister's clothes and the four layers of magazines stacked underneath them.

Dad came in to say goodnight and thank us for the lovely day, then insisted on a bedtime prayer.

'Dad!' Emma protested.

'Hands together, girls. Dear Lord, thank you for this wonderful day. And thank you for bringing the lovely Deirdre into Stephen's life. I'd always assumed he was gay. And, Lord above, we were wondering if Izzy managed to buy this week's *Enough!* magazine and see that article about the girl who cut off all her hair in a jealous fit of rage about her ex-boyfriend's new lover. Where did it get her? Nowhere, Lord, only bald and cold. So, thank you for helping Izzy make some progress recently as we were all getting a bit worried there for a while that she might end up doing something similar. And finally, sweet Lord, please help Colin Farrell to fall in love with our Emma and let it be the grace of God that she stops wearing that glittery pink eyeshadow as it does nothing for her. Amen.'

'Oi!' Emma protested.

'Sorry, girls, your mam wanted me to pass on those little bits and bobs to ye, but I didn't really have the heart to do it head-on so I wrapped them up into nice little prayers.'

I wondered if Mum was a mind-reader with the hair-and-scissors thing. I'd only entertained the idea for a day or two, tops. I knew I wasn't actually going to follow through as I'd already done as much of a Britney as I could handle by chucking the mother of all hissy fits for the whole world to see.

'Izzy, is my pink eye shadow hideous?' Emma asked, after Dad had left.

'No, it's not. You're just a very colourful, sparkly person, and if you like it you should keep wearing it.'

'You should be an advice-giver-outer in one of those magazines.'

'Emma, apart from knowing that you should keep wearing whatever eye shadow makes you happy, I know pretty much nothing else.'

'You know how to make me laugh.'

'Thanks,' I said, smiling in the dark.

'And you know how to get your hair to sit in really cute waves. I'm glad you didn't hack it all off.'

'Wow, Em. Now that I know I can get my hair to sit in really cute waves, I don't feel quite so much of a loser.'

'You're not a loser, Iz, you just got lost for a bit.'

'I hope you never feel that way,' I said, melting at the thought of my little sister ever feeling so unhappy.

'I hope I didn't upset you by telling you Cian and that transvestite were moving in together.'

'It's good to know these things, I guess.'

So why had he phoned me when he'd just moved in with *her*? To ask my opinion on interiors?

'I forgot to tell you about the hideous photo of her in *Social Scene*. You have to see it! She's wearing this awful dress that makes her look fat and her hair is a total mess.'

'You're kidding?' I perked up immediately.

Emma shot out of bed, turned on the light and rummaged furiously among the magazines, which were now scattered across the floor. 'Aha! Here it is!' She flicked through the pages of Ireland's celebrity magazine until she found what she was looking for, then thrust the open page right under my nose. 'See?'

I scanned the faces. People I vaguely recognized from last month's edition. Same faces, different party. Then I saw her and my heart sank. I lifted the page as close to my face as I possibly could without the picture going blurry. 'Emma, are you having a laugh? She looks *amazing*!'

'What? Are you blind? Look at her dress! Look at her hair!'

'I am, and it's killing me. She looks even skinnier than she did when I last saw her, her dress is a weird colour but stunning on her, and, yes, her hair does look a bit odd in a side ponytail but it's still amazing.'

'Well, I think she looks tacky. Like an eighties porn star.' Christ, Emma shouldn't be throwing such wild accusations around. She was a one-woman homage to Rainbow Brite and the Sprites.

I closed the magazine and threw it on the floor, feeling even worse about how stunning she was than I ever had before. 'No wonder Cian's moved in with her. *I*'d move in with her, just so I could stare at her all day.'

'You're insane. She's a tacky glamourpuss with no class and

no true beauty. My friend Millie was working at an event she was at recently and she said she was a right stuck-up cow, hanging off these loaded older men, getting them to buy her drinks all night. And who did she sleep with to get the part in your film? I've heard she's as loose as a pair of your After jeans.'

'Huh?' I said. I'd been imagining Edna fronting the new Cavalli campaign.

'Izzy, you've lost all the weight again. And more.'

'Really?'

'Really. You've never looked better. You may still be sad, Iz, but you've got a sparkle back in your eyes again . . . and, I don't know, a certain . . . glow.'

I was right. Emma had definitely been watching Danielle Steel movies. Just then Mum banged on the wall to tell us to stop talking and go to sleep. Like old times.

We whispered for a bit more about Stephen being a reformed slut and how he'd held Deirdre's hand the whole evening. It was so touching. He'd laughed at everything she said and couldn't help gloating about her achievements. And I mean *all* of her achievements. He even told us about the gold medal she'd won in an Irish-dancing *feis* when she was seven.

'Are you okay?' Emma asked, after a few minutes' silence.

'I can't be that upset about not winning an Irish-dancing *feis*, especially when I never even did Irish dancing.'

'No, Izzy, I meant about Edna. The magazine and all.'

'Yeah. I just really wish she wasn't in the film. It's like the final nail in the coffin.'

'Well, there may be one more nail. Teeny tiny one.'

'What?' She actually was fronting the next Cavalli campaign?

'I wasn't sure whether to tell you or not, but I heard that

172

apparently it was her and her mates who put the video up on Facebook.'

I blinked in the dark, letting the information sink in. I wasn't all that shocked, but what an almighty out-and-out *bitch*.

'Izzy?'

'I can't say I'm surprised.'

'It's her only form of attack. She's jealous that you were Cian's first love and that you're far more gorgeous and fantastic than she is. Underneath all that front, she has no self-confidence. That's why she feels she has to knock you.'

Sweet. If untrue.

'Screw it, Emma. I'm getting there, honestly I am, and I'm not going to allow this setback trip me up now . . . Besides, I have a plan to sleep with our rideable producer from London, so who cares about Edna and her amazing life and her stupid friends and Facebook?'

I thought about telling her that Cian had called and texted, but I didn't have the energy.

'That is *the* perfect plan! I'm so proud of you. I was going to make you sleep with this guy in my tutorial class, but now that you have your own bloke, I don't need to. That's great, Izzy. It's exactly what you need, some seriously hot rebound sex.'

Hear, hear!

Lying in a cocoon of my old teddies, I soon felt very sleepy. 'Night, Em,' I whispered.

'Night, Izzy. I love you.'

'I love you too.'

Snog Me Now, You Dublin Whore was well into its third week of filming and things were running smoothly. Or so Margaret kept telling me. I wasn't so sure, but she kept insisting that it was perfectly normal to witness people having panic attacks at random moments in random places around the set.

Today Margaret was in particularly foul form, and of course it was the one time I'd stapled the script together in the wrong order. Little did I know that the day was about to get a whole lot worse. Just as I was convinced Margaret was about to lob her coffee mug at my head, there was a bang on the door and it swung open. One of the assistant directors was standing there, looking as traumatized as I felt. 'Saffron needs you.'

Well, I needed her to piss off and stop destroying my life. 'Okay.'

I knocked on her trailer door, telling myself I wasn't going to take any of her crap.

'Isobel!' she cooed, as if we were long-lost friends reunited on *Oprah*.

Be strong. Be very strong.

'I need you to run an errand for me.'

'Of course.' Bollocks.

'If you could just pop down to the shops and get me a copy of *Social Scene* and a Diet Coke.'

Shoot me. I thought it was going to be something work-related, like printing off another script for her. But, no, she just wanted to exert her power over me by making me her personal lackey. 'Fine,' I said, not giving her the satisfaction of thinking it bothered me. 'I was just on my way out.'

I returned with her stuff twenty minutes later. (I'd got her a full-fat Coke 'by mistake'. Oops!)

'Come in! Come in!' she called.

'I have stuff to do . . .'

'Five minutes.' I'm not quite sure why but I stepped inside her trailer. I felt as if I was entering enemy territory and my back instinctively became rigid. I perched awkwardly on the edge of the couch, sitting on my hands in case I was over-powered by an urge to slap her.

'Oh, brilliant! My photo shoot! It's here!' she trilled, flicking through the magazine. 'Look!' she exclaimed, throwing it onto my lap.

'*Aaaah!*' I screamed. Jesus, Izzy, get it together. I tried to cover up by using Susie's excuse: 'Spider!'

Edna shrieked. 'Where?'

'Sorry, false alarm, it's only a bit of fluff.'

Calm. Pretend to take it all in as if you don't care. As if you have no idea who they are. Like the caption over the photos does not read: 'Stunning actress and Dublin socialite moves in with her hunky top-exec boyfriend.'

I disguised another scream as a cough.

Contrived shots of her and Cian cuddling on the couch, eating oysters in the kitchen, lying on the rug reading the Sunday papers.

My flipping rug! I'd given it to him as a present and now they were lying on it. 'Get off my rug, Edna McClodmutton!' I wanted to shout.

They were obviously living in her apartment, but in all the photos I could see pieces of my past life scattered about. I'd had sex with Cian on that rug, for Christ's sake. And they were *my mugs!* I'd hand-painted them.

Breathe.

Breathe!

She looked *stunning* in the photos. And even though I wouldn't wear a Black Halo dress on a Sunday afternoon to read the papers, it looked natural on her. She probably went jogging in Malene Birger cocktail numbers.

And there was Cian, happy and smug and *gorgeous!* Even though he was wearing snakeskin boots and, to the naked eye, I was pretty sure he had blond highlights, the ache in my heart suddenly became unbearable. I felt as if the walls were closing in on me. I eyed the door, knowing that if I didn't leave in the next three seconds and have a cigarette, I was going to die.

I glanced at Edna. She was scanning my face for tell-tale signs of trauma. I struggled to find something to say but, thankfully, I was rescued by a knock on the door. It was the AD again, Tom, still looking traumatized. Snap! He and I were so in sync.

'There you are, Izzy,' he puffed, out of breath. 'Emergency on-set. We need you.'

Wow. I felt like Superwoman. Until he told me what the 'emergency' involved.

Eight minutes later I was dressed in a Lycra training top, shiny pink tracksuit bottoms, skanky runners and big hoop earrings, with my hair scraped up into a ponytail/council-estate facelift. When I spotted my reflection in a window, I let out my third scream of the afternoon.

'Thanks for doing this,' Tom said, still out of breath.

I was about to say, 'What choice did I have after I was jumped by the costume department, stripped and re-dressed before I'd had time to object?' but I thought it probably wouldn't get me anywhere so I just nodded.

Why me?

Why today?

Honestly, *why*?

Some special extra had failed to show up apparently, and now they needed someone else to fill in ASAP. They kept repeating it and, believe me, I got the 'ASAP' of the situation when the wardrobe assistant gave me a chafe burn on my arse – she'd reefed up the hideous tracksuit bottoms too quickly.

Tom dragged me by the arm to O'Connell Bridge. 'She's

here! She's here!' he shouted wildly, when we were within earshot of the director. The entire crew clapped appreciatively when they saw me coming and I nodded shyly, wishing desperately that I could have stepped in to play someone glamorous in a puffball dress and cute peep-toes.

'Wow, they're one tight pair of pants, Isobel. But if you squint, you can't really notice the camel's toes.' *Arrgh!* Edna McClodmutton was absolutely fecking *everywhere!*

'Isobel, my darling! Thank you! Thank you!' the director called, as he approached me. 'Now, this won't take too long. Basically you just have to run down O'Connell Street with this tent as if you've just stolen it from a shop. That's all.'

That's *all*?

'Erm, really?'

'You're a great sport, Isobel. We really appreciate it. Now, we have to get going right away,' he chirped, ushering me towards the camera.

'I, er, didn't realize I'd have to actually *do* something,' I said to him quietly. 'I thought I was just going to be hanging around in the background.'

He laughed heartily. 'Okay, first positions, everyone!' he shouted. 'Now, Isobel, when I say, "Action," you just run and keep on running!' He handed me the tent. It was rather large and quite awkward to get a hold of, and as I was trying to get a proper grip on it, he shouted, 'ACTION!'

'Oooh, me?' I asked nervously.

'Yes, Isobel. ACTION! ACTION! ACTION!'

I started running, partly because the director had frightened me by shouting like that. I didn't hear anyone shout, 'Cut,' so I kept on running, as he'd said, hoping to God I didn't bump into anyone I knew. How odd was this? Legging it down O'Connell Street, carrying a tent, dressed like someone from Odds and Sods. Oh, please, God, may I not bump into anyone I know! Least of all Cian coming out of the homewares in Clery's with cushions to match my rug for his new love-nest.

Just when I was getting into some sort of rhythm, I felt myself being hoisted backwards, then lifted off the ground. I watched my legs still going mid-air, like a cartoon character's. What the hell?

'Where are you off to, young lady?'

I turned my head to see a store guard staring at me. 'Em, could you let me down, please? I haven't stolen this tent. I'm actually doing a scene in a movie.'

'Sure you are, love,' he said, still holding me off the ground at arm's length by the criss-cross back-strap of my Lycra top.

As I swayed there, like a decoration on a Christmas tree, I wondered if today would make it on to my growing list of the Worst Ever Days of My Life. I was fairly confident it would.

'Sorry! Excuse me! Sorry, sir, could you put her down, please?'

Hey! I recognized that voice. I peered at the figure pelting down O'Connell Street towards me.

Christ alive! It was Jonathan Ride Cunningham!

I was going to have to make a new list: Weirdest Ever Days of My Life.

'Hi, Jonathan,' I said, as he reached us, keen to seem semi-normal this time, despite the challenges at hand. 'How have you been?' I asked, trying to sound chipper.

'Fine, Isobel,' he said distractedly. He looked at the store guard. 'Please put her down, sir. The poor girl was filling in as an extra for the scene we're doing.' He took out his business card. 'I'm the film's producer, so if you could just let her come with me now that would be great.'

I felt like a prize turkey being bartered over at a farm fair.

All of a sudden the guy released his grip and I plopped back to my feet. Phew!

'You seem to have the most intriguing job, Isobel. I'm on-set for two minutes and I see you pegging it down O'Connell Street dressed like Vicky Pollard and almost getting arrested.'

'Regular day at the office.' I shrugged, trying to smile, which was quite painful with my hair scraped up so tightly. He smiled back and my stomach flipped. Good God, this man was divine.

Jonathan's mobile rang and he apologized, saying he had to take the call. I strolled back to the set. I couldn't wait to get out of those clothes. I knew Edna had been trying to rile me with the camel-toes comment, but I strategically placed the tent in front of me just in case.

Just then someone called, 'Oi!' Then again: 'Oi!'

I spotted a little man in dark clothes hiding behind the Daniel O'Connell statue, gesturing at me to come over to him. It was only when I'd nearly reached him that I noticed the giant camera looped around his neck. I flinched. I swear to Christ that if someone had just taken photos of me running down O'Connell Street in this clobber, with this tent so they could put them on Facebook . . .

'I saw you talking to the film crew a few moments ago. You're working on the film, are you?'

'Yes,' I said defensively.

'I'll give you twenty euro if you give me some dirt on Saffron Spencer.'

'What?'

'Fine, fifty euro.'

Fifty? I could buy that blouse in Topshop. And I could also get Edna back for exploiting my heartbreak on Facebook and generally ruining my life . . .

By the time I got back to the set office, Margaret had

calmed down substantially and was not holding any mugs of hot coffee so I relaxed a little. Jonathan popped by later to check I was okay after the O'Connell Street episode, and I was mighty happy not to be wearing my tight Lycra jogging pants this time. The 'I must sleep with him!' chant popped into my head and I closed my lips tightly.

'Listen, I have to head back to London tomorrow,' he said suddenly, 'but if you're around later and don't have any plans, maybe we could go for a drink or something.'

Good Lord! Had this cool, sophisticated, handsome producer really just asked me out for a drink? With my track record and all? Should I agree to go out with a guy who obviously had such bad judgement? Feck it! I couldn't be too fussy with the whole rebound-sex thing or it would never happen. I had to accept that Josh Hartnett was not going to be 'the guy' and just roll with what I got. Not that Jonathan Ride Cunningham was too bad a substitute. Hang on! He hadn't agreed to sleep with me yet, only asked me to go for a post-work drink.

One step at a time.

20

I spent the rest of the afternoon concentrating on not sweating because Jonathan Ride Cunningham was taking me for a drink after work and I wouldn't get an opportunity to change beforehand. The office was stuffy – it was essentially a metal Portakabin – and Margaret asked me had I hurt my shoulders when she saw me walking around with my arms set at Barbie-doll angles. I couldn't tell her it was to ensure air circulation to my pits as I was going for a drink with our gorgeous boss straight after work so I just said that, yes, I had hurt my shoulders – perhaps it was all the photocopying I'd been doing. She told me that a friend of hers had snapped a tendon in her finger from having to press the start button on the office shredder so I was to be careful.

Before I met Jonathan in Keogh's, I ducked into Brown Thomas to avail myself of the free perfume-squirting service they provided. I always made sure to look genuinely interested in the product before I spritzed some onto my neck and wrists from the sample bottle. I'd give it a thoughtful look before I replaced it on the shelf, too, my yes-that-is-nice-but-perhaps-I-should-shop-around-a-bit-more-before-I-decide look. It camouflaged the fact that I was just a scabby chancer. And then I'd be gone before a member of the Orange Brigade had bullied me into buying three different perfumes to get the free eye shadow I'd never use.

When I arrived at the pub it was bursting with office folk desperate to sedate their work troubles with a pint or two. I searched the crowd for Jonathan. I couldn't see him outside,

so I headed in. I scanned the bar and the lounge area, giddy with anticipation. I was wearing my nonchalant expression. It disguises my giddiness pretty well. I find it far more effective at times like this than the I'm-so-excited-to-be-here-where-is-he-*where-is-he* look of mania.

I wove in and out of any pocket of space I could find among the crowd, edging my way further into the bar. Where was he? Being small had its many advantages – such as when asking for piggybacks or playing drunken hide and seek – but coping with crowds was not one of them. I needed one of those mirror gadgets, like the ones MacGyver used for looking over walls. Just then, I felt a hand on my waist, gently steering me backwards. Before I launched into my 'Don't be such a sleazy pervert!' rant, I turned to see that the sleazy pervert was Jonathan. Not that he was a sleazy pervert, of course. Quite frankly, if he had been wearing a white tank top and spoken directly to my breasts for the whole night, I would have considered it rather charming. But he was dressed in a crisp, pale blue shirt, the sleeves rolled up casually. And he had the decency to look me in the eye when he spoke, which was nice.

He looked so lovely it was distracting, and I had to remind myself to answer him when he said hello. He leant in and kissed my cheek, which was a first. An awkward little moment followed when I thought it was going to be a kiss-on-cheek-with-added-hug manoeuvre. Jonathan, however, was opting for the simple kiss-on-cheek, which left me clinging awkwardly to his side.

'How has the rest of your day been?' he asked.

'Pretty good thanks. You?'

'Not too bad at all. Was lovely to bump into you earlier. And I'm glad I persuaded you to come for a drink.'

'Why? Did you think they'd have me fired by now?'

'No, not at all. Bright girl like you.'

We both knew I hadn't exactly put my best foot forward in the intelligence arena so far. What a cheeky bastard, mocking my apparent idiocy. Did he think I really was thick? I felt like telling him my Leaving Cert results, and that I'd got a B in Honours Irish.

'What time is your flight tomorrow?'

'Not until twelve, so I can afford to be a bit bold this evening. I can write you a sick note for the morning, if you'd like?'

'No, thank you. I take my job extremely seriously so I'll be bright-eyed and bushy-tailed at six thirty a.m. Might even go for a jog first.'

He laughed and shook his head. 'More power to you.'

I sincerely hoped he knew I was joking about the dawn jog. People who sacrificed an extra hour in bed to run around in the dark wearing Lycra were obviously in a weird cult and should be avoided at all costs.

'Oh, great!' he said, looking over my shoulder. Em . . . was Jonathan cross-eyed and I'd never noticed before?

'Sorry?' I responded, with a little wave, trying to get him to refocus on my eyes.

'Saffron's back with the drinks.'

I whipped around to see bloody Edna McClodmutton teetering towards us, clutching a pint of Guinness and a glass of red wine.

'Thanks, you're a star,' he said, taking the pint from her. 'Saffron, you've met Isobel?'

'Oh, God, yes,' she almost spat. She was clearly as shocked to see me as I was to see her. 'Yes,' she purred, regaining her composure, a fake smile spreading lazily across her face. 'Yes, of course we've met. How are you, Isobel? Have you recovered from your awful afternoon, being trussed up like a prize skanger and getting arrested?'

'Well, it wasn't exactly –'

'Oh, don't get me wrong. I'm *jealous*. I wish I could pull off a look like that to be more versatile in my work, but whenever I've tried, no one buys it. Not like you.' She smiled at me as if she'd just handed me the biggest compliment of my life. 'This is turning into a right work get-together, isn't it?' she said to Jonathan.

'Let me get you a drink, Isobel.' Jonathan disappeared into the crowd, leaving the two of us alone.

'So, uhm, how did your scenes go today?'

'Never knew you were so friendly with Jonathan,' she replied.

'Well, I'm not really . . .'

'Did you just bump into him? Are you here with a date?'

I despised this woman. How dare she? 'No,' I said, through gritted teeth.

'I never got a chance to tell Jonathan about the details of that Facebook incident. Oh, he's coming back now – it'll be a right laugh when I tell him . . .'

'I know it was you,' I interrupted, half terrified, half exhilarated.

'Excuse me?' she said, full of attitude.

'I know it was you who put it on Facebook.'

She shook her head slowly and smiled patronizingly. 'Oh, honey, I wouldn't even go there. You are so out of your depth.'

Jonathan rejoined us with a gin and tonic in hand. I smiled up at him, savouring the last few moments when he would believe, despite all my bad points, that I wasn't clinically psychotic. To my surprise, she didn't mention a word about my Britney episode, but she knew she had me on a tight leash because of it. I sipped my gin and watched her work her magic.

She flicked her hair flirtatiously and kept stroking the side of Jonathan's arm mid-conversation. After a while, it became clear that, with her, it was all just a glossy façade. As I listened to her, I realized her conversation lacked any real substance. She knew when to agree or disagree from someone else's lead, when to laugh and when to appear concerned. I tried to join in a few times, but any attempt was short-lived. Edna would tolerate me for a few moments, so as not to appear overly bitchy, but would then expertly steer the conversation back to herself.

How transparent. Schmoozing with the powerful producer who could undoubtedly get her parts in other movies. I decided to come in with a timely reminder of her fantastic relationship and that she was very much off the market.

'Saffron, that photo shoot of you and your wonderful boy-friend in *Social Scene* was so cute. Adorable, in fact. You guys look so . . . *together* . . . so *solid*.' And with that I excused myself and went outside for a cigarette.

I wasn't going to engage in a tug-of-war for Jonathan's attention. It wasn't like I really cared anyway. Who was he? Just some bloke I thought was cute. I'd only met him a hand-ful of times. I didn't know him. I just wanted to prove to myself that I was capable of liking a man who wasn't Cian. I could find someone else to have rebound sex with. Easy! Someone *nicer*.

I wasn't sure if he was getting a thrill out of two women vying for his attention, but I was pretty sure he was. Prick. He was loving it. Who invites two girls out on the same date? Hmph! Well, I certainly wasn't going to participate in this egomaniac's charade another minute. I stood outside, feeling proud of myself but disappointed too. It had been nice to have something to take my mind off a certain six-page spread in *Social Scene*. However brief.

Oh, well.

The atmosphere outside was so much better. I leant back against the wall and people-watched, savouring my cigarette. A group of office workers were getting rowdier and rowdier as the stack of empty glasses on their table continued to mount. There was a guy seated in a wooden chair, his tie knotted around his head, while a bevy of girls queued up to give him a kiss. I hoped it was his birthday and that he wasn't just another chauvinistic egomaniac indulging in a little 'me time'. When they launched into a semi-coherent version of 'Happy Birthday' I sighed with relief.

One of the girls saw me on my own and invited me to give Davo a birthday kiss. Before I got the chance to fob her off, she yanked me from my lookout post and shoved me to the top of the queue. Not wanting to spoil Davo's birthday, I went in for the kill and planted a smooch on his lips. It was met with rapturous cheers and a double shot of Sambuca.

Half an hour later I was best friends with the entire accounts department of the Dawson Street branch of TSB. After pilfering three more cigarettes and knocking back another two Sambucas, I decided I should probably go home. The threat of my six thirty a.m. start was sobering me up. I said goodbye to my new friends and apologized to Davo for leaving his birthday bash early, I'd never let it happen again.

The street was still bustling with pub-goers and I wriggled through them in a rather ungainly manner. Over the noise of banter and bustle, I could have sworn I heard someone calling my name.

'Isobel. *Isobel*!'

It was probably one of my TSB mates yelling, 'Give him hell! Give him hell!' to the next unsuspecting victim they'd found for Davo to snog. How easily I had been replaced! I'd have to review my friendship with that bunch.

Then I heard it again. Someone was definitely calling my name.

I turned. Jonathan was squeezing between two people, forcing his way towards me. Oh, come on! He wasn't going to act concerned, was he, innocently inquiring where I'd been all night? I'd been out here for *ages*. Enough time to make a whole new set of friends, even. He hadn't bothered to come and find me until now.

'Where are you going? Where have you been?'

For the love of God! What was he playing at? I had absolutely no interest in his schoolboy games. I'd been through enough already today. And all I really cared about was getting away so I could go home and crawl into my bed. I suddenly felt exhausted.

As soon as his path was clear he trotted up to me. 'You're not leaving, are you? I just came out to look for you. Where did you go?'

'I was just out here in the beer garden. Inside wasn't really my scene. Saffron doesn't like me. Personal reasons . . . doesn't matter.' I looked at the ground. 'Anyway, I'm sure she's a nice girl but I really wasn't in the mood for a strained conversation with her, so I decided to leave you guys to it. It's been a long day. Anyway, goodnight. Safe home tomorrow.'

I headed off. I felt really brave for having said that and not just going along with whatever Jonathan was saying.

'Isobel, wait a second.'

I turned back. A good few metres lay between us now.

He paused for a moment, then moved forward slowly, his hands shoved into his jeans pockets. I decided he didn't look like Josh Hartnett. It was probably the dark hair that had made me think so. That or blind optimism. He definitely had a Robbie Williams look about him, all right.

'Listen,' he blurted, when he'd reached me, 'I really wanted to spend a bit of time with you this evening. That's why I asked you for a drink.'

'Really? Did you want to spend a bit of time with Saffron, too?' I could hear the bitchiness in my tone, but I didn't care. I was getting angrier by the second at this guy's arrogance. I wasn't going to let every bloke on the planet, not to mention up-and-coming actresses, make a mockery of me.

Just as I turned to leave he slid his hand down my arm and clasped mine. What was going on here? I didn't try to pull away – it felt nice. We stood there for a moment or two.

'Really, Izzy, I did want to spend time with you this evening.'

I tugged my hand free. 'So why on earth did you ask Saffron Spencer along too? Who do you think you are? Robbie Williams?'

He looked confused, and I didn't blame him. God, I really should stop talking now. Had I not learnt my lesson that shock and alcohol don't mix well with me?

'Honestly, Isobel, she invited herself along. Just as I was about to leave to meet you, she cornered me and pleaded with me to go for a drink with her. I tried to get out of it but she said she'd been so miserable over the last few days, felt so isolated among her friends because they were jealous of her big break, that she thought she'd cry if she couldn't find someone to go out with for a drink.'

That girl was unbelievable.

I searched his face for signs of insincerity. He was either a really nice guy who was obliging someone because he thought they were lonely, or he was a player and an expert liar. Flip a coin?

'I swear to God,' he half whispered. 'She said she was just staying for one but I haven't been able to get rid of her. I've tried. I even tried to butt into other people's conversations in the hope they'd adopt her.' He edged closer to me, scooped both my hands into his and knotted his fingers through mine. I found it impossible to resist. I was totally captivated. 'So really,' he continued, 'all I wanted to do this evening was . . . this.'

He released his hands, placed them on my lower back and pulled me towards him. Then he kissed me. A lovely, soft, slow kiss that sent a shiver through me.

21

That Friday, all my social life aspirations were realized: I was blessed with the unrivalled opportunity of attending Eve's engagement party.

I kind of got the feeling it was a last-minute invitation – that morning I'd happened to call into the Lights! Camera! Action! office to pick up a parcel and she'd asked me. I flicked Gavin a quick look. He gave a masked nod, so I accepted. There was no way I was going if Gavin wouldn't be there.

'Marvellous!' she chirped, with forced enthusiasm. 'Bring a date! Or not . . . You're not going out with anyone, are you, Isobel? Hmm . . . well, sure just bring yourself so.'

I'd not known Eve and Philippe had got engaged and was surprised she didn't have posters up on billboards the length and breadth of Ireland, ads on the radio and flyers delivered through every letterbox in the city. Actually, she probably had, but I'd been so busy I'd missed them.

One thing I knew for certain: her party would fall into one of two categories – excruciatingly painful or highly entertaining. Either way, I was glad I had something to do this evening because I was in the mood to go out – and not in a bound-and-gagged-dragged-by-the-hair-kicking kind of way. I wanted to go out of my own volition.

Perhaps I was finally putting the past behind me. A lot had happened in the last little while. First and foremost, I'd snogged someone, which was super as I was beginning to get scared I'd forget how to do it and wondered if, at twenty-seven, I was too old to resort to practising on the back of my hand. Not only that, I'd managed to snog someone I happened to fancy the pants off. It had boosted my confidence no end. On the flip side, Cian had phoned and texted me, which was still bugging the shit out of me, there was the six-page spread in *Social Scene* and I had to work with Edna McClodmutton.

I showed Keelin and Susie those photos the day after I'd seen them, and Keelin got out a magnifying-glass to study them. (I'm not kidding. Whoever said girls were freaks was definitely on to something.) 'She has crows' feet!' she howled.

'And her left boob is bigger than the right!' Susie clapped.

'And she has awful fake tan marks under her armpits!'

And so it continued.

But even though the girls were doing their best to make me feel better about *The Cian and Edna Horror Picture Show*, I was actually feeling reasonably okay about it the next day. I still had the occasional urge to vomit, but otherwise I wasn't too bad, considering. It didn't matter how stunning she was or how fantastic she looked or what amazing parties she went to at the weekends, the truth was that she wasn't a nice person. So the other shite didn't really matter.

After work I darted home to get ready for the party. Knowing Eve, it would be a lavish function with no expense spared, so I chose my outfit carefully. I'd settled on a simple black cocktail dress. I don't care what anyone says about black, sometimes you just can't beat it. And it was a total lifesaver when all your meals on the day have been based on a toast theme – which doesn't work well with a tight evening gown.

The party was every bit as ostentatious as I had anticipated. Eve had hired an exquisite function room in the Four Seasons Hotel, decorated with clusters of red roses, golden balloons and silver streamers. Waiters in crisply pressed tuxedos offered guests fizzing flutes of champagne, the music was lively and the buzz was fantastic. By the time Gavin and I had arrived, the place was already bursting at the seams with 'dahlings', hordes of them in bejewelled dresses, spraytanned to the hilt, with long false talons. And that was just the men – I'm only kidding, but I did spot at least seven blokes who were *definitely* wearing fake tan. The tell-tale orange marks on their shirt collars said it all.

'Oh, hello, dahling!'

'Oh, hello, dahling! How wonderful to see you.'

'Oh, sweetie, you look simply stunning.'

'Oh, thanks, chickie, you too.'

I looked at Gavin. 'Drink, dahling?' he asked.

'Oh, you *are* a pet.'

As I waited for Gavin to come back from the bar, I couldn't help eavesdropping on a conversation that was taking place beside me.

'Yes, she's still away, helping orphans in Malaysia or Singapore or some Japanese country like that.'

A chorus of wows ensued. Then a blonde girl with seriously over-collagened lips said, 'So, like, are orphans kids with no parents or no gaffs or what?'

'Sometimes *both*,' her friend said.

'*Oh*, my God! What a focking nightmare.'

'Total and utter.'

'Now I feel bad we bought a second place in Marbella.'

'Don't, sweetie – you can't stop living just because others aren't as lucky. Make a donation online or something.'

Gavin and I huddled together in a corner and knocked back our champagne. Then we tried to come up with a list of things we possibly had in common with these people. Just in case we came face to face with one of them and were forced to make conversation. I planned to say that my friend Caroline had been to Marbella, that my dress was from a boutique on the southside (Boutique de Zara in Dundrum town centre) and that I'd tried gel nails once – as a result, my own nails had fallen off but I'd stop short of telling anyone that. If Gavin was cornered, he'd tell them that his cousin ran a spray-tan booth in Malahide, and after that he'd tell them to go and shite.

I told him he was so cool, so Colin Farrell.

We kept telling ourselves that after the 'next one' we really should go and find the happy couple and offer our congratulations. It would be terribly rude if we stayed there all night drinking champagne, then just left, wouldn't it?

Or would it?

A little later Laurence and Geraldine arrived and I could tell from Geraldine's expression that she was wondering why she'd come. 'I mean, Eve and I hate each other!' she spat. 'I feel like a total hypocrite.'

'Well, I wouldn't say that Eve and I are the best of friends either. But maybe no one here is. Maybe this lot came as a package when she booked the room, along with the balloons and the jazz band and stuff. Probably just have to tick a box on the application form that asks whether or not you wish them to provide friends for your party.'

'That sounds about right for her,' Geraldine chirped, then raised her champagne flute. 'To Eve, our dear friend.'

'To our dear friend.' We clinked glasses.

'I think Eve's problem is the music she listens to,' Laurence said authoritatively. 'I reckon all that yoga and find-yourself stuff is a load of old hooey. She needs to start listening to some decent feel-good sounds. Things she can have a good old bop to in the kitchen – Cliff, Dicky Rock, Hanson. And an hour of Westlife is as good as an hour in therapy. You laugh, you cry, you reminisce, you get angry, and then you forgive and forget. By the end you're as good as new. That's my gift to her.'

I totally agreed with him on the Westlife front.

'Ah, Laurence,' Gavin said. 'You got her some CDs. That's really kind.'

'Oh, no,' he said, taking a piece of paper out of his back pocket. 'I made her a list of one hundred of my favourite upbeat tunes.'

Aw. Laurence was so cute. And I just loved that he had no qualms admitting to his cheesy-pop-song fetish. He took his glasses out of his jacket pocket and placed them on the end of his nose. I bit my lip and Gavin shot me a glance. His eyes were dancing and I knew he was stifling a laugh.

'Right so. I've colour-coded the list so she'll know which songs she should listen to for whatever mood she's in. If you're down and feel a bit poo, try the songs highlighted in blue. S Club Seven's 'Reach For The Sky' is an exemplary number if you're struck down with a dose of the moody blues.'

'Come on, Larry, you big stropping hunk, you're dancing with me.' Geraldine pulled his arm and the two of them hit the floor, just as the DJ dropped some serious gangsta rap tune. Geraldine joined in, bellowing about her 'homies', clapping and shuffling from side to side. Every so often she'd punch the air and shout, 'Woo-hoo!' After she'd done that six or seven times, the dance-floor had pretty much cleared.

'I'm bloody roasting,' she called to us, fanning her pink face with her hands. Menopausal hot flushes cut heating bills everywhere. I couldn't imagine her shoulder pads were doing her any favours, though. There must have been at least six inches of stuffing in there. Geraldine had told me her outfit was some old yoke she'd found at the back of her wardrobe.

I hadn't known she was accumulating her own vintage clothing collection. She might have bought it in some expensive retro boutique in Rathgar or Killiney.

'Izzy! Join us for a dance!'

'Later,' I lied, plucking another drink from a passing waiter. I was wondering whether Jonathan Ride Cunningham was going to put in an appearance. Eve had mentioned he might come. She'd invited him because he was good-looking and important, an all-round perfect party guest. I could have done with another of his melty kisses.

'Iz, does Geraldine ever remind you of Mary FitzGerald from *How Do You Do?*' Gavin asked.

'Yes! Particularly when she wears eighties clothes. She looks *so* like her!'

'For me it's when she tells me to be careful with scissors.'

Poor old Geraldine. She often complained that she never had money for new clothes as all her cash had gone into straightening her eldest son's teeth. Nearly broke her heart when he slipped on the porch letting the dog out just after his brace was off, cracking his two front teeth in half. I thought she looked fantastic in her orange puffball dress. The giant orange plastic flower in her hair might have been a tad too much – but whatever. To hell with all those dahlings who were pointing at her and whispering things behind their hands.

My eyes drifted to the bar where Eve was chatting to an audience of perfectly coiffed women. They were all either extremely bored, didn't have a clue what she was on about or over-Botoxed. I couldn't tell. In the middle of her rant, she lifted her hand to fix her fringe, and I was momentarily blinded by a flash of light. I rubbed my eyes and looked at Eve again to figure out what had – Oh! It was her engagement ring! Shards of light beamed off it like lasers, catching the reflection of the mirrorball over the dance-floor.

'Phew!'

'Izzy, what are you doing? The limbo? If you want to dance I'll mind your drink. Go on down to Laurence and Geraldine.'

'I was trying to duck Eve's diamond light saber!'

Another few champagne cocktails and I was doing *Swan Lake* with Laurence – and new-found respect for the *Strictly Come Dancing* lot. I'd thought it looked easy and that they shouldn't be complaining about their blisters and dislocated vertebrae because they got to wear cool clothes – but this was seriously hard work! I begged Laurence to let me have a breather before I ended up in a neck brace. He agreed, on condition that I dance with him later on if they played any Lulu. My neck and I prayed for no Lulu.

On my way to the toilets to check in the mirror that my spine was still properly aligned, I was distracted by what seemed a familiar face coming through the door. I strained my eyes. Jesus – it was! It was *Edna*! Dear Christ, was Cian with her? I was hyperventilating as my eyes darted round the room. No sign of Cian. I ran into the cloakroom and forced myself to calm down.

After hiding behind a large anorak for some time, when I finally found the courage to emerge, the room was thronged. If Jonathan Ride Cunningham was here, I might not bump into him at all. Geraldine and Laurence were standing near one of the tables. Geraldine was chewing, her hand hovering over the mini smoked-salmon wraps, and Laurence was sniffing a vol-au-vent suspiciously. Geraldine whipped it out of his hand and stuffed it into her mouth, leaving him stunned.

Gavin was standing at another table, lost in conversation, his eyes narrowed. I shuffled through the crowd to get to him – but stopped suddenly in my tracks. He was talking to

Edna – but they weren't just chatting casually. She was leaning into him, her hand resting flirtatiously on his arm as she giggled coyly at his story.

What was going on?

I backed away, hoping they wouldn't notice me. I was in shock. He didn't fancy her, did he? She wasn't his type – although a very attractive woman in a tight-fitting ruby red cocktail dress with a plunging neckline might be *any* guy's type. And whatever about *types*, what about *Kate*? Why the hell was he flirting back with her like that? All of a sudden she leant forward and whispered something in his ear. I suddenly felt incredibly angry.

I stalked up to the bar and plonked myself down on a stool, flicked through the cocktail menu, ordered a Mojito and waited impatiently for it, my fingers drumming on the counter. After I'd drunk it I'd head home. I had so much to do tomorrow. I hadn't ironed in ages and I still hadn't registered for that barrier-free tolling on the M50. I didn't own a car, but you could never be too prepared, could you?

In the meantime, Eve had trotted up to the bar and squeezed herself in beside me, clicking her fingers for the barman's attention. Why didn't she just flash that rock in his eyes? I really wasn't in the mood for her right now, but I felt guilty that I hadn't spoken to her yet.

'Eve, hi.'

'Oh, hello, Isobel. Yes – I remember inviting you earlier on today.'

Why had I bothered?

'Eh, well, I just wanted to congratulate you once again on your engagement. It's a terrific party.'

'Why, thank you. Very kind of you. It was Philippe's idea, really. I mean, I would have been just as happy to sit at home with a bottle of wine and watch the telly [yeah, right] . . . And

197

he's *so* sweet – he even asked Saffron Spencer to come so I could have a celebrity at my party.'

Eve had been watching far too much of *My Super Sweet 16* on MTV.

'Have you seen her? She is here, you know!'

I nodded. 'Uh-huh, yep! I've seen her here, all right.' My brain was officially saturated with Saffron Spencer. *I* was officially saturated with Saffron Spencer.

'Excuse me, Isobel, but I can't stay and talk now. Yoo-hoo! Bar person! Over here!'

I downed my Mojito and left her to it.

I went over to Geraldine and Laurence to say goodbye. They told me they'd be leaving soon, too, and that we should all jump into a taxi together. I glanced about the room for Gavin – and spotted him in a corner, sitting at a table with Saffron. He was saying something to her, leaning in close to her face. Jesus, why did I have a knack for letting arseholes like him into my life?

Euch!

I had to turn away. I tried to look composed. 'Coming?' I asked.

'I'll get my coat, pet,' Geraldine replied.

I grabbed mine from the cloakroom and headed out of the door. Laurence had hailed a taxi, a mini miracle on a Friday night, and we began to climb in. I was afraid my voice would wobble if I tried to speak. I wanted to cry – Gavin had always been so kind when I got upset about Cian, calling him an idiot and telling me I was lucky to be rid of him. But now he, too, had shown himself to be two-faced and insincere.

Laurence was giving the driver directions so I whipped out my phone and texted Jonathan Ride Cunningham. I was fed up waiting around for my life to start while everyone else was living theirs with gay abandon. He texted back straight away:
Meet me beside the water feature out the back.

'Stop the taxi!' I shouted.

'Izzy, pet, we haven't even moved off yet,' Geraldine reminded me.

I jumped out and ran to the back of the hotel. Jonathan was there. Our eyes found each other and I marched straight over to him. He pulled me close and kissed me hard. Then, whispering in my ear, he asked had I ever stayed at the Four Seasons. Of course I hadn't. We hurried to Reception and booked a room.

22

Huge step. Major achievement. I felt like the Neil Armstrong of my own little world. I was officially moving on. Cian, the love of my life, was no longer the last person I'd slept with. Progress!

Now all I had to do was slip out of bed without waking Jonathan Ride Cunningham so I could fix my makeup in the bathroom and brush my hair before he woke up, saw me, screamed in horror and killed my buzz.

'Morning, you,' he mumbled sleepily, pulling me to him with one lovely strong-man arm. Oops, too late. However, he didn't appear to have any prejudices against the scruffy Goth look. Maybe I owed it to myself to seal the deal. Just to make sure. Just in the name of progress . . .

'Izzy, I'm so proud of you.'
  'You've come so far.'
  'All the hard work.'
  'And the dedication.'
  'And it's finally paid off.'
  Wow. I really *did* feel like Neil Armstrong. I didn't want to dilute all the praise by telling them it hadn't been *that* difficult. We'd just booked a room and taken our clothes off. I also didn't want to tell them that I'd felt like a slapper when we were checking out the next morning and I was in last night's dress with mascara smudged beyond my eyebrows. Or that I'd been caught nicking the toiletries from the chambermaid's trolley and was told that they did not appreciate that sort of behaviour at the Four Seasons, thank you very much.

'And he's such a ride. That's the cherry on the cake. I'd love to see Cian's face now!' Susie laughed.

'He can keep his lame Edna McClodmutton. You've trumped him with the delicious Jonathan Ride Cunningham!' Keelin came back out of the kitchen with a pot of tea and a plate of Skittles.

We sat on the rug, blowing on our tea and catching up on the events of the week. We laughed over the newspaper articles about Edna's 'true identity'. I'd had no idea that the tabloids would print literally *anything* without researching it or double-checking the facts. Everything I'd told that paparazzo on O'Connell Street the day of the shoot had ended up in the celeb-gossip columns.

'Saffron Spencer's true name revealed . . . Edna McClodmutton!'

'Saffron Spencer's next role . . . a transsexual maneater!'

'Saffron Spencer's ex-boyfriend reveals how his penis fell off after contracting rare sexually transmitted disease!'

'Priceless, Izzy,' Keelin gasped, as we split our sides laughing again.

'I guess you really can't believe everything you read.'

'I told you that, Izzy, when you read in *Zelebs* that that actress in *Fair City* could read rabbits' minds and were convinced it was true.' Susie shook her head.

'I just wanted her to tell me Dermot wasn't traumatized by that rabbit-flavoured dog food Keelin brought home.'

'I'm pretty sure Dermo can't read and therefore had no idea what was in the tins,' Keelin said.

'Anyway,' Susie interrupted, 'back to Edna. She deserves whatever's in those gossip columns because she's a sneaky, nasty person who's been bitchy to you whenever she's had the opportunity.'

'Hear, hear!' We clinked our mugs together.

Enough about Edna McClodmutton. I didn't want to talk about her any more. I couldn't get the image of her and Gavin together at the party out of my head, and it really bothered me. I wasn't sure why.

I attempted to change the subject. 'I bags the last red Skittle,' I said, swooping in and snatching it from the plate. I caught Keelin grinning. She'd been doing it quite a lot lately. 'What's up with you?' I asked her.

'Who – me? Nothing,' she said, and was grinning again.

'Out with it,' Susie ordered. 'Either you've bought yourself a new pair of shoes or something's happened with Simon.'

'Something happened with Simon.'

'No way!' I yelped. Had she drugged him, then dragged him off to some lonely spot up in the mountains? Did she know that didn't count? Not to mention the fact that it was illegal. To start with I'd been amazed that Simon hadn't seemed interested in her. But now I was shocked that something had actually happened after months of nothing. What had changed? 'Tell us!' I was itching to hear all the details.

'Well, last week I volunteered to do this soup-run thing for homeless dogs around the city centre. We all have to do a few every year as our boss likes the firm to be seen doing charity work.'

'Do dogs drink soup?' Susie seemed genuinely curious.

'Suz, that was one of the most ridiculous things I've ever heard you say. We give them our own dog food.'

'Do you just walk around town with buckets of it looking for hungry stray dogs?'

'Exactly. So, anyway, there I was, heading off with my bucket, when Simon joined me. Apparently he'd been assigned to come with me. I was so chuffed I almost started dancing.'

'Like you did in Topshop that time you found those shoes left in your size and we were asked to leave by the security man before you got a chance to pay for them because he thought you were drunk?' Susie asked.

'Yeah, a bit like that. A whole night with Simon. On my own! I couldn't believe it! A chance for me to work my magic properly! Unlike Simon, who looked suitably unimpressed that he had to escort me. And then I just thought, Well, screw you! If he wasn't interested, fine, but he didn't have to act like he hated me, right?'

'Right!'

'So I just headed off and did my own thing, thinking, Sod him!'

'Sod him!' we repeated. This was fast turning into some sort of Simon-bashing cult.

'Well, I'd fed two terriers and a Jack Russell when I was approached by this big collie cross. He looked so sorry for himself, his coat all matted and dirty. Little did I know he was a pervert!'

'The collie?' I asked. I hadn't known dogs could be perverts.

'Yep. Started humping my leg, and then, he tried to mount my back!'

Susie and I burst out laughing, and Keelin sort of did too. But then she told us we weren't taking her ordeal seriously enough, so we quietened down.

'I was screaming like a mad woman in the middle of Temple Bar, trying to get the brute off me. There were loads of people standing outside the pubs, but no one would help me. They were all too busy laughing.'

I couldn't look at Susie in case I started laughing again.

'Then I saw Simon pegging it towards me out of nowhere. And he just wrestled this animal off my back with his bare hands.'

It was a dog we were talking about here, wasn't it? Not a bear?

'He was so nice and kind and not at all rude like he'd normally be. He was checking to see I was okay, and making sure I wasn't hurt. And then I said to him, "Why are you being so nice to me, Simon? You hate me."

'"I don't hate you," he said. "I just don't like your carry-on."

'"What carry-on?" I asked, brushing dog hair off my black jumper dress.

'"Give it a rest, will you?" he said, and started to walk off.

'"No, what carry-on, Simon?" I said, like a dog with a bone, fittingly enough. "I don't understand. What are you talking about?"

'He turned round. "Stop playing with me," he said.

'"Playing with you?"

'"Yes, Keelin. All this carry-on where you patronize me by pretending to be interested in me, like it's some sort of game, like I can't see you're using me just to get a reaction."

'I was completely shocked. But I wanted to grab him and hug him because he looked so embarrassed. He folded his arms and stared at the ground.

'"I can't believe you thought I was flirting with you as a *joke*! Or to be cruel! What kind of a horrible person must you think I am?"

'"Oh, come off it. How would a girl like you ever fancy someone like me?"

'I was dumbstruck, girls. I said, "Someone like you . . . what?"

'"Someone who is the complete opposite of what you are. Keelin, you're this stunning, stunning girl who's crazy and funny and wild and outgoing. And I'm just . . . not. And I'm okay with that. But you are so way out of my league."

'He had absolutely no idea how gorgeous he was! "Simon, I fancy the pants off you," I said to him. "And it's not a joke.

I can't believe you thought that. You've been driving me crazy! First I wondered if you had a girlfriend. And then someone said you might be gay, but I said no way. So then I just assumed you weren't interested in me."

'We stood there, staring at each other.

'"So all this time," he said softly, "I've been going out of my mind wanting to kiss you and I could have?"

'"Anytime you'd wanted."'

I had goosebumps listening to her.

'Go on, go on.' Susie was hooked too.

'Well, he pulled me to him, looked straight into my eyes, then leant in . . . and kissed me.'

'Oh. My. God.' I was mesmerized.

Susie's jaw was in her lap. 'That's the sexiest thing I've ever heard,' she said.

'I know! Right?' Keelin beamed.

'I love it,' I gushed. 'It's just so fantastic.'

Aidan arrived, breaking up our tea party.

'How are you, Aidan?' Keelin asked him, through gritted teeth.

'Good, yeah. Just been at home all morning practising my trade . . .'

Drug-trafficking? I wanted to ask.

'Gotta keep on top of the game, be at my physical peak. So I've taken up kick-boxing and I'm learning how to use nun chucks too.'

To be fair, he was in pretty good shape, but it sort of hurt my eyes to look at him when he was wearing that 'Pain is Love' Jason Streatham T-shirt. I couldn't resist just one teeny-weeny nibble at the bait.

'You know what's great to have on your CV as an actor?' I said in my best helpful voice.

'What's that?' He was all ears.

'Horse-riding. Your parents have that unbelievably plush stud down the country, right? You should take advantage of it.'

He ignored me. 'Are we off, Susie?' Then he added, 'Saved this for you.' He dropped a newspaper onto the rug. 'That's your mate, isn't it?'

I looked at the photo on the front page. Edna McClod-mutton? Certainly no mate of mine. But who was that in the photo with her? The guy she was kissing?

Gavin.

Later that evening I hooked up with Jonathan for a drink. I'd been excited to hear from him and happy to get out of the house. Susie would be gone for the rest of the day, Keelin was going on an 'official' date with Simon, and I didn't want to be stuck in the house on my own asking Dermot why Gavin had snogged Edna McClodmutton.

'So, when are you coming over to London for a visit?'

'Hmm?' I'd been a million miles away. 'When do you want me to come?' I'd tried to sound flirty. It hadn't worked: I'd sounded more like one of those voiceovers on the late-night sex-line ads. I reminded myself that the guy I'd been pursu-ing for the past few months was sitting in front of me – *and* I'd slept with him *and* there might be more opportunities to sleep with him if I acted normal.

But at the end of the evening when he invited me back to his hotel, I told him I should probably head home, that I had some work to finish off for an early-morning meeting. That part was true. Gavin and I were having a meeting about the storyboards. I didn't know now how I felt about that. Should I just tell him I thought he was an absolute dickhead for cheating on Kate, and then demand to know how he could have snogged Edna McClodmutton when he was supposed to be my friend? Bile burnt the back of my throat.

Jonathan was doing his best to cheer me up, but it just wasn't enough. And then I got *another* bloody text from Cian.

Izzy please, why wont u answer me? Pls, I really wanna talk. Cian. x.

Jonathan put me into a taxi, we kissed goodnight, and he told me he'd be in touch over the next while. I headed home to ask Dermot why Gavin had snogged Edna McClodmutton.

23

The next morning I stood at Gavin's door with my story-boards under my arm and my mind made up. I was going to come out with it. I knocked loudly.

'Morning, you. Come on in.'

'Why did you kiss Saffron Spencer?' I blurted out.

'What?' he asked, taken off-guard.

'Why would you do that? You're supposed to be my friend. And you told me you thought she was a muppet. So, what now? You've met her and you think she's a total babe? Like *everyone* does? And what about Kate? Why would you do that?'

'Izzy, step inside,' he said crossly. 'I'd prefer if all my neighbours didn't know my business and perhaps then I can defend myself before you throw any more wild accusations at me.'

I looked around: two of them were on their porches, pretending to check their postboxes.

'I saw the photo in the paper,' I continued, once I was in his living room.

'For a start, that photo was nonsense,' he said, no trace of humour in his voice.

'Well, I read that you'd hooked up at Eve's party.'

'Well, maybe you shouldn't believe everything you read.' Everyone had been saying that to me lately.

'But the photo . . .' I was confused now.

'If you'd stayed around long enough to get the *whole* picture, you would have discovered that the entire thing was an elaborate set-up by yours truly.'

'What?'

'That *muppet* Saffron Spencer found out about your little chat with that photographer guy and decided to get her revenge. Apparently she'd heard through the grapevine that you and me sort of had a thing going, and this was her attempt to sabotage it.'

'You and me? No way! Who told her that? Who *thought* that?'

He shrugged. 'Anyway, she came to the party with her social-diarist photographer in tow, made a beeline for me, and Bob's your uncle. Totally lunged at me with her big ugly flytrap mouth.'

'You didn't enjoy it?'

'Izzy, what have I told you? I don't find her attractive. I don't like her. I was only playing along with her little game so I could tell her how pathetic she was for treating you the way she had and that she should just fuck off and leave you alone.'

I was almost overcome by the urge to cry. 'Really?' I asked, touched by his loyalty.

'Anyway, she jumped on me and that bloke took the photo before I knew what was happening. What a total muppet. She seriously needs to get a life.'

'Thank you, Gav,' I said, wanting to hug him. 'And I'm sorry for sort of putting you in that position.'

'She's poison – she would have done it anyway, Izzy. Now if we're done with talking about her, can we get down to some business, please?' He looked at the storyboards in my hand. 'Hand them over.'

I showed him the series I'd done so far and was chuffed when he said he thought they were incredible and even better than he'd anticipated. I told him I still had a lot of work to do and we chatted about the additions we thought would look good. Just as he began to tell me about the progress he'd made with the initial researching and filming he'd done, a thought struck me. 'Gavin, what about Kate? Did she see the photo? I can tell her I know exactly what Edna's like and that –'

'Izzy.' He sighed heavily, running his hands through his hair. 'Kate and I have broken up.'

We sat in silence for a moment or two.

'When?' I asked quietly.

'A week or two ago.'

'I'm so sorry. What happened?' I wasn't sure he wanted to talk about it. 'I thought you guys were solid.'

'It's been on the cards for a long time. We were just going in two very different directions, and we'd grown apart because of it. But she's a fantastic girl, and I think we ended on okay terms, all things considered.' It hadn't been right for ages, he said, and, in a way, now that it was over, he was relieved. They hadn't been arguing as such, but something didn't fit any more. Things had come to a head when he'd told her he was entering the documentary competition. She couldn't understand why he'd want to spend so much time on something that might never happen, even though he'd told her what the prize would entail and that it had always been his dream. Her career path had been structured so she couldn't see the point of putting in a lot of work if you weren't necessarily going to reap any reward.

'I don't think she ever really respected what I want to do, Izzy, or what I have to do to make it happen. That it may not be straightforward, but it'll be worth it because, whether I win this competition or not, I'll be doing something I love and truly believe in.'

I could sympathize with that.

And I had no doubt that he would succeed at it, once he was given the opportunity to prove himself.

'So there it is, really,' he said softly. 'Kate's such a great girl and I just hope we can stay friends.'

He was so noble and gracious. I had so much to learn.

'So, what next?' he asked, nodding towards the story-boards.

I hadn't a clue. After his revelation my head was all muddled and I couldn't think straight for the life of me.

When I got back, the house was empty so I chatted to Dermot while I made some dinner. Keelin had left a note on the fridge to say she was at her aunt's, delivering the Tins of Death for their Schnauzer. Just as I was filling Dermot in on Gavin's reaction to my storyboard, my phone rang.

'Hey, Iz. It's Keelin. I've left my keys behind. Will you be in for the next while?'

'Sure.'

'Great. I'll see you in a bit.'

'Keelin?'

'Yeah?'

'Grab some Ben and Jerry's on the way, will you?'

'Sure.'

Twenty minutes later the bell rang and I skipped to the door, trying to guess which flavour she'd chosen.

'*Jesus.*'

'Hi, Izzy.'

My stomach lurched into my throat and I thought I was going to be sick.

'Can I come in?'

I stared at him blankly, unable to move, speak or think. His eyes were fixed to the floor, his hands shoved deep in his pockets.

'Okay,' hovered on the tip of my tongue, but I couldn't say it. Another minute passed.

The silence pressed unrelentingly against my ears. I found myself fiddling with the latch on the door.

He cleared his throat. 'Izzy?' he said.

I nodded silently. My head spun and black dots flitted before my eyes. I clung to the door for support as Cian walked past me and into my house.

24

I asked him if he wanted to sit down, but he said he didn't. I offered him a cup of tea, but he refused it. So I sat on the couch, wondering why I'd suggested tea. It had been over-generous. Next I'd be offering to run him a nice hot bath or iron one of his shirts.

But what do you say when the former love of your life knocks on your door on a Sunday evening and you're in the middle of cooking dinner? What do you say when the person you've spent months trying to forget shows up with his hands in his pockets, asking if he can come in?

'Are you sure you won't have some tea?' I asked again. What was I like? He'd probably think I'd done nothing over the last ten months except watch *Father Ted*.

'No, honestly. I'm fine, thanks . . . The place looks different.'

'Keelin felt she needed a bit more colour in her life.'

He walked around the room, peering at the books and DVDs on the shelving unit, knowing that would stall any proper conversation. I went with it willingly. This way I could look at him. Drink in every inch of him. I could only do that when he wasn't staring at me with those dangerous blue eyes.

I studied his profile, his shoulders, torso, arms and legs, as I'd done a million and one times before. But it felt different now. As if I shouldn't be looking, as if it was wrong to look because it was too intimate. I knew him too well: every inch of his skin, every freckle on his chest, how his hair curled when it was too long, the scar on his elbow.

He had dark circles under his eyes and his hair needed a cut. He was wearing the T-shirt I'd bought to thank him for painting my bedroom walls when the girls and I had moved in here. He'd known I hated those green walls, and he'd painted them cream for me as a surprise.

And here he was now. Standing in my living room, reading the back of *The Big Lebowski* DVD.

What was he doing here?

I felt nauseous again.

'You're probably wondering what I'm doing here,' he said, slotting the DVD back into the rack.

'I'm a little surprised to see you.' I was delighted I hadn't come out with another offer to put the kettle on.

He twiddled with the fairy-lights hanging from the book-shelf. 'That day,' he started, 'when I saw you in the shop —'

'It was horrible,' I interrupted, putting my head into my hands.

'I know. Just horrible. I felt so bad. And then Saffron getting the part in the film. So . . . I just . . .'

'Stop,' I said. The confusion, the panic, the shock that had been swimming through me since he'd appeared had turned into bubbling fury.

So here he was: Cian. The shithead who had nailed my heart to the bottom of a pit seventeen feet deep, covered it with seventeen layers of cement, then walked away. The prick who, after three years, had dumped me so casually you'd swear I'd been a one-night stand. The arsehole I hadn't heard a peep from since.

'I tried calling you,' he said quietly.

Except for the phone call.

'And texting.'

And the texts, of course.

After ten long months a twinge of guilt had prompted him to call over and apologize for how he'd behaved.

'Big deal, Cian. Jesus! Did you think I was still hanging around waiting for an apology? It's funny but tonight was the first night I hadn't spent out on the porch, waiting for you to come, holding a banner over my head, saying, "Hoorah, you're back"!' I barked sarcastically. 'Waiting for you to explain why you'd gone off me. How you'd fallen in love with someone and failed to inform me of the joyous news. And why you'd felt it had been acceptable to do relay races between my bed and *hers*.'

He was gazing at the floor, flicking the corner of the rug with his runner. 'Izzy, I'm so sorry.'

'Oh, fuck off, Cian,' I spat, and marched into the kitchen. I couldn't sit there any longer and look at him. Besides, a stream of hot tears was rolling down my face and I didn't want him to see how upset I was. I'd done enough crying over him.

In the kitchen, I took deep breaths and wiped my cheeks with the back of my hands, shocked by how easy it still was for him to unravel me. My hands were trembling and there was a painful lump in my throat.

I should be stronger than this.

Why was I *still* crying over him?

I hadn't heard him follow me, but he was suddenly behind me, wrapping his arms around me, tucking me into his chest, resting his cheek on the top of my head, stroking my hair. I folded into him, as I had so many times before. I knew how to do it. It was easy.

'I'm so sorry, Izzy,' he whispered, as I cried into his chest. 'I'm so sorry.'

His smell. His arms. His hands. His voice.

I cried and cried and my head spun like a fairground waltzer. He squeezed me tighter.

Suddenly an image of him and Edna McClodmutton

together in *Social Scene* flashed into my mind. I struggled out of his embrace and pushed him away. 'Fuck off,' I said, unable to look at those hypnotic eyes. 'Just fuck off.' I marched out of the kitchen, swiped my keys from the hall table and ran out of the front door, slamming it behind me.

By the time he'd caught up with me, I was nearly at Stephen's Green. I never knew I could run so fast. Good to know, I suppose, if I'm ever being chased by an axe-murderer.

'Can we talk?' he said, trotting up behind me. 'I understand if you don't want to, but I need to know you're okay.'

'I'm fine,' I said, out of breath.

'No, you're not.'

'I am. I just don't like you very much, so if you pissed off, it would cheer me right up.'

'Please,' he persisted, overtaking me and standing in my path.

'You came and said your apology. Well done. I'll send you your certificate in the post. Now *fuck off*!' I shouted.

An old couple with a Jack Russell sitting on a bench nearby tutted loudly. 'They're probably on drugs,' the woman said, and stood up. Her husband took her arm and they moved off.

I dodged out of Cian's way and kept walking. I could hear him following me, keeping the same pace.

We continued like this for another twenty minutes until I decided I wanted a rest and slumped beside the pond.

He sat down beside me.

Neither of us spoke.

I watched the ducks, meandering apparently aimlessly in different directions. Then a kid with a bag of bread ran to the edge of the water and they quacked excitedly, pedalling furiously towards her.

A group of teenage Goths were opposite us, drinking cans

of cheap cider. The girls seemed awkward and the boys apologetically self-conscious. They were all dressed in the same uniform: black trousers, black jumpers and Doc Martens. I wondered if Goths ever wore shorts or flip-flops or if they ever went to the beach. Maybe they could get that white makeup with an SPF in it.

Cian cleared his throat. 'I thought about you for days after I saw you in the shop.'

'Well, I thought about you for months after you dumped me.'

Another silence. I watched the ducks fight for the bread as the little girl tossed pieces into the water.

'I've missed you.'

'*Sorry?*'

'I've missed you.'

'Oh, piss off.'

'I have, Izzy. I know I have no right to come and say this to you now, after everything I've done, but . . .' his voice dropped '. . . I can't stop thinking about you.'

My heart was pounding and I broke into a sweat. Was this a dream?

'I fucked up. Big-time. I wish I'd never met her,' he continued, his voice wavering. He was nervous.

But not half as nervous as I was. I tried to slow my breathing in the hope that my heart would stop banging so violently against my ribs. So this wasn't just an apology? It was . . .

'You have no idea how much it killed me knowing I'd hurt you so badly. But it all just spiralled out of control. She was so demanding and it had gone too far and I felt so sick with the guilt. I knew you'd never forgive me . . .'

'So you picked her.'

'It wasn't like that.'

'What was it like? Enlighten me.'

'I got to the stage where I hated being around you because I was so ashamed of myself. You didn't deserve to be treated like that. I knew I'd messed it up for us. But she kept calling and calling and . . . it just sort of became something. I'd never intended that to happen.'

'Were you ever in love with her?'

'No,' he said, after a moment or two.

'Did you fall out of love with me?'

'No,' he said.

'Then why?'

'Izzy, I don't know. You must think I'm so weak.'

'At this stage, I'd say that weakness was one of your better features.'

'You have every right to. But . . .'

'But what?'

'Well, we hadn't been getting on too well. You and me.'

'What?'

'You seemed distant a lot of the time.'

'For Christ's sake, Cian! What did you expect me to be like? You were so bloody stroppy. I could never win with you. You'd get so moody, not to mention the effort it took you to show me even the slightest bit of affection. Until, of course, the guilt got to you and you'd sweep me off my feet with some over-the-top romantic gesture. So don't turn this around on me, you prick.'

I watched him pick the petals off a daisy and toss them into the water. They sat in a bundle on the surface briefly, then spread out lazily.

'She's nothing like you.'

'I don't want to know.'

The little girl with the bread was hopping towards the gate with her mother, and the crowd of Goths had finished their cider. It was getting dark now and the warmth was seeping out of the day. I shivered. He tried to put his arm around me. 'Don't.'

'Sorry.'

He picked another daisy and tore at its petals. He loves me, he loves me not. He loves me, he loves me not. 'Izzy, I still love you.'

I closed my eyes tightly and allowed a tear to tumble down my cheek. 'Please don't.' I got to my feet. My head felt so heavy and my neck could hardly hold it upright. I wanted to curl up in a ball and sleep. I wanted to be at home with my mum, on the couch with a cup of tea. I wanted to close my eyes and forget the world.

I walked towards the park gate, Cian behind me. I went down Grafton Street, not sure where I was going. Home? I turned into South Anne Street and passed the Bailey. I decided to go in. I went straight up to the bar and ordered a double vodka.

I could sense him behind me. He ordered a pint of Guinness. We stood at the bar for an hour, drinking and not talking. Then we got a taxi back to his place.

As soon as we got there, we ripped each other's clothes off.

25

I hadn't slept a wink the night before and I knew I wouldn't sleep tonight. Getting through today had been a challenge, and by the time I finished work, all I wanted to do was go home and sprawl on the couch. But if I did, I'd blurt everything to Susie and Keelin. And I couldn't face the consequences of that. They'd lock me in the cupboard under the stairs because I was a liability to myself. They'd tell me it was for my own good and they'd probably make it comfortable, with pillows and chocolate and self-help books and stuff.

The next morning I went into the Lights! Camera! Action! office to sort through some files and discuss interest rates and over-budgeting with Laurence. Blah blah blah profit share blah blah twenty-six per cent blah blah return on investment. I think I managed to pull a muscle in my neck from all the enthusiastic nodding I did to hide the fact that I didn't understand or give a shit what he was on about.

Eve purred sarcastically that they'd all missed me 'terribly' since I'd been working on-set.

'We have, pet,' Geraldine put in. 'Gets very serious in here altogether when you're not around.'

'That's because there's work to be done, Geraldine,' Eve said authoritatively. 'It can't always be fun and giggles.'

'Heaven forbid! Why don't I organize some hair shirts for us and some electric-shock computer keyboards so we can rule out the possibility of extracting any joy whatsoever from our jobs?'

'Now, now, ladies,' Laurence remonstrated. 'We don't want to put Izzy off coming back to us.'

'I'll make you a cup of tea, love, and you can tell us all the gossip on-set.'

'Damn right,' said Laurence. 'I want to know everything about the actors. Especially any information on what Gavin Reed was doing with Saffron Spencer in the conservatory at Eve's engagement party!'

Even though I knew the truth, the sound of their names in the same sentence still unnerved me.

'They would make such a gorgeous couple – their children! Go and put the kettle on,' Eve interrupted, removing her glasses and folding them up neatly. 'Ten minutes and then back to work.'

'Thanks for that, Your Majesty. Do let me know which toilet breaks you've pencilled me in for,' Geraldine muttered under her breath and, still sitting in her wheelie chair, propelled herself to the sink and flicked the kettle on.

We sat nursing our mugs of tea and chatted about what I'd been getting up to on the set and what I'd been missing in the office. Even though I'd seen them a few days ago at Eve's engagement party, it was a good excuse to put our feet up and do as little work as possible. I was all for that. Especially today. I told them about Saffron Spencer and what a pain in the arse she was, how she carried on as if she owned the place, and how rude she was to the crew members she thought were beneath her. Eve refuted this, saying she thought she was a complete dote when she'd spoken to her at her party. Now why didn't that surprise me? When Geraldine asked if Saffron was going to be one of the bridesmaids at her wedding, Eve failed to detect the sarcasm in her voice and replied that she'd have to think about it.

Geraldine told us that Ger was in hospital with an ingrown

toenail, and you'd swear his body was being amputated from the waist down, with all the moaning and complaining he was doing. Not to mention the late-night phone calls she was getting from him saying he couldn't sleep for the stress.

Eve told us she'd booked a castle in Scotland for the wedding reception in January. And how she was going to arrive to the church in a Swarovski-crystal-studded husky-drawn sledge. She had always dreamt of a winter wedding, and if it didn't snow, she was going to hire a fake-snow machine. She said that Philippe was going to arrive on a snow white horse and she'd enrolled him for riding lessons up in Enniskerry. The last time he'd been on an animal's back it had been a donkey in Dublin zoo when he was seven. He'd fallen off and broken his arm. Now he was petrified of the entire equine family. Nice for Eve to have taken that on board.

Suddenly we heard Fintan's door handle turn and we all whipped back to our desks. I put on my work face, the one that belies the fact I'd rather be slicing out my own retina with a scalpel than doing any work.

'That 1.46 per cent making a bit more sense now?' Laurence beamed proudly at me from his desk, thinking he'd inspired some mathematical genius in me.

So my work face had the desired effect. Nice one.

I got through the rest of the day, flicking through files and sorting out the scraps of paper that littered my desk. Eve made me type up some stuff for her on the computer — apparently I looked as if I needed a 'challenge'. I did it to avoid an argument but left in a few typos so she'd have to redo it after I'd gone. I hadn't liked the sarcasm with which she'd imbued 'challenge'.

Just as I was about to leave, Geraldine asked me to give Gavin a buzz and ask him if he'd be in tomorrow or would he be still off gallivanting on the other, more exciting projects.

Oh.

I didn't want to call Gavin. I wasn't sure why. Perhaps I'd tell him everything that had happened the night before and he'd think I was a fool.

Which I was.

I pretended to punch his number into my phone. 'Engaged,' I said, then grabbed my bag and ran out of the office.

I'd felt numb all day, as if my body had been injected with an anaesthetic, but I could still see and hear everything around me. Now, though, the numbness was abating and a frisson crept in. Of shame.

I'd slept with Cian.

I'd actually slept with Cian.

He had called to my door to say he was sorry, that he had made a mistake, that he missed me. Did I slap his face for having the gall to show up out of the blue like that? Did I kick him in the balls and wallop him over the head with a rolling pin? No. I decided to have sex with him.

Gloria Gaynor would be so ashamed of me.

Not that I even owned a rolling pin. Didn't think I'd even seen one since my *Blue Peter* days. But it was my weapon of choice for inflicting pain on Cian in my head. That or a pitchfork. Which I didn't own either. Wow. I really hadn't thought it through properly. In truth, I'd not expected to hear from him again. Not after ten months. Inflicting pain on Cian had been something to entertain myself with, like when I was bored waiting in a queue, or on a bus, or in work talking to Laurence. I'd never imagined I'd get an opportunity to do anything about it.

When we got back to his place last night, I was like a mad woman. All the anger, hurt, regret and betrayal that'd been planted in me ten months before grew roots, branches and more branches until I thought I was going to explode. I needed to get them out of my system. *Now!* I could have thrown every plate in his kitchen at his head, but that would only have made me feel worse.

The only thing I could do was respond when he touched me.

He pushed my back to the wall and kissed me hard. He dragged my T-shirt over my head and undid my belt buckle. I grabbed at his jeans buttons and ripped at his shirt and before I knew it we were standing in his hall in our underwear. He lifted me up and carried me to the kitchen table. There, he continued to kiss me. Everywhere.

I couldn't wait. I needed him inside me. *Now!*

It was quick and furious and uncomfortable. And then it was over.

'Izzy, I love you.'

'Get the fuck off me.' I shoved him away with the only shred of energy I had left.

'I'll run you a bath,' he said, and left me lying there. I counted eight separate damp patches on the ceiling. One looked like the face of an old woman, another like Gonzo from *The Muppet Show*.

I sat in the bath for an hour, letting occasional tears roll down my face and plink into the water. When I got out, he wrapped me in a towel and gently patted me dry. I crawled into one of his T-shirts and he led me into his bedroom and rolled down the duvet.

I got into his bed and he tucked himself in beside me and held me to his chest. We lay like that for hours, not talking, not sleeping, not moving. Until I bolted up. I needed to get out of there.

'Where are you going?'

'Home.'

'Izzy, stay. Please.'

'No.'

'Please,' he implored, as I climbed back into my clothes.

'No, Cian.' I pushed his hands away.

What on earth was I doing? I was here with Cian. In his house. *In his bed!*

I ran down the stairs and out of the front door and looked about frantically for a taxi. I spotted one with its light on, stopped at the traffic-lights down the road, sprinted to it and jumped into the back.

My phone beeped in my bag. I pulled it out. His name was flashing on the screen. My eyes glazed and I wanted to throw up. But I didn't have enough money to pay the driver's soil-age charge, so I forced myself to hold it down. Not that he would have noticed – he was too busy having a one-way conversation with the late-night talk-show host on the radio: 'Recession, me hole! The politicians have just nicked all the money and are hiding it for themselves somewhere. It's probably in some cave down the country!'

I got into my house and found a note from Keelin:

Where the hell did you disappear to? Thought you'd slipped on one of those water-chestnut yokes you put in your stir-fries and were lying unconscious on the kitchen floor. Got bored standing on the porch wondering whether you were alive or not so I called over to Will, Caroline and co. till Susie came home. Anyway, turns out you hadn't slipped on a water-chestnut on the kitchen floor so I assume you got a better offer and headed off out for the night. You lucky bitch. I sat in and watched some programme about courtship rituals in Carlow in the 1800s on TG4. And it didn't even have subtitles. God, this note is long. I have a cramp in my hand. Night x

I scribbled, 'Had to go home, Emma had a fake-tan emergency. Me and Mum had to soak her knees and elbows in nail-polish remover' at the bottom of her note. Hopefully she'd see it before she left for work in the morning. It wasn't very inventive, but it was all I could think of. And, knowing Emma, it wasn't beyond the realms of possibility.

I couldn't tell her where I'd been. I couldn't tell anyone. Not Keelin or Susie or Emma or Mum or Gavin or anyone.

My phone beeped in my hand and I watched Cian's name flash on to the screen again.

26

'So you really think it's too much?'

'Keelin, I can see the tops of your nipples.'

'But if I wear my hair down it'll cover them up a bit . . . no?'

'Keelin, you have a bob. I don't care how pert your boobs are, they can't be that pert. And all the male guests will get a simultaneous erection, which will make things awkward.'

'But it's my birthday. And that's always been one of my fantasies.'

'To be in a room with twenty horny drunk Irish men?'

'You make it sound so unsexy.'

'May I remind you that Aidan will be there?'

'Oh, sweet Jesus.' She raced over to her chest of drawers and pulled out a black string top and put it on under her dress. 'When you say stuff like that you make me want to go to confession and do two hours of Hail Marys.'

'Much better,' I said.

She stood in front of her mirror and lifted the hem of her dress until it rested dangerously just below her knickers.

'Keelin!'

'Okay, okay,' she said, letting it drop to mid-thigh. 'Since when did you get all Taliban?'

'You look gorgeous as you are. And he's already noticed you – you don't have to try so hard any more.'

She looked doubtful.

Simon was coming to the party tonight and I could tell she was petrified.

'It's just . . . What if he gets bored, meeting my friends and stuff? It might take the mystery out of it all. I mean, it's fine at work. But what if it doesn't translate to the real world?' She plopped onto the bed. I'd never seen her so insecure about a guy before and found it endearing: if she hadn't felt a bit vulnerable, she wouldn't have cared that it might not work out.

'You might get lucky tonight yourself, Iz. Plenty of top totty coming. And you're on a roll in the sex department.'

I picked at my nails to avoid looking at her.

'How long has it been now?'

Four days. 'God, I dunno. A few weeks . . . Jonathan,' I said instead. 'Let's hope I don't have to wait as long again, eh?' I guffawed over-enthusiastically. She glanced sideways at me. Did she know I was hiding something?

'When are you going to see him again?'

'Who knows? Anyway, it was good fun, did what it was supposed to do. Better go and get ready.' I got up off her bedroom floor and headed into my own room.

'I wanna see some tit!' she called after me. 'We're gonna try and get you some action tonight. It's like breaking the seal. Once you go, you need to keep going!'

Jaysus, easy on there, I thought. Was Keelin turning into Hugh Hefner in her old age? I pulled open my wardrobe.

As it was her birthday she'd decided earlier in the week that she wanted to have a big party in our house to celebrate. She was afraid no one would come on account of the drugs fiasco, which nearly everyone in Dublin had heard about – she'd had a text from someone asking if there was going to be hardcore knackers there or what was the *craic*. She'd been a bit worried by that and had sent a group text to everyone: **Just to assure you that the type of craic we'll be having is of the fun variety, not the narcotics. And although I'm very open to multi-culturalism, no drug dealers**

will be at the party. But if you do have friends from any other ethnic backgrounds, all are welcome! Snacks, mixers and police protection will be provided. A workmate of Will's had spent a summer in Ibiza as a male stripper for hen parties. The policeman routine with the cuffs and the baton was his most requested performance. It was close enough.

I raked through my wardrobe. I'd bought a top in All Saints on my lunch break: what could I wear it with? Rats! I'd forgotten to shave my legs in the shower even though I'd been in there for half an hour. The shampoo-rinse-conditioner-rinse-shower-gel-rinse routine had only taken about four minutes, so what had I been doing for the other twenty-six? Watching the mildew grow on the tiles? I'd been preoccupied over the last few days certainly, but a to-do list in the shower would be taking things too far. I stuck my head around the door to see if Susie was still in the bathroom. Plumes of steam were billowing out from under the door and there was chipmunk singing coming from inside.

I'm not sure why Susie morphed into a chipmunk in the shower. It was the strangest thing. She had a beautiful voice normally, but whenever she sang in the shower she sounded like a helium-sucking cartoon caricature.

By the time she'd finished I wouldn't have time to shave my legs – it was already seven thirty and people would start arriving at eight. A skirt was out. I sauntered back to my wardrobe and sighed. I was in no mood to get dressed up and host a party. If someone had offered me the choice of hosting the party or working the late shift in that scary chipper on Pearse Street, I would have chosen the latter. At least then I wouldn't have had to do the looking-nice thing and make small-talk with a collection of drunks. Instead I could have looked gross and basked in misery as I served battered

229

burgers to battered people. At least you knew where you stood with battered drunks who loitered around Pearse Street: always be afraid. Happy drunks, on the other hand, were an entirely different matter. There was always one lunatic who'd seem to be having the time of their life, but would suddenly be bawling crying and accusing you of hating them, even though you'd never met them before in your life.

I still hadn't told anyone about Cian. No one knew except him and me. And a snail on the wall outside the Lights! Camera! Action! office. I told it when I was on a cigarette break yesterday morning. It was sitting there beside me and I doubted it'd mention it to anyone else. It didn't seem too bothered about my problems. I told it that Cian had called at least ten times a day since Monday, leaving the same message every time: 'Izzy, don't be scared of this. Please believe me. I love you.' And every time he called I zoned out. And then I told the snail that the wall I'd built around my heart was being slowly taken down brick by brick by the man who had forced me to put it up in the first place. At this point the snail had had enough: it retracted its head into its shell as if to say, 'At least you won't get eaten by a blackbird.'

I stared into my wardrobe. What was I going to wear? Wedged between a pair of combats and a white linen skirt, a pair of jeans caught my eye. I fished them out, pulse quickening, and held them up in front of me.

My lovely skinny Citizen of Humanity jeans . . .

The ones that wouldn't fit any more after I'd decided to go right ahead and put on fourteen stone. Okay, so it was more like *a* stone but, like one human year is to seven dog years, one actual stone is to fourteen mental ones. Some people call that dysmorphia. I call it rejection – the feeling that you're now the ugliest, fattest, most unlovable blob of lard in the whole world.

I laid them out on my bed and twittered around them like

a giddy budgie. I hadn't been so excited in days. Not since before I'd decided to sleep with the man who'd made me mentally obese. I didn't want to get my hopes up too far, though. My Wayne Rooney days were over, I had two eyebrows instead of one and you could no longer plait my leg hair – but had I lost the mayonnaise deposits around my belly? Would I get back into my Citizen of Humanity jeans?

I thought back to the chocolate chip muffin Geraldine had force-fed me yesterday morning and my heart sank. I hadn't even wanted it. 'Damn you to hell, Geraldine!'

'What?' Susie had poked a giant towel-wrapped head around the door.

'Damn you to hell, Geraldine!' I repeated.

'I thought that was what you'd said. I have no idea what Geraldine's done, but has anyone ever told you that you sound like Skeletor from *He-Man* when you're pissed off?'

'Never.'

I traipsed into her room to see what she was going to wear. She pulled out a pair of black trousers and a silvery-grey long-sleeved round-neck top.

'Okay, I may sound like Skeletor but you dress like him. We should get together as a double act for Hallowe'en.'

'Do you think it's a bit . . . conservative?'

'Yes,' I replied bluntly. 'How about this?' I fished a beautiful blue and green sundress out of her wardrobe. 'I haven't seen you wear it in ages.'

'I don't know. I think it's a bit tight.'

'Try it on. Please.' This dressing-down thing was all to do with Aidan – he was such a jealous idiot. He'd slowly picked away at her self-confidence because he knew only too well that she was far too good for him. And he thought that if he knocked her down a bit, he'd be the good guy in her eyes when he picked her up again.

She slipped into the dress. 'Do you not think I look tarty in it?' she said pulling at the neckline.

'No. You look beautiful. It's classy and elegant. And if you put your hair up like this . . .'

She brushed my hand away. 'Izzy, stop. I don't want to wear it.'

I watched her change into her safe clothes. The ones that hid every inch of her body so that Aidan wouldn't get angry and accuse her of looking for attention.

I felt sad for the Susie I'd known nearly all my life. I missed her. The one who had shown me how to shave my legs and walk in high heels. The one who had lent me my first push-up bra for a school disco. The one who knew how to flirt without looking desperate (the only one, in fact). The Susie who on holiday three years ago had been so comfortable in her own skin she'd entered the Bikini Cowgirl Poolside Drinking Competition (long story) and won.

Now she was sliding into her grey, flat slip-ons. 'What are you going to wear?' she said, with a forced smile.

'I dunno. Something.' I headed back into my room to find out the answer to the 'Are you still carrying too much chunk?' challenge.

The first guests to arrive were Jackie, a friend of Keelin's from college, and some bloke called Ian, who was even more orange than she was. I wondered if there was a fake tan out there labelled 'Bright Orange'. There had to be. There were just so many orange humans around these days. I used to think they only lived behind the Brown Thomas counters, but you see them everywhere, travelling to work on buses, getting educations in universities, flocking around the shops during the day, going to house parties on Friday nights, living and breathing among us.

I looked at Orange Ian. His shirt was unbuttoned halfway down his chest, revealing tufts of black hair and a pair of dog-tags – even though, judging by his manicured hands and plucked eyebrows, I imagined the closest he'd ever got to the army was buying Ralph Lauren combats.

Was he gay?

No, apparently not. I watched him smack Jackie's orange bottom as they headed into our living room. (I didn't actually see the colour of her bum but an expert fake tanner like her would tan it to match the rest.)

'What's the storeeee?' she shrieked, as she hugged the birthday girl.

I handed them both a cocktail as they headed into the living room. I hoped they wouldn't leave giant orange outlines on our couch, like some *CSI* crime scene.

Susie and I were in the kitchen, shaking up Sea Breezes and quoting scenes from *Cocktail* when more people arrived. I was delighted that Marcus was among them as I was about to incorporate his surname into the *Cocktail* quote game. I'd been waiting patiently for his arrival.

'Stop feeling so sorry for yourself, Flanagan!' I called from the kitchen, and Susie burst out laughing behind me. I was so funny I was considering doing a circuit of Edinburgh this summer.

'What?' Marcus replied, a bit confused. 'I'm not feeling sorry for myself. I just stubbed my toe on your porch step and it hurts a bit.'

'Oh, go invent a floogilbinder,' Susie retorted, and I collapsed on the floor in a fit of giggles.

By ten thirty the house was rammed with people. I had been so busy making cocktails – and knocking back the end of each jug of Sea Breeze – that I hadn't noticed the time flying by. I told myself that liquid diets were the only way forward. I told Susie as well, but she said she was too into bagels. I mean, I hadn't given up entirely on the Liquorice Allsort Diet, but the Cocktail Diet seemed much more fun. All the goodness of fruit juice mixed with vodka to make you happy! Give it a week or two, and you'd be a skinny bitch. Or an alcoholic and unemployed but . . .

'Cocktail sausage?'

'Oooooh! Yes, please!'

Fuck!

Okay, liquid diets weren't going to work out for me.

But they were *cocktail* sausages, so maybe they were allowed.

I followed Keelin and the cocktail sausages into the living room to mingle with our guests. Caroline took over the cocktail-making.

The party was in full swing and, as with any good party, a fight was going on over the music beside the CD player. Will was holding a Destiny's Child album over Orla's head, laughing as she tried to jump up to reach it.

'Bully!' I said, as I passed him. Then I wished I hadn't because he wrangled me into a headlock. Which gave Orla an opportunity to grab the CD off him. After I'd wrestled my way out of Will's armpit, we launched into a seizure-type dance, convinced we were 'doing it just like Beyoncé'. A few songs later, with my lower back going into spasm, I decided to sit down. I needed to figure out how to get the heel of my shoe out from between two floorboards first, though . . .

By one o'clock, I was lying on the patio out the back with Keelin on one side and a guy called Ronan, who'd nicked my last fag, on the other. A little bit of heel was missing from my left shoe. I puffed on a Marlboro Red, and tried not to cough. I told Keelin that her shoes were lovely and sparkly. Grinning inanely, she told me Simon had brought them earlier. He'd bought them as a birthday present after he'd seen her ogle them on a website at work. And I told her that was the loveliest thing I'd ever heard.

'Top-ups?' Caroline called from the patio door, brandishing a jug in her left hand.

'Yes, please!' I purred, holding out my Granny Loves You Best mug. Some thief had stolen my tumbler earlier (knowing Ronan, it was probably him), so I'd resorted to my Easter egg mug from last year.

Caroline wobbled over to me and poured an uncoordinated splash of alcohol in the general direction of my mug. 'No Sea Breeze left. Whiskey and orange juice.' She plonked herself down between Keelin and me. 'Are you having a good birthday?'

'Yes,' Keelin replied. 'All of the party guests are charming.' She took a glug out of the jug and winced as it slid down her throat.

'Where's Shymon? I wanna meet him!'

'Me too, Keelin, get him!'

We'd started calling him 'Shymon' earlier that week because Keelin kept telling us he was shy and we'd have to make an effort with him.

'He's in talking to some of the boys.' She sighed, all gooey. She was in love. I was going to have to find Shymon in a bit and hug it out.

'I can't believe I've spent the last God knows how long hung up on these oddballs only to fall for the most normal bloke I've ever met.'

'One's man's meat . . .'

'I know! Can you believe it? Have I ever been after one man's meat for this long?'

Caroline shot me a look and we laughed.

Much later, on my way back from the bathroom, I let out a yelp when I saw what could only be described as a kaleidoscope of ginger shifting around at the bottom of the stairs holding up a plastic bag with a goldfish in it. I brought my whiskey-blurred vision into focus and saw that it was none other than . . .

'Greg!'

'Fish!'

'Greg?'

'Fish!'

'What?'

'Fish!'

Had he forgotten how to say any other word?

'Fish!'

Yes, he had. And he wouldn't remember any other until he'd hypnotized me into a ginger trance when I'd want to kill myself and go to ginger hell.

'Nice to see you,' I said. I didn't sound convincing.

'Caroline said over Sunday stew last week that you guys might be having a party tonight for Keelin's birthday. I usually watch Pat Kenny on a Friday, but it's the summer so he hasn't been on. Who's your favourite guest that Pat has ever interviewed? No, top five. No, top ten. No, top fifteen. No –'

'What's with the fish?'

'Fish!'

Images of me dunking Caroline's head down the loo for her Sunday-stew revelation flashed temptingly before me.

'Well. So. There I was thinking, What should I get Keelin for her birthday? You know how you have to ask yourself that before you buy a birthday present for someone? So, I remembered you all love that bunny of yours. David?'

'Dermot.' I took a swig from my mug. They used whiskey to distract you from pain in the good old days and I hoped it still worked.

'Dermot. Well, here's to add to your brood! I thought you

236

and Susie might get jealous so I bought you one each. I've already named them. I hope you don't mind?' He held out the bag to me. 'This little creature of God's is your one.'

I took it from him and studied the white sticker flattened onto the front. 'Irene.'

'I thought what with you all mad for calling animals human names . . . Case in point: Duncan.'

'Dermot.'

I wobbled my way into the kitchen to fix Greg a ginger ale. Fitting. It was the least I could do since he'd been so kind as to bring Irene into my life.

'Hey, Iz! Meet Grainne!' Susie was standing beside the fridge holding up a plastic bag much like mine with a gold-fish in it.

'Hi, Grainne.' I waved.

'Keelin's got Ursula outside.' Susie was swaying and I feared for Grainne's safety. 'I'll go and put them in a bowl,' I said, and took Grainne from her.

'Great party, Izzy. Careful, you can get salmon poisoning from handling fish. My brother nearly fuckin' died after he cleared out his fish tank at home once, then ate a packet of Tayto straight afterwards without washin' his hands first. He puked so much a bit of his stomach came out his nose.'

Euch. Aidan. I'd already been lynched by him earlier in the evening. He was on his best behaviour tonight, which was sickening, and he looked ridiculous. His attempt to prove to all of us that he had reformed was to wear a tie. But he was still wearing his usual Ireland tracksuit. He was attractive, though, so he could almost get away with it – but I couldn't help laughing when I heard someone ask him if he'd been told the party was fancy dress.

I teetered back into the living room with the twins. Okay, I knew they were triplets, but I had yet to meet the elusive Ursula.

Everywhere was cluttered with bodies, lit by the fairy-lights hanging on the bookshelves. On the couch, a bevy of beauties were crooning along to some weepy Jeff Buckley number. A girl I'd never seen before sat in a crumpled heap in the corner, sobbing into her glass of chardonnay while two blokes over by the fireplace were chatting about 'Riding'.

So, your typical house party when it's three a.m. and everyone's locked. I'd have to keep my eye on the emotional wreck in the corner, though – at any moment I might be accused of hating her. And, before I knew it, I'd have agreed to go for lunch with her next week and make her godmother to my firstborn.

Gavin was by the CD player, chatting about some new band to a workmate of Susie's. Thankfully, Eve and the others weren't here. Gavin knew Will through some other friends, so he usually turned up when we were having a major get-together.

'You guys still going on about cords?' I called over. 'It's the summer, for heaven's sake. You'll be in heavy trousers long enough over the winter months.'

Susie's workmate threw me his best you're-such-a-pathetic-girl look, which I accepted graciously and smiled back at him sweetly. He turned to Gavin and said, 'Later, man,' then went to join the 'Riding' discussion.

'You trying to start fights, young lady?'

'Maybe.'

'Get things going a bit. You should go over to your one having the breakdown in the corner there and tell her she'll probably never meet a man. That'll spice things up nicely.'

'Good advice,' I said, and turned to head over to her.

He grabbed my arm. 'Izzy, I was kidding.'

'Me too.'

He rolled his eyes. 'Well, I'm glad you were. I think she's crying because her boyfriend, Mr Sensitive over there in the yellow T-shirt, is discussing their sex life with the pervy-looking one in the white jumper.'

'What a prick.' The emotional wreck in the corner had sunk into the foetal position on the floor, and her boyfriend was gesticulating all sorts of crudities. 'Nice guy. When I grow up, I want a boyfriend just like him.'

'What's going on with Irene and Grainne?' he asked, studying the names on the plastic bags I was holding.

'Bizarre gift from Caroline's brother. I'm gonna put them in a bowl before some sushi-loving genius eats one.'

I tried to reach for the glass bowl on the top shelf, but it was too high so I turned to ask Gavin if he could reach it for me. I found him staring at my arse. 'What?' I asked, straining around to get a look. 'Have I sat in rabbit shite?'

'No.' He laughed. 'I was admiring your jeans. They look great. Are they new? I'm now grossly aware that I sound gay. To correct that, may I add that you look fit in them?'

'I love you!' I gushed, jumping on him and knocking him back against the wall. He struggled to keep hold of me, Irene and Grainne. 'They're my lovely posh jeans, but Cian made me physically chubby and mentally obese so I haven't been able to fit into them in ages, but I tried them on tonight and now they fit. I'm so glad you noticed because no one else has.'

My nose was practically shoved into his as he held me off the ground with his right arm.

'Your butt looks exquisite.'

'Thank you.'

After he'd made sure both my feet were planted firmly back on the floor, he reached for the glass bowl on the shelving unit and emptied out the sequins and buttons that'd fallen off our clothes over the last four years. We were still getting around to sewing them back on.

We hunched down on our knees and untied the knots in

the plastic bags. For such a simple task, it took an extraordinarily long time because we'd been drinking for approximately six hours.

'Look at Irene – she's going nuts.'

'Same with Grainne. They can't wait to get in there.'

'I don't think Irene likes being away from Grainne.'

'No, and Grainne certainly doesn't like being kept away from Irene.'

I watched Irene wiggle about excitedly in the bag. He smiled at me, and I studied all the new freckles he'd got across his nose from being in the sun.

'I know how Irene feels.' He'd said it quietly but the words screamed in my ears. The blood rushed to my head and I barely heard myself when I told him I missed not being in his apartment. His expression remained the same, but he held my eyes, his face so close to mine that I could hear him breathe. And even though the room was spinning because I was half cut, I couldn't look away. I just stayed there, entranced by the flecks of gold in his green eyes as Grainne flipped about wildly in the bag in my right hand.

'Don't forget Ursula!'

We jumped back as Susie plopped herself on to the floor and emptied her bag into the glass bowl. 'Keelin is so irresponsible.' She peered into the bowl. 'Put the others in!' She clapped. Gavin caught my eye and winked. I could feel myself blushing.

We poured Grainne and Irene into the bowl and sat back as they whirred around in circles in their new home. Irene ate a stray sequin and promptly spat it back out. Ah, Irene, you're so mad, I thought.

Gavin took my empty mug and his empty glass off the shelving unit and said he was going into the kitchen to fill them up. I gazed dreamily at his lovely toned arms as he moved across the room. 'Gavin just lifted me up. He's so strong,' I cooed to Susie

'Were you guys doing *Dirty Dancing* moves?'

'Not really.'

'Gavin's great,' she squeaked, through a hiccup, and fell back on to the sheepskin rug.

'He is, isn't he?' I said, joining her on it.

'I think those guys are talking about threesomes,' she said, after a moment or two. I lifted my head a few inches and looked at the three horn dogs sitting at the other end of the fireplace. Yellow T-shirt's girlfriend was still sobbing in the opposite corner. When I turned back, Susie was fast asleep.

I struggled to my feet and went to the kitchen to find Gavin. He was shaking up some gross cocktail of Guinness and whiskey. When I told him there was no way I could drink it, he lashed in some apple juice. At that point I realized my bladder was about to burst and made for the bathroom.

Before I used the loo, I decided to check my makeup in my bedroom – technically, I'd applied it yesterday so Heroin Chic might have struck during the course of the evening. I opened my bedroom door, sashayed over to my dressing-table and tripped on something. I landed flat on my bed. The 'something' turned out to be Caroline and Marcus in a passionate clinch.

'Snared, you secretive secret keepers!' All Caroline could do was giggle and I said a heartfelt prayer of thanks to the patron saint of vestments that they were both fully clothed. 'Get back to work,' I said, left the room and shut the door behind me. The hotpress light was on, so I flung open the door to make sure no one had put the cocktail sausages in our linen basket. The only thing in the linen basket was a man's leg. The other was braced against the wall, and Keelin was perched on Simon. I was about to ask her why she'd have sex in the hotpress, which was the size of a kitchen cupboard, when she had her own double bed across the landing, but I realized it might ruin the moment for them – their first time and all that.

'Hi, Shymon!' I said.

'Don't mind her, she slurs when she's pissed.' Keelin slammed the door before I could say anything else. For the best, probably.

It was like a brothel up there. I headed for the bathroom, hoping I wouldn't find someone having a shag in the bath.

I sat on the loo, rocking from side to side, and decided I'd probably have to pass on Gavin's latest concoction. It had been such a good night, though, hadn't it? My tummy muscles were sore from laughing. Nice one – gyms were so overrated. Just get locked and laugh your arse off with your mates instead. What was the big deal? Why had I been dreading tonight so much?

It was only when I tried to remember, through the fog of alcohol, what I'd been trying to forget all night that it hit me.

I'd had sex with Cian on Monday. He had reappeared in my life, telling me he was still in love with me, that Edna had been a terrible mistake and he wanted me back. Holy shit. The reality of what had happened crashed into me with the force of a charging bull, and nearly knocked me off the loo.

Cian was back.

And I'd slept with him four nights ago.

Oh, my God!

I got off the loo, zipped myself up, washed my hands and headed out of the bathroom like a robot. I walked down the stairs, straight out of the front door, climbed onto my bike, not without some difficulty, and pedalled off to find him.

27

After I'd rung the bell I sat on Cian's porch and waited while I listened to someone moving about upstairs. My heart was in my mouth as the sound of his footsteps descended the stairs. What if Edna answered the door? No, she wouldn't – they'd been living at her place together. Keys jangled and the Chubb lock clicked, the latch slid back and the door creaked open.

'Hi,' I said.

'Hi.'

He sat down on the porch beside me. He studied my face as I looked at the houses on the opposite side of the road. We were silent for a while.

'You want to come in?'

'I'm not sure.'

'Okay.'

A black cat jumped down from the wall across the road and stopped in its tracks when it spotted us. The moonlight glinted in its eyes before it darted off behind a group of bins.

'I'll come in.'

'Okay.'

He led me into his sitting room, where he flicked on a small lamp over the television. I stood there awkwardly. 'I'm not sure why I'm here.'

'I'm glad you are.'

I looked at him. His arms were folded and his shoulders were propped against the wall. He was wearing a pair of boxers, his hair was messy and his eyes were groggy with sleep. 'I'm sorry I woke you.'

'You've woken me every night this week.' He smiled. 'I just can't get you out of my head.'

'Have you been listening to Kylie Minogue?'

'Huh?'

'Nothing.'

Another silence fell. I inched my way over to the couch and perched on the edge, wishing my mind was clearer and my balance steadier. I willed myself to sober up, but started hiccuping instead.

He disappeared into the kitchen and came back with a glass of water. He got down on his hunkers in front of me, took my hand and closed it around the glass.

'Thank you,' I said, between hiccups. Water splashed out of the glass onto my jeans. 'Oops,' I said.

'Iz? You okay? Try and drink some.'

'I think I may have to lie down.' I started to lean to the left, in the hope that I'd eventually land in a horizontal position on the length of the couch. But Cian got there first and caught me.

'Come on, you.'

'No, I'm fine here. Night, night.'

'No arguments. Come on.' He started to lift me.

'Excuse me, Professor H two O,' I said, shrugging him off. 'I'm fine here.'

'Why don't you just lie on the bed? You'll be much more comfortable.'

'Because I don't –hic – want to – hic – have sex with you.'

'No offence, baby, but I'm not exactly turned on right now.'

'Don't be such an arsehole,' I said, trying to punch his arm, missing and whacking the side of the couch instead.

When he'd eventually wrestled me up to his room, he laid me on his bed and took off my shoes.

'Enough!' I said gruffly. 'I'm – hic – staying in my clothes.' I pulled his duvet around me and told him he could sleep in the cold for being a two-timing prick.

He climbed onto the other side of the bed.

'Where's Saffron tonight?'

'Izzy, I've told you. We've broken up. If I can't have you, I don't want anyone.'

I smiled in the darkness and closed my eyes. The room went quiet and I was asleep in seconds.

I woke up the next morning convinced that if I didn't get water into me in the next seven to ten seconds, I'd die. I flicked off the duvet and jumped out of bed, heard a dull thud and landed back in a crumpled heap on the mattress.

The dull thud, I found out when I came to four minutes later, had been the sound of my skull hitting Cian's bedroom wall.

'I forgot I was here,' I said groggily, looking up at him as he collected me in his arms and cradled me.

'You all right?' he said, trying to hide a smile.

'No.' He rubbed my head as it throbbed. 'I forgot I was here,' I repeated. 'You can't jump out of that side of the bed, I remember now, because it's pushed up against a wall.'

'That's correct. You have to get out my side.' He brushed my hair away from my face and stroked my forehead with his fingertips. I swallowed hard and tried to figure out whether to move or not. I discovered I didn't want to.

His smile slowly disappeared and his expression changed. His eyes bored into mine. I held my breath as he moved his hand and knotted his fingers with mine.

'I hate you,' I whispered.

'Well, too bad, I love you.'

He bent his face to mine and kissed me softly. In slow motion we removed each other's clothes. He touched me gently yet passionately and the familiarity of his hands made me want to burst. He kept his eyes on mine the entire time we made love, and when it was finished, he rolled over and pulled me onto his chest, stroking my hair and my back. His fingers swept down my arm, and he grasped my hand tightly.

'I'm so glad you're back,' he said, twirling my hair between the fingers of his other hand. I searched for something to say or some definitive emotion to cling to amid the rush of a hundred. Was I back? I gave up, buried my face in his neck and waited for him to speak again.

'Will I get you that glass of water?'

'That would be great.' I giggled. 'And a hard hat in case I entertain any more notions of getting out of bed.'

I watched him slide out of bed and climb back into his boxers.

'Do you want some toast?'

'Do you cook now?'

'I know how to burn a thing or two.'

'Lovely. I'll have a slice of burnt toast, so.'

As soon as he left the room I fell back on the bed, aware that my entire body was as tense as a taut rope. I wanted to smile, but I wanted to scream too. What happens when he comes back with the toast? Does the world really work like this? Is Fate telling me that the one you're meant to be with shows up again in the end? After all that's happened?

My train of thought was interrupted by Cian's mobile vibrating under a bundle of clothes on the floor. My heart jumped into my mouth as I bolted upright in the bed. Cian's mobile phone and I did not have a good history. I shouldn't look. But I had a right to, didn't I? After the last time? I needed to look, just once – I mean, why was someone calling him at nine thirty on a Saturday morning? Or should I say *who*?

I jumped off the bed and scuttled onto the floor, rummaging furiously through the clothes to find his phone. When I unearthed it, I stared at the screen incredulously as it flashed in my hands.

A girl's name. One I didn't recognize.

My breathing got shallower and quicker as I waited for a voicemail to come through. As soon as it did, I watched myself press the buttons to listen to it. I could hear my heart banging as I waited for it to connect. *You have one new voice message.*

'Baby, it's me again . . .' It was *her*. 'Look, I know you're cross with me, but you have to believe me that it was a once-off. I was drunk. He means nothing to me. It didn't mean anything, I *swear*! How many times can I say it? Come on, Cian.' There was a pause while she sighed heavily. 'You can't just keep ignoring my calls. Call me back.'

There are no new messages. Beep.

I threw the phone hard against the wall and watched it smash before it landed in pieces on the wooden floor.

28

Rathmines village was inconveniently busy. It was Saturday morning and the shops had just opened their shutters. I hated being there among the congested pockets of people, aimlessly wading through them, desperate to get away and out of my clothes, which smelt of Cian's bed. To crawl out of my skin, which still tingled from his touch. To shut out my mind as it screamed to me of what had just happened.

Mostly I wanted to rip my heart out of my chest. My cheeks were scalded as hot tears washed down my face. I couldn't hear myself crying, but I could feel the sobs as they resonated in my chest.

I searched the streets for a taxi, but there was none in sight. I had been in such a hurry to get out of his place, I'd left my lovely bike behind. That was another reason to hate him. I went to the nearest bus stop, failing to apologize as I bashed into people. I stood in front of the twirly bus timetable thingy and spun it distractedly, not even knowing what bus I should be looking up or if I was even on the right side of the road.

'Excuse me,' I wailed, to the blurred blob on my left. 'Does the thirty-nine stop here?' Jesus, I was actually wailing like a child in a toyshop pestering for a Barbie.

'I'm not sure. I only ever get the one sixteen.' The human being inched away until I couldn't see him at all any more.

'Oh,' I howled, spinning the bus-timetable thing fruitlessly again.

I plonked myself down on a low wall behind the bus stop and scanned the road for an approaching bus. Nothing.

A little girl in a cute green duffel coat was skipping down the path hand in hand with her mother and I managed a half-smile as she stared at me inquisitively.

'Look, Mum, a junkie!' she said, pointing at me. Her mother tugged her away, hissing at her to be quiet and remember what she'd told her about junkies having 'those dangerous needles'. I wanted to laugh, but I cried some more instead.

In fact, I cried pretty much all the way home on the 39. I cried all the way up Pearse Street, past Odds and Sods, up my road and into my house.

'Oh, fuck.'

Keelin stood in the living room, staring at me, as I let a gut-wrenching wail escape from my lungs, just in case she hadn't already gathered the state I was in.

Susie ran out of the kitchen with a wedge of folded bread hanging out of her mouth. She pulled it out and said, 'Oh, fuck.'

I dropped to the floor, crawled over to the sheepskin rug and collapsed onto it. I wanted to climb into the fireplace, up the chimney and hide there for the rest of my life. Keelin and Susie fell to their knees and followed me on to the rug.

'Where have you come from? I thought you were in your room.'

'I was at Cian's.'

'Oh, Jesus.'

Susie grabbed a tissue and rubbed at the unsightly snot trails loitering on my top lip. 'What happened?'

I could barely get the words out as they battled against the sobs.

'He arrived here out of the blue on Monday evening,' I started, not caring what they'd think. I was too crushed to deal with this on my own. 'We fought, I cried, he said he was still in love with me, that Edna had been a huge mistake, that he wanted me back . . .'

Susie and Keelin gasped and went pale.

'Then I told him to fuck off. I left the house but he followed me and we ended up in a bar and then back in his place. We had sex on his kitchen table. It was horrible.'

'Oh, Jesus,' they breathed in unison. Susie pulled me into a hug. I cried my heart out into her chest. She pushed the tear-soaked hair away from my face.

'I couldn't think straight all week. Just when I thought that door was closed, he came back and flung it open again. I was doing so well, I'd made so much progress, I'd been trying so hard to forget him. The selfish *bastard* . . .' My face crumpled again. 'He's been leaving messages all week saying he still loves me, that we can get through this together, that he's back for good and I won't be able to change how he feels, no matter how hard I resist.'

'So what happened last night?' Keelin asked.

'I left here about three in the morning. I had to see him all of a sudden. The enormity of it all just struck me. All the feelings I had for him, have for him, that I've been trying so hard to block out, suddenly it was like I was allowed to feel them again . . . So I left and cycled over to his apartment, which was not a good idea as I skidded and now not only do I have a broken heart but I have a broken light too. *And* a graze on my knee! And I left my bike *behind*!' I knew I was being a touch too dramatic, but I didn't care. 'I was fairly pissed at that stage, so he put me in his bed, fully clothed, and I conked out. But this morning . . .' The words choked at the back of my throat and fresh tears brimmed. 'I've never got over him.'

'We know,' Susie said, her arm still around me. 'Go on.'

'We had sex again, but it was different this time. He kept looking at me in this way that was different . . . and it was amazing . . . and I thought that maybe, you know, we *were* still in love with each other . . . that it was mutual . . . that my life could get back on track again . . . that someone had put this horrible pause on it for the past ten months and now I had it back . . . and maybe I had him back too . . . that I could stop pretending I was fine without him . . .'

'What did he do, Izzy?' Susie's eyes were filled with concern.

'He got up to make breakfast, and just as I was lying there trying to make sense of it all, his mobile rang. I couldn't resist looking.'

'Oh, no . . .'

'It was her. It was Edna. It was fucking *déjà vu* all over again.' I had to catch my breath. 'She left a voicemail and I listened to it. She'd done the dirt on him. She was on the phone, pleading with him to call her back so they could sort it out. He's not still in love with me,' I said, looking at them. 'He was only using me to get back at *her.*'

Keelin fell back against the sofa, which prompted me to curl up into a ball and sob into the sheepskin rug.

'I don't know what to say, Iz,' Susie said. I sat up and pulled the fluff out of my eyes. My lungs were tired, my head was heavy and my heart broken.

For the second time.

He'd done it again.

This time round, though, the pain was compounded with shame because I'd gone back for more.

'He used me. Totally and completely used me.' My voice sounded far away, as if I was in another room.

That night I lay in my bed, staring at the ceiling, trying to convince myself that I was asleep. It wasn't working. I looked at my alarm clock: 03:55. I shut my eyes tightly and prayed for the night to be over. This insufferable, never-ending stretch of sleepless agony. I wished there was someone I could talk to – anyone – just to distract me for five minutes.

But there was no one I could call at this hour of the night. Did I know anyone in Australia? Only Kylie Minogue. But she didn't know me. So that was a non-runner.

Anyone in America, perhaps? I could ring Abercrombie and Fitch and get them to talk me through their autumn collection.

I threw off the duvet and slung on my dressing-gown. A chat with Dermot was probably my best option, given that I didn't really know anyone outside my time zone.

As I stared blankly at the Discovery Channel, I told him I reckoned Cian could be used in a case study for bi-polar. All you'd have to do was get someone happy and bubbly, persuade them to sleep with him and watch them sink into manic depression. I wiped the tears off my cheeks with my sleeves. Jesus, I was like a camel – where was all this water coming from after the endless crying I'd done today?

'I'm so fed up thinking about you.' I sighed into the empty living room. 'Not you, Dermot,' I said, stroking his soft warm ears as he looked up at me. 'The Bi-polar Inflictor.'

And now here was a fresh stock of new thoughts to torment me. I was haunted by the extent of his cruelty. How could he do this?

So there it was. All the I-still-love-yous, the I've-made-a-terrible-mistakes, the pleas, the humility . . . utter and complete lies. They didn't even involve me. It had all been about him, a way to make himself feel better, to get back at her. He was just playing with me. Like a cat that's caught a mouse but will neither kill it nor let it go, tormenting it for its own amusement.

The way his expression had changed when he walked back into the room this morning. It had been as stark as flicking a light switch. As soon as he saw me hunched on the floor, in utter shock, his mobile phone lying shattered beside me, he'd known he'd been caught out.

Worst of all, he hadn't even tried to fight it. He'd shrugged. 'She slept with someone else.'

'I never, ever thought you could stoop this low,' I said, hanging my head. 'Cian, you broke my heart.'

'It wasn't like that.'

'Shut up. You broke my heart, and then when I felt like I was just about getting over it, you came back into my life and made me believe you still loved me! How could you do that? How?' I shouted.

'Izzy, you have it all wrong,' he protested. 'Initially, yes, I'll admit it, I wanted to hurt her. She'd gone off and shagged this nightclub owner, and then I saw her in the papers kissing some guy and I wanted to get my own back and I knew being with you would do that. She was always so insecure about you, which is a huge compliment to you, really.'

'I'm sorry?' I didn't understand how that could be remotely positive for me.

'No, no, hear me out. What can I say, Izzy? I'm a fucking idiot. But I think I got slowly brainwashed by Saffron's scene. It's just so vacuous and insincere. Everybody's out for themselves. They're all your best mates to your face, but not one of them would help you out if you were in trouble. Not one.'

'So, not all it was cracked up to be?' I asked sarcastically.

'No. But, Iz, listen to me – when I saw you again I realized I still loved you and wanted you back. She's had nothing to do with it since then.'

'I can't believe you'd use me to get at her. What did I ever do to you to deserve that? Especially when it involved *her*? Cian, did you know that she put that clip up on Facebook? Do you know the humiliation I've been through – and how long it's taken me to get back on my feet again? It nearly destroyed me.'

'Izzy, I swear to you, I only found out a few weeks ago that she did it. You have to know I would never have allowed that. You see? That's what I mean! They're all so two-faced and insincere, cruel for their own gain without so much as a thought for anyone who might be affected by it.'

'Hurts, doesn't it?' I said, looking straight at him.

'Izzy, fuck her! I've realized how much I love you – that's what's important. I love you so, so much.'

I shut my eyes tight and listened to the words I'd prayed for him to come back and say to me over the last ten months. He approached me slowly and sat down on the floor beside me, wrapping me in his arms. 'I've missed you so much, my sweet, sweet Izzy. The kindest, most down-to-earth, most beautiful girl I know.'

I sat there numbly, letting him rock me.

'You'd never do that to me,' he whispered, stroking my hair.

'You fucking scumbag,' I said quietly.

'What?'

'I said, you fucking scumbag.'

I pushed him off me and got to my feet. I reached for my jeans and climbed into them.

'Izzy? What did I say?'

'You said that I'd never do that to you.' I stopped what I was doing and turned to face him. 'You've only come back to me because you got hurt and your ego's been kicked and you've had the fright of your life because you thought you were untouchable. You've realized that if you play with fire you get burnt. And now you want me to nurse it all better for you. You've scuttled back to your safe place, like the coward you are, so you can lick your wounds before you go back out there and do it all over again.' My whole body was trembling. '*Well, you can go to hell,*' I exploded, taking myself, as much as Cian, by surprise.

'Oh, for God's sake,' he huffed, rolling his eyes. 'Izzy, please.'

I looked back at him. 'All this time I've been fantasizing

about someone else. It wasn't you, just a better version of you, with the same name and the same face.'

His eyes misted over. And for the first time in my life, I thought I was going to see Cian Matthews cry. But I couldn't feel sorry for him. He looked too pathetic. Had I *really* been in love with this man?

'I never want to see you or hear from you again for the rest of my life. Ever. Do you understand?' I said, looking at him one last time.

I left his apartment. He didn't try to stop me. Why would he? The game was up.

I woke up on Monday morning with Keelin's nose pressed to mine.

'What are you doing, Keelin?'

'Checking you're still breathing. There's a packet of paracetamol on the kitchen counter and I thought you might have knocked them back with a flask of whiskey during the night. I'm glad you're still alive.'

'Christ, I'm not suicidal. I had a headache.'

She dragged me out of bed, pulled me into the bathroom, turned on the shower and instructed me to wash.

Monday morning. It was here. And it brought with it as much disappointment as it did relief. On the positive side I had work to distract me, but on the negative, I had the burden of pretending life was grand. Skipping around the set doing a million and one odd jobs and carrying on like life was a big bowl of cherries. The big bad world didn't allow you let on that over the weekend someone had come along and pissed all over you. I practised my fake smile in the bathroom mirror, but my eyes still held a blankness I couldn't dispel, no matter how hard I tried.

The day passed — it was like watching a movie with the sound turned off. I said hello to people when they nodded at me, answered questions when anyone asked me anything and fulfilled the menial tasks assigned to me. But no matter what anyone said to me, all I could hear was, 'Cian only had sex with you to get back at Edna McClodmutton.'

I came back after lunch and plonked myself down in my chair in a huff. I couldn't believe the lady behind the sandwich counter had told me I'd never have sex with anyone else like I'd had with Cian and that any lover from now on would be like your man from *Ryan's Daughter*, roll-on-in-out-grunt-roll-off-fall-asleep. She'd really asked did I want butter or mayonnaise, but that wasn't what I'd heard at the time.

The only time I was marginally cheered was when a few of the actors came over to the production office to look for the script editor. It was like watching the Battle of the Egos. I should have placed a bet. I knew the lad from Cork was going to win.

'Bullshit!' he snapped, at the bloke from Dublin. 'Seventeen words was all you had – I counted dem, boiy! *Twenty-four* was what I had!'

'I told ya before, ya bleedin' muppet, the nods don't count.'

'They do, they mean "yes".'

'Yeah, but you're not actually saying the word so it doesn't count.'

'You haven't got a clue what you're on about, boiy!'

Ruth, one of the trainees, got up from behind her desk in a bid to hush them, which I thought was a pity: watching two actors fight about which one of them had had more words to say in their last job was far more entertaining than folding pieces of paper and putting them into envelopes.

'I want to speak to the script editor. *Now!*' God, sometimes the Cork accent really did sound like an injured dog crying to be put out of its misery.

'Isobel? A word?'

Snared by Margaret again, the seventh time today, for

doing no work. This was getting embarrassing. I headed into her office and she closed the door behind me. She sat at her desk and looked at me earnestly.

Oh, Lord! She wasn't going to fire me, was she? I held up my little finger pitifully in the hope she'd notice my paper cut and see that I'd done at least *some* work!

'Isobel, I've put a lot of thought into this, and I've decided . . .'

Here it comes! This was officially the worst few days of my entire life. What next? My entire family had been wiped out by a freak hurricane that'd only hit our house in Blackrock? All my friends hated me? Doctors had found a Fisher Price farm animal in my stomach – I'd swallowed it when I was a child – it had travelled up to my heart and I was going to die?

'We need someone to go to London for us in ten days' time. And, well, I figured you'd be the best person. They'd love you over there.' She told me what I'd have to do.

'Oh.'

'Isobel?'

'Yes!' It had taken me a moment to grasp that I hadn't just been fired.

Wow. I'd been chosen to go to London, to BCM, on a mini business trip. How fantastic! Although it was entirely unnecessary, I was thinking of buying myself a briefcase. And a calculator. And a diary. All proper business people had them. I only had to hand deliver the film rushes to the BCM office – they couldn't risk losing them in transit with a courier – but so what? I felt like a pretty important business person. I'd stop off in that office-supplies place on my way home. I might even grab myself a *Financial Times* and see how the Footsie was doing.

First things first, though, I had to get my suitcase from Gavin's house. I whipped out my mobile to see if he was about tonight so I could call over.

29

Gavin pulled the suitcase out from under the bed in the spare room. 'I've hidden a few grams of cocaine in the front zip pocket for when you go through Security at the airport. Thought you might like a bit of class-A-drug drama. It's been a while now since your last bust, hasn't it?'

'Yeah. And I miss that buzz. Did I tell you what one of my neighbours said to me when we moved back in?'

'No,' he said, already laughing.

'I was on my way back from Odds and Sods when I got ambushed by Mrs Gibney from number eleven. You know her? The one with the headscarf that's constantly out polishing her brass doorknob and screaming at all the children?'

'Intimately.'

'Shut up, you – anyway, she pegs it over to me, waving me down with her brass polisher. "Come here, young one!" she yells. "Did yous lot all get arrested for hiding illegal immigrants in your house?" And I said no, that it had been a mix-up with the guards. Then she says to me that she saw a girl a while back with short dark hair, of "foreign descent", scuttling shiftily from our house one day. I told her that had been Keelin, that she'd had a fake-tan disaster and was trying to run back to the salon without anyone seeing her.'

'Did that really happen?'

'Yeah! Sure my dad thought she was Indian when he popped round the next day. Started speaking to her the way parents do to foreigners – shouting slowly like the person has a severe mental disability.'

'What did she do?' he asked, agog.

'The salon said there was nothing they could do, that their tanning technician was only learning and that's why Keelin had got it so cheap.'

'They're called tanning technicians?'

I nodded. 'They have nail technicians too.'

'Well, that's news to me. I didn't even know that UCD had added Beauty Engineering to the basic engineering degree.'

We headed downstairs to tuck into the pot roast Gavin had made us for dinner. I really was going to have to learn how to cook one of these fine days. Everyone was putting me to shame. I mean, even Keelin, who'd lived on pepperami and processed cheese for the entirety of her third-level education, could cook now. When had they all learnt how to do it? Where had I been when all this culinary expertise was being absorbed? Trawling through Tiffany replicas on eBay?

We sat down on the couch and Gavin told me about the shite that Aidan, the drug lord himself, had been spouting at the party. He'd told Gavin he wanted to get a new tattoo that said 'Life is Pain' over the Nike tick he already had on his back to mark his life's struggles. Poor Aidan. I'm sure a life of opulence and summer holidays in Cannes had been torture. I could just see him now, spreading his caviar on his doorstep-wedge of pan, watching *The Snapper* over and over, trying desperately to perfect the accent. He should be a contestant on the lifestyle equivalent of *Stars In Their Eyes*. He could come out in his private-school uniform, his hair parted and combed, saying, 'Tonight, Matthew, I'm going to be . . . *a complete scumbag*!' The audience would cheer and he'd pop backstage to complete the transformation into the little shit we knew and didn't love today.

Wasn't it lovely to be able to sit, chat, laugh and take my mind off the fact that the world had ceremoniously shat on me over the weekend? It was the first time since Saturday morning that I'd laughed properly, and the first time I knew it would all be okay. I'd get over it. Really, I would. And if any good had come out of what had happened, it was a massive slice of closure. There was no going back now. I could finally let Cian go. Because now I *had* to.

Just being in Gavin's apartment lifted my spirits. Maybe it was the smell of the pot roast. Or that he always had my favourite white wine in the fridge. Or that his couch was one of those cool L-shaped ones that you can sprawl out on. Or perhaps it was just Gavin.

'Izzy, I wanted to give you something as a thank-you.'

'Gavin, you did *me* the favour. You reminded me how much I love this and how much I've missed it.'

'I'm so happy you've said that because, Izzy, you really are so, so good. You've no idea.' We looked at the storyboards as they stood against the shelving unit in front of us. I was so pleased he was happy with them, and it was great that I had them finished so I could bring them over with me this evening to show him.

'Your present is beside you.'

'Where?' I said, looking around me.

'Try beside the cushion.' I pushed my hand down and, sure enough, it came across something. I tugged it out. A little velvet pouch.

'Open it,' he encouraged me.

I untied the knot and felt inside. There was a box and I pulled it out. I inhaled sharply when I saw the colour. The signature turquoise blue. *The Tiffany colour.* So many of my daydreams were made up of these little blue boxes. And now I had one of my own! Maybe there was something inside it! I'd have been happy enough with just the box . . . I shook it. It rattled. *Oooh!* I lifted the lid slowly – and melted.

'I'd heard you mention Tiffany and I thought it was either that singer from the eighties or this one. I went for this one, although you very nearly ended up with a best-of album from Tesco.' He scooted down the couch, lifted the bracelet from its little blue nest and fastened it around my wrist. 'It's a charm bracelet. And I hope you don't mind but I took the initiative in getting you started.' A little silver paintbrush and palette hung from one of the links. It twinkled as it swung around and caught the light.

I was speechless. I stared at him and finally found my voice. 'Thank you so much.'

'Thank *you*,' he said, smiling.

Somehow I was unable to tell him how wonderful he was for hearing what I'd said and acting on it. No one had done that before.

'So, did you see them?' he said.

'Huh?' I said, rejoining Planet Earth. 'Did I see who?'

'Your man Greg and Keelin's twin getting it on together in the wee hours of Friday night.'

'No way!' I said aghast. 'But, he's, well, the guy who buys people goldfish and listens to Eurovision music, and she's so virginal!'

'Literally dry-humping.'

I choked on my wine as I tried to laugh and swallow at the same time. 'I don't believe you.'

'Cross my heart and hope to die,' he said, making a criss-cross over his chest.

Wow, even my ginger tagalong had moved on. I was definitely losing my mojo. And Keelin's twin? Dry-humping? It was like trying to process one of those mad maths theorems in school – they made no sense but you had to try to take them in anyway. Keelin's twin couldn't have been more *pure*. When they were born, Keelin was three pounds heavier than

Aoife, and I'm convinced she got all of the DNA that was meant to be Aoife's fun, wit and sex appeal. There was no way you'd think they were sisters, let alone twins. You'd be hard pushed to imagine they were even of the same species.

'Let's see . . . what else did you miss after you crashed out? What time did you head to bed at?'

I sighed heavily into my glass of wine. 'I didn't exactly go to bed. Well, technically I did. But not to mine.'

'Did you end up crashing in with Susie and Aidan? Lucky you,' he said, winking.

I circled the rim of my glass with a finger, wondering whether to tell him or not. I probably should, I thought, so I'm not living in denial about the whole thing. If I wasn't honest about it, I wouldn't be facing up to it. Jesus, I'd done enough pretending. If I was honest with Gavin, it would never happen again. Right? God, I hoped so. Just thinking back to Saturday morning rattled the clarity I'd felt only moments ago about everything being okay.

'You did *what*?'

His eyes glazed with an expression I'd never seen in them before. I shuffled nervously on the couch. Perhaps I should have kept it to myself. I couldn't expect him to be as understanding as Keelin and Susie – he wasn't one of my girlfriends. Also, my case evokes much more sympathy when I'm telling it while roaring crying. Without the tears and the snot, it can sound slightly pathetic.

'Well, you see . . .' I started in a fluster '. . . he called over last week, trying to get me back . . . and it was really hard. I tried my best to be strong.'

What was going on? I'd never felt so nervous around Gavin before. I didn't know where to put myself, whether to look at him or not. I felt like I had when I was a child and I'd let my dad down. Now I was sinking under an unbearable weight of disappointment. I felt as if I'd let myself and Gavin down. Was that ridiculous? It had had nothing to do with him – so why did it feel like it did? I wanted him to shrug and laugh it off, tell me playfully what an idiot I'd been. I searched his face for some sort of resolve along those lines that I could grab on to.

Nothing of the sort. Just that expression in his eyes. It rattled me further. What must he think of me? 'Believe me. I know how stupid it was.'

'Good,' he said sarcastically.

'Gavin, please. I really don't need a lecture. I feel bad enough about it already. I shouldn't have told you.'

'I'm glad you did, actually.' His tone was laced with disdain.

'Just leave it, will you?' I said, shifting myself to get up.

'Why *did* you tell me, Izzy?'

'Well, I just thought . . .'

'What? That you'd tell me and that I'd be happy to just sit here and pick up the pieces with you – *again*? After listening to you go on about that fucking gobshite I don't know how many times before? The same fucking gobshite that isn't worth one millionth of what you are. Did you honestly think I'd just sit here and tell you that you're the best in the world and not to be so silly for worrying about doing the most stupid thing in the whole fucking world?'

His words tore through me and I swallowed hard to dispel the rising lump in my throat.

'How do you not know your worth, Izzy?'

I was so shocked at his anger that I couldn't find my voice right away. I got to my feet and shrugged my shoulders awkwardly. 'Well, you'll be happy to hear I've learnt my lesson now. Things didn't go too well afterwards.'

'Why am I not surprised?' he said, the sarcasm returning. 'And, no, I'm not happy to hear anything.'

This was horrible. What the hell was going on here?

'When did you become judge and jury?' I said, trying to remain calm.

'When you told me you slept with your arsehole of an ex-boyfriend, Izzy.'

'Fuck this,' I said, grabbing my coat and bag. 'Cheers for being a mate.'

'Don't throw that in my face. I've been a damn good friend to you.'

'I know,' I said quietly, battling with the lump in my throat again. 'I'm going to go now.'

'Yes, I think you should. Goodbye.'

I stalled for a moment or two. God, I just wanted to crawl onto his lap and hug him. Try to fix whatever had just gone wrong. But he was so angry. And I was too raw to attempt to convince myself that it might be a clever or rational idea.

I left his apartment.

I stood in the street, confused. Had I just had an awful row with Gavin? With *Gavin*? I hadn't imagined it possible. Okay, we'd had a tiff a couple of weeks ago, but that had just been a misunderstanding. We'd had a laugh about it and got over it. This was different.

Oh, Izzy! What have you done?

Should I go back? But what could I say? I couldn't change what he thought – that I was a slutty little doormat – or take back what I'd told him. I bit my lip. I felt utterly rotten – worse than I'd felt all weekend. I could try to deny it as much as I liked, but what had happened with Cian was a *fait accompli*. How much more proof had I needed? Had I really thought there would be a happy ending?

But I'd done what I'd done. *My* decision. Why did Gavin have such a problem with it?

I supposed he was right, though. I'd been looking for sympathy from him, and reassurance. And for him to cheer me up. Like he always did. Because he was loyal and funny and kind. Did I do enough for him? I should have asked him if he was okay about Kate. Why is it always just about *me*? God, I was a selfish bitch.

I'd go back and ask him about Kate. I'd show him I could cheer him up like he did me. And I'd tell him I knew it was time for me to grow up and hear some cold hard truths about myself. He was only being honest and that was what true friends were. Even if it hurt sometimes.

I marched back towards his apartment, full of intent and purpose. But as I stood poised at his door, I realized how childish I was being. And, again, how selfish. I only wanted to fix things so I could feel better. He didn't want me there, asking how he was about Kate or telling him a joke. It would be insulting to him. And I'd only end up making even more of a fool of myself than I'd done already. And what joke was I going to tell him? I racked my brains. The only one I could think of was: What's a shih tzu? A zoo with no animals.

Pathetic.

I stared at his door. The crack in the wood down the left-hand side. The key scratches around the lock. The weather-beaten brass number 9. It was all so familiar. Had I lost Gavin's respect? Maybe even his friendship?

I walked away, wondering if I'd ever again be welcome to the door with the crack in the wood, or the key scratches, or the weather-beaten number 9.

30

The last time I was at Dublin airport the sleeve of my jacket got caught in the suitcase carousel and I thought I was going to die. And I don't mean in a when-I-discovered-there-was-no-milk-for-my-tea-I-thought-I-was-going-to-die kind of way. I mean, I thought I was *actually* going to die. Two very different things. The latter makes you scream like a wild pig, which is neither cool nor dignified when it happens in a highly populated public place. As with any crisis, all my brother and sister could do was laugh and point. Although after I'd been dragged a good few feet, Emma decided that she shouldn't be pointing and laughing – she was putting her Dublin-airport street cred at far too much risk by doing that. Instead she turned away and hid her face in shame. Stephen, great brother that he is, dutifully kept up the laughing and pointing. Mum was off 'doing a wee' and we hadn't seen Dad since we'd stepped off the plane. He had a strange fixation with airport trolleys and always dashed off in a panic to find one in case, God forbid, there weren't enough to go around. What can I say? He was a war baby. Rationing must have scared the shit out of him.

Anyway, back to me nearly dying. Some American dude with a handlebar moustache and a Kiss Me I've Been To Ireland cowboy hat jumped onto the carousel and pulled me to safety just before I disappeared behind the black plastic flaps into the suitcase-mulshing chamber . . . *for ever*.

It took me a further four minutes to stop doing the wild-pig scream. And when you think about it, that's a significantly long time to keep screaming when you're no longer facing death, simply standing at a suitcase carousel beside a big American in a silly hat.

Emma said afterwards that I wouldn't have died, even if I had been dragged into the suitcase-mulshing chamber, that I'd just have come out the other side with a flat-packed buggy stuck up my arse. Stephen said I would have been dumped in overweight baggage after all the eating I'd done on the trip away. He's such a knob.

So here I was, back in Dublin airport, still alive but with a mild phobia of baggage carousels. I passed a sign pointing to Baggage Reclaim and thought I was going to wee a little bit. (I didn't, by the way, which was good.)

I spotted the Aer Lingus check-in desk at the opposite end of the hall and ran over to it, even though I was in no rush. It always made me feel as if I was in a movie when I did that.

'I'm going to London. I need to get on that plane!' I said breathlessly, to the lady behind the desk.

'Okay ... Ms Keegan,' she replied, looking up from her computer with my passport in her hand. 'That shouldn't be a problem. Your flight doesn't leave for another two and a half hours.'

I beeped when I passed through the security checks, as I *always* did. I keep asking Mum if I have a metal plate in my head that I don't know about, from some operation as a young child. She keeps telling me I don't, that it's probably just my underwired bra, but I'm not entirely convinced.

I knew I'd have to be frisked so I glanced at the bunch of security personnel to see which one would make the first move. A butch-looking woman stepped forward to perform the task. Her hands scooted over my arms and legs and down my back, and then she waved me through. That was probably the only action I was going to get for quite some time now that Cian had turned sex into an act of hate for me.

I sauntered through the shops, telling myself not to buy things I didn't need. Like the turquoise beaded shawl from Accessorize that I could only get away with wearing if I lived in Fiji. Or the burnt-orange Mac lipstick that I could only have pulled off if I'd had hair, eyes and skin of an entirely different colour. I still bought them, though. Sure, why not? I decided to get a pair of sunglasses too, seeing as they were reduced after the summer. And they might disguise the bags under my eyes from the stress-induced lack of sleep.

I put them on and looked at myself in the mirror. Much better. Now perhaps I could find a *burka* to hide the rest of my head.

As soon as we touched down in London, I fished my mobile out of my bag and switched it on, silently praying for a message. One came through and I held my breath.

It was from Mum and I needed a first-class honours degree in cryptography to decode it. **Padd t7gp, luш Mtm кк**, which roughly translated as 'Safe trip, love Mum xx'. She reckoned she was getting the hang of predictive texting. Any day now, I'd told her.

Still no word from Gavin. Not that I was expecting to hear from him, but you live in hope.

I tried to avoid eye-contact with the stewardesses as I left the plane in case they tried a last-ditch attempt to make me buy something else. The Aer Lingus alarm clock they'd talked me into having was more than enough for one flight, thank you very much. I'd only had it five minutes before I gave it to the little boy sitting beside me in the hope that he'd stop trying to stick his blue crayon into my ear.

Okay, confession time. I did something awful when I got

to Baggage Reclaim. I put my sunglasses on and asked a man nearby if he could help me retrieve my luggage from the carousel. It was either that or never pluck up the courage to collect it myself in case I was dragged to my death again. But I did give a pound to the lady collecting for guide dogs on the way to the Underground in the hope that it would pay off any karma debt I'd incurred at the baggage carousel.

I'm not sure when I'd told myself I'd be staying in the Ritz Carlton. Probably around the same time that I'd told myself I might pick up a few bits and bobs in Harrods. Had I forgotten I was the office runner for a small production company in Dublin and not Scarlett Johannson? Yes, I had, I concluded as I checked into the Stockwell Arms in South London. Picture a derelict pub in a council estate that someone had painted pink and yellow, with an 'Accommodation' sign over the front door. That was pretty much my hotel. Only everybody had London accents instead of Dublin ones and the local scary hoodlums had Staffordshire bull terriers instead of horses.

''Allo. Name?'

'Isobel Keegan.'

'Room three one five. Don't use the lift as it gets stuck and my hearin' ain't great so if you get trapped and start screamin' there's a good chance I won't hear you and you could be in there for a few days.'

Christ almighty.

'Okay.'

'Just use the apples and pears.'

'The what?'

'Stairs, mate, stairs. Cockney, innit?'

'Right.'

'Breakfast is served in the morning between eight and

eight fifteen. We have corn flakes and Shreddies. There's your key.'

'Right.'

I took it and headed up the stairs, waving goodbye to my Ritz-Carlton-and-Harrods fantasy. However dingy my dwelling, I was relieved to be out of Dublin for a few days. My head was swimming, and the temporary change of scene could only be a good thing. And it was probably for the best that Jonathan Ride Cunningham was in America, as I wasn't doing too well with the men in my life at the moment. I was safer with girls and rabbits. I mean that in a far less kinky way than it sounds.

31

The BCM office was everything I'd imagined it would be, and then some. It was a very impressive glass building right in the heart of London's West End, with an endless stream of important-looking people whirring through the giant brass revolving door. Everyone looked like they belonged in the movies, even if they weren't actors, and I suddenly wished I'd worn something a bit funkier. Or that I'd managed to dry my hair properly before the hair-dryer had burst into flames.

The girl at the reception desk with a head-set microphone took my name and asked me to sit in the waiting area. She told me Jonathan wouldn't be long.

'Jonathan?'

'Jonathan Cunningham? You're here to see him?'

'Oh, no, he's in America. I'm here to see . . .' I fished out the business card Margaret had given me '. . . Vivienne Shortt.'

'Miss Shortt replaced Mr Cunningham on the US trip at the last minute. So, if you'll just take a seat . . .'

I sat down and took out my mobile phone for the thousandth time already that day. Nothing from Gavin. The awful feeling crept back and nestled in the pit of my stomach. What would I do without him? What if I never spoke to him again? You hear of friends drifting apart, break-ups, splits, and if someone doesn't want to see you any more you just have to respect it.

'Izzy?'

'Jonathan. Hi.'

'Great to see you. I was delighted to hear they were send-
ing you over.' He winked.

We stood there grinning at each other, and I tried to think
of something interesting to tell him, like I'd taken up a night
course in astrology or cycled all the way to Wexford without
stopping. Couldn't think of anything. Only that I'd had a row
with Gavin over sleeping with Cian. But Jonathan Ride Cunningham probably didn't need to know that.

'Come on . . . I'll introduce you to the man himself.' As I
followed Jonathan up the marble staircase, with the rather
delectable view of his butt ahead of me, I reminded myself
that although the head of BCM was revered as royalty in
our Lights! Camera! Action! office, he was not *officially* a
king, therefore to curtsy when I met him would be plain
ridiculous.

For the second time that day, I attempted to dry my hair.
They weren't overly concerned with health and safety at the
Stockwell Arms, I thought, as I turfed the spare hair-dryer
from Reception into the bin after another pyrotechnics display.

I looked at the bed. I really wanted to crawl into it, pull the
duvet up around my ears and watch *Coronation Street*. Mind
you, I could only get reception for the telly if I stood by the
window, which didn't appeal. No, I just needed to get going
and I'd be fine. And once I saw my foxy date, I'd perk up.

The restaurant was located in the corner of a beautiful
cobbled courtyard not too far from Soho. I wrapped my
shawl tighter around my shoulders as an autumn chill crept
into what had been a beautiful summery September day. I
walked across the cobbles, trying not to snot myself in front
of all the elegant diners. Walking in heels on cobbles is difficult enough, but when your heels are so high that they've

already given you a mild bout of altitude sickness, it's even trickier.

Gosh, it's beautiful, I thought. Clusters of fairy-lights sat in the branches of the trees that lined the courtyard, blinking and twinkling – the sky seemed to have been drizzled with glitter. The sound of laughter and clinking wine glasses bounced off the stone walls. If only I could rally myself into feeling just a *little* bit excited. I'd been thrilled when he asked me out that morning after all the flirting that had gone on between us. I'd run through it once more, I decided. He was gorgeous, check. He wanted to take me out for the night, check. I was young, free and single, check. The last person I'd been with was Cian, check. I needed to change that ASAP so he wasn't hovering over me like an awful sex shadow, check, check, check.

So, what was the problem?

'Izzy?' I turned. He was seated in a candle-lit alcove, start-lingly handsome in the flickering light. Might have to upgrade him to Jonathan Absolute Total Ride Cunningham. He stood up and kissed my cheek. Very gentlemanly, considering he'd already had my ankles around his ears. His aftershave lin-gered in the air as he sat down again. My skin tingled where his stubble had pressed. As he poured me a glass of cham-pagne, I realized I was happy to be there. Check. I began to relax for the first time in days.

'You look lovely.' His eyes were jet black in the soft light.

'Thank you. So do you.'

Maybe things were on the up. Here I was in a beautiful restaurant, on a date with an absolute hottie, in this amaz-ingly romantic setting, *enjoying myself*! I smiled as he handed me a champagne flute and made a toast to 'us'. Maybe it was time. Maybe I was finally moving into a new phase in my life. I'd no idea what might happen between Jonathan and me but perhaps I was now officially over the Cian Years. Christ alive, it had taken me long enough.

Jonathan was fantastic company. We drank and laughed and chatted about life and work and the film. I told him I was thinking of exploring another facet of the industry, maybe something a little more creative. He said he could introduce me to a few art-department heads while I was in London. I thanked him but said I'd rather do that another time: I'd just helped a friend with some storyboards so I'd concentrate on that for a while. Jonathan was trying to play it down, but I could tell from his stories that he was a big deal. He was meeting the director of his next project in LA next week to do some castings.

LA? *Wow*.

He told me about his home town in Hertfordshire, where he'd grown up, and I told him about my mad family, about Dermot and about Will's new girlfriend in work. He told me about how Will had once come to visit him when he was about nine and seduced a girl called Penelope by tying one of her plaited pigtails to the branch of a tree so she couldn't run away when he tried to kiss her. They'd remained pen-pals for three years afterwards. That was an *eternity* in pen-pal years.

When Jonathan told me that as a teenager he'd sleepwalked naked during a party his parents were hosting I laughed so much that I couldn't help slapping the table – it tells the person I'm with that I'm laughing so much, I can't breathe. It's a strange thing I do, but he didn't seem to mind.

By the time the waiter brought the dessert, I was smitten. The way he kept looking across the table at me made my stomach dance. When he took my hand, I thought I'd explode. I put all thoughts of Dublin firmly out of my mind.

We left the restaurant and made our way to the Soho Lounge, a basement nightclub not too far away. We bought

Mojitos at the bar and slugged them back as we chatted some more, our conversation ever more ridiculous as the rounds clocked up. We danced among the other uninhibited piss-heads and, in a moment of pure madness (note to self for future: Mojitos may cause moments of pure madness), I showed Jonathan my *Thriller* dance moves. For the record, it was right in the middle of the Madonna remix set that I became convinced I wanted to go home with him. Tonight.

We hailed a taxi, bundled into the back seat and snogged all the way to his apartment in Hoxton. Jonathan threw the driver a twenty-pound note as we got out – and whoever said men couldn't multi-task had been wrong: he managed to unbutton my dress before we'd got out of the lift. We burst into his flat in a flush of heated passion and headed straight for his bedroom. My head spun with the thrill.

He released me from his grip to go to the window and draw the curtains. I watched him loosen his tie and lift it over his head. He unbuttoned his shirt and slid it off his smooth, tanned chest. I was going to enjoy myself this time. The last time had been a blur because I'd been angry with the world, but tonight – Imagine thinking I'd never want to sleep with a man who wasn't Cian! Well, I was moving on. *Hoorah!* I whipped off my bra in celebration and flung it across the room.

Then I stood beside the bed, looking across at him, this oh-so-beautiful man, and wondered why I was having to work at this, why it wasn't coming naturally and easily. I realized I was talking myself into it – into him. It shouldn't be like this.

My brain whirred, and suddenly I knew what was wrong, and why I had to leave his apartment immediately.

32

My period was more than three weeks late. It was never, *ever* late. I'm someone who can predict the exact minute it will come. I've never been caught out in a pair of white trousers, or muttered, 'I couldn't believe it – of all things I got my period,' because I always know. And I'm ready with ten kilos of chocolate, my comfy oversized Dunnes tracksuit and my box set of *Will and Grace*.

But it was now more than three weeks late.

Three weeks and four days to be precise.

Three weeks and four days of walking around in a trance, watching my life slip further and further away from me.

I hadn't done a pregnancy test. I was far too scared. And it would only tell me what I already knew.

I hadn't told anyone. Except Dermot, who always remained calm in a crisis.

I was pregnant.

Pregnant!

How stupid had I been? The thought of contraception had never even entered my head because I'd been on the pill when I was going out with Cian. Had I thought I was immune to getting pregnant because I was angry? Because I was hurt? Because I'd chosen to believe we were 'working things out'? It was Cian's baby. It had to be. Jonathan and I had used protection.

Only a month ago I'd thought my world was changing for the better. I'd thought maybe everything would fall into place. Well, I'd *hoped* it would.

After the Jonathan Cunningham thing (I've removed 'Ride' from his name because I already feel like a total prick-tease so I don't want to draw attention to the fact that I was once attracted to him), I got back from London and started trying to figure out what I could do to (a) patch up my friendship with Gavin and (b) get over Cian's betrayal.

What a mess. Tears fell down my face and I shook with sobs. I wondered if the baby would look like him. If it would have blond hair and blue eyes with the same angular nose. And if it did, how I'd be able to resist naming it 'Shithead' after him. Shithead Keegan. Mum and Dad would never forgive me. I'd never get away from Edna McClodmutton and Cian. They were probably back together by now. I'd be stuck in hell with no way out, no life, no Gavin, no nothing. Just an eternity with my Cian-clone child. Cian and Edna would probably get married and my child would end up loving its stepmother more than me – people I loved tended to get bored with me and like her more. It was awful to admit it, but I didn't want this baby. I would've done literally anything not to have spent those two nights with Cian.

'Hello? Bladder nearly bursting out here! Izzy, have you got the scuts, love?'

'Out in a sec,' I called, trying to sound cheerful.

That was the problem with working in this rabbit hutch. Not a second of privacy. I longed to be back on the film set, where there were so many people running around, you could easily skive off if you needed to. *Snog Me Now, You Dublin Whore* had wrapped last week, so I was back at the Lights! Camera! Action! office – back in the shoebox where I was nearly driven demented wondering if and when Gavin would show up. I hadn't seen him in more than five weeks. Not since the fight. And no word from him either. Laurence said he was in Belfast working on the company's next project and didn't know when he was coming back. 'Any day now I'd reckon,' he'd said, at least a week ago. No wonder I was a nervous wreck.

I unlocked the toilet door and found Geraldine standing there, legs plaited around each other.

'Dodgy curry? I'd love a bit of that so I would. It's basically like free colonic irrigation, isn't it? Nothing like a good old clear-out to feel a pound or two lighter.'

'Yeah,' I said, ducking away from her as I passed so she wouldn't see my blotchy red face.

'What's wrong with you?' It was Eve's best attempt at sounding concerned, even if her tone still implied that she wanted to kill me in a slow and painful way. I wished she would. What had I to live for? A child who would want his stepmother to adopt him.

'I'm fine,' I replied, as I sat down at my desk and hid behind a few manila files.

'Have you been crying?' This time her tone was lighter.

'No,' I lied. 'I was just chopping onions.' What? She'd never buy that. Should have told her I had a cold.

'You fucking oddball! In the toilet? You have far too much time on your hands, Isobel. You can sort this lot out.' She dumped a ten-foot pile of paperwork in front of me. 'That is, unless you have plans to pluck a few chickens or peel a bucket of potatoes with your letter-opener before lunch?'

I wasn't in the mood for arguing, so I reached for the top file. If I jumped out of the window behind Laurence's desk, would I kill myself or only break a limb or two?

That evening, on my way home from work, I passed a pharmacy and stalled outside. I really should buy a pregnancy test. It might help me come to terms with what was happening. I couldn't keep running off 'to chop onions' in the loo at work.

Then, at least, I could start making decisions. Like when and how I was going to tell Cian. And my parents – they'd have a simultaneous coronary. It would have been bad enough if I was still with him, but getting pregnant after two impulse shags when I'd spent the last ten months crying over how badly he'd hurt me?

I'm not sure my parents even knew I'd had sex. I mean, they must have had their suspicions seeing I'm twenty-seven years old, but the only reference my father had made to it was when he warned Emma and me about the responsibilities that come with 'heavy petting'.

After I'd spent half an hour sniffing the Nenuco shower gels until I was the only customer in the shop, I scuttled up to the counter. I didn't want to take any chances. It was guaranteed that any other female customer would play golf with Mum, and after she'd witnessed me buying a pregnancy test, she'd hose me down with Lourdes holy water, then print five hundred copies of 'Isobel Keegan is a slutty pregnant whorebag' to pass around at the next Ladies' Day coffee morning.

When I got to the counter, my resolve melted away and I was paralysed with fear.

'Can I help you?' the pharmacist asked.

'Yes.' I could feel the sweat gathering on my top lip.

'Are you sick?' he asked, in a concerned voice. Maybe he would take pity on me and I could go and live with him instead of in some horrible bedsit with net curtains and brown and mustard Paisley wallpaper, with just enough room for me and a cot. I could earn my keep by mixing the potions for him or sticking the white labels on the little containers.

'Ma'am?' he asked again.

I couldn't do it. I couldn't say the words 'pregnancy test'. This wasn't my life. This wasn't what was supposed to happen. I wanted to leave my job and do a graphic-design course and get proactive about work and have a fantastic career. I wanted to be in love and for all this to happen the *right* way. I wanted to continue living in the house with the girls. I didn't want to be a lonely single mother.

'Is there anything I can help you with at all?'

I stared blankly at him as he stood poised to assist me.

'Do these lollipops contain vitamin C?' I asked, pointing at a big glass jar containing about a hundred different-coloured ones.

'Ah, yes, they do,' he replied, evidently flummoxed.

'Fantastic. I'll have a green one and a red one, please.'

I left the shop and threw the lollipops into the bin.

33

I turned to find Gavin looking at me from my bedroom door, arms folded, head leaning against the wall.

'What?'

'Nothing,' he said quietly. 'Am I not allowed look at my girlfriend when she's getting dressed?' I loved how he looked in half-light.

'I suppose.' I reached for my jeans and started to climb into them.

'Hold it there.' He walked over to me and pulled me to him. I loved how small I felt in his arms when I was in my bare feet.

'Don't you dare even think about it, Mr Reed. I'm gonna be late. And I've just done my makeup and you haven't shaved yet today – you'll give me stubble ra–'

'Ssh.' He silenced me with a soft kiss that made my stomach flip. When I opened my eyes, his face had morphed into Cian's. 'Take it off,' he whispered, pulling at my bra.

'Off?'

'*Off!* Izzy! Turn it *off*!'

What, in the name of Jesus . . .?

I opened my eyes. Susie was standing at the bottom of my bed.

'What?'

'Your alarm clock! Would you turn it off? It's been ringing for the last fifteen minutes.'

'Sorry. I was in another world.'

She headed out to the bathroom and I turned over stiffly to hit the button. I flopped back on to my pillow.

I got dressed and brushed the knots out of my hair. My reflection in the mirror shocked me. I had smoky-look eyes although I wasn't wearing any makeup. Naturally achieved smoky-look eyes are not as flattering as they are when you've carefully applied kohl eyeliner and a charcoal shadow. I looked like one of those ghouls you can get down in Dunnes to put on your porch for Hallowe'en. Well, it was Hallowe'en next weekend, I suppose, so maybe I wouldn't look too out of place. People might think I was a bit old for dressing up, but I'd tell them to feck off. I was young at heart.

Keelin was cross-legged on the sheepskin rug, glued to the television, when I got downstairs. 'Izzy, do you think it's wrong to still fancy Phillip Schofield?'

'Maybe,' I answered, smiling.

'I just want to corrupt him – he looks so angelic. I mean, when I was a kid, I fancied him cos he was mates with Gordon the Gofer, but now, I don't know, he's still sexy. I'd love to run up to him completely nude and say, "Tits," just to see what he'd do.'

'He'd probably call the police, Keelin.'

'I've often wanted to do the same thing to Pat Kenny. Not in a sexual way of course, oh, God, no – he looks like your dad – just to see his reaction.'

'My dad looks nothing like Pat Kenny!'

'I was trying to make something up so you wouldn't think I fancied Pat Kenny. Which I do. I can't help it. It's like Marmite. You're kind of repulsed and intrigued at the same time.'

'I have no idea what to say to you. I'm picturing you with Pat Kenny and it's turning me off my breakfast.'

'Isobel. You pervert. Get your own sex thoughts. Stop stealing mine. Anyway, you can talk! You wanted to marry Tony Hart and live with him and Morph.'

'I was eight.'

'I don't care. It's all relevant. Ask Freud.'

Susie came downstairs and threw herself onto the rug next to Keelin. Then we abused her for ten minutes about her obsession with Ian Dempsey when she was a young one.

'You can talk Izzy, you fancied Tony Hart,' she piped.

'Does *everyone* remember that?'

'Yes,' Keelin said sternly, looking at me as if I had a terminal illness.

'At least Ian had a lovely smile. Tony Hart was just an ageing weirdo,' Susie said, trying to defend herself. It was on the tip of my tongue to tell her that Tony Hart, Phillip Schofield, Pat Kenny, *anyone*, in fact, was more fanciable than Aidan but I held it back. I shouldn't make everyone else's life a misery just because I was turning into a cynical wench. A pregnant cynical wench.

When was I going to tell them?

I'd have to face the music soon. All this chat about trivia was well and good, but it was just an escape. I had to tell them.

I felt sick. I wasn't sure if it was the shocking truth that I had once fancied Tony Hart or morning sickness. I decided to skip breakfast, and left Susie and Keelin watching a few more minutes of early-morning telly before they left for work. As I shut the door behind me, I could hear them cracking up laughing over some story about a singing gerbil in Wales.

I wished we'd all had the day off. Then we could have watched stupid television all day long and forgotten about the real world.

When I got to the office, I was the first in, so I made myself a cup of tea and took advantage of being able to stare into space for a while without being called lazy or weird – both compliments Eve had bestowed on me. Laurence was convinced I wanted to become an actress, which was why I had come over 'all strange' lately.

He had beckoned me over to his desk the other day for a quiet chat.

'What's up, love?' he'd asked.

'I'm fine.'

'Honestly, did you get a taste for the acting when you were down on-set? It's addictive. I still miss it. I can't stay away from it altogether. I've been working on that piece from *X Men*.' I hadn't seen it. 'The bit where your man goes off to get his revenge? It's not a classical piece by any means but I do like it. Maybe one day this week we'll get lunch and sit in the park and I can do it for you. See what you think.'

'Of course,' I said. Laurence was so cute.

'So is that why you're down? The film has finished up and you're stuck here in the office and you want to be back on-set, but as an actress this time? You know, I always thought you had an Audrey Hepburn look about you. I think it's time for an Audrey with blonde curly hair.'

'No.' I laughed. 'I definitely don't want to be an actress. I dunno . . .' I stumbled over my words '. . . I guess I'm just a bit fed-up at the moment.'

He cocked his head to one side, studying me. 'Is it your heart that's in trouble?'

'A bit,' I said quietly.

'The path of true love never does run smooth, Izzy. Sometimes it feels more like a dirt track, doesn't it?'

He was right. Why did I think *I* was so special? Everyone had been shat on at one time or another. Millions of women had faced what I was facing now. Well, it was time to grow up. I was going to do a pregnancy test. Then I was going to tell my friends and family. And then I was going to tell Cian.

I didn't even notice I was crying until Laurence wiped a tear from my cheek.

'Thanks,' I whispered.

'Why don't you call Gavin, see when he's coming back from Belfast? You two are as thick as thieves. And you always manage to put each other in good spirits, no matter how stressed out you are.'

After a moment or two I managed to find my voice. 'Yeah,' I replied, and moved back to my desk before I choked up entirely.

That Thursday, as I stared at my untouched Cup-a-Soup, wondering how on earth those coloured flecky bits turned into fully fledged vegetables with just a splash of hot water, Gavin walked into the office.

He was here.

Jesus Christ.

Standing right in front of me. Just like that.

I wanted to be sick. Proper projectile hose-type sick. The kind that sprays a hundred metres and looks much like the lumpy vegetable slop that was congealing in the mug in front of me.

But what caught me off-guard most was the overwhelming attraction I felt for him. It was radiating out of my pores. I couldn't hide it. It was so physically overpowering that I was convinced everyone else would see it. A neon sign must have lit up over my head flashing, 'GAVIN, PLEASE REMOVE YOUR CLOTHES SO I CAN HAVE SEX WITH YOU.'

I wanted to hide.

I wanted to walk over to the filing cabinet, chuck all the files out and climb inside.

How had I failed to notice until now what a complete and utter *ride* he was? I mean, I always knew he was handsome but, honestly, my head was going to explode with the amount of blushing I was doing. *Jesus, look at him!* His pale blue jumper made his eyes glow a beautiful golden green and his skin look like toffee. His dark hair had grown since I'd seen him. It hung around his face, messy and unkempt, but so incredibly sexy. Okay, I knew I'd missed him, but this was different. I certainly didn't feel this way about all my friends when I hadn't seen them in a few weeks. I had flashbacks to that night in my house when I'd wanted to kiss him. And that dream.

I kept my eyes firmly on the Cup-a-Soup and began stirring it fiercely, not knowing what else to do. I mean, even though I wanted to, crawling under my desk, shutting my eyes and sticking my fingers in my ears wasn't a valid option.

'You beating an egg, Isobel?' Eve asked, her face scrunched up in disgust. 'You going to make yourself an omelette for lunch? Chop a few onions in the loo for it, perhaps? You've been watching too much *Ready, Steady Cook* if you ask me. I'll tell you something, though, you could probably cook the omelette on your head with the heat your face is generating. Why are you so red?'

Had Eve actually said those words? Out loud? In our tiny office? With Gavin standing only a few feet away?

'You're nearly purple. Did you put on too much blusher this morning? You probably buy that cheap supermarket stuff. Awful on you now, I have to say, just awful.'

God, make her shut up!

'Are you sick, Izzy, love?' Geraldine joined in. 'Have you still got the scuts?'

Why were they saying these things?

'A bit of white bread will clog you up lovely.'

Oh. Fucking. Hell.

We still hadn't made proper eye contact. I just kept stealing little glances at him while he was looking away. He chatted to the others for a bit, then unloaded his stuff onto his desk. Eve started speaking like she was in a Bond movie again, her preferred tone whenever Gavin was about. She must have thought it was sexy. To me she sounded as if she had tonsillitis.

Geraldine filled him in on all the goings-on in her domestic hell. That her daughter was in third year now, and even though it was only October, she had already developed mild alopecia over the stress of the Junior Cert, and her son had taken to blaring Metallica at three thirty in the morning in protest at not being allowed to get Sky Sports installed.

Next Laurence was telling him about his new colour-coded system for production-manager receipts. 'Don't be scabby, don't be mean, if you have production-manager receipts, file away under green.' Gavin repeated it back and told Laurence that secondary colours didn't get the recognition they deserved any more and that he should set up the Secondary Colours of Ireland Association to preserve their heritage.

'Oh, that's right, mock me.' Laurence laughed. 'We have missed you, though, Gav,' he said, under his breath. 'Eve is driving us mad, imposing her wedding plans on us. Maybe you can get her to shut up for five minutes. I swear to God, if I hear another word about Egyptian cotton napkins or gold-embossed place cards I'm going to ram my stapler down her throat. You are definitely a sight for sore eyes in this Godforsaken place. Isn't that right, Izzy?'

'Huh?'

'Haven't we missed Gavin?'

'Um-hum,' I mumbled, in the hope that no one would know what I was talking about and leave me alone to get on with wanting to die.

Laurence's phone rang and he ducked away to answer it, leaving Gavin and me entwined in a horrific awkward silence.

If my face could have gone any redder, it did.

'Hi,' he said, after a moment or two. He smiled, but it didn't reach his eyes. My stomach lurched with disappointment.

'How are you?' I said, in what might just have passed for English, but came out more like Japanese. My heart was racing and my hands slid off the desk with all the sweat my palms were producing. They landed on my lap like two dead fish.

'Fine. Everything's cool. You?'

Well, I'm pregnant. A complete and utter mistake from a complete and utter other mistake. Which is shit, really, because I want to jump your bones. I didn't say that because I live in the real world and not some Hugh Grant movie. Unfortunately.

Was I in love with Gavin?

Holy shit!

'Fine, fine,' I said, in real-world speak.

'That's good,' he said, turned away and switched on his computer.

This was awful.

I put my hands to my head and prayed for the day to end. It did, eventually. But not in the five seconds I'd asked Mary, Jesus and Holy St Joseph for. Oh, no, just the regular sixty-minutes-in-an-hour way. The painfully slow way.

When the clock finally dragged its minute hand to five o'clock I jumped up and turned off my computer.

''Bye, guys,' I said, trying to be chirpy. I had endured three hours of pure hell. Three hours of staring at the back of Gavin's beautiful neck in an agonizing silence as he worked away. Wanting to kiss it. Wanting to scream. He never looked around. Not once. And I thought I'd suffocate with sadness.

''Bye, Izzy,' they chorused, as they packed up their bags and got ready for home.

34

I woke up in a panic at two twenty-five a.m., shaking and sweating. I had to tell someone. I felt so alone, so scared, that I had to let somebody help me through this nightmare. I had to tell someone about Gavin, about the baby.

I jumped out of bed and scurried through the dark to Keelin's room.

'Keelin!' I cried, flinging her door open. 'Keelin, are you in here?'

'What? Of course I am,' she answered groggily. 'It's my bedroom and it's night-time – where the hell did you think I'd be? Outside picking daisies?'

'Keelin, I'm scared.'

'Izzy, it's just a credit-card bill. We all get them. Just bring a few things back. Or hide it under your bed for a few more days until you've come to terms with it.'

'I'm pregnant. Remember I had sex with Cian? Well, now I'm pregnant.'

'*Whaaat?*' That had come from Susie's room.

Next thing I knew we were all sitting on the kitchen floor, drinking sweet tea. I'm not quite sure what the sitting on the floor was about, but nothing says 'crisis' like it. Like you're too traumatized even to contemplate furniture.

'Is anyone else's arse getting numb?'

'A bit.'

'How long have we been sitting here?'

'An hour.'

Dermot was at our feet. He was delighted to have nocturnal company.

'You know, I was just thinking . . . I mean, it's an option . . . maybe.'

Keelin and Susie looked at me.

'It's – well, some women do go to England, you know, and –'

Susie took my hand. 'I don't think you really mean that.'

I looked down at Dermot. No, I didn't suppose I did. You clutch at straws when you're desperate, but I couldn't really see myself going down that route.

'Izzy,' said Keelin, 'we're going to get a pregnancy test tomorrow. We can figure out where to go from there. Yeah?'

I bit my lip. Where would I be without these girls?

The next afternoon Keelin and Susie headed off to Boots while I stayed at home. They were afraid I'd wrestle the kit out of their hands at the last minute, not wanting to face the music. And they had a point. So I sat with Dermot on the couch, ran through baby names and wondered whether or not it would be cruel for my child to take rides on his back every now and again. I mean, he was a very big rabbit.

The doorbell rang. That couldn't be the girls back already? I lifted myself off the couch and shuffled to the front door, praying it wasn't Aidan. I couldn't handle him this morning, going on about Guy Ritchie and London gangsters. I might have to pour my glass of water over his head. But then he'd petrol bomb our letterbox and shred the contents of my wardrobe and . . .

'Hi.'

'What the hell do you want?' I spat, shocked at how little I could hide my distaste.

'Izzy, please, just hear me out,' he said. 'I know I don't deserve any more chances, but I want to give you something.

That's all. And afterwards, if you never want to see me again, I promise I won't bother you.'

'What is it? A signed copy of *Social Scene*?' I asked, with stony sarcasm.

'I deserved that.' He hung his head.

'Cian, what are you doing here? Saffron didn't take you back so you need to use me again in another bid to get her attention?'

'Please, Izzy, I just came around with your bicycle and to give you this. I don't want to fight.'

'How noble of you,' I said, incensed by his woe-is-me charade. 'Go away.' I started to close the door. I didn't want him there when the girls got back. I wanted time on my own. Time with my own thoughts and then with the people who *really* cared about me.

'Izzy, wait.' He stopped the door with his hand. 'Just read this. That's all I ask. Please.' He had a letter in his hand and held it out to me, pleading with his eyes. 'Just read it,' he repeated, after I'd taken it, and walked away.

I sat on the couch with the envelope in my hands, staring at the familiar handwriting. I flipped it over, tore the seal open and lifted out the folded piece of paper inside.

Izzy,
First, words cannot express how disgusted I am at my own behaviour. If I hadn't acted like the biggest prick on the face of the planet, I wouldn't have had the need to sit down and write you this letter in the first place. But I did. And you will never, ever know the extent of my remorse because of it. If I never get you back, well, that's just the regret that I'm going to have to live with for the rest of my life. The knowledge that I fucked everything up by being a stupid, selfish, immature idiot.

Izzy, I want you to know that you have always been my girl.

And whatever temporary loss of insanity I suffered that made me stray from you, I'll never understand. But if you take me back I swear to God I'll spend the rest of my life making it up to you.

I'm lost without you Izzy, please let me love you again.

Cian xxxxxxxxxxxxxxx

I rested the letter on my lap. It was all I'd ever wanted to hear from him. And as the tears trickled down my face and onto the page, I cried for everything that had changed, for bad timing, for knowing that this had come too late, and that I didn't love him any more.

I was head over heels in love with Gavin. It was like a light-bulb had flicked on in my head. I was in love with Gavin. I loved Gavin. There it was. Simple.

Except not simple at all because I was carrying Cian's baby. I was stuck in no man's land with a life I didn't want. And the one I did want so temptingly close, but so utterly unreachable.

What was I like? I didn't know if Gavin even felt the same way. He probably didn't. I mean, he probably would have said something if he did. I wished I'd figured it out before I'd got pregnant, so then if he'd told me he only saw me as a friend I wouldn't have died wondering. It would be difficult, but I'd eventually get over it.

I looked at the Tiffany bracelet on my wrist. All the hints I'd given Cian over the years and it had never even struck him. And Gavin had given me this beautiful and thoughtful present out of the blue.

Said everything, really.

I sat in the middle of the room, like a figurine in a snow globe waiting for the pieces of her fragmented world to settle around her.

Not long after he'd gone, the doorbell rang again. Here we

go. He was back. I didn't love him, but we had a responsibility to do the right thing. Maybe we could make things work for the sake of the baby. I took a deep breath and opened the door.

'*Jesus!*' I screamed.

'Wow, you really weren't expecting me, were you?' he said, half smiling.

I rubbed my eyes, blinking furiously, making sure it was Gavin who was standing in front of me and not Cian. 'What – what are you doing here?'

'Izzy, what's wrong?' he said.

'Nothing, it's just –' He swooped in and wrapped his arms around me tightly. I collapsed into him, so upset, so confused, so angry with myself for realizing everything too late.

He led me into the living room and sat me on the couch, brushing my hair from my face and wiping my tears away with his hands. 'Izzy, I may be the biggest fool in the world for saying what I'm about to say, and possibly an even bigger fool for hoping you might feel the same.'

Now it was as if someone was violently shaking the snow globe and I wanted to get out. But I was trapped, alone, scared. I couldn't look at him – it was too hard. I got up and walked over to the window.

I cursed the early-evening moon and the Hallowe'en fireworks that burst into enchanting sparkles across the velvet blue dusky sky. I cursed the love songs that floated out from the radio in the kitchen. I cursed them all because they spoke of love and romance and hope. For other people. Not for me.

Gavin had followed me. It was killing me that I could sense his anxiety and do nothing to make it easier for him.

It was so unfair. My body trembled with anger, regret and frustration. I had spent the last year worrying that I would never find someone like Cian ever again. Only to discover I was in love with someone ten billion times more amazing than him. My friend Gavin. My funny, kind, intelligent, gorgeous friend Gavin.

But I could never have him. Even though he appeared to want me too. Instead I was bound eternally to a half-life I didn't want. And to a man I didn't love. And who didn't love me.

Gavin stood behind me and wrapped his arms around my waist, pulling me to him. A lump rose in my throat.

We both stood looking out ahead of us, his chin resting on the top of my head as the fireworks shattered into a myriad bright splinters. I could have stood there for ever.

'Are you cross with me?'

I shook my head. I squeezed his arm with my hand and he buried his head in my neck. 'Izzy,' he whispered, 'I'm mad about you.'

The world around me flooded my senses. The taste in the air, the feel of his breath on my skin, the smell of his aftershave. And the heat of the tears as they gathered in my eyes. When they fell, I didn't dare wipe them away for fear he'd see.

'Everything that's happened over the past few months was down to you. None of it was your fault, but I couldn't have helped it if I'd tried. I couldn't help falling for you. You made me realize I wasn't in love with Kate. She's a fantastic girl, but she's a second-rate you. Everyone is. Who was I trying to kid? And I wanted to tell you the night of Eve's party but you'd left before I had the chance. Then Laurence told me you'd met up with that Jonathan tosser and I knew I'd missed my chance. I hear he's quite a nice guy, but I still like to think he's a tosser.'

I smiled sadly. He hugged me tighter.

'And then when the Cian thing happened, I just couldn't

do it any more. I couldn't be around you, feeling the way I did, while you told me you'd been with him. Fuck. I was so jealous. I fucking hate that prick. And I just thought, This has got to stop. She's not into you, mate. It's made me realize one thing, Izzy. I can't just be your friend. That might make me a sore loser, but I can't do it any other way. I'm too in love with you.'

The tears streamed down my face and I swallowed hard against the sobs in my chest as they gasped to get out.

'I really don't want to lose you as my friend. I used to love just being around you, just to be near you and spend time with you. But I want it all. I can't do it any other way. Izzy, if you don't feel the same, I promise I'll leave you alone.'

We stood in silence, wrapped up in this beautiful bubble, his words floating in the air around us. And I knew I was about to shatter that bubble any second. For ever. Would Gavin still want me if he knew everything? If he knew I was pregnant with Cian's child? The answer was no.

His remarks about relationships and timing taunted me, and I closed my eyes tight in the hope that they'd go away.

They didn't.

This was it.

I mustered every nerve in my body to help me. I didn't think I'd be able to do it, but I did.

I shook my head.

He stood still, but I could hear his breathing change.

After a torturous moment or two, he finally spoke.

'Okay,' he said, releasing me gently. ''Bye,' he whispered, and kissed the top of my head. Then he was gone.

35

The third time the doorbell rang I wondered would it be Tommy Lynch, the guy from St Killian's I'd gone out with for two months in fifth year. Well, everyone else had called to the door in some Hallowe'en-ghosts-of-my-past way, so why not him?

It turned out not to be Tommy. It was the girls back with the pregnancy tests. Before I ran out of energy completely, I sat them down to tell them about my decision.

'Did you tell him you were pregnant?'

'No, not yet. But at least I know how he feels about me, right?'

They both looked down at the letter again and nodded. Neither of them seemed convinced.

'Izzy, you know you don't *have* to stay with Cian because of the baby. It's not nineteen-twenties Ireland here. We're not going to send you off to a Magdalene laundry if you don't marry him,' Susie pleaded.

'We'd support you, you know that. And your family would, too, once they were over the shock.'

I could see the sadness in their eyes and I knew they weren't buying it. But I'd spent too much of my life being the victim, coasting, flitting from one thing to the next without any conviction. This time, when it mattered, I was going to take responsibility for my actions and step up to the plate. 'Guys, all I want is for you to be happy for me. Maybe Cian and I were meant to be. I mean, how lovely is that letter?'

'Lovely.'

'Lovely.'

I smiled at them. 'I'm okay with this, really.'

Keelin looked down at it. 'He does have lovely handwriting.'

'And he's a good speller,' Susie added.

Well, there you go. What more could anyone want?

An hour later, we sat on the bathroom floor and stared into space, our rear ends completely numb. Confused, knackered and speechless.

We'd done five tests. All negative. We'd come to the conclusion that it'd been a dodgy batch and they were all broken. Then Susie jumped up and said she'd do one, just to check I was doing it right. That came out negative too. She'd nearly fainted on the loo from hyperventilating.

'Suz, what's the matter with you?' Keelin asked. 'You can't get pregnant by taking a test.'

'It's not that,' she wheezed.

'Then what? I keep telling you that you wear the belt on those jeans too tight.'

'What if I ever got pregnant with Aidan's baby?' she yelped, nearly passing out again.

Keelin and I looked at each other. 'Well, honey, it is a possibility. It always is when you're sleeping with someone. That's just the shitty reality.'

'It's not meant to terrify the living daylights out of you, though, is it? I mean, we're adults. It's not like it would be a crisis teenage pregnancy. Okay, it may not be planned, but if you're in love . . .' Her face crumpled and she started to cry.

'What is it, Suz?' Keelin asked gently, rubbing her arm.

'I don't . . . I don't think I could do it. I couldn't have a baby with Aidan. It's too difficult. *He's* too difficult. It would break me. I know it's insane, and I know you can't understand how I fell for him. But I did. I really, really fell for him.

I never meant to. It was never the plan. I just wanted to be a bit wild for a while. Show my parents that I wasn't this perfect person who had to fit into the mould they'd created and live by their rules for the rest of my life. And I knew Aidan was all wrong for me – *is* wrong for me. But that didn't mean it wasn't unbelievably exciting. And it was the first time I'd ever been really physically attracted to a bloke in my life. I mean *really* attracted. And I've never had sex like it. And what if that's just the way it is for me? That I can only have chemistry with the arseholes? Because, believe me, I want to be with a man who is kind, and uncomplicated and makes me feel good about myself, but I won't be satisfied if I don't want to rip his clothes off. And I'm afraid I won't find someone who has it all for me.'

'You know what, Suz?' I offered. 'I'm in such a messy place right now that perhaps I'm not the best one to be offering advice here, but I gotta tell you, from my own experience, my ideas of what I thought I found sexy have changed so much that I barely recognize what I used to find attractive. I thought I had a type – cocky blond blokes with an overbearing sense of self-importance. What I thought I was programmed to look for in a man turns out to be what makes me miserable. And misery is not sexy. Happy is sexy. Honestly. And I don't think it has to be a second-best or self-preserving not-as-exciting alternative. I've come to see that self-tortured sexy is just so *boring*.'

'Iz has a point,' Keelin said. 'Don't limit yourself into thinking that you now have a type you're attracted to and that's the only way it can be. Look at all the crazies I went out with. All those loud arty types, unpredictable musicians, temperamental blokes into all sorts of drugs, tortured writers and stoners. And, sure, it was exciting because it was different and they were crazy. They were the sexy, moody, brilliant-

298

in-the-sack blokes. But I never fell in love with any of them. And now look at the guy I'm with. An accountant! Who's uncomplicated and principled and so *normal*. And I've never felt so wild and alive and out of control in my entire life.'

'Keelin, are you in love?' I asked, grinning at her.

'Shut up. No, I am not. Get a grip.' She tucked her knees under her chin defensively. 'Okay, maybe. Just a little bit.' We all smiled.

Then Susie said, 'Oh, guys, I know there's no future with Aidan. So what am I doing?' She looked so lost, it nearly broke my heart. Her eyes welled and then the floodgates opened.

We huddled together and held on to each other as Susie cried and cried. Even though she was devastated, I was relieved that it had dawned on her now instead of ten years down the line when she had kids and a mortgage. She had difficult decisions to make now, but she'd be okay. I knew she would.

And Keelin was in love? Just a little bit? If Susie hadn't been so distraught, I'd have opened a bottle of champagne to celebrate.

'What are you going to do now?' Susie asked, a little later, after she'd gone from sitting on the bathroom floor to curling up on the bathmat.

'I'm going to the doctor tomorrow to get a proper test done.'

'If you're not pregnant, will you please, please, go and tell Gavin you feel the same way about him? Please?'

I hadn't lasted too long with my decision not to tell them about Gavin. The frustration over the pregnancy tests had broken my resolve. I had also told them I was pretty sure that I hated, rather than loved, Cian.

Now everything was messed up. And it was so much more

complicated than just telling Gavin I felt the same way.

I sighed heavily, feeling even more exhausted. He'd been so brave to come straight out and tell me exactly how he felt. And I had turned him down point blank. He wasn't up for playing games. He'd hate me for messing him about. How could I tell him the real reason I'd rejected him? I shut my eyes tight and pulled my knees into my chest. It was far too shameful.

I already missed him. And now I couldn't even have him as a friend.

Well, that was the price I had to pay for being such an idiot.

And, anyway, I knew I was pregnant. I just knew it. The doctor would confirm it tomorrow. I looked at Keelin and Susie, hunched on the bathroom floor, the moonlight spilling through the window making their faces glow a pale blue.

'Now, Isobel.'

I snapped out of my daydream and shuffled nervously on the cold steel chair in the surgery.

'I have your test result.' Dr O'Reilly folded his arms and stared at me. I'd been mortified at coming here today, but I hadn't known where else to go. Dr O'Reilly had been our family GP since Stephen was born, so it seemed only natural to consult him. I'd made him cross his heart and hope to die that he wouldn't say anything to my mum and dad.

'So, here it is.' He coughed.

I was having a baby. I braced myself.

'You're not pregnant.'

'What?'

'You're not pregnant.'

'What?'

'You're not pregnant, Isobel.'

I woke up on the floor with Dr O'Reilly taking my pulse.

'Am I dying?'

'No.' He half laughed. 'You're not dying. What you are, Isobel, is exhausted.' He helped me to my feet and sat me back in the chair. 'You fainted from shock. Or relief, to be more exact. Your system has been under an awful lot of pressure lately. That's why your periods have stopped. Stress, Isobel. You're going to have to start taking better care of yourself. Are you sleeping?'

'Not really.'

'Have you had a stressful time lately?'

I instantly thought of Cian. 'Yes. I suppose I have.' Then I thought about Gavin. About thinking I was pregnant with Cian's child. And what kind of a life I thought I'd been facing up to two minutes ago. 'I'm not pregnant?'

'No.'

I started laughing and crying at the same time. Dr O'Reilly handed me a lollipop. Did he think I was still five years old? That was worrying, considering I'd come to find out if I was pregnant or not. 'Sorry. You must think I'm very immature.'

'Not at all. The lollipop is to raise your sugar level. Clearly it's only a short-term measure. You need to get at least eight hours' sleep a night, and make sure you're eating properly. Doing things like getting massages or taking up yoga can be extremely relaxing for people under stress.'

'Thank you, Doctor.'

I left the surgery, went straight to the corner sweet shop and bought a humungous bag of apple drops, a Twix, two packets of Smarties and some Skittles. Doctor's orders. Far nicer than having to go to the chemist and take a rake of nasty antibiotics. Or being pregnant for that matter.

I wasn't pregnant. If I'd figured that out a few weeks ago I'd have saved myself an awful lot of anguish.

So . . . what now?

36

I started putting my life back together bit by bit. I did my best to get eight hours' sleep a night, to eat well and do some relaxing exercise, like walking up the escalators in Brown Thomas. I even went to a yoga class with Susie. She loved it, but I wasn't sure it was for me. I found the middle-aged women farting and the men in tight Lycra pants quite traumatizing.

Most of all, though, I savoured the freedom of *not* being the mother of Cian Matthews's child and everything that came with it, like getting my arse into gear about my career. I'd already applied to do a night course in graphic design when the new term started, and I was giddy with excitement about it.

I hadn't seen Gavin in weeks, but I'd heard through the grapevine that not only had he been chosen as a finalist for the documentary competition, he'd already been head-hunted by a production company based on the strength of his submission. I was over the moon for him and texted to congratulate him. He texted me back saying he was delighted and thanking me again for my contribution with the storyboards. And that was it.

I couldn't believe how much it was still affecting me. One day, when Emma asked me how he was I burst into tears.

'What's up with you?' she asked, looking at me as if I was an alien.

'Nothing. It's just I'm going to miss him if he goes and works for another company.'

'Izzy, you have to toughen up. You've made great progress

in getting back out there and socializing, but don't start putting the shits up me that you might relapse and start crying in public again. Get a grip! You don't know the damage control I've had to do on your behalf over the last year. I even told people in college you were on a drug trial that'd gone horribly wrong.'

'Sorry, sorry. Absolutely. No, you're right, I'm fine,' I said, wiping my eyes and breathing purposefully. I grinned bravely, but she was still looking at me sceptically.

I was feeling an awful lot better overall, though. I was heading out most weekends and enjoying myself. Or spending time at home watching *Nationwide* with Mum, singing Céline Dion duets with Dad on the karaoke machine and taking the now-shaggy-again Doris out for walks.

Eventually my period came back.

The relief.

The *overwhelming* relief. I mean, I clearly knew I wasn't pregnant (five failed pregnancy tests and confirmation from a doctor), but it proved to me that I was getting back to normal. That I was moving on.

But one thing still troubled me. One thing continued to wake me in the middle of the night. I'd hoped that if everything else more or less fell into place I would forget him. That maybe it was never meant to be. But it was impossible. Forgetting Gavin would be like forgetting to breathe or eat or think.

Susie ended it with Aidan. Again, I was tempted to open a bottle of champagne, but thought it more sensitive to let her get over it first.

Then one evening she arrived in the pub for a post-work bevvy and made an announcement.

'So what do you think?'

'I think you're absolutely dead right and you should go for it.'

'Really?'

'Really.'

She smiled broadly. 'I'm going to book it.'

Susie had decided that she needed to get away for a bit. Everything to do with the Aidan break-up had sort of imploded in her shortly afterwards, forcing her to stop and assess where she was in her life. 'I just can't believe I allowed myself to be taken over by the situation. I'd always thought I was stronger than that. How could I not have seen the writing on the wall when it was *so* bloody clear all along?'

'Suz, don't be so hard on yourself. You've said yourself that a lot of it was down to your own issues, and once you've acknowledged what they are and resolved them, there's no way you'll allow it happen again. It's time you accepted yourself for who you are, a fantastic, clever, beautiful, funny woman.'

'Iz, you sure you don't want to come on the yoga trip with me? You sound so hippie and zen and, well, perfect for it, really.'

'No, thanks. I'll leave you to your Lycra and your dangerously gaseous downward-dog positions. Besides, my course will be starting shortly and that's now my main priority.'

'Good for you!'

'Good for us!' I said, raising my glass. We toasted ourselves, and I wanted to hug her. So I did.

We texted Keelin to join us and she turned up a while later . . . *with* Simon! Susie and I nearly fell off our stools! Keelin *never* brought a guy with her to meet us. She always said she wouldn't burden us with the obligation as they were usually too odd to maintain a normal conversation. Well, 'Shymon' was far from odd. Yes, he was shy, but in a lovely, unassuming and gentlemanly way. And I could totally see what Keelin meant about his quiet, mysterious sexiness. Jaysus, they were smitten with each other. When Susie told them the pub was on fire to see if she could catch their attention, all they said was 'Really?' in dreamy voices without breaking their mutual gaze.

We decided to leave them to it. Susie and I got chips and walked home arm in arm to Google all the cities in Italy she was going to and start planning her trip. I was so happy for her that she was doing it. *And* doing it on her own. How brave. I told her she'd come home all bendy and fluent in Italian with her issues resolved, and she said she liked the sound of that.

As we walked home, I felt a sort of resolve that I hadn't felt in a long while. Perhaps we were all getting wiser and growing up. And sometimes it's nice to be able to acknowledge that the shit times had opened your eyes, and be okay with that. Without them, you wouldn't have come out the other end to be where you were now, having learnt all you had.

My final lesson in the whole ordeal came when I met up with Cian finally to put things to bed – not literally. I thanked him for the letter, but told him it was definitely over. For good. I didn't say anything intentionally to hurt him or make him suffer. I just said it like it was.

And what did he say in return? 'Whatever. Saffron and I are probably going to give it another go anyway.'

What a tosser. Thanks be to God I'd seen the light and dodged that bullet. 'Well, I think you should,' I said earnestly, 'because, Cian, in all my life, I have never met two people more suited.' With that, I left him sitting in the coffee shop, firmly closing the door and leaving behind that chapter of my life.

37

It was the day before the world première of *Snog Me Now, You Dublin Whore* and, with the excitement and furore, you'd have sworn we were getting ready for George Clooney *and* Brad Pitt to descend on us. Geraldine had had hair extensions put in for the occasion. Eve had arrived in in a Roland Mouret dress, 'in case I got papped by any photographers' on the way to work. When I asked her why on earth they would want to take photos of us, she removed her Chanel sunglasses, shrugged her shoulders and said, 'You never know!' God help us. She'd probably made poor Philippe stand outside the office with a camera all day just so she could make herself feel important.

Everything was pretty much ready for the première and we were finishing off the last few bits and bobs. I was quite looking forward to it. Eve kept annoying everybody by saying she was keeping the guest list top secret until the night. Honestly, did she think we were going to be that impressed by the celebrity chef from Leitrim we already knew was coming? (Although, I have to admit, I was *slightly* impressed, and I was even contemplating quizzing him on how he managed to get his meringues so fluffy.)

We were all being put up in the Shelbourne Hotel courtesy of BCM, and that was the bit I was most looking forward to. I couldn't wait to get there, run myself a luxurious bubble bath, swan around in a lovely soft terry robe and steal all the mini shampoos, body lotions and soaps from the bathroom. I was also looking forward to the free piss-up after the film screening. It was an invitation-only party and I'd managed to get *everyone* on the list. Keelin, Susie and Emma were 'models'. Will, Marcus, Caroline and Orla were in a 'pop group' called Mix 'n' Match. And Stephen and Deirdre were down as Bono's children. Eve hadn't batted an eyelid when I'd passed the list to her, just scanned it briefly and said they were all in, and that she'd probably got them on her list anyway.

I was kind of hoping Gavin would be there, but I had a feeling it might not be his scene. Then Laurence told me he was stuck in Belfast, finishing his preparatory work on the next project he was doing for Lights! Camera! Action! before he left us for good. Gradually he was slipping further away from me and soon he'd be gone altogether.

Just as I was thinking I was ready to pack up for the day and go home to beautify myself, Fintan landed at my desk with a very scary look on his face. 'Well, Isobel? What possible explanation do you have?' he fumed, his face all red and sweaty.

'Sorry, Fintan, I don't know what you're talking about,' I stammered. Christ, I'd never seen the man so angry.

'I'm going to be the *laughing stock* of BCM, thanks to you!' he bellowed, making me shrink in my seat. I racked my brains to think of what I could possibly have done. Perhaps he'd seen the guest list and knew only too well that Stephen and Deirdre weren't Bono's offspring. Or maybe he'd overheard me saying to Geraldine that I was going to fleece the goodies in the bathroom at the Shelbourne.

'How could you do this, Isobel?' he demanded.

The room went quiet and I could see Geraldine and Laurence blinking at me like two scared rabbits.

'Er, sorry, Fintan,' I said cautiously, after a few moments of silence. 'What have I done?'

Even by the time I'd walked the whole way home, I was still trembling with anger. How could she have done that to me? How could she have blamed me like that, when it had had absolutely nothing to do with me?

Keelin and Susie were both at home when I got in. Keelin was on the couch French-plaiting Dermot's fringe and Susie was sitting on the floor with a bucket on her head. I raised my eyebrow at Keelin in the hope she would enlighten me.

'She read online that meditating in total darkness can help you exorcize your break-up demons. She couldn't find her eye mask, so she's using the bucket from under the stairs instead. She's hoping to get in the zone before she goes on her trip.'

Susie removed the bucket and said hello.

'How's it working out for you?' I asked.

'Not great. I'm still so angry about it. As much with myself as Aidan. Maybe you really need to use an eye mask to make any sort of progress.'

'You're looking a bit frazzled, Izzy. Maybe you should wear the bucket for a while,' Keelin suggested.

I slumped down on the couch and told them about the nightmare that had just unfolded at work. Eve had been in charge of organizing the posters for the film, but there'd been some mix-up with the order, and it had turned out they weren't going to be ready by tomorrow night. But instead of Eve owning up and admitting to her mistake, she'd told Fintan it was *my* fault because *I* had placed the order. And now they couldn't even get hold of the designer to ask him to run a few copies from the original. I felt so helpless. The more I'd tried to defend myself, the angrier Fintan had got. And when Geraldine and Laurence had tried to stand up for me, he'd told them they could leave if they had a problem.

Obviously this had been a serious fuck-up. And Fintan

had kept ranting that he'd never been to a première in his life where the film's poster hadn't been on display. I'd stared at Eve, imploring her to do the right thing and own up. All she could do was straighten her fabulous Roland Mouret dress and gaze out of the window, avoiding my eye.

And now here I was, stunned, hurt, angry and potentially unemployed. Susie and Keelin were both outraged and Keelin said she was going straight to Eve's house, wherever it was, to read her the Riot Act. I told her she lived in Castleknock. Then Keelin said she wasn't sure how to get there but could you get the number fifty-six from Eden Quay? I told her to leave it, that Eve wouldn't give a damn – she'd just slam the door in her face. Just as Susie was trying to convince me to wear a hidden tape recorder into work tomorrow and get Eve to confess to the crime when we were alone my mobile rang.

'Hello, Izzy?'

'Yes?'

'It's Jonathan.'

'Jonathan *Ride* Cunningham?' I asked. Had I just said that? Out loud?

'Sorry?'

'Eh, hello. Can you hear me? The connection's breaking up. Who did you say was calling?' I winced, hoping to God I could come out of this with my decency still some way intact.

'Isobel, it's Jonathan Cunningham,' he said loudly and clearly.

Oh, God love him. 'Ah, yes, Jonathan! I thought I heard you say that! How are you?' This was awkward: the last time I'd spoken to him, I was whipping off my bra and flinging it across his bedroom.

'Listen, Isobel, we're in the shit here, big-time. Fintan told me about the poster fuck-up.'

Oh, no. I was semi-naked in both our minds' eye, and now he was firing me as I stood there with my tits out. 'Jonathan, you have to believe me. I had nothing to do with posters.'

'Don't worry about that now. There's nothing we can do about it at this stage. What we need is a replacement.'

'Right. A replacement for me?'

He laughed, and for a second I thought he was an awful arsehole, even though I had denied him sex at the last minute so he was *sort of* in his rights to be a little rude to me. But then he told me that I'd misunderstood, and we urgently needed a replacement poster.

'And that's where you come in, Izzy.'

'It is?'

'Remember you were telling me you were into art and graphic design and that you'd helped your friend out with some storyboards?'

'Yeah – but, Jonathan, it's only a hobby. I'm not qualified in anything like that!'

'Who cares? If you can do it, you can do it. And you know the film better than any freelance designer we'd find this late in the day.'

'What – where – how many – why?'

'Isobel, will you do it?'

Well, why not? What was the worst that could happen? If I failed, I couldn't be any worse off than I was right now. And maybe, just maybe, there was a chance I could pull it off.

I got off the phone and ran back into the living room. I told Keelin to get on with her plaiting and Susie to put the bucket back on her head: I was locking myself into my room to sort my life out and I probably wouldn't see them until tomorrow.

Keelin threw her eyes to heaven. 'The two of you and your mad new-age self-help strategies.'

*   *   *

'Please!' I wailed, holding on to the Spanx for dear life. 'Why are you doing this to me?'

'Mother of God, Isobel, you're the biggest drama queen I've ever met. Now let *go*!' shouted Keelin, slapping at my hands.

'No! Please! Just let me wear them!'

'No!'

All of a sudden Keelin and Susie flipped me on to my back and wrestled them off me. I lay on my bedroom floor, feeling worn-out and violated. 'Why?' I whimpered. 'Just tell me *why*.'

'Because you don't need them, that's why,' Susie answered. 'Now, on your feet! Snap to it!'

Well, I needn't have worried about Susie regaining her confidence after Aidan, that was for sure.

'Fine,' I sulked, dragging myself to my feet.

'Arms up! Up! Up!'

'Susie, that fitness bootcamp you're going to is having some serious side-effects.'

'UP!'

I screamed and put my arms up obediently. She slid the dress over my head, and pulled it down my body, fixing and straightening it as she went, then zipping up the side deftly. Keelin started clapping like a seal and Susie's face came over all trance-like. Great, did that mean she was going to ease up on the shouting? 'Look at yourself!' She took my shoulders and twisted me towards the mirror.

Oh. My. God.

I inhaled sharply and clung to her for support. The dress was *stunning*. I couldn't speak for the first few moments so I just stood there grinning at myself like a simpleton. I hadn't a clue when I'd get an opportunity to wear such a fabulous dress when I'd bought it in Brown Thomas all those months back but now here I was. And I loved it even more than I had when I'd bought it.

'You like?' Keelin asked.

I nodded emphatically, still unable to find my voice.

'See? You don't need those Spanx. Izzy, you look amazing,' she said, smacking my arse.

I looked at myself again.

The dress was exquisite: a corseted bodice that cinched in perfectly at my waist, only to slink back out again with layers of oyster silk puffing their way to my knees and a surface layer of fine gold lace. The effect was simply breathtaking. 'I can't believe it's mine,' I whispered dreamily.

We whizzed around the house, applying our final layers of lipgloss, making sure we had our hairbrushes, eyeliners and lipsticks in our bags. Keelin made us knock back the cocktails she'd invented earlier in honour of the night: Dublin Whores, she'd named them. She thought they might catch on, but I wasn't sure that peach schnapps and *crème de menthe* mixed together too well.

On the way to the cinema, we dropped off our stuff at the Shelbourne. Keelin and Susie were bunking in with me but I'd bagsed the toiletries in the bathroom just to avoid any last-minute misunderstandings. We were meeting Emma, Caroline, Marcus, Will, Stephen and Deirdre at the after party. I'd even managed to sneak Simon on to the guest list at the last minute as a celebrity dog-trainer.

I still didn't know what was happening on the poster front. I'd told Jonathan I'd leave my design into the Lights! Camera! Action! office first thing in the morning and someone could collect it when I'd gone as I didn't want to see anyone. And all I knew was that I hadn't been fired.

By the time we got to the Savoy Cinema on O'Connell Street, we were running a bit late so we scooted in through a side-door because I spotted Edna McClodmutton getting her photo taken out on the front steps. Cian was with her and, for the first time ever, it didn't bother me in the slightest. Anyway, it was hard to feel anything except nausea with him dressed in that navy blue velvet suit. The girls reckoned he was a shadow of his former self and miserable to boot. I'd say he was probably fed up that he was Saffron's arm candy and she was stealing the limelight.

Inside, the Savoy was jam-packed, with hordes of people filing into Screen One. We squirrelled our way to an usher to ask where we could get the popcorn and the pick-and-mix before the film started. He looked at us as if we were serial killers, so we took this to mean that it would possibly be a touch uncouth to gorge oneself at a première. Shite – I'd been looking forward to some fizzy worms.

We followed the stream of people into the auditorium, and I kept my head down in case I saw either Eve or Fintan – I didn't want to talk to either of them. My blood was still boiling over Eve's lies and accusations. Why had Fintan taken her side so quickly and not even considered that I might be telling the truth? Eve was such a two-faced bitch.

We located our seats in row M and gossiped about who was there and who wasn't. Then Geraldine scooted down the row after us, polishing the people who were already seated with her bum as she shuffled past them. She gave me a big hug. 'Izzy, Laurence and I are ignoring Eve. And I managed to get her seat moved so she can't sit beside us. And, just so you know, I plan on spilling red wine all down the front of her dress later.'

All of a sudden the room went quiet, the screen lit up and the opening credits were rolling. We sat back and watched the film that had taken over our lives for the past year. A year of my life that I would never get back.

* * *

What a pile of crap. The bit where the mum throws her boy-friend over O'Connell Bridge? Or the bit where the old man comes on to the girl who works in Clery's? Or the bit where Saffron's character stabs the thug with the heel of her shoe? Christ. It was like watching *Days of Our Lives* with Irish accents. With a bit of *Pulp Fiction* thrown into the mix, and a soupçon of fourth-year school play to finish it off. And Edna McClodmutton's acting?

Shocking.

At the end, all I could think was: Was that it? I wondered if everyone else was as disappointed, confused and all round mentally abused as I was. But they were applauding. Luna-tics. Maybe they were pissed.

Keelin and Susie were crying and clapping wildly. Well, that wasn't too much of a shock, I suppose – Susie had cried for a week when Ailsa died in *Home and Away*. The director took to the podium to thank everyone for coming and the crowd went crazy. Mentallers. What had I been doing, spend-ing the majority of my waking hours contributing to some-thing I honestly didn't care about? I'd known it was going to be no *Shawshank Redemption*, but I'd hoped I'd feel proud of it. In that moment, I was overwhelmed by how unfulfilled I felt and how fed up I was with my job. It really wasn't me at all. Roll on the graphic-design course.

What was me, however, was copious amounts of cham-pagne and a live jazz band in a beautiful function room at the Shelbourne Hotel. Two huge Christmas trees stood in the lobby, dripping gold and silver decorations, while red velvet bows curled their way up the magnificent staircase. The red carpet that had been laid out for the party was sprinkled with specks of pearly white glitter like snowflakes under the chandelier.

The guests spilled in for the party, occupying every corner, perching on chairs at large round tables covered with crisp white linen tablecloths, forming neat queues at the bar to avail themselves of the free drink, and clustering in small groups to chat and laugh and enjoy all that an evening of pure indulgence had to offer.

Keelin, Susie and I claimed a spot close to the bar and toasted ourselves with champagne. Shortly afterwards, the others arrived and promptly joined us. And the more we toasted, the more the world became this shiny happy Christmassy place full of people I loved. Stephen was telling a story about how Deirdre had fixed the boiler system in her flat and wasn't that amazing? I loved Deirdre. I had yet to get to know her properly, but what was there not to love? And she was handy in a DIY crisis. And there was Keelin, wrapped around Simon like a python, smiling so much I wondered had she given herself lockjaw and was too embarrassed to say. And just when I thought I couldn't possibly feel any more warm and fuzzy inside if I tried, who comes and pisses all over it?

Edna McClodmutton.

'Fuck!' I said, jumping at the sight of her. The others gave a communal yelp behind me as I gawped at her. She peered down her nose at me and I remembered how intimidating she was up close.

'Nice dress,' she said disparagingly. 'So, anyway,' she cooed breezily, 'I thought you should know I've dumped Cian so you can have him back if you like. No hard feelings.'

'But you arrived with him?'

'So? Doesn't mean I have to leave with him. There are some very interesting options in the room, and I have to put my career first.'

Wow. Harsh!

No hard feelings? Was she for real? I started to rack my brains for a comeback, then realized I didn't give a shit any more. I was so over the both of them. And it hit me how foolish I'd been wasting so much of my time obsessing over this woman. And you know what? I could see what the girls meant about her not being beautiful. She looked as if she was trying too hard – the overtanned skin, the false eyelashes, the sequined dress that was cut too low.

'So, your friend Gavin, is he here?' She cocked an eyebrow at me. 'He's the talk of the industry. He's going places, that guy. Maybe we could all meet up and go out for a drink some time.'

I stared her square in the eye and spoke with icy calm. 'I'd rather have my eyes gouged out and fed to a tank of sharks.'

She recoiled as if I'd slapped her face. 'Huh! Well, fine. I don't give a shit. I have bigger fish to fry, sweetheart. Colin Farrell's here.'

'He's welcome to you, Bernie. Go knock yourself out.'

I'd finally caught her out. Saffron Spencer wasn't her real name. I should have known it was a stage name all along. Laurence had shown me her actual name on one of her payslips during the week and I'd almost burst with joy when I saw it – Bernie Hoare. Bernie Hoare! Edna McClodmutton had actually been a step up for her!

I thought nothing could top that until Geraldine bounded up to tell me that a producer had just asked her to be the lead in a new feature film. She dropped her voice to a whisper and said it was going to be a Celtic soft porno called *Queen Maeve and the Bullocks.*

Before I'd had a chance to digest this outrageous piece of information, the crowd hushed and I saw Jonathan Ride Cunningham standing on a podium at the far end of the room. Sorry, Jonathan Cunningham. He tapped his microphone loudly and asked for silence. 'Now most of you probably didn't know this, but yesterday we were thinking that this première night might not happen,' he started, 'largely because our posters for the film were nowhere to be seen. And who has a movie without a poster? They're a vital advertising tool.'

I shrank with panic and apprehension as I listened to him, stomach churning like a cement-mixer. I glanced around to see if I could spot Eve or Fintan. Had they used my design? Maybe they'd sourced the original and had it printed off.

'So without further ado, ladies and gentlemen, may I present to you, fresh this minute from the printers, the poster for *Snog Me Now, You Dublin Whore*.' The crowd parted and a giant mobile poster unit was wheeled into the centre of the function room . . . with a huge copy of *my design* emblazoned on it.

Emma caught me just before I fainted. She propped me up and forced me to drink something – more champagne, which only made my head spin faster. Everyone was clapping.

'Izzy, congratulations! It's amazing!' Keelin, Susie, Orla, Marcus, everyone flocked to me, each passing me to the next when they'd hugged me.

Then Jonathan was standing beside me. 'Congratulations, Izzy. They all absolutely adore it. We scanned your design this morning and it's being printed as we speak so we can send it off around the country first thing tomorrow morning.'

'Holy shit!' I exclaimed. 'I don't know what to say.'

'Well, we discovered that it was Eve who'd screwed it up and, to punish her for lying, Fintan demoted her to your position of junior office assistant.'

'Oh. So where do I go?' I asked, wondering if this was his polite way of telling me that, despite the success of the poster, I was out of a job.

'Well,' he started, 'it's early days but there may be an opening for an internship in one of the design departments. I've already had quite a few colleagues asking for your details.'

'Get lost!' I half shouted, which made him laugh.

'I know you Irish folk have funny ways of expressing your-selves, but should I take it that you'd be interested if I passed on your business card?'

'Yes! Thank you! Thank you so much! But I don't have one.'

'She's crazy. Crazy drunk,' Susie interrupted. 'She'll have it with you by next week.'

But I wasn't drunk!

Susie dug me in the ribs – she'd predicted what I was about to say. 'Shut up,' she said, out of the corner of her mouth. 'This is a fantastic opportunity to get you started as a designer, Izzy. Take it.'

'Get it to me as soon as you can.' Jonathan smiled.

'Thanks so much.' I beamed at him again, overwhelmed.

'It's not me you should be thanking.'

'No?'

'It was Gavin at Lights! Camera! Action! who contacted me after it all blew up yesterday.'

'Gavin?' I asked, almost wanting to cry.

'Yes, Gavin Reed. By the way,' he asked, suddenly intrigued, 'is that *the* Gavin?'

Bollocks. I was kind of hoping he wasn't going to bring that up. Somewhere between deciding that I didn't want to sleep with him that night and actually leaving his flat, I'd managed to blurt out everything about Gavin. Just what every man wants – the girl he'd wined and dined in a posh restaurant to start blabbing about some other bloke she'd just realized she was in love with. Classy date.

'Ehm, heh heh,' I chuckled self-consciously, 'I don't remember mentioning a, eh . . . Gavin, was it?'

He grinned. 'Well, I'm sure he's very proud to see the poster anyway.'

'He would be, if he wasn't stuck in Belfast working on the latest Lights! Camera! Action! project.'

'Huh? I just saw him at the bar – at least, I thought it was him.'

What?

Keelin came over with a fresh glass of champagne, saying we needed to make another toast to me, the most artistic person in the Shelbourne. We clinked glasses and then Jonathan got chatting to everyone. While Keelin was telling him how much she'd loved the film, Susie took me aside and said that although it was a bit weird, given my history with him, she thought he was gorgeous and did I mind if she flirted with him? I reminded her that I wasn't attracted to him now and if she didn't go and put the 'Ride' back into Jonathan Cunningham, I was never going to speak to her again.

I left them all and made my way through the crowd as best I could. I wasn't sure if it was the champagne, the news that Geraldine was becoming a porn star, the fact that I might be inching closer to landing my dream job, or that Gavin was supposedly in the room, but I was quite unsteady on my feet.

Why wasn't I taller? I wanted to ask the man in front of me if he could lift me on to his shoulders so I could have a quick scan of the place, but he might have been one of the colleagues Jonathan had mentioned. I didn't want to embarrass myself.

An arm went around my waist. Oh, yes! Oh, wow! Gavin! I spun around to him.

Ugh! Cian! I grappled his hands off me. 'Piss off.' I could see in his eyes that he was in a drunken, lecherous mood.

'Izzy, you're the love of my life,' he slurred.

'Piss off,' I repeated, slapping his hands away. 'Change the

319

bloody record. I already know Saffron's dumped you again, so if you have your sights set on ruining my night because you've been humiliated and you need your ego massaged, go and annoy some other idiot.'

Suddenly he lunged but I swooped out of the way just in time. Christ, he was annoying when he was drunk.

I swung round to walk off – and Gavin was in front of me. I smiled widely, so happy to see him, but he just looked at me icily, then turned away.

'Gavin!' I called after him. 'Wait!' I had to knee Cian in the balls to get him off me, which I rather enjoyed.

'Gavin!' I shouted, running down the marble staircase, my shoes disappearing into the plush velvet carpet that spilled down the steps. 'Gavin!'

'What is it?' he asked gruffly, when I caught up with him in the foyer.

His harsh tone stung. 'I just . . . wanted to say . . . hi.'

'Hi,' he said, turned his back and walked away again.

'Jesus, Gavin, I know you said we couldn't be friends but you don't have to carry on as though you hate me,' I blurted, trying not to cry. My God, it was so fantastic to see him – I wanted to hug him, hold him, spill my heart out to him. Well, why not? Why didn't I? What was holding me back now?

Nothing! And if he didn't want me, at least I'd know. It was now or never.

I took a deep breath. 'I need to tell you something right away, and if you don't mind I'm going to say it all in one go because if you interrupt or if I stop to think about what I'm saying there's a good chance I won't be able to do it. Gavin, I love you. And not as a friend but with the whole of my heart and my soul. I've been utterly miserable without you and I'd be the happiest girl in the whole entire world if we could just take what you said to me at the window that night in my house and what I'm saying to you now and fuse them together right here and ignore all the bullshit that's happened in between.'

He stared at me without speaking for what seemed like an eternity. Then he looked at the ground and shook his head. 'It's too late,' he said sadly, and my heart broke. 'I'm not doing this any more.'

'Doing what?' I asked, trying to keep my composure, trying to keep the tremble from my bottom lip.

'Cian. This unfinished business you have with him.'

'Gavin, it's so totally finished!' I implored.

'No, Izzy,' he said sternly, looking me straight in the eye. 'Not now because it suits you. Not now because you've happened to bump into me, or because you've just had a row with him in there. If you really felt this way, why haven't I heard from you?'

Now probably wasn't the time to tell him that I'd thought I was pregnant with Cian's child. I stood there, mute, willing him to understand and believe what I was saying.

'Good night, Izzy,' he said softly. 'You look beautiful tonight. You really do.'

And with that he was gone.

38

The next afternoon the girls and I had arranged to meet up for lunch in the Metro Café to dissect last night in minute detail. I'd spent the night on my own in my bedroom suite after Susie had shacked up with Jonathan (yay!) and Keelin fecked off home with Simon. I didn't mind: it'd meant I could sit in the bath and cry and drink my way through the mini-bar without feeling I might be keeping anyone awake.

When I'd arrived Keelin and Susie were already there. They started clucking like a pair of hens when they saw me, ordering me to sit down immediately before they exploded.

'You will *not* believe all of this.' Keelin giggled as she took a newspaper from her handbag.

'This is *priceless*!' Susie enthused, taking the paper from her and passing it to me proudly.

I looked at the front page and screamed. I turned to the other customers and apologized profusely, then turned back to the paper.

Oh. My. God.

There on the front page was a picture of Edna McClod-mutton from last night under a giant caption that read, 'Aspiring actress's dreams put on hold as performance is panned by film critics.' I screamed again. I couldn't help it. This was too much.

'And there's more!' Keelin laughed, turning the page. The caption 'Stars come out in their droves for première night' was spread across both pages. I could barely contain myself as I looked at the photos. I covered my mouth before I screamed again. There, in a colourful two-page spread, was a collage of all my friends. Pictures taken on the red carpet on their way into the party. Orla, Caroline, Marcus and Will from the new Irish pop sensation Mix 'n' Match, Bono's children Stephen and Deirdre (who looked a bit perverted as they were holding hands and seemed to be extremely in love), dog trainer to the stars Simon Morrissey, and top models Keelin and Susie. I laughed until I thought I was going to pass out.

'There's more!' Susie clapped.

'No, stop, I can't take it,' I wheezed.

'We have *the* best gossip ever from last night,' Keelin said calmly and slowly.

'Gather yourself, Izzy. Are you ready?' Susie said, taking over.

I nodded warily.

'Guess who Jonathan and I stumbled on in a very compromising position when we took the wrong room key and ended up in another bedroom.'

'Who? Who?' I demanded giddily.

'Your Laurence with Eve's fiancé, Philippe!'

I fell off the side of my chair and landed with a thump on the floor. No way! That was madness! But it all made such perfect sense. Laurence was *gay*? And had been caught with Eve's fiancé?

'Serves her right, the cow!' Susie said, almost reading my mind.

'Oh, and while you're down there,' Keelin added, 'your sister snogged Colin Farrell.' All I could think was how excited Mum would be before I half passed out.

We stayed there for the entire afternoon, ordering pot after pot of tea as we made our way through the entire dessert menu. I told them about Gavin. And although they listened patiently, I think they were far too excited about their own goings-on to appreciate my heartbreak. But I was happy to listen to Keelin chat about Simon, and Susie about Jonathan.

'Jaysus, he's a handy man to have around for some rebound sex all the same, isn't he?' Keelin sniggered. Susie and I burst out laughing. 'Better keep his number in case things don't work out between me and Simon.'

We left when we realized we were the last people there, and that if the lady at the counter coughed any more to get our attention, she'd rupture a lung. On our way home, Susie said Jonathan had asked her to tell me that a copy of my poster was waiting for me to collect in the Shelbourne.

'Really? I'm sure I can get one in work. Will we not just head straight home?' I whined. I was shattered, emotionally and physically, and the only thing I wanted to do was change into my pyjamas and hang out with Dermot on the couch.

'Izzy, please,' Susie said, 'I'm trying to impress him. Don't let him think I didn't do the one thing he asked me to do.'

Wow. Sounded as though she liked him. 'Fine,' I said sulkily, as we plodded towards the hotel.

They said they'd wait outside and have a smoke while I went in to collect it.

'I'm here to collect a poster,' I said to the concierge.

'Isobel Keegan?'

'Yes.'

'Upstairs and to your left.'

'Thank you.'

I passed the bar off the lobby. It was jammed with people singing Christmas carols and joyously getting into the spirit of the season. I climbed up the stairs, turned left and found myself outside in a little courtyard. Oh? The concierge must have given me the wrong directions.

I stood there breathing in the fresh winter air. There was something so enchanting about it that I paused to take it in.

Despite myself, I was smiling. The fairy-lights looked magical twined over the rose bushes. It was another clear evening, and the sky was like a gorgeous navy blue velvet blanket. I sauntered over to the fountain. Closing my eyes, I danced my fingers along the surface of the water.

'Hey.'

I jumped and spun round. Gavin was standing in the doorway. 'Christ,' I breathed. 'What are you doing here?' Gavin? Here? My heart was racing.

'I'm glad the girls delivered you safe and sound.'

'The girls? What did . . .' I was dumbstruck. Had he *set this up*? I wasn't sure and I didn't want to jump to any conclusions in case I fell flat on my face yet again.

We stared at each other. The sound of 'White Christmas' drifted up from the bar. All of a sudden he marched right up to me and scooped me into a hug. I laughed into his chest. 'Gavin . . . God, I don't know where to begin. I never got a chance to thank you for calling Jonathan about the poster. It would never have happened without you.'

'Yes, it would. But perhaps a little later than last night. I'm so proud of you, Izzy.'

I held on to him tightly. I wanted to never let him go again.

'Anyway, I owed you for getting me started on the documentary.'

'I'm so happy for you about your new job,' I said. 'But you've no idea how much I'll miss you at work.'

He looked down at me, holding my eyes. I could have gazed into his green ones for a lifetime and never tired of it.

'Well,' he said softly, 'I'm kinda hoping we won't have to miss each other too much.'

'Really? Are you going to carry on doing freelance for us?'

'No, no. What I mean is . . . We're not very good at this, are we? There always seems to be something in the way. Last night, Izzy . . .'

'Gavin,' I whispered, close to tears, 'you don't have to apologize. I understand why you don't want to be with me. Why you can't be with me. I've messed everything up royally. I know that. So please don't feel bad. I have you back as a friend, and I can't tell you what that means to me. Please . . .'

'Izzy, Izzy, Izzy,' he murmured. 'I don't want to say sorry any more. And I don't want you to say sorry any more. Last night I thought I couldn't take it all. But later I realized I'd had enough of *this* – of wanting you but always letting other stuff get in the way.'

Dear God in heaven, did he just say he *wanted* me? Oooh, maybe I'll let him finish first, maybe he wants me to do something for him . . . like more storyboards. I didn't want to pre-empt anything in case it wasn't what I wanted to hear and I crumbled entirely under the disappointment. I was on tenterhooks as he went on, 'I'm sorry I walked out on you like that last night. It's just . . . when I saw that prick, Cian, and I thought . . . But I met Keelin outside and she calmed me down and explained a lot of things. I know it's over between you and him.'

'Gavin, that man was never in love with me. It just took me a long time to figure it out. And, yes, it is completely and utterly over. I don't want him in my life, with his nastiness. I've learnt a lot about myself over the last few weeks, and I know where I want to take my life next.'

'Oh? And would there be room in it for me?'

All the feelings I'd been keeping bottled up suddenly flooded out and I started to cry. Gavin pulled me closer, holding me tight. It felt so . . . right. Hindsight is a marvellous thing, all right. When Cian held me like this, it always niggled at the back of my mind that he wasn't fully with me, wasn't really in the moment. But now, being held by someone who was incredibly present ... Cian had never really loved me. Love felt like a warm protective shield around you, keeping you safe. Love felt like this.

When I could speak again, I placed my hand on his face. 'Gavin Reed, I'm in love with you. Instead of having room for you in my life, or room for me in yours, how about we share the same one?'

He stared at me, smiling, then he leant in and kissed me. My stomach flipped. It was the most amazing kiss of my life. In that instant, I thought I was going to burst with happiness. I wanted to hold him for ever.

'Come with me,' he said.

He took my hand in his and led me down to the rose bushes, stopping when we reached a gold pot with a tiny Christmas tree in it. My head felt all light and fluffy, and he scooped me under his arm, kissing the top of my head.

'What's this?' I asked, as he hunched down to it.

'This is the Tiffany Christmas tree,' he said, smiling up.

'Wow. You name trees. You're so cute and weird. Who's that one?' I asked, pointing to the next tree over.

'That's Dave. But we don't need to concern ourselves with Dave right now.'

'Okay.'

'Do you think this one looks a little different?' he asked.

'Well, it's the only tree out here that isn't decorated. Gavin, is this your way of telling me your next documentary is going to be about horticulture because, I gotta tell ya, I can't see it doing so well . . .'

'Come here to me.' He pulled me down to him. 'I can tell you now that I'm not doing a documentary on horticulture.'

'Phew!'

327

'Are you sure this tree doesn't have any decorations on it?' he asked, brushing the hair from my face in a way that made me want to rip off my clothes.

I decided to humour him, whatever he was on about. I bent forward and stared at the branches of the tree, looking for . . . *What* exactly?

And then I saw it. Dangling from a tiny branch in the middle of the tree. A gold heart charm. I held my breath as I turned to him.

'It's for the bracelet. I think this is a pretty important one. It's just so you know, if you don't already, that you have my heart.' He lifted it off and placed it in my hand. Then he folded me into his arms again and we grinned inanely at each other, as if we knew something the rest of the world didn't.

'Oh, Gavin,' I said, kissing him with all the happiness that was bubbling inside me. 'I love it.'

'I'm very happy, Izzy,' he said.

'So am I.'

I held my heart tightly as we kissed. Both of them.

Acknowledgements

My sincerest thanks to Patricia Deevy and Michael McLoughlin in Penguin Ireland for making a big dream come true for me. I'm still walking on air and pinching myself every now and again just to check that it's real. (Let's hope it is, and this whole thing isn't some elaborate and cruel wind-up!) Many thanks also to Cliona Lewis and Brian Walker at Penguin. And to my literary agent, Faith O'Grady, and all at the Lisa Richards Agency for helping me to juggle my acting and writing commitments when I was having mild heart-attacks about not knowing when I'd have time to do both. Thank you for keeping me calm at all times and telling me it would all be fine. And on the work side of things, a huge thank you to Rachel Pierce, my editor, for teaching me so much, helping me so much and making me laugh so much. (Finally an apology and a cheeky thank-you to the Shelbourne Hotel because I gave it a courtyard and a fountain that it doesn't have. I gather that's called artistic licence.)

To my fantastic family, for all your love and support. I'd be lost without you. Mum, Dad, my brothers Mark and Paul and my cousin Noeleen, who feels more like a sister, I love you all very much.

Along with the love story, the heart of this book is about the merits of friendship. Female friendships, to be more precise. And the inspiration for me comes because I have been blessed with the best group of girlfriends any girl could ask for. Thank you all so much for all the laughter, support, advice and fun, and I'm so looking forward to all there is yet to come. And a special word of gratitude to Olivia, Joanne, Mandy and Lynne, who read the early drafts and told me I wasn't crazy for attempting to write a book, and encouraged me to keep going.

And sometimes you've got to save the best for last. So thank you to my fiancé, Brian. My one and only, always.